Murdered But Not Dead

A *James "Bonnie" Dundee* *Mystery*

By Anne Austin

Originally published in 1939

Murdered But Not Dead

© 2015 Resurrected Press
www.ResurrectedPress.com

Published by Resurrected Press

This classic book was handcrafted by Resurrected Press. Resurrected Press is dedicated to bringing high quality classic books back to the readers who enjoy them. These are not scanned versions of the originals, but, rather, quality checked and edited books meant to be enjoyed!

Please visit ResurrectedPress.com to view our entire catalogue!

For updates on future releases, LIKE us on Facebook:
http://www.Facebook.com/ResurrectedPress

ISBN 13: 978-1-943403-05-9

Printed in the United States of America

Resurrected Press Books in A. E. Fielding's *The Chief Inspector Pointer Mystery* Series

RESURRECTED PRESS CLASSIC
MYSTERY CATALOGUE

Journeys into Mystery
Travel and Mystery in a More Elegant Time

The Edwardian Detectives
Literary Sleuths of the Edwardian Era

Gems of Mystery
Lost Jewels from a More Elegant Age

Anne Austin
One Drop of Blood
The Black Pigeon
Murder at Bridge

E. C. Bentley
Trent's Last Case: The Woman in Black

Ernest Bramah
Max Carrados Resurrected:
The Detective Stories of Max Carrados

Agatha Christie
The Secret Adversary
The Mysterious Affair at Styles

Octavus Roy Cohen
Midnight

Freeman Wills Croft
The Ponson Case
The Pit Prop Syndicate

J. S. Fletcher
The Herapath Property
The Rayner-Slade Amalgamation
The Chestermarke Instinct
The Paradise Mystery
Dead Men's Money
The Middle of Things
Ravensdene Court
Scarhaven Keep
The Orange-Yellow Diamond
The Middle Temple Murder
The Tallyrand Maxim
The Borough Treasurer
In the Mayor's Parlour
The Saftey Pin

R. Austin Freeman
The Mystery of 31 New Inn from the Dr. Thorndyke Series
John Thorndyke's Cases from the Dr. Thorndyke Series
The Red Thumb Mark from The Dr. Thorndyke Series
The Eye of Osiris from The Dr. Thorndyke Series
A Silent Witness from the Dr. John Thorndyke Series
The Cat's Eye from the Dr. John Thorndyke Series
Helen Vardon's Confession: A Dr. John Thorndyke Story
As a Thief in the Night: A Dr. John Thorndyke Story
Mr. Pottermack's Oversight: A Dr. John Thorndyke Story
Dr. Thorndyke Intervenes: A Dr. John Thorndyke Story
The Singing Bone: The Adventures of Dr. Thorndyke
The Stoneware Monkey: A Dr. John Thorndyke Story
The Great Portrait Mystery, and Other Stories: A Collection of Dr. John Thorndyke and Other Stories
The Penrose Mystery: A Dr. John Thorndyke Story

The Uttermost Farthing: A Savant's Vendetta

Arthur Griffiths
The Passenger From Calais
The Rome Express

Fergus Hume
The Mystery of a Hansom Cab
The Green Mummy
The Silent House
The Secret Passage

Edgar Jepson
The Loudwater Mystery

A. E. W. Mason
At the Villa Rose

A. A. Milne
The Red House Mystery

Baroness Emma Orczy
The Old Man in the Corner

Edgar Allan Poe
The Detective Stories of Edgar Allan Poe

Arthur J. Rees
The Hampstead Mystery
The Shrieking Pit
The Hand In The Dark
The Moon Rock
The Mystery of the Downs

Mary Roberts Rinehart
Sight Unseen and The Confession

Dorothy L. Sayers

Whose Body?

Sir William Magnay
The Hunt Ball Mystery

Mabel and Paul Thorne
The Sheridan Road Mystery

Louis Tracy
The Strange Case of Mortimer Fenley
The Albert Gate Mystery
The Bartlett Mystery
The Postmaster's Daughter
The House of Peril
The Sandling Case: What Would You Have Done?

Charles Edmonds Walk
The Paternoster Ruby

John R. Watson
The Mystery of the Downs
The Hampstead Mystery

Edgar Wallace
The Daffodil Mystery
The Crimson Circle

Carolyn Wells
Vicky Van
The Man Who Fell Through the Earth
In the Onyx Lobby
Raspberry Jam
The Clue
The Room with the Tassels
The Vanishing of Betty Varian
The Mystery Girl
The White Alley
The Curved Blades

Anybody but Anne
The Bride of a Moment
Faulkner's Folly
The Diamond Pin
The Gold Bag
The Mystery of the Sycamore
The Come Back

Raoul Whitfield
Death in a Bowl

And much more!
Visit ResurrectedPress.com
for our complete catalogue

**For updates on future releases, LIKE us on
Facebook:
http://www.Facebook.com/ResurrectedPress**

FOREWORD

Anne Austin is one of those writers that flourished during the 1930's and then disappeared as times and tastes changed. She got her start as an author writing romance novels, but switched to mysteries starting with *The Black Pigeon* in 1929. Many of her novels first appeared in serial form in syndication to various newspapers in the US and Canada. In all, she authored six mysteries and six novels in the romance genre.

Five of the mysteries feature James "Bonnie" Dundee, a young detective who becomes a Special Investigator in the District Attorney's office, with *Murdered But Not Dead*, published in 1939, being the final installment in the series. There is a gap of seven years in the series between this book and the previous work, *One Drop of Blood* (1932). This may have been the result of Austin's involvement with Hollywood as a result of the filming of one of her non-mystery novels, *The Wicked Woman* as a movie of the same name.

The Hollywood connection is carried over in *Murdered But Not Dead* which deals with Yola Canova a film actress who is trying to restore a flagging career with a cross country publicity tour. When the tour lands in Hamilton, there are a number of people who are convinced that Conova is really Madge Smith, a housemaid, who left Hamilton some ten years earlier after conceiving a child out of wedlock. The mystery surrounding the actress deepens when her body is discovered hanging from a bridge the night of her arrival in town.

As with several of the other mysteries in the series, much of the story deals with the clash between the small town attitudes of Hamilton, a mid-sized city whose location is never specified but which probably was meant to be in Ohio, and the wider world, in this case, the world of Hollywood and New York. As an author, Austin was concerned with the psychology of her characters, which play a larger role in her books than the actual mechanics of the crime. The method of detection followed by Dundee is to understand the motivations of the various suspects rather than concentration on the clues. Yet, despite this focus, the mystery is supported by a chain of evidence intricate enough to please most mystery fans.

It's quite clear that Austin's mysteries were targeted towards a feminine audience, especially working women in their twenties. The detective Dundee, young, handsome, and considerate, was certainly designed to appeal to this group as the model boyfriend. The setting, a small, industrial mid-western city, reflects the realities of the times, the end of prohibition and the middle of the Great Depression. The subject matter involves areas that would have been relevant and of interest to women of the period, illegitimate sex, failing marriages, problems relating to alcoholism. One of the strengths of Austin's works is that she does deal with these matters in a realistic manner. As the series progressed, the tone of the books became more mature and darker, the failings of the characters, both victims and suspects, more pronounced and believable.

Though not well known today, the mysteries of Anne Austin are well worth reading. It is with pleasure that Resurrected Press presents this new edition of *Murdered But Not Dead*.

About the Author

Born in 1895, Anne Austin began by writing romance novels about young women in the mid 1920's but soon turned her talents to producing a string of mysteries through the 1930's, some of which appeared as serials in newspapers.. Many of these mysteries feature as the detective "Bonnie" Dundee, Special Investigator for the District Attorney, including *Murder Backstairs, The*

Avenging Parrot, Murder at Bridge, and *One Drop of Blood.* Several of her mysteries were translated into French, including *Le Pigeon Noir* and *Le Crime Parfume.* Despite her success as a novelist, Anne Austin disappears from the public record after the 1930's.

Greg Fowlkes
Editor-In-Chief
Resurrected Press
www.ResurrectedPress.com
www.Facebook.com/ResurrectedPress

I

MURMURING "PARDON ME!" "So sorry!" and "Thank you!" James F. Dundee forced his way past belligerent knees and unforgiving glares to the one vacant seat in Row M of the new Egyptian Theater, Hamilton's not too modest copy of the Hollywood original. The metal numeral on the back of the upholstered chair corresponded with the number on the stub of the ticket which had come to him so mysteriously that afternoon just as the district attorney's office was closing for the day.

"I was told not to answer no questions," the messenger boy had insisted. "My orders was to give this here envelope to Mr. Bonnie Dundee and to nobody else but, so if you are the guy with a dame's moniker—"

"I'm Dundee," the special investigator admitted, flushing, as he reached for the envelope.

"That's his underworld moniker, kid," District Attorney Sanderson confided mendaciously, "Other cities can have their Pretty Boy Floyds and their Baby Face Nelsons, but Hamilton's proud of its 'Bonnie' Dundee. Now, beat it, sonny. What you got there, Dundee? Well, I'll be—A free ticket for the show tonight. I had to cough up five bucks apiece for my pasteboards. Gordon said the free list was positively suspended tonight. Personally, I'm getting sick of this 'personal appearance' racket. If anyone asks *me*, the place for a movie star is in the celluloid, not 'in the flesh.' But Penny didn't ask me. She *told* me—to get the tickets, so I got 'em. The worst henpecked husband in Hamilton. That's me!"

"And don't you love it?" Sanderson's secretary, Rose Berman, interposed, as she gathered up gloves, hat and handbag. "Gosh! I'm so excited I don't know whether I'm standing on my head or my feet. . . . Where's *my* ticket? I know I put right here in my bag, and now it's gone. If I've lost it or some lowlife has swiped it— Oh, thank heaven! Here it the precious thing! I'll say it's precious! Cost me three dollars—second balcony, extreme right, and the last seat to be had any price. But I wouldn't take ten bucks for it."

"Who said there was a recession?" the district attorney marveled. "Why any sane girl will pay three dollars to find out whether another girl is as pretty off the screen as she is on—"

"Who said anything about wanting to see Yolo Canova?" his secretary interrupted. "A couple of years ago I'd have paid more than three dollars to see her in the flesh, but she's just a last year's hat now. It's Clinton Risher I'm simply dying see, and I'll bet you the price of my ticket, Mr. Sanders, that it's Clinton Risher your wife is all excited about."

"Who's Clinton Risher?"

"Why, Mr. Sanderson!" the girl exclaimed. "Don't you really know who Clinton Risher is? You must be kidding! Why, he's the personification of masculinity. He's sex appeal plus. He's more thrilling than Charles Boyer, more virile than Clark Gable, handsomer than Robert Taylor, more appeal than Spencer Tracy—"

"Good Lord!" Dundee groaned. "Commit the girl to the psyke ward for observation, Sandy. She's obviously nuts—"

"Nuts to you!" Rose Berman retorted. "And if I *am* gaga about Clinton Risher, I'm no worse than all my girl friends. And if you must know, I was simply quoting Kay Loring."

"Kay Loring?" Dundee repeated blankly.

"Don't you even know who Kay Loring is?" The girl's tone was scornful. "She's the star girl reporter and the movie and dramatic critic on *The Sun*. She's the cleverest, snappiest—"

"What the devil has this Clinton Risher ever done?" Sanderson interrupted. "I've never heard of him before, and I'll bet Penny hasn't, either."

"He's jealous," his secretary giggled. "So's my boy friend. We had an awful row about him last night, so I had to buy my own ticket, at the last minute. Clinton Risher has appeared in only two pictures," she enlightened her audience, her eyes glowing "In the first one, 'Lord and Lady,' he only had a bit. He wasn't the lord, but he stole the picture, and he got so many fan letters that World-Wide simply had to give him a real part in 'Born to Sin,' and was he grand. Terrific!"

"One of those South Seas pictures, wasn't it?" Sanderson grunted "I thought it was lousy, but I remember now that Penny sat through it twice"

"I saw it three times," the girl said. "Well, good night, everybody! I've got to dash to the beauty parlor."

"On the chance," suggested Sanderson, "that God's gift to women will spot you in the second balcony, extreme right?"

"Stranger things have happened," the secretary called over her shoulder, as she disappeared through the door.

"Women are the damnedest fools!" the district attorney exploded "Who do you suppose sent you that ticket, Jimmy? Some girl on the make?"

"For me—with Clinton Risher in town?" Dundee grinned; but as he began to turn the pasteboard slowly between his fingers his blue eyes sobered, then narrowed. "Look, chief. This ticket's an 'Annie Oakley.' See the holes punched in the stub? Whoever sent this ticket didn't have to buy it.

"Couldn't have been Gordon, manager of the Egyptian. He wouldn't give you a song-and-dance about suspending the free list, and then send a mere special investigator a comp ticket."

"Maybe the manager of the personal appearance tour sent it," Sanderson suggested. "Wanted to make sure a real detective would be on the job. There's always a bunch of nuts and crooks trying to horn in on a stunt like this. After all, since Yola Conova is one of the most famous women in the United States, she's a shining target for cranks and crooks."

Dundee shook his head. "Doesn't sound reasonable, Sandy. If Weinberg—I believe that's the tour manager's name—wanted a representative from this office, wouldn't he tip us off what to be on the lookout for? Besides, he's from New York, I understand, so he never heard of me in his life. And if he did, it wasn't as 'Bonnie' Dundee. . . . What a nickname! What a cross to bear!"

"Fits you like a glove, laddie."

"Furthermore," Dundee continued, "there'll be two or three plainclothes dicks in the audience, as a matter of routine, addition to the extra detail of patrolmen inside and outside the theater."

"All right. I'm wrong—as usual. The manager didn't send the ticket to you. What's your guess?"

"I'm probably wrong, too," Dundee said slowly, "but I have a hunch this ticket was sent by a newspaperman. All press tickets are punched like this."

"Why should a reporter be so cagey, sending you a ticket?"

"For no reason at all, unless he happened to be working a hot tip that there's likely to be something doing in my line tonight."

"*Your line,* eh?" Sanderson chuckled. "Maybe Rose Berman's hotheaded boy friend has threatened to shoot Clinton Risher on sight. I'll take a shot at him myself if Penny lets out just one bleat about his being the personification of masculinity."

"Don't shoot, chief. Be subtle. Pant with passion while Conova's doing her turn."

"That won't be hard," Sanderson admitted. "I don't think I've missed a picture of hers in the last seven years. She may not be what she used to be, but I'll bet there's life in the gal yet, Archy, what the hell! If I weren't married I'd be tempted to cook up an excuse to have the

Incomparable Conova brought before the district attorney for questioning."

"Maybe I can find an excuse for you, Sandy," Dundee grinned.

Now, as he settled in his seat in the crowded theater, the district attorney's special investigator felt uneasily that perhaps he was being made the butt of some obscure joke. For, in neither seat adjoining his, was there a newspaperman. Crowding the narrow chair on his right sat a stout and impressive matron in evening dress. Except for the glare with which she had received his apologetic efforts to squeeze past her plump knees, she had taken no notice of him at all. Now, through a jewel-handled lorgnette, she was studying her program, her mouth pursed, the nostrils of her aquiline nose flaring in and out with a peculiar unpleasantness.

On his left was a young girl. In fact, two-thirds of the big audience seemed to be girls and women. Out of the corner of his eye Dundee saw that his neighbor, small and young, was devouring a copy of the large "souvenir" program which was being peddled in the lobby. Another Clinton Risher fan, undoubtedly. Dundee felt unreasonably annoyed, and looked away. If this same crowd had stormed the theater, gladly paying an exorbitant price to see Yola Conova, he would not have been surprised or contemptuous. After all, Conova was a real actress, almost a great actress. For years she had done splendid work on the screen—fine, sincere work. She had not depended upon beauty and sex appeal, although she had an abundance of both. Why, three years ago she would have been mobbed by her adorers, if she had come to Hamilton on a personal appearance tour! Just when had Conova ceased to be the rage? And did she know that her day was done? Backstage now, did she guess that it was not she but a boy unheard of six months ago whom all these women and girls were waiting to see?

"Are you *very* angry, Bonnie Dundee?"

The question, with laughter rippling through it, caused Dundee to jerk his head toward the left. The girl, both hands raised, was taking off her brown velvet tam, whose color exactly matched the eyes which were staring up at him. Round, wide, solemn eyes. He was startled, and showed it.

"I know," the girl murmured sadly. "The first sight of me affects nearly everyone like that. I never know whether my hair—" She ran quick fingers through her cap of short rust-red curls—"or my freckles. It's probably both. It takes time, but you get used to them, really. I used to try to cover them up with powder—the freckles, I mean, but it took such frightful lot, and what with the depressions and recession and all—"

"I'm afraid I don't quite—I mean, I haven't—" Dundee began, flushing.

"The honor of my acquaintance?" the girl helped him. "But tell me—who did you think sent you that ticket?"

"I proved myself a poor detective," Dundee admitted. "I deduced, after a really brilliant train of reasoning, that came from a newspaperman."

"Bravo!" the girl applauded softly, and shifted in her seat so that her head almost touched his shoulder. "Bend your head low, unless you have a crick in your neck," she commanded. "And don't blush and bridle like a coy girl. I'm not trying to pick you up. . . . Really, I think you were wonderful to hit the truth."

"But—"

"The new dictionaries," she twinkled, "will right an ancient wrong. Immediately after the word, 'newspaperman,' there will be, in parentheses, 'Noun. M. or F.'"

"You mean *you*—"

But she interrupted him again. Was she going to be one those annoying girls who never let a man finish a sentence?

"Yes, I'm a newspaperman. To tell you the truth, while I'm not angry, I'm terribly, terribly hurt that you didn't recognize me. I've been flattering myself that practically every man, woman and child in Hamilton knew me by sight at least. I'm not exactly inconspicuous, you know, and—"

It was Dundee's turn to interrupt. He grinned down at her with sudden assurance as he said: "I'm delighted to meet you at last, Miss Loring. I read your column every day, and simply can't wait to tune in on you—"

"Liar!" she chuckled. "I wouldn't admire you half so much as I do if I thought you read all the rot I write. For heaven's sake, stop blushing! I admire you because you're a damned good detective. Every newspaperman in town knows you're big-league stuff as a criminologist. Which explains why I sent you that ticket."

Dundee's pulses began to hammer. So his hunch had been correct!

"You're all agog, aren't you?" Kay Loring was amused. "Your nose is positively twitching at the scent of a new case"

"Is my nose wrong?"

"It's a very nice nose," she decided, after a solemnly critical inspection. "So nice that I hate to disappoint it, if it fancies it has caught the scent of blood. There's nothing I'd like better than to work with you on a murder case, but the best I can offer is—blackmail."

"Blackmail!"

"Control yourself," the girl whispered. "Unfortunately, we have very close neighbors. . . . Yes, blackmail! But I can't tell you any more until after I've seen Yola Conova 'in person.'"

"'Yola, Conova!" Dundee repeated, not too brightly; but before he could ask a question the sixty-piece orchestra crashed into the overture from "Tannhäuser."

Wagner's turbulence seemed to cow Dundee's companion. She sighed, sank low in her chair, and again began to study her program. Dundee, watching her with amused interest, saw her hold the booklet at arm's length, then bring it slowly almost to the tip of her short nose. Finally she dropped the program into her lap again, shaking her head and sighing in deep perplexity.

With a "May I, please?"—which Wagner drowned out—the detective reached for the program. It was open at a full-page portrait of Yola Conova.

Although Dundee had seen hundreds of photographs of the star, and had sat through the screening of nearly every picture in which she had appeared since her sudden rise to stardom seven or eight years before, he studied her features now as he saw them for the first time.

Here was not the face of a conventionally beautiful woman. The brow was too low, the dark eyes too deep-set, the cheek bones too high, for classic beauty. But there was something blood-stirring, something darkly exciting, in that face. An odd face. The face of a vital, passionate woman. Not the face of a happy woman, but of a woman who could suffer gallantly and even smile with a wry, twist of humor. The nose was good—clean-cut, with sensitive nostrils. Critics, he remembered, had always claimed that Conova could put more emotion into the quiver of a nostril than most actresses could register with their entire set of features. The mouth was thin-lipped and more than a trifle too wide, but at the height of Yola Conova's popularity her mouth had become the fashion, making the bee-stung Cupid's bow look silly and insipid.

In the portrait before Dundee, the actress was resting her chin upon her laced fingers. Her slightly raised eyes seem to give him look for look, but their dark depths were filled with secrets. Sultry, brooding eyes they were, their somber lines lightened a little by the whimsical curve of her left eyebrow. The right eyebrow lay low and flat, a gleaming, straight stretch of black silk, but the left winged upward—following a gay, humorous career of its own. Some critics maintained that Yola Conova owed her fame to that eccentric left eyebrow; others that—

"What do you think of her?"

With a start Dundee realized that the overture had thundered to its triumphant conclusion, and that the lights of the theater were slowly growing dim. But he could still make out the shower of golden freckles on Kay Loring's absurdly youthful face, tilted now against his shoulder. Tomorrow morning he'd undoubtedly find a fiery red hair or two, clinging to the tweed cloth of his coat. Luckily, there'd be no wife to discover them.

"I think she's grand," Dundee answered sincerely.

"Good! I thought so long before—But, tell me! What class would you say she belongs to? I mean, would you say she's—patrician?" Kay Loring amazed him by asking.

"Patrician? . . . No," Dundee answered slowly. "I'd say, regardless of the claims of her press agent, that she's of peasant stock. There's a sort of earthiness about her. A peasant's stockiness and strength, in spite of her slimness, which is, I imagine, the result of constant dieting. Why?"

"I just wondered," the girl murmured. "So you really, like her a lot?"

"I'm not a movie fan, but I believe she's my favorite screen star," Dundee told her. "In fact, a while ago I was angry for her sake. Remember you asked me if I was *very* angry? When you were trying to 'pick me up,' you know."

"Yes," Kay chuckled. "I thought you were furious because it was only me that had sent the ticket."

"I was simply boiling at the thought that the fickle public, as represented by this audience tonight, will, probably break Conova's heart—if other audiences haven't already broken it."

"I'm afraid it's been broken—a long time," the girl said, her voice very grave and low. "Shh! We can't talk any more now. Mr. Gordon's going to spout and gloat."

The theater manager did indeed spout and gloat; but the detective's ears were closed to his platitudinous and ungrammatical speech. Dundee was shamelessly beset with curiosity. What did this "newspaperman" beside him really know? Was it possible that he—Dundee—was lending himself and the dignity of his connection with the district attorney's office some publicity stunt? But almost instantly he dismissed the idea. This girl was flippant and possibly too hail-fellow-well-met, but she was straight and decent. She was too proud of being a "newspaperman" to use her press connection for monkeyshines. Somehow Dundee was very sure of that. And he was equally sure that she had something so serious on her mind, something that actually frightened her so much thi she was acting a bit too hard in an effort to conceal it. Yola Conova—Blackmail.

"And now, ladies and gentlemen, I take great pleasure in introducing to you Mr. Max Weinberg, manager of this personal appearance tour for these two great stars of World Wide Pictures—the incomparable Conova, and the new sensation of talking pictures—Clinton Risher."

The theater manager had been interrupted by a slight spatter of applause at the mention of the actress' name, but a perfect storm of hand-clapping followed his ringing pronunciation to the male star's name. Dundee involuntarily clenched his fist then grinned at his own fierce partisanship.

"Me, too," said a voice near his shoulder.

'Who raved in print about 'the personification of masculinity'? Who said this Risher headache was 'sex appeal plus more virile than Clark Gable, more—'"

"Who's been telling on me?" the girl demanded. "He's really all I said he was, but I'll hate him to pieces if he hogs the show tonight. I want Hamilton, of all places, to give her a big hand. It simply *must*, I tell you! I wish I had ten pairs of hands to clap when she comes on."

"Why Hamilton, particularly?" Dundee wanted to know but the stout lady on his right turned and glared at the whisperers so fiercely that they both subsided.

Mr. Max Weinberg seemed to be an uncommonly jolly little man. Beneath a thatch of tight gray curls his ruddy face beamed with good humor. He spoke with exuberant briskness, but as his slightly accented voice rushed on, Dundee became convinced, oddly enough, that the little man was not feeling half so jolly and cocksure as he would have his audience believe.

"Now, ladies and gentlemen," the manager of the tour was saying, after his preliminary remarks, "I am not going to keep you on tenterhooks. I know what all of you are saying to yourselves: 'We didn't pay five dollars for a ticket to hear a guy named Weinberg make a speech. We came here to see our favorite star of the silver screen. We came here to see—*Yola Conova*!'"

He brought out the name, after a pause, as if he were trumpeting it through a megaphone. Then he waited, his curly gray head cocked, his eyeglasses gleaming expectantly. There was a spatter of applause, which Kay Loring and Dundee tried to swell to the proportions of an ovation.

"Well, folks," Weinberg beamed, "I'm not going to keep you waiting. I'm going to introduce to you the Incomparable Conova, the Duse of the screen. . . . Come, my dear!"

The curtains of royal purple velvet were parting slowly, to reveal a dais, in the center of which was a tall gilt chair. And, in the chair like a queen on her throne, sat a slender, dark woman. For a full minute she remained very still, ignoring the manager's invitation, her hands loosely clasped in her lap, her head slightly bent, her dark eyes brooding upon the audience. There was a deep hush, broken only by quick-drawn gasps of admiration, then a storm of applause, augmented by whistling and the stamping of feet.

"She's got them going, thank God!" Kay Loring breathed. "Isn't she divine? And—isn't America a strange and wonderful country?"

Dundee was too engrossed to ask her what she meant. Probably nothing half so cryptic as she made the platitude sound. . . . He leaned forward tensely. Conova had risen. Standing motionless for a moment beside her throne she looked every inch the queen. The form-fitting sheath of her black velvet gown, cut extremely low, made

her seem much taller than she was, and slender to
fragility. But it was not her exotic beauty that made
Dundee draw a sharp breath. The actress, he felt sure,
was not posing beside her chair for effect. She was
waiting until her trembling legs could carry her across
the stage.

"Poor thing!" whispered Kay Loring. "She's simply
dying of stage fright. To think she's still timid, after all
these years—"

Yola Conova was walking now, but with a stiffness
and jerkiness which made the stately gown itself look a
bit awkward, almost absurd. Somewhere a girl giggled
convulsively. Before others could follow suit Max
Weinberg had sprung the star's side, taken one of her
hands in his, and thrown affectionate, protective arm
across her bare shoulders.

"Say a few words to all your friends out there, Yola,
darling," he urged in a loud, hearty voice. . "You don't
have to make a long speech, child. *She's got stage fright
folks!*" he confided to the audience, with a broad smile.
"Tell her to be afraid of you! Tell her you love her! Come
on, now! All together now—W*hat's the matter with Yola?*"
he shout like a Rotary Club chairman.

The little man was irresistible. The audience, in one
great, good-natured voice, bellowed its answer: *"She's all
right!"* The actress smiled, a frightened smile that jerked
her lips oddly.

"Thank you—so much," she gasped. "I—I *am* a little
frightened, I think. Appearing before an audience is so—
different from acting before the camera and the
microphone. But I want you all to believe that I am happy
to be here. Proud and happy. So—so very proud to be in—
Hamilton—"

At the strange emphasis on the name of the town Kay
Loring 's hot fingers closed suddenly over Dundee's left
hand.

"—more proud than any of you can guess," the star
continued, her voice suddenly full and clear. "It's like a

dear, dream come true, this being face to face with those who—" Suddenly, out of the balcony, came the shrill voice of a girl: "Where's Clinton Risher? *We—want—Clinton—Risher!*" Instantly the cry was taken up by at least fifty female voices.

The words were shouted in a strange, primitive rhythm: "*We—want—Clinton—Risher!*"

Kay Loring covered her face with her hands.

Dundee clenched his fists.

"Damn, damn, *damn* these fool women!" he muttered; but his eyes, fascinated, clung to the woman on the stage.

He saw her head go up in a proud, swift gesture. Her famous nostrils flared, and her mouth became a thin streak of scarlet. To Dundee her scorn seemed magnificent. He knew she was not afraid of her audience now. She despised it.

It was not until that ugly sound had died completely and had been succeeded by a breathless, frightened hush, that Yola Conova spoke. There was not a tremor in her voice, and, to Dundee's amazement, not a trace of arrogance or anger.

"It is my great pleasure," she said, "to introduce to you in person one whose screen personality made so instantaneous an appeal to all of you. One who, because you love him, is soon to be made a star. . . Clinton! Come along, Clinton!"

Kay Loring had dropped her hands from her flushed face, on which tears were glistening.

"Isn't she wonderful, Mr. Dundee?" she gasped in a broken whisper.

"Really wonderful," the detective nodded gravely. This was no time to ask her why she cared so tremendously.

From the wings a young man stepped. At first sight of him the audience broke into a wild storm of applause. Dundee, prepared instinctively to dislike the public's new idol, and to criticize anything he might do, wondered cynically just how this Clinton Risher would respond to the ovation. But the almost hysterical enthusiasm of the audience apparently have no effect upon him at all, save to make him run the last few steps that carried him to the star's side. And there he did a strange thing—did it with just enough awkwardness to make the gesture seem lovably impulsive, rather than theatrical. He knelt upon one knee, took Yola Conova's hand in both his, raised it to his lips and kissed it.

On his feet again, the boy whirled to fate the crowd, and Dundee saw that his cheeks were red with a violent blush. "Gosh!" the young actor exploded. "I never kissed a girl's hand before in all my life—not even in a movie! But the funny thing is, I don't feel half as foolish as I must have looked. Fact is; folks, I just couldn't help myself. Imagine being introduced on a real stage by a great star like *Yola Conova*! Gee, folks! *Yola Conova*! If the Queen of England called a private out of her army to come and stand beside he that soldier couldn't feel near as honored and grateful as I do today, to be privileged to stand up here beside Yola Conova and have a little share in the grand welcome you're giving her. Of course, compared to *her*, the greatest actress on the screen—"

Something, possibly a strange, choking sort of exclamation from Kay Loring, made Dundee turn his eyes from the boy to Yola Conova. The effect of this passionate championship was a queer one, certainly. The actress had retreated a step two, as if she wished to escape. Her head was tilted toward a hunched right shoulder, and her right hand, palm outward, was raised to her forehead, as if to shield her face from a blow. And in her dark eyes there was an expression so piteous, oddly humble, that Dundee's heart contracted sharply.

"—I don't amount to a hill of beans," he heard the actor crying out vehemently. "But traveling with her, like I've been doing, and having the great privilege to know her personally has been such an inspiration to me that I give you all a promise right now to try to learn to be a real actor."

Almost as soon as the boy had begun to speak, the fog of cynicism and contemptuous dislike through which the detective had seen him but dimly began to melt, dispelled as if by the beams of a strong sun. And now he had to acknowledge that the young man was extraordinarily handsome. In the powerful spotlight the boy's thick, slightly curling hair was the color of amber, his skin a golden tan, and his wide-set eyes, beneath the most nobly modeled brow Dundee had ever seen except in the statues of Greek youths, seemed to be of the same luminous amber. As for the boy's body—again a Greek statue seemed the only possible comparison. But how strange to hear a Praxiteles sculpture speak with the Texas drawl and in the homely Texas idiom! Strange, but somehow endearing.

From the neighborhood of his left shoulder came a low murmur: "Ironic, isn't it? He's head over heels in love with Conova, and to save his life he can't help ruining this tour for her. But isn't he a dear?"

On the stage little Weinberg was speaking again:

"—just to meet you folks, and say hello. But you'll have a chance to see them again, after the showing of Miss Conova's great new picture, 'Magnificent Sin,' when both Miss Conova and Mr. Risher will appear in a fine little one-act play written especially for them. And on behalf of these two fine artists of the silver sheet I would to thank you—"

While the applause was still raging, although the lights were being dimmed for the showing of the feature picture, Kay Loring rose suddenly in her seat.

"Come along!" she urged Dundee. "Leave your hat and coat."

He obeyed without question, or argument, but not swiftly, stumbling past obstinate knees, till he reached the aisle.

"Being a runt is occasionally an advantage," his leader assured him, as she grasped his arm firmly and hurried him—not toward the rear of the theater, but toward the stage.

"Are *you* going to make a speech?" Dundee protested.

"If you weren't a very poor detective," Kay Loring told him severely, "you'd have deduced that we're going backstage."

"But why? . . . Oh, sorry! I was forgetting your exalted calling. Are you going to permit me to be present while you interview our visiting celebrities?"

"I'm not looking for an interview now," she told him, as she opened an inconspicuous door to the left of a tier of boxes.

"Then why—"

"Because I'm sure now," she told him cryptically, but spoiled the effect slightly by adding, in a troubled voice: "Almost sure."

"Sure of what?"

"I'll tell you when I'm sure I'm sure. . . . Come on. But watch your step. And don't get in the way of the scene-shifters. They aren't a respectful crew, and not even a special investigator attached to the district attorney's office impresses then noticeably. Down this way, I think. I suppose she'll have the same dressing room Helen Hayes had—Oh! Wait a minute!'

Puzzled, but unprotesting, Dundee allowed himself to be pulled into a cavern beneath a flight of rickety stairs. These backstage regions were cold and drafty, entirely unromantic. He wished for the overcoat he had left behind him.

"You're trembling," he accused the girl, with sudden solicitude. "Or just shivering? It's cold as a tomb back here—"

"Shut up!" she commanded, in a sharp whisper, her little fingers digging mercilessly into his upper arm. "Just look—and listen!"

Dundee looked. He saw a man coming toward them from the opposite direction, as if he might have arrived by way of the stage entrance in the alley. A typical actor,

Dundee told himself, with the slight contempt characteristic of men of more virile professions. As typical an actor as that boy, Clinton Risher, was typically not an actor in personality and speech. In the raw light of an unshaded globe swinging from a ceiling cord, the detective saw that the man was an Englishman or at least an imitation of an Englishman. A cane. A monocle on a narrow black ribbon. Evening clothes of impeccable smartness. A top hat. And, on his pallid, thin face, an expression of vacuous superiority. A sort of embalmed sniff.

"I don't like to look at him," Dundee complained to the girl.

"Then just listen," she scolded, in her husky whisper. "By the way, if you don't know, that's Conova's husband. His name is Geoffrey Arundel."

"Inevitably," Dundee sighed.

"I don't understand his being here," Kay whispered, a frown pleating her freckled forehead. "He's supposed to be in New York, rehearsing for a stage play. Listen!"

They were not too far away, in their cavern under the stairs, to hear the subdued rapping of his gloved fingers upon a dressing-room door. He knocked, and was then elegantly bored and impatient at being kept waiting. At last he raised his stick and knocked with the thick round head of it, three staccato raps. This time he did not have to wait. The door was opened a few inches, and the eavesdroppers under the stairs saw a blonde and pretty head appear.

"Miss Conova cannot be dis—" they heard the blonde girl begin, then, after, a startled "Oh!" she stepped into the narrow corridor, closing the door soundlessly behind her. Her next words were low-spoken but quite audible: "Oh, Mr. Arundel! What a surprise! Miss Conova isn't expecting you—"

Kay Loring giggled—a tiny sound smothered in her handkerchief. "Look at him!" she begged, in her husky whisper. "That's what is known as drawing oneself up to one's full height. In this case, a full five feet seven, if an inch. You'd think he was playing a part on the stage—"

"Now you shh!" Dundee interrupted, for if he was going to be an eavesdropper he wanted to be a thorough one.

"How do you do, Miss Patton?" they heard the English man say, with condescending cordiality. "Nice to see you again. And how is Mrs. Arundel?"

Fortunately for the listeners under the stairs, the blonde girl seemed to have no doubt of being alone with the man, for her words, in their crisp eastern accent, were delivered with great distinctness:

"I'm really quite worried about her, Mr. Arundel. I'm afraid she's more upset this evening than usual. She's just come off after the introduction, you know, and I've persuaded her to lie down and sip a hot drink I had ready for her. So—"

"Too bad! Too bad!" the actor interrupted in a quick clipped voice. "You're being very watchful—very careful, I trust, Miss Patton?"

"Oh, yes, sir!" the girl assured him earnestly, her hand clasped for a moment against her heart. "I try never to Iet her out of my sight, and I do everything I possibly can to cheer her up, to keep her interested and amused, just as you told me—".

"Quite! Quite! Good girl! I was sure I could depend upon you, Miss Patton. . . . Now, will you be so kind as to tell my wife I am here—"

Kay Loring's fingers dug into Dundee's arm, which was beginning to be sore from so much clutching.

"What's it all about?" she breathed, and Dundee, looking down at her, saw that her childish, freckled face was white milk.

"Strange he doesn't barge right in," the detective muttered.

"Not so strange," Kay contradicted. "According to the tatbloid keyhole peepers the Conova-Arundel romance has gone ph-t! But who is the blonde Venus? A sort of— keeper? Oh! I wonder— Yes, I bet that's it! Oh!"

"What's what?" Dundee demanded almost irritably, for he was growing a bit tired of mystery heaped upon mystery. But Kay did not answer. Her eyes, very big and round now, were fixed upon the actor, who, kept waiting again, was tapping an impatient patent leather evening shoe, as he delicately scratched the tiny mustache on his long upper lip.

"He isn't really a bad actor, in sophisticated comedies," the newspaper girl whispered, as if bent on giving the devil his due. "But the public simply can't go for him. Not having any at any price, thank you. Poor Conova tried to cram him down their throats for a year or two after she married him, but the result was rising gorge. It hurt her more than it did him, very literally speaking—"

The door opened again, and again was closed noiselessly behind the blonde girl.

"I'm awfully sorry, sir," they heard her apologize, "but Miss Conova says she cannot see you this evening. Perhaps tomorrow about noon—"

The actor stepped back at the rebuff. He gasped and sputtered incoherently for a moment, then his manner changed suddenly.

"I quite understand," he said, in his clear, clipped voice. "Quite! . . . Too bad! Too bad! Poor girl!. . . By the way, Miss Patton, I am stopping at the Hamilton Hotel— just in case my wife changes her mind this evening, you know. Please try to persuade her to do so. My train leaves for New York at 7:55 in the morning—beastly hour!"

"I'll do my best, sir."

"I'm quite sure you will, my girl," the Englishman agreed. "In any event, continue to keep me posted. By wire, if necessary. If my poor wife does not improve by the end of the week, I shall insist upon her giving up this beastly tour—and contract be hanged!"

"Yes, sir."

"Remember now! This evening, if possible. But I shall quite understand if it cannot be managed. . . . Good night, Miss Patton!"

"You can depend on me, sir. Good night."

The watchers saw the Englishman turn and walk away toward the alley exit. But his step had lost its jauntiness. His stick was tucked under his arm now, not swinging blithely as when he had arrived.

"Poor devil!" Dundee whispered, with sudden sympathy "It's not all beer and pretzels, being married to a temperamental—"

"Look!" Kay commanded, in a sharp whisper.

Dundee obeyed. The girl whom Geoffrey Arundel had called Miss Patton was taking cautious, tiptoe steps down the corridor, in the wake of the departing husband, apparently to make sure he was really leaving the theater.

"Damned funny, if you ask me," Dundee muttered, as the girl tiptoed out of sight.

"Look!" his companion again commanded, and Dundee's eyes followed hers obediently.

Although there had been no sound of its opening, a door almost directly opposite the star's dressing room now stood wide; and, framed in it, a man was standing.

"Clinton Risher!" Kay Loring breathed. "His door must have been ajar all the time. He heard it all—"

Just then the blonde reappeared, running lightly and swiftly. At sight of the young actor she stopped suddenly, gave a great sigh of relief, and passed a hand wearily over her forehead. "He's gone at last," she said. "I thought I'd never get rid of him."

"You knew I was listening?" they heard the boy ask, in curiously rough voice. "Well, I was! And I'm not ashamed either! It was all I could do to keep from butting right in am telling that 'Quaite-quaite' son-of-a-gun just what Yola thinks of him, and that he's wasting his time trying to make it up with her—"

"Shh, Mr. Risher! He might come back," the Patton girl pleaded.

"Let him! Let him!" the boy stormed. "It doesn't suit me at all to play hide-and-seek. If Yola hadn't made me promise to stand by and do nothing until this damned tour is over—"

"But you did promise, Mr. Risher," the blonde girl insisted, in a pleading, soothing voice. "You know how she is now. Don't, *don't* make it harder for her by being rash—"

"Yeah! I know! I'm trying to be patient, ain't I? But— Oh, *Lord*!"

And the door slammed behind him, as the boy plunged back into his own dressing room.

"Isn't love wonderful?" Kay Loring breathed. "The hopes of a million girls doomed to perish—"

"Yours among them, I suppose," Dundee interrupted, in his normal voice, since the Patton girl had also disappeared behind the door of the star's dressing room.

"Yes, 'Here lies love'," Kay quoted flippantly. "But I must be brave. Duty calls. The show must go on. Come along."

Seen at close quarters when she responded to Kay's knock, Miss Patton proved to be not quite so pretty or so young as she had seemed at a distance. In the raw light of the unshaded electric lamp the fine lines around her blue eyes were only too evident, as were two deeper lines between her carefully plucked eyebrows. Under that light, too, the roots of her hair, exposed along the side parting, showed a dull brown, in contrast with the bright gold of her carefully set curls.

"I must speak with Miss Conova on a matter of urgent importance," Kay was saying.

"I'm sorry, but Miss Conova can see no one until after the show," Miss Patton told her crisply.

"I think she will see *me*," Kay persisted. "Tell her it's Ginger—'Ginger' Loring. Tell her it's terribly important. And be sure to say it's Ginger that's calling."

The star's companion or maid, or whatever she was, looked surprised, almost startled. She seemed about to ask a question, but caught it. Her voice was quite unruffled as she said:, "I'll give her the message, of course, but—You'll pardon me for closing the door?"

"'Ginger'!" Dundee repeated, and chuckled, his eyes on her mop of rust-red curls. "May I call you that, Ginger?"

"No, you may not!" she retorted. "I haven't let anyone call me that since I was a kid—not since I was big enough to fight with some chance of winning."

"*Big* enough?" Dundee laughed "You're not big enough now to lick a ten-year-old boy, Ginger. So you knew Yola Conova when you were a kid. That's what all the mystery means, is it?"

Before the girl could reply, the door was opened again at the Patton woman stepped out, closing the door behind her.

"I'm sorry, Miss Loring, but Miss Conova cannot be disturbed. And she asked me to say that she knows no one called 'Ginger'."

"She—really said—that?" Kay whispered, her little freckled face quite white. Then, with a sudden snap of her fingers, at an impish grin on her face, she spoke loudly: "O.K.! I hope she's quite sure. It takes a big load off my mind. If she never knew 'Ginger' Loring, then she never knew a man call 'Dink,' and everything's just lovely. Quaite! Quaite! . . . Good night, Miss Patton! I hope your—*patient*—rests well."

II

JAMES F. DUNDEE, Special Investigator, was not a patient man, nor was he naturally a docile one. Neither was he experienced in being treated as a piece of furniture by girls who accepted him as an escort. Of course this girl who was ignoring him so completely had not "accepted" an invitation from him. She had commanded his presence and supplied the ticket! All of a piece with the rest of her behavior this strange evening.

Dundee, sitting very straight and stiff in his seat in the theater, so that she could see how indignant he was; stole a glance at Kay Loring without turning his head. Silly little idiot! Just look at the way she was eating up that ridiculous movie! A dyed-in-the-wool picture fan! *She*—a critic? Why, she had no more discrimination than any of these other fans. Not as much, apparently, as some. That fat woman on his right, for instance, must have good taste enough to be bored or disgusted with cinematic trash, for she was leaving. Good riddance! More room for his elbow. . . . The audience, on the whole, was enduring the picture rather than enjoying it. And quite fair of them, too, Dundee conceded, in spite of his partisanship for Yola Conova. The photography was superb, but not even the tropics gorgeously filmed could turn "Magnificent Sin" into anything more important than tawdry trifling. As for Yola Conova. . . . Where was that fire, that strange dark vitality, combined with a suggestion of hushed listening to untellable secrets, which had made this woman a star almost overnight, seven or eight years ago? All gone now, Dundee discovered unhappily. And in their place only a deadly indifference. No, not indifference. Fatigue and dull anger, rather, as if the woman who had strolled and drawled unwillingly through this silly picture had been fully conscious that she was through. All washed up. If only, Dundee thought suddenly, motion-picture stars and presidents of the United States could die at the very height of their careers, how much suffering could be spared them and how much disillusion spared the public. Only the fortunate, like Warren Harding and Jean Harlow, died "in office," and were spared the ignominy of living on, as dethroned monarchs. Yola Conova had been a queen, worshiped by enraptured millions. She was a queen no longer. She was just a tired, sick, resentful woman, hating the one-time subjects who had weaned of her rein. Why did she not 'abdicate gracefully? Surely she was a very rich woman. And if she really was as tired and ill as she seemed in this picture, surely retirement—with much money—would be "the better role."

With a start Dundee, realized that he had forgotten his grouch against Kay Loring. Grinning at himself and at her, he glanced at the girl again. Funny little piece! Not pretty with those freckles and those wiry red curls, but—rather bright. Her lips were parted now, in breathless interest, like a child's. How old was she? Not less than eighteen, surely; certainly not more than twenty. But she looked no more than fifteen, with her tiny, immature body, and those absurd freckles.

What was her game, anyway? Why had she—clever enough—inveigled him into sharing her pair of tickets to show that was a sheer waste of his time? Sanderson, he knew would have guessed instantly that the girl was trying to "make" him. But Dundee knew that, whatever else she might be, Kay Loring was not a flirt. Romantic, and in love with mystery and intrigue—yes; but not—

Suddenly the girl leaned back in her chair, and looked at him, her brown eyes filled with laughter.

"Quit trying to psychoanalyze me," she said, in a clear undertone. "I haven't been taking you for a ride; I'm not a silly kid playing at mystery-hatching; and you haven't been wasting your precious time. But I can't explain till the show is over. Now, smile pretty for the lady!"

"Brat!" he muttered at her, but he smiled. "And *you* quit reading *my* mind. It upsets me, Ginger!"

She jerked straight again. "Quick! The picture's ending. Clap! Clap for all you're worth, Bonnie Dundee! Clap, damn you!"

Feeling like a fool, Dundee obeyed, smiting palm against palm with all his strength. And such is the psychology of the mob that the example of two madly applauding fans stirred those around them—slowly, it is true; but in less than a minute nearly the whole of the audience was applauding.

"Thank God for that!" Kay Loring sighed piously, as she breathed upon her reddened palms to cool them. "And thank *you*, Bonnie Dundee I couldn't have managed alone."

"At last I know why you wanted me here," he answered "You'd heard that I have unusually big hands. So glad your one-man claque made good."

"You can laugh if you like," the girl whispered fiercely, "but if I can help it that poor thing shan't commit suicide in Hamilton."

Dundee's jaw dropped. Literally, for Kay Loring leaned toward him and with her small fist gave an upward thrust at it, giggling as she heard his teeth click.

"You're a dumb egg," she accused him, almost tenderly. "What on earth did you suppose Arundel and that nurse were talking about?"

Dundee flushed. Damn the brat's insolence, and her egotism! But—she *was* keen-witted. Almost psychic. Look at the way she had read his mind from the very first. With real humility, he reviewed that strange conversation between the Patton woman and Geoffrey Arundel. How had the Englishman phrased it? "You're being very watchful, very careful, I trust, Miss Patton?" . . . Yes, those were his very words. Thank heaven for the kind of ears that registered accurately. And what had the woman replied? Something about never letting Conova out of her sight, trying to keep her interested and

amused—'just as you told me," she had added. And from
nothing more than this the girl beside him had
constructed a whole theory of contemplated suicide, with
the star watched day and night by a nurse in the employ
of a worried husband. A husband who, strangely enough,
in view of his evident solicitude, was so estranged from
his wife that she would not even see him after he had
journeyed from New York to be with her for a few hours.

The lights were dimming again. The motion-picture
screen had disappeared, and the rich velvet curtains
waited to be drawn upon the one-act play in which Yola
Conova and Clinton Risher were to make their "personal
appearance." And Max Weinberg was preparing the
audience for the treat in store for it, as he phrased it.
Dundee did not listen. He was watching the girl at his
side.

She sat slumped in her seat, her head tilted against
the high back, her eyes closed, her arms extended limply
along the arms of her chair. She looked very small and
very tired—a most exhausted. There was a pitiful droop
to the corners her childish mouth, and, to his amazement,
Dundee saw traces of tears among the freckles on her
now pale, almost wan cheeks. For the first time, then, he
took her seriously. Whatever all the mystery might be,
this child was not enjoying it, not making a lark of it. He
was suddenly sure it was terribly real to her, and really
terrible—whatever it was. She looked, he decided, with a
rush of pity, as if the dark wink of tragedy had brushed
across her face.

"Wake up, Ginger!" he whispered, for the curtains
were parting slowly. He touched one of her limp hands. It
was ice cold.

"I wasn't asleep," she protested, in a forlorn little
voice. "I was thinking—and remembering."

"And why were you—crying?" he whispered.

"Because I was terribly hurt tonight," she confessed,
her lip quivering. "Oh, look! It's a lovely set, isn't it? . . .

Doesn't she look marvelous in that wine-colored gown? She always loved that color—"

Dundee sighed. He might as well contain himself until the show was over and he could make her explain. No use speculating on this new angle to the mystery.

The playlet proved to be unexpectedly good, and well suited to the couple it was exploiting. A "Fata Morgana" sort of theme, showing an awkward, innocent, idealistic boy, worshipfully in love with a glamorous, disillusioned woman of the world. Never seen, but well realized, was the equally young and idealistic girl the boy should have loved. In a climax that was really moving, almost tremendous, the older woman—played by Conova, of course—deliberately killed the boy's love, because she loved him and knew herself unworthy. Disgusted him in the one sure way—by offering her body with the casualness of a prostitute, when the most he had dared dream was to kiss her hand reverently. Shocked him, saw him run from her—straight to clean youth, she knew; and then, as the curtain slowly fell, sought about for means of committing suicide in the least painful, least disfiguring way.

"Oh, the damned idiots!" Kay Loring almost sobbed. "To give *her* a play with an ending like that!"

Dundee nodded, sympathetic with her distress. But as the applause thundered on and on, he was trying to put his finger on exactly what had seemed strange about the star's performance. She had overcome her stage fright, apparently, but there had been a stiffness, a lack of ease in her acting which surprised him. Actually, she had seemed amateurish. Of course she was an amateur before the footlights.

"Wasn't Clinton Risher wonderful, the way he built her up and subdued himself?" Kay Loring murmured. "Bless the boy, for a very Christian gentleman! Shall we beat it now, before the rush?"

They were among the first to leave, but in the lobby Kay collided with a distinguished-looking, middle-aged man who had run down the stairs from the balcony.

"So sorry, Professor Martin!" she apologized. "Are you looking for Mrs. Martin? She left in the middle of the picture. Did you see the show yourself? I was wondering why you weren't here."

The man flushed and muttered an inarticulate reply, for which Kay did not wait, but she was laughing as she led the way out of the too-warm theater into the too-cold November night. A raw wind was whipping up the day's debris in the gutter, a nasty, unfriendly wind that snatched at hats and coattails, and flung grit into eyes and nostrils.

There were few people abroad, except for the crowd that would soon be pouring out of the theater. At the intersection of Main and Houston an overcoated traffic cop beat his gloved hands to and stamped his feet to keep warm. On the corner, their eyes on the Egyptian Theater, stood two patrolmen, idly swinging their billies.

"Let's cut through the alley to First Street," Kay suggested, shivering and wrapping her shabby muskrat coat more closely about her narrow hips.

With heads lowered against the wind they started down the alley, Dundee's hand gripping her elbow firmly, for it seemed to him that a particularly strong gust might sweep her off her feet.

Halfway through the alley she stopped suddenly, flung up her head, and pointed.

"Stage Entrance!" She read aloud the words painted above a closed door. "Were you ever a stage-door Johnny, Mr. Dundee?"

"How old do you think I am?" he protested "Stage door Johnnies were extinct even before the war, I'd have you know—"

"Quaite! Quaite!" she laughed. "But you're going to be one now. And me, too!"

"You don't mean—?"

"Of course I do! I've got to see her close, as close as I can get, before I spin my yarn for you, Mr. Special Investigator.

"She won't be long, I'll bet. . . . There's a car now, turning in from First. One of those sedans with a chauffeur that you can rent by the day or week from the Randolph Hotel's garage, if I'm not mistaken. Yowser! My eagle eye does not fail me. That's the chauffeur they always give our visiting celebs. He has the grandest legs ever seen in a pair of Cordovan puttees—"

"Stand back, Ginger!" and Dundee jerked her out of the path of the shining black sedan, just as it rolled to a smooth stop directly in front of the stage entrance.

"Told you I'm famous," Kay reminded her escort proudly, when the chauffeur, upon descending from the sedan, had touched his cap and murmured; "Good evening, Miss Loring."

"Let's wait on this side of the car. We'll be practically hidden until she gets in, and then we can see her very clearly through the car windows. Here comes the nurse. Bend low, so—"

"Another stage door Johnny," Dundee interrupted, in a whisper.

"Where?" Kay demanded, and straightened from her crouching position to peer around the back of the car, in the direction of Dundee's gaze.

A peculiarly unattractive man had just turned into the alley and was sauntering, with cocky insolence, toward the stage entrance. On his narrow head was tilted a green velours hat, and beneath his sharp Adam's apple an orange tie was knotted. The face between, these splendors was long, thin, and, yellow, with pale, lashless eyes, and the teeth of an ancient horse. The knob of his long nose was peculiarly like a nearly ripe boil.

Only a mother could love such a creature, Dundee was sure; but after all, the man was no Frankenstein monster. Nor half nasty enough, really, to cause Kay Loring, esthetically sensitive though she might be, to shudder and cling.

"Ginger!" Dundee whispered, patting the two small hands clamped about his arm.

But she did not seem to hear him. Still clinging to him, she was staring straight through the sedan windows to the door which Yola Conova was following the Patton woman. And so Dundee stared, too.

The screen star, hatless and still in the wine-red evening dress she had worn for the one-act play, was shivering as she wrapped an ermine coat more closely about her. With the suddenness of a snake striking, the man in the green hat and orange tie was at the star's side, had seized one of her hands, and with an almost savage gesture, shoved up the wide sleeve of the ermine coat toward the woman's shoulder, so that her right arm was exposed.

The chauffeur's gloved fist crashed against the man's head, bent so low over that exposed arm that he seemed about to bite it. The green hat rolled in the dirt of the alley.

"Police!" shouted the chauffeur.

Kay Loring swung her weight on Dundee's arm. "Don't interfere yet," she said, pulling him back. "Look! Listen!"

Dundee had no need to be told to look, for, if this strange girl would not permit him to use his fists, he had every intention of using his eyes to the best advantage.

The man who had dared lay hands upon the star was grinning—an evil grimace of triumph that showed all of his horsy teeth.

"Call the police! O.K. by me," he challenged the chauffeur, but his eyes were upon the white, pinched face of the star, who seemed to be almost fainting in the arms of her blonde attendant. "How about *you*, Miss Yola Conova? O.K. by you for the police to give me the third degree?"

The star did not answer him, but, as if her limbs were suddenly freed of paralysis, she plunged into the sedan, dragging Miss Patton with her.

"To the hotel!" they heard her order the chauffeur. "And don't stop for the police or *anyone*!"

For a moment, before the driver could take his place under the wheel, the star's face was so close to Kay Loring and Dundee that they could have touched it, if the window of the car had been lowered. And so it was that the detective looked, for one brief, illuminating moment, into the depths of those dark eyes, before they swerved from his face to that of the girl clinging to his arm.

III

"YOU'RE NOT OLD ENOUGH to have an apartment all by yourself, Ginger, my girl," Jimmy Dundee announced severely, as he settled more deeply into a Cogswell chair. "What's more, you're far too young to be entertaining a male visitor at midnight unchaperoned. But you're old enough, by a miracle of precocity, to make the best coffee I ever drank."

Kay Loring beamed at him from her nest of pillows at one end of the big couch. "I also made the walnut cookies, of which you've eaten seven. And I'm not too young for anything. I'm twenty-two years old—come Christmas. And I haven't an apartment all by myself. My stepmother lives with me. I'm sorry you can't meet her tonight. She went to the show, too, but she must have left early, because she's already in bed. I peeped into her room while the coffee was perking, and found her asleep."

"Then we mustn't disturb her," Dundee said, lowering his voice. "Now, I want you to tell me all about the mystery of Yola Conova. How did you first meet her, and why should it hurt you so for a Hollywood snob to deny your acquaintance?"

"It's sweet of you to mind," Kay said softly, "but you're being just a bit stupid. You don't really understand at all."

"I understand this much. Yola Conova recognized you tonight, and then tried to pretend she didn't."

"You think so, too?" Kay cried. "Then I'm surer than sure. Although I didn't really have many doubts all evening. And I wish it weren't true, for her sake. . . Dink is sure now, too, and I don't know what's going to happen—"

"Dink?" the detective repeated. "The poisonous gentleman in the green hat? But look here, Ginger! We've

had enough of riddles and mysterious hints. Wipe the
tears off those darling little freckles and then tell me all
about it. From the beginning, spang up to the present
moment."

"I want a cigarette first," she answered, her brown
eyes very meek and her mouth still trembling. "Then if I
cry I can pretend it's smoke in my eyes. Thank you Mr.
Dundee."

"'Thank you, Jim,'" he corrected. "By the way, I'm
trying to live down the nickname you used on the ticket
envelope."

"'Bonnie'? Why, it's as appropriate for you as Ginger is
for me. Shall we compromise on Jimmy? Well, to begin
this story. . . When I was two years old my mother died,
and later my father married again. When I was four-and-
a-half, Pauline—my stepmother—had a little baby boy.
There was something wrong with his spine. Chris never
even sat alone in all his life. . . . Damn this cigarette
smoke! . . . All newspapermen cuss like sailors," she
stopped to explain huskily.

"So I've heard tell," Dundee assured her.

"I simply adored Chris. So did Dad. He was the
sweetest, dearest, brightest—I'm *not* crying! I practically
never shed a tear. Of course Pauline was devoted to
Chris, too, but she isn't the kind that pets and pampers.
The born spinster-schoolteacher type of woman. Cold and
strict. Even Dad was awfully respectful to her, and never
a bit familiar."

"Hum-rn-m."

"You, needn't feel sorry for me!" Ginger flared,
interpreting his look. "I'm just telling you because—
Anyway, Chris couldn't go to school, of course, so when he
was five Dad found a sort of combination nurse and
governess for him, and let her teach me, too—"

Suddenly a harsh voice cut across the girl's low-
spoken confidences: "Kay! Time to go to bed! Send your
young man home at once!"

Dundee sprang to his feet. To his annoyance he felt his cheeks flushing hotly, as if he had been caught at something.

And the woman in the doorway looked as if she had convicted him as well as the girl, without benefit of trial. Tall, thin and incredibly grim, she stood there swathed in a flannel dressing-gown, regarding them both with cold suspicion.

"My stepmother, Mrs. Loring, Jimmy," Ginger faltered. "This is Mr. Dundee, Pauline. He brought me home from the theater."

"Very kind of him, I'm sure," Mrs. Loring commented in her harsh, flat voice, ignoring the introduction. "But now that you're safely home there's no need for him to keep you up till all hours. . . . Good night, young man!"

"Good night, Mrs. Loring," Dundee said, with a slight bow. "I'm sorry if we disturbed your rest."

"Mr. Dundee was just leaving, Pauline," Ginger said meekly. "Good night."

The door closed with a bang. The sound of slippered footsteps died away, down the little hall.

"I'm sorry," the girl whispered. "I did want to explain a lot of things before I showed you something. Now there won't be time. But if you're a real detective—"

She walked, a trifle unsteadily, Dundee thought, to the table near the outside door, where she had left her hat and handbag, and returned carrying an envelope so that Dundee could read the address.

It was a cheap white envelope—the kind sold for ten cents, 'a pack' in every drugstore and stationer's—and was addressed, in typing:

Miss Kay Loring, Movie Critic,
The Sun,
City.

"This thing came to the office late this afternoon," she told him, as she removed a single sheet of white paper.

"You'll notice that it was addressed to me personally. Also, that whoever typed the letter made a carbon copy. . . . Wait! I'll show you how I know that."

And, still holding both envelope and letter, she ran to a small typewriter desk in a far corner of the living room.

"I write short stories in my spare time," she whispered loudly enough for him to hear, "and I always make a carbon of the last draft, and I've noticed that— Oh!"

The detective cleared the room in long strides. "What's the matter, Ginger?"

He heard her shuffling among a litter of papers that lay beside her portable typewriter before she turned to face him, empty-handed.

Even her freckles seemed to have paled. "Nothing's the matter, nothing . . ." she denied in a rapid, shallow voice. "I've just changed my mind. That's all! I—I was playing a joke on you! It was *all* a joke. Do you hear? And you fell for it." She laughed hysterically.

"Ginger!" Dundee stopped her sharply. "You're not telling the truth."

"Don't shout," she giggled, "unless you want Pauline to join the party and hear the joke on you. Please go now. I'm—tired," she added, her voice breaking and tears starting suddenly out of her, brown eyes.

"I'll be damned If I will—".

"Please! And forgive me," she pleaded. "It was a stupid joke. I—I didn't realize you would be so—so sweet. I'd heard about how clever you are, and what a wow of a detective, so I— Please, please go! And forget all about this whole silly evening."

"I'm afraid I can't promise to do that," Dundee said stiffly. "I've enjoyed it too much to forget it. Goodnight!"

His anger, being a feeble thing at best, cooled quickly in the biting winds which whipped about him as the detective walked the few blocks to one of Hamilton's erstwhile mansions, on whose top floor he maintained bachelor quarters.

It was nearly one o'clock and he was very tired, but somehow he could not bring himself to undress and go to bed. Instead, he removed the big black silk square from his parrot's cage, gravely returned old Cap'n's sleepy greeting, and flung himself asprawl into a big leather armchair.

"I don't like it, Cap'n," he sighed, as he filled his pipe. "A practical joke? . . . Hunh! She *must* think I'm a fool! I wish I'd stayed to shake the truth out of her—poor little scared liar! . . . You know, Cap'n, the funny thing is, I'm damned sure Ginger Loring is, ordinarily, neither a timid soul nor a liar."

The parrot thrust his head through the bars of his gilt cage and yanked a lock of the detective's tousled black hair. Cap'n's idea of a caress.

"Hey! Leggo!" Dundee commanded sternly, but his blue eyes were smiling with affection. He swung the cage so that the parrot was at a safe distance but available for one of those queer, largely one-sided Watson-and-Holmes dialogues in the course of which the detective had untangled many a knotty problem during the years since he had acquired the bird as a sort of prize for solving the murder of old Mrs. Hogarth. How quickly the years had passed since that warm June night when a strange old woman had been strangled, with only her taciturn parrot as a witness! But what a witness! The newspapers still called old Cap'n "The Avenging Parrot," and the bird had long since become a symbol of the quick and deadly efficiency of the district attorney's young special investigator, when murder had been done.

"Ho, hum, Cap'n!" Dundee pretended to yawn, in the hope that it would make him sleepy. "We've had us a time, haven't we, old boy? How long has it been?" and he glanced at the loose-leaf calendar on his desk. "Thursday, November 18," he mused aloud, then scowled as the date seemed to ring a bell in his memory. Suddenly he snapped his fingers so loudly that the parrot clucked angrily. "Hey, partner!" the detective sang out. "Know what day this is? My birthday! Thirty-four years old today."

The bird cackled harshly.

"Oh, yeah? Who says so?" Dundee answered his parrot's mocking laughter. He drew a watch from his pocket and looked at it. "Laugh's on both of us, Cap'n," he admitted. "*Yesterday* was my birthday. Today is Friday, November 19. It is now forty-five minutes past twelve midnight—and I'm forty-five minutes along in my thirty-fifth year. Good Lord! Thirty-four whole years behind me! When I came to Hamilton and stumbled onto poor old Mrs. Hogarth's murder I was cocksure I'd be a big man in criminology by the time I was thirty. *I* was going to write big, fat, learned books on the psychology of criminals. Sure! *That* was me! Remember me, Cap'n? Laugh, damn you! . . . Well, what if I do stick around here? I'm having me a good enough time, even if it is the slack season for murder. What with depressions and recessions, guess I'm just plain lucky to be making enough out of a hobby to live comfortably."

The parrot laughed again, still more nastily; then deliberately, insultingly, he turned his back on his owner.

"Well, it *was* a hobby—to begin with," the man defended himself. "I was going to ride my nice little hobby of crime-detecting until I 'found' myself as a very serious writer. And now my hobby rides me, and I couldn't get away from it if I tried. . . . Thirty-four years old and no future. Not even enough salary to—have a real home, and a—"

"Shut up! Shut up! You're driving me crazy!" Cap'n exploded shrilly, whirling on his perch.

"Jealous, hunh?" Dundee taunted. "No girl would want to be a stepmother to you, you—you million-year-old hellion! I bet Ginger would get a great kick out of you. If you behave your fool self, I'll bring her to see you. But if you nip her, you limb o' Satan, look out! Because my money's on Ginger. How she's kept that much spunk with a battle-ax of a stepmother like that! Father dead. Little brother dead... I wonder what the devil she was trying to tell me when that woman butted in and, for some strange reason, scared the wits out of the kid. Let me think—" and Dundee screwed his eyes tight shut in deep concentration.

The parrot turned rapidly about on his perch, then squawked: "Bad penny! Bad penny!"

The detective was startled—illogically enough, since the words had, for nearly three and a half years, been a part of the parrot's vocabulary. But since those words had, indirectly, been the chief clue in the solving of the Hogarth murder mystery, Dundee never heard them without feeling his scalp prickle. . . .

"Bad penny," he repeated, then suddenly sat erect to stare at the bird. "Good Lord! Of course! Ginger is right. I'm stupid tonight.... So another bad penny has turned up in Hamilton! A bad penny that has been gold plated, but is still phony. . . . God! How that poor movie star must have felt, showing herself in Hamilton! What pride, and what terror! But even with the threat of blackmail hanging over her she must have gloated a bit, and laughed."

If Kay's stepmother had not interfered—after having eavesdropped, perhaps—what strange tale of a nursemaid's disgrace would Kay Loring have unfolded to him? Dundee wondered. For he was absolutely sure now that it was under the burden of such knowledge that the little newspaper reporter had been jittery all evening. Knowledge shared by how many others in that huge audience? Certainly by Dink, that evil-looking creature of the green hat and orange necktie. Was Dink the author of the blackmail letter which Ginger had inexplicably, decided to withhold?

"She was telling me that a carbon copy, had been made," Dundee said aloud. "It is undoubtedly Ginger's theory that the copy was sent to Yola Conova. If she is right, Conova must have been terrified when Ginger tried to see her, thinking she was there as a reporter and because she had received the original of the letter. If she really has been in a suicidal frame of mind lately—"

With sudden energy he hitched his chair closer to the desk and reached for the telephone.

"Randolph Hotel? . . . I want to speak with Miss Conova!"

The voice of the hotel switchboard operator was bored and weary as she answered: "Miss Conova has left orders that she is not to be disturbed."

"This is James F. Dundee, of the district attorney's office," the detective announced crisply. "Please ring Miss Conova's room."

There was a significant change in the operator's voice "Please hold the line, a moment, Mr. Dundee. . . . Randolph Hotel. . . . No, *ma'am*! I've told you three times already I can't ring Miss Conova for you. Please don't call again. Hello, Mr. Dundee! I'm sorry, but I really can't ring Miss Conova, At 12:45 she gave orders she wasn't to be disturbed again, and then she left the receiver off the hook Shall I connect you with the manager's office?"

Dundee considered, frowning. Then: "No, thanks. I'll call in the morning"

But he had scarcely replaced the receiver when he removed it again, to dial another number—that of Police Headquarters.

"Dundee speaking. Let me have the night chief, please. . . Hello, Kelly! Dundee. . . . Fine, thanks. Listen, chief! Do you know a fancy-dressed bird whose first name or nickname is Dink?"

"Sure!" came back the night chief's lazy drawl. "Dink Garnet, that'd be. Runs a pool hall over on State Street. Quite a char-*act*-er. I've had, my eye on that baby for years, but we ain't got nothin' on him. . . . Why?"

"I was just wondering," Dundee evaded. "What's his history?"

"Well," Kelly drawled, "he's been runnin' that pool hall for ten years or so. Before that, he worked for old John Kenyon, big produce man, who died a couple of years ago. Just a billin' clerk, Dink was, but suddenly he marries a gal that worked as a maid in the Kenyon home, and sets hisself up as proprietor of this here pool hall. There was a lot of talk at the time—"

"What kind of talk?" Dundee interrupted eagerly.

"'Well, the gal he married disappeared right after the ceremony," Kelly told him, "and folks said old Kenyon had paid Dinka good hunk o' dough to marry her. Young Bruce Kenyon was engaged to be married to a society girl by the name of Helen Winter, but when he come home from college after Dink's jumped-up weddin' he lit out, and didn't show up again for months. His marriage with the Winter girl didn't take place until late that fall, though the date had been set for June. Folks put two and two together, but whether there was any truth in the scandal they cooked up, I don't know. All I know is, Dink always acted mighty free and easy with old man Kenyon, and Kenyon stood for it, in spite of the fact that he was proud as Lucifer. On the other hand, young Bruce can't bear the sight of Dink, and don't make no bones about it."

"What was the name of the girl Dink married?"

"I disremember," Kelly confessed. "I never saw the gal, myself but I understand she was pretty as a picture, and kinda foreign-lookin'. The gossips said she worked for several families here, and got into trouble with every one of 'em. Jealous wives, I reckon."

"Are Dink and the girl divorced?"

"Reckon so. Dink's been married again for six or eight years."

"You said you had your eye on Dink, chief," Dundee reminded him. "What's he suspected of?"

"Runnin' a gamblin' joint upstairs over his pool hall," Kelly answered. "He's been raided twice, but so far he's too slick for us,. Got anything on him yourself?"

"Maybe," Dundee answered. "Thanks a lot, Kelly. I'll be seeing you."

Dundee hung up the receiver and swung his chair to face the parrot again.

"A nasty business, Cap'n," he muttered. "I like it less and less. Why the devil did Yola Conova risk appearing in Hamilton? . . . Afraid to refuse to include it on the tour, I suppose."

The parrot swung upside down on his perch. "Bad penny! Bad penny!" he croaked hoarsely.

"You're a malicious old bird, Cap'n," Dundee reproved him. "I doubt if she's half as bad as you tell me. At any rate, I'd swear that Ginger loved her. . . . But what can I do? If I staged a raid on Dink's joint tonight, single-handed and without a warrant—and was lucky enough to get the goods on him, he'd be out of the jug on bail by ten o'clock tomorrow morning. And Conova is to be in Hamilton until Sunday. Oh, hell!"

He groaned and shook his head, as if it ached. For he was remembering the apprehension in a pair of dark eyes.

"We *can't* have her committing suicide in Hamilton, Cap'n" he insisted vehemently, and was unreasonably incensed when the parrot chuckled. "Shut up, or I'll wring your neck. . . What the devil can I do to help her? Ginger tried to help her, and she wouldn't even see her— By George!" His blue eyes kindled. "I wonder if Ginger can really write! Yes, I believe that would turn the trick! . . . Listen, Cap'n! Ever hear the old proverb about grasping the nettle firmly and it soft as silk remains? Well, tomorrow morning I'm going to call on Miss Yola Conova and do my damnedest to sell her the idea of nettle-grasping on a large scale With Ginger, who loved her then and who still loves her, to write the story of her life in Hamilton, her blackmailer, whoever he or she may be, will find himself holding a very empty bag. And Conova herself will have laid a ghost that undoubtedly, has haunted her all these years. If Ginger can really write. . . ."

But it was the young man rather than the detective who lost himself then in a vision of a very small girl hunched over a typewriter, her freckled face very solemn and very pink with excitement. He saw her frail, almost transparent wrists arched over the keys, and suddenly, a wave of indulgent tenderness rose up in his heart. He closed his eyes and lay back in his chair, smiling.

The telephone on the desk startled him out of a sleep almost as profound as stupor. But he awoke instantly and as he reached for the instrument his scalp began to tingle with a premonition of disaster.

"Hello! Yes, Dundee speaking. *Who?*"

The harshly urgent voice at the other end of the wire answered him: "Hepburn, manager of the Randolph Hotel. Is Miss Conova, with you, by any chance, sir?'"

"With—*me?*"

"I thought it was just possible—You see, Mr. Dundee, one of our switchboard operators told me you tried to get in touch with Miss Conova earlier this evening on a matter of urgent importance."

"Yes, I did, but—What time is it? I was asleep—"

"Terribly sorry to disturb you, Mr. Dundee," the agitated hotel manager apologized. "It's very late, I'm afraid. A quarter to three. But the fact is that Miss Conova is not in her suite, and is not with any other member of her party. Certain circumstances make her absence rather—well, disturbing. Of course these movie people think they're a law unto, themselves, and—"

"How do you know she is with none of her party?" Dundee cut in.

"As soon as I learned she was missing," Hepburn explained rapidly, "I had Branagan, the hotel detective, enter the suite occupied by Risher and Weinberg, on a pretext of looking for a sneak thief. He searched their parlor and both bedrooms thoroughly, without letting on to the gentlemen whom he was really looking for. These movie stars being what they are, I thought it likely the lady was paying a little visit to the Risher boy—"

"I see!" Dundee, feeling unreasonably angry, cut him short. "Have you checked on the husband?"

"Husband?" the hotel manager repeated, in obvious astonishment.

"Geoffrey Arundel," Dundee informed him curtly. "Registered at the Hamilton Hotel. Got into town late this evening, I understand, and has been trying to see his wife. But never mind, Hepburn. I'll check that angle myself. If I don't call you within five minutes to say I've located her with Arundel, you'll know I'm on my way to your place. In the meantime, don't notify the police until I've looked the situation over. No use stirring up a hornet's nest, if everything is all right."

"God knows I don't want the police mixed up in it," replied Hepburn. "She's probably safe and sound with her husband—"

"Probably. Good-by!" Dundee snapped.

Quickly he dialed the number of the Hamilton Hotel.

"Please ring Mr. Geoffrey Arundel's room," he requested.

"Mr. Arundel is not in his own room just now," a girl operator's voice answered. "One moment, please. Say, Grace! What's the number of that room Mr. Arundel's visiting, in?. . . 617? Oke!"

"Wait, operator!" Dundee commanded sharply. "I don't want to disturb Mr. Arundel if he is busy. Can you tell me—?"

"Oh, it's all right to ring him," the voice assured him "He said to, if any calls came. He's just playing bridge with some of our other guests. They've been playing ever since the show was over, and looks like they're going to make an all-night session of it. I'll ring him for you."

"No, thanks. I've changed my mind. But wait! Who are the other players?"

"Three of our gentlemen guests, but the hotel doesn't give out names—"

"Good girl!" Dundee applauded, hung up the receiver, and ran toward the door.

But as he was about to take his hat and overcoat on the way out the detective halted, considered for a moment, then strode back to his desk and snatched up the telephone directory. If Kay's name was listed, Yola Conova could have found it, too, and with it her former little charge's address. . . Yes, there it was!

Ginger answered so quickly that Dundee knew she had not been aroused from sleep.

"Hello!" he heard her eager voice answer; then, with a note of disappointment: "Oh! It's you, Jimmy. . . Are you still angry with me?"

"No. Are you alone, Ginger?"

"Alone?" She seemed puzzled. "Of course, except for Pauline. But why—?"

Satisfied with the information he had received, Dundee hedged as he answered: "I'm sorry I disturbed you, but I was wondering if you had changed your mind about telling me the truth, Ginger."

"I—I can't talk now." The low voice seemed strangely troubled. "Good night."

Fortunately Dundee had not garaged his car, but had broken a minor city ordinance by leaving it parked in front of the house, so that in just fifteen minutes from the time the hotel manager had called him the detective was entering the spacious, rather somberly furnished lobby of the Randolph. He found Hepburn awaiting his arrival with nervous anxiety.

Only the night clerk, a trio of bellboys, and two scrubwomen witnessed the meeting. It was three o'clock.

The hotel manager was as fashionably dressed as a floorwalker and as pompously dignified as a United States senator, but his usually florid cheeks were almost as gray now as his hair.

"Then she isn't with—" he began, but checked himself in obedience to Dundee's warning gesture. "Shall we go up to the star's suite?" he asked in a low voice. "Miss Patton's there, with Branagan, the hotel detective. . . . Pogue!" The night clerk listened obsequiously. "Relay any calls for me to Suite—"

"Just a moment, Mr. Hepburn," Dundee said, his voice calm and matter-of-fact, for he knew he was dealing with a man on the verge of panic. "Suppose we step into one of the writing rooms first. Before we question Miss Patton, I'd like very much to hear what you already know."

"I know damned little," the hotel man, confessed, as he ran a distracted hand through his thick, iron-gray hair. "This all right? . . . Certainly you may close the door, but there's no one around to listen, at this ungodly hour of the morning.... Well, Dundee, these are the few facts I have. At half past two, Pogue, the night clerk, 'phoned and woke me up. He said he had just had a call from Miss Patton, in the Conova suite—"

"Miss Patton has a bedroom in the star's suite?" Dundee interrupted.

"Yes, yes," Hepburn answered impatiently. "The suite consists of two bedrooms, two baths and a parlor. The bedrooms are separated by the bath belonging to Miss Conova's room. But—"

"Just a moment," Dundee stopped him again. "Are the telephones on separate lines?"

"No. The rooms in Suite 4-B are never let separately, so there is only one main line to the switchboard, with extensions in every room. The suite is usually taken by a family, or by a wealthy guest who wants his servant to be always within call. I don't know Miss Patton's exact status, but I gathered she was a sort of companion to the star. Miss Conova called her 'Miss Patton' and treated her as an equal, so far as I had a chance to observe."

"Thanks, Mr. Hepburn. Please go on."

"Well, Pogue said Miss Patton had just called him to ask if he'd seen Miss Conova since one o'clock this morning," the manager continued. "When Pogue said she had not passed through the lobby, the Patton woman began to cry and carry on at a great rate. Hysterical, Pogue said. Naturally I dressed and—"

"Sorry, Mr. Hepburn, but what were some of the things Miss Patton said? You've talked with Pogue since, haven't you?"

"Yes, while I was waiting for you," the manager admitted, mopping his brow. "He says she babbled a lot of nonsense about it's being all her fault, and that if Miss Conova was dead she'd never forgive herself. And, oh, yes! That Conova had tricked her, but that she—Miss Patton, I mean—should have known it was all a trick to get rid of her."

"I'd better tackle her now, I suppose," Dundee said.

"None of the elevator boys took Miss Conova down after she went to her, rooms before midnight," Hepburn volunteered, as he led the way to the nearest lift. "I made inquiries, of course. So far as I can learn no employee of the hotel saw Miss Conova after midnight. Fourth floor, Lloyd."

One of the advantages of Suite 4-B, as room clerks always pointed out to wealthy guests, was that it was so far removed from all elevators that no faint sound of their opening and closing doors could possibly penetrate into its luxurious privacy. But Dundee noted, automatically, a door with a red light above it, at the end of the thickly carpeted corridor on which 4-B opened.

"Stairs or fire-escape, Mr. Hepburn?"

"Stairs," the manager answered. "For emergency use. The building is thoroughly fire-proofed, so there are no outside fire-escapes."

"Do employees use the stairs?"

"Only if the service elevator is temporarily out of order, which doesn't happen once in a blue moon."

"Then," Dundee began thoughtfully, "she could have walked down three flights of stairs without running much chance of being seen. And there are three or four side doors, by which she could have left the hotel if she had watched her opportunity."

Hepburn frowned. "Only one side door is left open after one o'clock. The one by the flower shop on the Fifth Street side."

"One door is enough," Dundee reminded him, and the manager, raising a hand to knock on the door labeled 4-B, did not contradict.

The hoarse, strained voice of a woman called "Come in!" and the two men stepped into a small foyer, through which they passed into a very large and very beautifully furnished "parlor." Huge baskets and innumerable vases of flowers filled the room with a funereal fragrance, made doubly oppressive by the waves of steam heat which poured from concealed radiators.

"Can't we have a window open?" Dundee asked. "This room is a furnace."

But the woman who dragged herself up out of a low, overstuffed chair protested, with chattering teeth, as Hepburn strode toward the nearest of the heavily draped windows.

"I—I can't stand—any more—wind." She shivered. "I'm freezing, to death. I've g-g-got all the heat on, and I I—I c-c-can't get warm— Oooh!"

"Never mind the window, Hepburn. . . . Lie down on that couch, Miss Patton. You're having a bad chill. . . . Hepburn, get me some whiskey. Have you a hot-water, bottle, Miss Patton? . . . No, no! Lie still. We'll fix you up in a jiffy."

And they did. Within five hectic minutes the shivering, sneezing woman had been wrapped in down comforters, her icy feet had been chafed by Dundee's own warm, big hands, and then propped against a blue hot water bottle. The stiff dose of Scotch which had been poured down her throat was bringing color into her cheeks and melting the ice in her veins.

"Feeling better now?" Dundee asked briskly, as he drew up a chair to the couch.

"Much better," the woman whispered, without opening her eyes.

"Where's Branagan, the hotel detective?"

"He's searching the hotel—empty rooms and cupboards, and balconies!" she whispered faintly, and shuddered.

"Miss Patton," Dundee began slowly, "do you know where Miss Conova is?"

"Of course I don't!" the sick woman gasped.

"What do you suspect she is doing—or has done?" the detective asked, with unmistakable significance.

"I don't know what you mean," she protested. "Naturally I was alarmed when I found Miss Conova wasn't here. But I should have kept quiet—"

"Why?" Dundee cut in sharply.

"Because, if there isn't anything wrong— I mean, if she's just out on—on private business or—or pleasure," the woman floundered, "she'll never forgive me for causing a scandal—"

"Miss Patton," Dundee interrupted curtly, "how did you happen to discover Miss Conova's disappearance, or absence, if you prefer?"

"I—I went to her bedroom just before half past two, and she was not there. She had not been to bed at all. I lost my head. I didn't stop to think—"

"Why did you go to Miss Conova's room at such an hour? How did it happen you weren't asleep yourself? . . . I may as well tell you now that I've looked into your own bedroom. Your bed has not been slept in either."

"I was out," she gasped. "If I'd been here Miss Conova couldn't have left like that—"

"And you—were *you* out on business or—pleasure?"

All color drained out of the blonde woman's cheeks. Her blue eyes looked almost green against her yellowish pallor.

"Miss Conova sent me out on an errand. But there's no use asking me what the errand was. I won't tell, unless—" and a chill seized her again.

"*Unless*—" Dundee pounced.

"Unless Miss Conova herself gives me permission to tell," she concluded.

"I suggest that you intended to say, 'Unless Miss Conova does not return'," Dundee said sternly.

The woman covered her eyes with trembling hands. "Oh, I don't know what to do!" she moaned.

"The only sensible thing to do is to tell anything and everything you know that may help us in our search for Miss Conova."

"No, no!" she sobbed. "I can't do that. I promised not to. Oh, please leave me alone! She may walk in any minute—Wait! I forgot something! Her husband's here! Of course that's where she is! Oh; haven't I been an idiot?" and she began to laugh and cry hysterically.

Dundee shrugged, glanced at the hotel manager's distressed face, then shook his head slowly, as if confessing helplessness.

"Miss Patton," he began gravely, "I'm very sorry to have to tell you that Miss Conova is not now, and has not been, with her husband tonight. Please try to control yourself. Hysterics are worse than useless just now. . ... Exactly what is your relation to Miss Conova, Miss Patton? Are you her personal maid?"

Color flamed suddenly in the pallid cheeks of the woman on the couch. "Her *maid*? Certainly not!" she flared. "I was —I *am*—Miss Conova's companion."

"Thank you. . . . Now, Miss Patton—By the way, what is your full name?"

"Louise Patton."

"A very pretty name," Dundee commented cheerfully, and the woman gave him a piteous little smile. "Now, Miss Patton, I'm sure you can have no objection to telling me just how Miss Conova spent the day and evening— until she sent you out on that errand."

"I don't see what harm that could do," she agreed, with a deep sigh, then sneezed violently three times. "I'm taking an awful cold," she shivered, and pulled the down comforter more closely about her shoulders. "Well, our train got in just at noon. The station was packed and jammed with people to see the stars—"

"Did anything unusual happen at the station?" Dundee asked, leaning toward her with sudden intensity.

"Why, yes, but Miss Conova made light of it. She says a fan couldn't do anything crazy enough to surprise her. That's the reason she hates personal appearance tours, she says—"

"Just what happened, Miss Patton?"

"You know that sloping runway from the train shed up to the station? Well, it was roped off today to keep the crowds back," the star's companion explained. "But so many people pressed against it that the rope broke, and a good-looking, tall, dark man—about thirty-two or -three years old—fell right against Miss Conova, before Mr. Risher could pull her out of the way. This man caught her arm to steady himself, and looked at her for a minute in the strangest way—not smiling or apologizing or anything. Well, we walked on, but I looked back and I saw the funniest thing—"

"Yes," Dundee prodded impatiently, as she paused.

"Another man was talking to this good-looking man, and laughing, and all at once the good-looking man hauled off and slapped this other man right in the face—hard!"

Dundee whistled softly. "And the second man, Miss Patton? What was he like?"

"Flashy! Cheap-looking!" she answered promptly. "He had on a green hat and an orange necktie. But that wasn't the only time I saw him. Tonight, when Miss Conova and I were leaving the theater this same man had the nerve to grab hold of her arm. Of course, Miss Conova can't afford bad publicity, so she wouldn't let me call the police."

"I see," Dundee agreed gravely, and was silent for a moment. In his own mind there was little doubt as to the identity of the "good-looking man". So Bruce Kenyon, as well as Kay Loring and Dink Garnet, had taken pains to get a close-up of Yola Conova. "Now, Miss Patton, as to the rest of the day?"

"Mr. Gordon, the owner of the theater, took us all from the station to the hotel in his car," the woman continued. "We all had lunch together right here in this room. Miss Conova won't ever eat in the public dining rooms, because of the crowds that would gather to stare at her. Well, after lunch I persuaded her to take a nap, because she hasn't been very well for a long time, and she was awfully tired and nervous yesterday. There were a lot of reporters trying to see her, but she wouldn't give out any interviews at all—"

"Why not?" Dundee cut in sharply.

"She says she's sick and tired of publicity." The star's companion was on the defensive. "She wouldn't see the reporters in Chicago, either, and some of them were quite nasty about it—in their newspapers, I mean. But Mr. Risher saw the reporters yesterday, and explained that Miss Conova was tired, and not feeling well. They were all very nice about it, except one—"

"Yes?"

"A Miss Loring—she's the movie critic on the evening paper—was the only one that wouldn't take no for an answer," the woman told him, with sudden hostile vehemence. "Tried to trick me into letting her see Miss Conova in her dressing room last night. *You* ought to know! You were with her. She pretended she was an old friend, and had to see Miss Conova on important business," she added scornfully.

"Tricks in all trades, you know," Dundee reminded her. "Did Miss Conova know Miss Loring was a reporter?"

"I told her so myself," Louise Patton answered. "I'd seen her name over the movie column in the evening paper."

"And after her nap, what did Miss Conova do?"

"We all took a drive. Mr. Weinberg, the manager of the tour, has hired a car and chauffeur for our exclusive use while we're here," the woman told him, a touch of pride in her voice. "Mr. Risher held out for a sedan, instead of a limousine, because he wants to drive himself most of the time. He's just crazy about cars," she added indulgently. "All four of us went driving. I sat beside the chauffeur, and Miss Conova was on the back seat between the two men. She seemed to enjoy the drive, and kept telling the chauffeur which way to turn. I got the idea that Miss Conova had been to Hamilton before, but she didn't say so."

"Quite likely," Dundee agreed casually. "Where did your drive take you?"

"Nearly everywhere. Miss Conova particularly wanted to see the river front. I don't know why, because there wasn't much to see besides warehouses and factories and wholesale houses. Then we went all through the residential sections, and on out to Mirror Lake. It's certainly pretty out that way!'"

"Very," Dundee agreed. "Did Miss Conova seem to be especially interested in any one section?"

Miss Patton frowned, as if trying to remember. "Why, yes!" she exclaimed eagerly. "She had the driver turn into a street that had two rows of grand old maple trees, and then go as slow as he could along it. I turned back to say something to her, and I saw the strangest thing! She was leaning way over, to look at an old white Colonial house, set far back on a big lawn with an iron deer on it—"

"The old Loring homestead," Hepburn interrupted. "It's quite a showplace. I suppose the architecture interested her."

"The funny thing was," Miss Patton insisted, "she looked at me when I spoke to her and there were tears in her eyes. I didn't say anything, of course, but—" She checked herself suddenly and looked at the hotel manager with wide blue eyes. "Did you say *Loring*? Then maybe she did know that Loring girl—Oh! I'm terribly sorry—"

"Sorry because you did not tell Miss Conova the name of the reporter who was calling?" Dundee interrupted sharply.

"Yes, sir," the woman confessed. "I knew she didn't want to be bothered by reporters, so—" and she began to cry weakly.

"Don't distress yourself, Miss Patton," Dundee said gently. "I'm sure you were merely trying to do your duty by your employer." But his heart felt strangely lighter, and the last of his resentment against the star for having hurt Kay Loring melted away.

Miss Patton huddled deeper into her down cocoon. "If she used to live here," she remarked, almost cheerfully, "I guess she's just slipped out to call on some people she used to know, and—"

She was interrupted by the ringing of the telephone. Dundee stretched out a long arm for the instrument, conveniently placed on a small table at the end of the couch, before the manager could reach it.

"Suite 4-B. No, Miss Conova is not here. Who's calling, please?"

A twangy, male voice at the other end of the wire answered: "This is Shear, down in the hotel garadge. I jis' sorta thought I'd find out if Miss Conova had got in all right—"

"Why?" Dundee interrupted sharply.

"Well, because I was kinda uneasy about her, seein' as how she'd took the car out alone, and now we get word, that the car's been abandoned on Old Bridge—"

"On—*Old Bridge*?" Dundee repeated.

"Yes, sir," the twangy voice answered. "I gotta go bring it in now, but bein' kinda uneasy about Miss Conova, I thought—"

"Wait! I'm coming with you, Shear. This is Dundee, of the district attorney's office. Miss Conova has not returned."

When the detective hung up the receiver he discovered that the sick woman had flung off her covers and was on her feet, swaying drunkenly.

"Lie down, Miss Patton!" Dundee commanded sternly, "We don't want you fainting."

"What's happened, Dundee?" Hepburn asked hoarsely.

While the detective was explaining, the woman struggled to her feet again, and steadied herself by clutching the back of a chair.

"I'm going with you!" she panted, when Dundee had finished, and was hurrying out of the room. "I've got a right to go! I'm her nurse!"

"Nurse?" Dundee repeated, his hand on the door knob.

"Yes!" she almost screamed. "A nurse hired to guard Yola Conova's life! And I've failed! I let her trick me! If she's dead, it's my fault, and I wish to God I were dead, too!"

But she did not go with Dundee. He left her lying on the floor unconscious.

IV

"Gosh! I sure wouldn't pick out a night like this to disappear in," declared Shear, night attendant of the Randolph Hotel garage, as he took his place beneath the wheel of a coupe. "Thermometer outside the garadge doors is down to thirty, and still droppin'."

"Neither would any other sane person, Shear," Dundee agreed.

"Gee, Mr. Dundee!" ejaculated the keen-eyed but otherwise nondescript-looking young man. "You don't figger there's been foul play, do you?"

"Suicides, Shear, are usually of unsound mind—temporarily, at least," the detective explained himself. "And we have reason to fear that Miss Conova has committed suicide. By the way, how did you learn that the car had been abandoned on Old Bridge?"

"The cop on that beat's a friend of mine. It was him that rung up the garadge and warned us we'd have a stolen car to worry about if we didn't have no better sense'n to leave it out all night with the key in the switch," Shear explained. "Told us it had a flat, so Mac—he's the other night man at the garadge—picked on me to go bring it in. But like I told you over the 'phone, I felt kinda uneasy—"

"And very sensible of you, too," Dundee praised him. "Were you on duty when Miss Conova took the car out?"

"Sure! It was me that give her the car. Said she didn't want no driver, when I told her her shofer had went home for the night. Showed me a California driver's license. Said she could drive anything on wheels. So I didn't see no harm in letting her have the car—"

"Of course you couldn't refuse," Dundee assured him. "How'd did she act? Worried? Nervous?"

Shear considered. "Yeah. Fact is, she said she was nervous and wanted to take a drive to calm her nerves, so's she could sleep. Lots of folks do that. I thought maybe she was afraid somebody in her party might try to stop her from going out alone, the way she kept lookin' over her shoulder. She seemed in such a hurry to get away that I was considerable surprise when she stopped to pick up a handful of maps."

"Maps?" Dundee repeated. "What kind did she ask for City? State?"

"Didn't specify. Just said she'd forgot to get some maps she wanted, and went over to the big rack of maps that we keep up near the front of the garadge, near the desk where she signed out for the car. She took quite a handful, but I didn't pay no attention. Guess I was lookin' at her, more'n at what she was doin'," the truthful Mr. Shear confessed. "It ain't every day I git a chance at a close-up of a famous movie star—"

"A *handful* of maps," Dundee repeated thoughtfully.

Shear laughed. "Ever'body does that. Partly because they're free, partly because maps are kinda—well, fascinatin', if you get what I mean. Must be a lot of money in the map busines since cars come in."

"What time did Miss Conova take the car out?"

"Five minutes to one o'clock on the dot," Shear told him promptly. "I had to write the time down on a card. She had me wheel the car out into the alley for her, instead of the street. . . . Gee whillikins! It's cold down here on the river front! This wind's like knives made out of ice."

The car had turned into a wide street, more than half of whose width was taken up by railroad tracks and sidings, on which freight cars stood at intervals. Hamilton's wholesale district, concentrated along the river front, was a welter soot-grimed old buildings, most of them not more than two storeys tall. An exception to the general architectural dreariness was the new brick and concrete home of the Kenyon Wholesale Produce Company.

Shear, with coat collar up and shoulders hunched against the bitter wind, drove silently and swiftly along the deserted street, until the last of the grimy old buildings was passed, and the railroad tracks deserted the river front to curve away toward the imposing new Union Station. Tall apartment houses and family hotels, with an occasional "mansion," all boasting a river view, now began to flash past the coupe's steamy windows.

They were nearing their goal.

"I thought Old Bridge was closed to all but pedestrian traffic," Dundee remarked, his teeth showing a tendency to chatter in the cold. "I know it was condemned as soon as the new suspension bridge was finished."

"That's right. It's officially closed. Got signs posted all over, sayin' there's a ten dollar fine for drivin' acrosst it," Shear told him. "But it ain't guarded, and ever' once in a while a couple of neckers turn off the road onto the bridge and park for a pettin' party. The cops don't make no trouble unless a car actually crosses the bridge. I used to park this end of the bridge myself, 'fore I got married. Kinda romantic to set there in the moonlight, lookin' at the water. . . . Well, here it is, mister! And there's our sedan; with no lights on."

A string of wooden "horses," from which swung red lanterns, stretched across the approach to the bridge, but the "horse" at the extreme left had been turned at right angles to the others, so that there was just room for the coupe to pass through.

Except for the feeble glow of the lanterns the old concrete structure lay in darkness. As Dundee descended from the coupe a blast of icy wind threatened to tear the overcoat off his tall, sturdy body.

"Holy Moses!" he muttered. "Give me your flashlight, Shear. Thanks!" Then, in silent comment as he labored toward the sedan, closely followed by Shear: "Fancy choosing to commit suicide outdoors on a night like this!

Why the hell didn't she do it comfortably in her own room after she got rid of the nurse? Taking no chances, I suppose, on the Patton woman's coming back too soon, or on her tipping off the hotel detective that the lady was to be watched."

Shear had parked his coupe at an angle so that its headlights shone full upon the sedan.

"This tire's sure God flat, all right," he commented now, idly kicking at the collapsed rubber. "Guess I'd better put the spare on now, hadn't I?"

"No. Wait till I've had a look around," Dundee answered.

He had decided to inspect the inside of the car as thoroughly as possible without actually entering it. Not that there was any logical reason why he shouldn't step inside the car, but the police were jealous of their prerogatives, especially where the district attorney's office was concerned. So he contented himself with standing at the one open window of the sedan—the one to the left of the steering wheel.

On the maroon cushion of the driver's seat lay a woman's handbag, a large flat one of the envelope type, obviously an expensive one, made of the thick, scaly gray skin of some sort of snake. A bag for "daytime or sports wear," as the advertisements would say. Half hidden by the bag was a white handkerchief of very sheer linen—crushed but snowy clean. And nothing more—no other trace of the missing woman that a flashlight playing over the whole interior of the car could reveal.

"That's the pocketbook Miss Conova was carryin', all right," Shear, looking over the detective's shoulder, assured Dundee. "I took particular note of everything about Miss Conova, so's I could tell my wife. She's quite a picture fan—"

Dundee stepped upon the running board and reached for the bag, taking care not to touch the steering wheel or any other surface that could register fingerprints. Not that he expected fingerprints to play any part in this case, but routine was routine—and inexorable.

Seated upon the running-board of the sedan, while Shear held the flashlight for him, Dundee examined the contents of the bag. A large compact, for powder, rouge and lipstick. A tiny phial of perfume. A somewhat worn, tooled-leather billfold carrying a California driver's license and strutted with a neat sheaf of greenbacks totaling sixty-five dollars. A small coin purse of the snakeskin, containing three pennies, a dime, a key ring with several keys of different sizes. And, last, a magnificent ring. Yola Conova's engagement ring, probably, for it was a large diamond solitaire, square-cut, and set in platinum.

Dundee sighed heavily as he shut the bag and slipped it into his overcoat pocket. An eyewitness, he told himself, could hardly have spoken more clearly. For the handbag was mute but eloquent testimony that it had been deliberately abandoned by an owner who would never again have use for keys and cosmetics and money. No, Dundee corrected himself; the owner had not "abandoned" the handbag, in the strictest sense of the word. She had left it behind but had demanded that it render her one last service: it must stand in lieu of a suicide note.

"One sure thing, mister," Shear spoke with nervous urgency, "the poor girl wasn't robbed and done away with. Guess there ain't no two ways about it—she come out here on purpose to jump off the bridge and end it all. Though how she knew about Old Bridge, her being a stranger and all—Say! Listen! We're fergittin' about that flat tire! If she set out on foot to git help, she may have got lost, being a stranger and all—"

The wind howled a long hoot of derision. The wind knew, and Dundee knew, and Shear knew the answer to that, but Dundee put it into brutal words:

"Just strolled off, leaving her handbag! It's no use, Shear. Pull yourself together. You'll have to help me look about a bit before we call for help to search the river bed. Not enough water down there now to carry the body away, but plenty to hide it."

Dundee's words turned his own stomach. For the first time that night the icy wind was a boon. Feeling suddenly weak, he wished he had remained seated on the running board of the sedan But directly before him was the low broad concrete wall of the bridge—about the height of the deck rail of a ship. He lurched forward, his right hand groping for the support of one of the iron spikes set at intervals along the top of the wall.

As suddenly as it had come, the feeling of nausea passed conquered by a thrill of horrified excitement. For the detective's fingers had closed, not upon cold iron, but upon the unmistakable roughness of rope. As if the coils had been those of a snake, Dundee snatched his hand away and raised his flashlight.

"God God!" Shear ejaculated. "That looks like tow rope! The sedan had a tow just like that—"

"See if it's missing out of the tool chest," Dundee commanded sharply. Then, silently, he gave himself orders: "You've got to look! That's what you're here for."

And the still-unhardened young detective forced himself to train the flashlight downward, and to look.

If he had never seen her alive, if he had not, for one unforgettable moment, looked deep into her tormented dark eyes it would not have been so cruelly hard for him to look at the thing now revealed by his flashlight.

One end of the rope was tied in a clumsy double knot to the spear-headed iron spike. Far below, the other end was tight around the neck of something to which the wind gave a horrible semblance of life—now causing it to swing far out, now banging their head with sickening thumps against one of the concrete pillars which supported the bridge.

For a moment only the beam of Dundee's borrowed flashlight shone full upon the slightly upturned face of the corpse. But it was enough. Blue and bloated though that face was, and bruised by that horrible banging, it was recognizable.

His first duty, of course, was to make absolutely sure that life was gone, Dundee reminded himself, with a shiver of loathing for the job.

"Tow rope's gone from the tool chest," Shear announced. "Is she—"

"Yes. We'll have to haul her up somehow. Give me a hand, will you, old man? A nasty job, but it can't be helped. . . . No, no! Don't touch the knots. Got to leave them as is, for the police to observe and photograph. . . . That's the stuff. Careful of the spikes, Shear, or you'll gore yourself. All set now?"

They labored silently, each man breathing in gasps that occasionally turned into grunts of pain, until the rope's burden could be lifted over the spikes.

"Open the rear door of the sedan," Dundee panted. "I'll hold her. . . . Turn on the dome light. . . . Now, give me a hand. . . . Easy now! . . . That's right! . . . Whew!"

"Stiff as a board, ain't she, sir? What a sight! Poor little thing!" Shear gasped, as they laid the body on the back seat of the big car. It made an ample bier, for Yola Conova had indeed been a little thing.

"Rigor mortis has set in, hastened by the freezing temperature," Dundee explained, as he knelt to feel for a pulse that was obviously still and to listen for a heart that would never beat again.

Yola Conova had dressed very simply for her rendezvous with death. Stout little brown Oxfords, well-polished but far from new, looked comfortable and inexpensive, as did the fur-lined tweed coat, which Dundee had unbuttoned to make his futile examination. Plain and serviceable too were the dark red jersey dress and the tightly fitting felt beret of the same warm color, which, according to Ginger Loring, Yola Conova had always loved.

They had laid the body flat, but the rope-strangled neck had stiffened in such a way as to turn the face slightly upward and sideways. Now, as Dundee still knelt beside her, he felt a strong impulse to brush the pretty red cap clean of those fine particles of cement which it had collected during those hideous bangings by the wind. She would have so hated to look untidy.

But something incredibly strange caught his eyes and shocked his interest away from the dusty beret. Nothing more than the tip of a glove finger. But it was with almost sickening excitement that the detective lifted first one, then the other of those little stiff hands in their new pigskin gloves, to study each palm and every finger.

"Couldn't we cover her up with the laprobe, Mr. Dundee?" Shear asked huskily. "She looks so awful cold— "

"She doesn't feel the cold now," the detective comforted him. "But it would be only decent to cover her poor face."

Thinking how odd it was that a woman who had made a profession of beauty should be willing to make her last "personal appearance" with that beauty completely destroyed, Dundee swivelled on his heels to reach for the laprobe slung across a bar set into the back of the front seat, but as he did so his foot-struck something hard. It was a crank, lying on the floor of the tonneau.

"Yeah, we leave one layin' out in plain sight in all the rent cars," the garage man answered Dundee's question. "Can't ever tell when a starter'll go dead on you."

"That's right," Dundee agreed absently, and again reached for the robe. But he stayed his hand. "Look here, Shear!" he commanded. "Do you see anything out of the ordinary? Anything that doesn't look *natural* to you?"

The garage attendant leaned far into the car to peer about obediently. For a moment the detective, waiting tensely, was afraid he was to be disappointed.

But, "Well, I'll be damned!" exclaimed Shear. "Say, Mr. Dundee, no wonder that poor girl run into a curb and got a flat tire, if she had herself all swaddled up in that-there laprobe! Women drivers *will* do the craziest things— Gee! I didn't mean any disrespect—"

"You're dead sure, Shear, that that laprobe has been used since Miss Conova took the car out?" Dundee interrupted, his heart pounding with excitement.

"Sure as shootin'!" Shear insisted. "Why, I folded up that robe myself, after Green brought the car in long about midnight! Folded it up neat as you please, fur side out and all the edges even! Us Randolph garadge men take pride in our work, believe me! You got to, to hold a job these hard times! Sure it's been used! Jis' look at the any-old-which-way it's been put back."

But Dundee had not stopped looking since the strangeness of the laprobe's appearance in that interior of studied elegance had first caught his eye. It was folded so unevenly that no two corners touched, and hung so crookedly that the rod cut an almost true bias across the exposed plaid lining of the fur robe.

"Gosh, Mr. Dundee!" Shear commented, in an awed voice. "Don't it make you feel kinda funny when you think of that poor girl takin' the trouble to fold up that blanket and put it back in its place, the last thing before she—"

"Very funny, indeed," Dundee admittedly grimly, as he descended from the tonneau of the sedan, without having touched the laprobe. He switched off the overhead light, then closed the door. "So you think she ran into a curb, do you?"

"That's my guess," Shear replied. "'Cause that tire's been bruised bad, jis' the way it would be if that's what happened."

"Near here?" Dundee asked.

"Well, sir, it either happened right near here, or else she drove with a flat," the garage man explained. "Which can be done, but it's sorta hard for a lady to steer a car that's got a flat."

"Could you tell, by taking the tire off and examining it, whether she drove any distance after it went down?"

"Sure could! Want I should yank it off, and have a look?'

"It's irregular, but—" Dundee muttered to himself. "Yes, go ahead, Shear! And make it snappy. I'll keep a look-out for that cop who spotted the car. He ought to be passing this way again almost any minute now."

As Shear hustled about his task the detective tramped back and forth across the wind-swept bridge. He wondered if Ginger was asleep. She had certainly been awake when he had telephoned at a quarter to three. If she was awake now, and if there was anything in the theory of telepathy, what a state the poor child must be in! Should he himself break the news to her gently? But what a stupid phrase that was! Who could convey such hideous news gently?

"She and Louise Patton will outdo each other, taking the blame for what's happened," he reflected "Of course, if Ginger had told the whole truth, and had told me early in the evening, I might have been able to prevent what's happened But I doubt it if anyone could have saved Yola Conova. . . . Or am I only trying to excuse Ginger, because I—"

He swung abruptly back toward the sedan. "Nearly finished, Shear?"

"All but tightening up these nuts, sir. Car's been driven some distance since the tire got that bruise, but I'm pretty certain it went down gradual. Tube ain't tore— just pinched Listen! I hear footsteps. Sounds like that cop at last."

Five minutes later Dundee left the sedan in sole charge of a dazed and guiltily apprehensive patrolman, from whom he had extracted the following information:

1. That the sedan, to the best of the policeman's knowledge, had not been parked on the bridge when he— McGurk—passed that way on his rounds at approximately one o'clock that morning.

2. That he—a reluctant admission—had spent the entire hour between one and two o'clock in a lunch wagon stationed on a side street in the wholesale district.

3. That he had first observed the car shortly after two o'clock and that he had not investigated the car at that time, thinking it occupied by a sweethearting couple, and feeling no call to disturb them if they did not linger indecently long.

4. That at three-thirty, the car still being there, he had strolled up to it, had seen that it had a flat front tire, and, recognizing its license number as well as the car itself, telephoned the garage direct, rather than bother the police department.

5. That he had not noticed the rope tied to the bridge spike, because he had had no cause to look in that direction.

6. That the streets on his beat, which extended from Old Bridge down through the wholesale district, were flushed by the street-cleaning department every morning between twelve and one o'clock—answering a question which seemed to puzzle him sorely.

"To police headquarters, Shear," Dundee directed.

"Yes, sir," the garage man assented dubiously. "Gosh! I wish it had been anybody but me with you when you found her. I don't relish the idea of being a witness at an inquest. But say, Mr. Dundee! There's something kinda interestin' I noticed—me bein' what you might call car-conscience."

"A splendid word, Shear," Dundee grinned. "What did you notice?"

"See that speedometer of mine? . . . Well, sir, I'm kind of a nut about watchin' mileage, and I've got into the habit of turnin' my trip speedometer to zero ever' time I finish a run, matter how short it is. Do the same thing with all the cars I take care of in the garadge. Sort of automatic-like—"

"I understand," Dundee prompted impatiently.

"Well, sir, it's a funny thing, but the trip speedometer on that sedan shows exactly the same mileage as this one does."

Dundee whistled. "That's pretty keen of you, Shear. What conclusion do you draw?"

"Well, sir," Shear began, obviously flattered, "there am but one conclusion to draw: the lady made a bee-line for the bridge, jis' as I did. Come any other way, and you'd run an eighth to a quarter of a mile more mileage sure shootin'."

"Good man!" Dundee applauded. "You've made a task I've set myself seem a lot easier. . . . Being car-conscious, Shear, you'd have no trouble identifying treadmarks left by the sedan's tires, I presume?"

"Sure I wouldn't," the garage man boasted. "I been thinking to myself we'd oughta look for the place where Miss Conova bumped the curb, and I knowed you had it in mind, too, when you asked the cop about the street flushin'."

"Really, Shear? That's amazingly clever of you," Dundee told him.

"Aw, shucks!" the gratified young man protested. "I'm car-conscience—that's all. . . . Best way, sir, is for me to get out and walk along the curb while you drive as slow as you can. Not likely to have been another car, besides this one, on this street since it was flushed; but in a few minutes more the place'll be swarmin' with early customers for the wholesale produce houses. It's past four o'clock now."

When Dundee took the wheel the car had been driven about an eighth of a mile since leaving the bridge, the minimum distance Shear estimated that the sedan had traveled on a flat tire. In defiance of traffic regulations, the detective drove on the wrong side of the street, keeping the car, which seemed scarcely to move, close to the man who walked near the curb in the glare of the headlights.

"Here we are, sir!" Shear called suddenly. "Miss Conova bumped the curb right here, or I don't know an automobile from a baby buggy. . . . See!" he excitedly urged Dundee, who had leaped from the car to join him. "There's the print of her tire tread, plain as a book to read. Judgin' by the angle, she slewed right across from the middle of the road spang into the curb. . . . Of course, she might have skidded, if she come along while the street was still wet from the flushin', but them tires is new, and—"

"I don't think she skidded," Dundee interrupted, bending over the clear print of the tire tread in the thin crust of dried scum which lay in the gutter. "The Street must have been nearly dry by the time Miss Conova drove past here, if McGurk is right about the car's not being on the bridge at one o'clock. He says the street was flushed tonight not later than half past twelve. This muck in the gutter wasn't dry then, but the street was."

Before returning to the coupe he made mental note of the exact location. The sedan had struck the curb in mid-block, almost directly in front of the Liberty Storage Warehouse.

"You take the wheel again, Shear."

The garage attendant had driven only four blocks when the detective sharply ordered him to halt. Without confiding his purpose, Dundee descended from the car, and, flashlight in hand, himself began to search gutters for whatever interesting information—if any—they might have to give him.

"Can I trust you, Shear, to bear witness to a couple of discoveries I've made, and to keep them strictly under your hat until—or if—you are officially required to tell what you know?" Dundee asked gravely, when he had returned to the coupe.

"Sure, mister!" the garage man promised solemnly. "I'd a heap ruther not know a thing more about this business, but if you need me, reckon I gotta do my duty as a citizen. I give you my Bible oath I won't open my trap till you've given me the word yourself."

"Then come along!"

When, after a bit, Shear took the wheel again he reiterated his expert conclusions with puzzled shakes of the head:

"Yes, sir! No manner of doubt about it! There's been three cars here tonight since the street was flushed. All of 'em parked long enough for a bit of oil to collect on the pavement... Funny business. Our sedan and another car with new Longwear tires parked right in front of the Kenyon produce house, and a car with nearly new. More miles parked spang across the street There ain't a tire tread I don't know. You can bank on that. . . . What do you make of it all, Mr. Dundee?"

But the detective did not answer that question then, nor when it was put to him by the night chief of police, to whom he made a brief report.

He said only: "If there are any death-watch reporters hanging around, Chief, say, 'It looks like suicide.' Which is the exact truth, by the way, but now, with your permission, I'm off to rout Captain Strawn of the Homicide Squad out of his warm bed."

For what the special investigator attached to the district attorney's office made of it was this: that before Yola Conova had arrived upon Old Bridge to keep her rendezvous with Death she had kept another appointment; and at neither strange rendezvous had the unhappy star been alone with her host.

V

IT WAS SIX O'CLOCK on the morning of Friday, November 19.

Captain John Strawn, in charge of Hamilton's Homicide Squad, and James F. Dundee, special investigator from the district attorney's office, were just finishing a hearty breakfast which had been served them in a parlor-bedroom-and-bath suite on the second floor of the Randolph Hotel. The manager, Hepburn, had almost tearfully urged Dundee to make the hotel, and, particularly, this luxurious suite, his headquarters until, as he put it, "this ghastly business is finished."

"Meaning until a coroner's inquest brings in a verdict of suicide," his non-paying guest had remarked, with a grim chuckle, to Captain Strawn. "But he may wish he had not been so lavish of the hotel's hospitality before this business is really finished."

And then, of course, he had had a lot of explaining to do.

"Thank God for coffee, to say nothing of bacon and eggs," he pronounced grace informally but piously, as he drained his third cup. "I feel like two new men, and you, Captain—you've swallowed your grouch along with your Java."

"I'm gettin' to be too old a man to be cheerful over having two hours cut off the best end of a night's sleep," Strawn growled. "And murder ain't the picnic for an old-tinier that it is for a young squirt like you."

"Then you agree that it *is* murder?"' Dundee asked quickly.

"I ain't agreein' to nothin'," Strawn denied, working at his teeth with a toothpick he had insisted upon the waiter's providing. "Fact is, Bonnie, everything you've told me—all your deductions about the Conova woman bein' a servant girl in Hamilton years ago and gettin' into trouble, and about her husband hirin' a nurse to watch her, so's she couldn't commit suicide, and all the rest of it, points straight as an arrow *to* suicide! . . . Why, even the first one of them extras, slung together before the newspaper boys had a chance to interview anybody—" and the Captain pointed to a heap of newspapers on the floor between them—"has the dope on how this movie star tried to bump herself off in Hollywood a month or so ago, and how she was known to have melancholia. Looks like the whole world knew she was sick of living."

Dundee crashed a fist upon the breakfast table. "But that's just it, Captain! My whole contention is that her murderer made use of her well-known state of mind! Never—he must have congratulated himself—had a killer played in better luck!"

Strawn shook his grizzled head slowly. "That'd be a mighty pretty theory, boy, if you had a few tangible facts to back it up. . . . No, wait a minute! You've had your say. Now let me have mine. First, we'll take up them clever deductions of yours about the car. And I *mean* clever! Don't get your back up, kid! . . . Well, you've got evidence to prove, and an expert witness in Shear to back you up, that Miss Conova's hired sedan and two other cars were parked in front of the Kenyon Produce Company's building after the street was washed, that is, after half past twelve. . . . All right! More evidence of suicide, in my opinion!"

Dundee could restrain himself no longer. "You think, of course, that the poor girl went to call on her old lover, Bruce Kenyon, and that the nature of that interview so depressed her that she lost no time in killing herself."

"A bull's-eye!" Strawn grunted.

"The only trouble with that sad and sentimental picture, Captain, is that there was a third party present at that rendezvous or waiting for it to end. Now, for what it's worth, I offer a fact I know to be true from personal observation—that Bruce Kenyon drives a Lincoln cabriolet and his wife drives a Chrysler coach. It will be interesting, but not necessarily conclusive, to check up on the make of tires on those two cars."

Strawn snorted. "Got it all figgered out that a jealous wife followed her husband's paramour and persuaded her to let her hang her from a bridge. . . . Real accommodatin' of Miss Conova, I must say!"

Dundee grinned. "It's a beautiful theory, Chief, but it isn't mine—yet. I'm just looking at facts. Clues, if you like the word, pointing so far only to murder—not to the murderer himself. Those three cars in that particular spot within a fairly well-established, period of time we can lump together as Fact One. Fact Two—"

"Yeah, I know," Strawn interrupted. "That laprobe you made such a point of. Well, I've thought of an explanation of that. Let's suppose Kenyon got to the meetin' place ahead of Miss Conova. She drives up. He gets out of his car and joins her in hers. It's a bitter-cold night. He reaches back for the laprobe and tucks it about her knees while they talk—"

"Just a moment, Captain," Dundee cut in. "It is true that the night was cold, but Miss Conova was driving a closed car, which is automatically heated. Furthermore, she was very warmly dressed."

"Makes no difference," the old man contended. "Puttin' a laprobe around a lady's knees would just be what you might call a gallant gesture, especially if they used to be lovers, and Bruce was crazy enough about her to go huntin' for her when he found out his daddy had married her to another man. Which is what you yourself made out of the gossip Kelly told you."

"And the third car?" Dundee asked pleasantly. "Is it your theory that the driver of the third car joined the tête-à-tête in the sedan? Because, you know, it is quite certain that the third car was also parked for several minutes—long enough, as were the other two cars, to drip a little puddle of oil upon the pavement."

"What's your Fact Three?" Strawn demanded gruffly.

"A crank lying on the floor of the sedan's tonneau," Dundee told him. "A useful and very handy 'blunt instrument,' if one end of it was well wrapped up—say in a neck scarf. If we find that Miss Conova was not strangled by human hands before she was strangled with the rope, the handy presence of a blunt instrument may loom up importantly. Which reminds me that I want to call Dr. Price at the morgue. I suppose he's busy on the autopsy by this time. Carraway must have finished photographing the body and the rope knots an hour ago I also asked him to go over the car for fingerprints, of course. But first let me tell you Fact Four."

"Just bristlin' with facts, ain't you?" Strawn jeered, but a gleam had come into his cold gray eyes.

"Fact Four," Dundee began impressively, "concerns the dead woman's new pigskin gloves. The gloves on her stiff dead hands. The gloves she must have been wearing when she tied the knots in that thick, tough rope—if she committed suicide! Now, Chief, I found those gloves intensely interesting. In fact, they were my first clue to murder!"

"What are you drivin' at?" Strawn was impatient of dramatics. "Guess you're gonna tell me the gloves showed no signs of havin' been worn by the hands that tied knots in thick, oily rope."

"That's clever, of you, Captain," Dundee conceded. "But the murderer was smart, too. But not quite smart enough. First, let me describe those gloves. I found them so interesting that I gave Carraway specific instructions about making some nice, big 'close-ups' of them. Well, they are new glove of light-tan pigskin, with brown-stitched outside seams. They are size seven, at least a whole size too large for a snug fit—'

"Hold on!" Strawn commanded. "My wife always buys her driving gloves a size larger than her dress gloves."

"Oh, yes!" Dundee agreed. "Loose gloves for sports wear are fashionable. I'm not questioning the fact that the gloves belonged to Yola Conova. And I'm further granting that the gloves were worn by the hands that tied the knots into that tow rope. The palms and fingers were slightly scratched and stained, as I expected to find them. But—and here's what made me almost fall over backward when I first observed it—the tips of three of those glove fingers were empty. By this time Carraway should be developing pictures which show those glove tips folded over—"

"I don't get you," Strawn frowned.

"No?" Dundee was incredulous. "Visualize Yola Conova's gloved hands tying that rope. Can't you see that the pressure exerted would have forced her fingertips— all of them—into the very tips of the glove fingers, even if she had put the gloves on carelessly in the first place, which would be unlikely?"

"She may have taken her gloves off after she got the rope ready—for some reason or other," Strawn suggested.

"To powder her face?" Dundee contributed sarcastically. "But I believe, if she had been thinking that much of her personal appearance at such a tune, she would have been the more likely to smooth the fingers of her gloves as she drew them on. . . . No, Captain. There is no doubt in my mind that the murderer, having concealed himself on the floor of the tonneau under the laprobe, while Miss Conova was temporarily out of the car—say, with Bruce Kenyon in his office, found the automobile crank conveniently at hand, and prepared his 'blunt instrument' while waiting for the star to return to the car. She returned, drove away alone—"

"Then you're eliminatin' Bruce Kenyon," Strawn interrupted.

"Not at all!" Dundee protested vigorously. "I'm accusing no one yet, and eliminating no one. I'm trying to construct a theory from the actual facts at hand, a theory which is concerned only with the manner in which the murderer accomplished the deed, not his identity."

"All right, all right," Strawn agreed impatiently. "Your theory is, then, that he reared up from under his laprobe and clouted her over the head with the crank, when she'd driven two blocks away from the produce house, accounting for the way she banged into the curb at that point."

"I'm inclined to think he did nothing worse than to startle her, at that time," Dundee said slowly, his brows drawn together over his gleaming blue eyes. "To hear a voice behind her when she thought she was alone would be enough to make any woman lose control of a wheel for a moment—long enough to run into the curb. For I think the murderer was there for a chat—not a friendly confab, certainly; but my guess is that he did not come intending to murder or prepared to murder. . . . Well, they headed straight for the bridge, and whether Yola Conova was driving—under orders —or whether the murderer made her surrender the wheel we have no way of knowing. And I don't think Carraway will find any fingerprints to help us, since, on a night like last night, practically, everyone who was out in the weather wore gloves."

"Must have been somebody who knows Hamilton, and had the bridge in mind as a good spot for a private row," Strawn suggested. "Even if the Conova woman did live here ten years or so ago, she wouldn't have known about the bridge being condemned."

"Exactly!" Dundee applauded. "The bridge, I think we can safely conclude, was the murderer's own idea, to which Miss Conova, if she was still conscious at that time, as I believe she was, was forced to agree. It is also safe to assume that she did not call for help, either because she did not fear violence, or because she could not risk a scandal. At any rate, the sedan did reach the bridge. How long murderer and victim talked we don't know, but, as I dope it, the murderer saw fit to strike her down. Possibly as they talked his plan had been born— murder to look like suicide, since he, as well as the rest of the world that keeps up with movie gossip, knew that she had attempted suicide. He had a choice of two possible ways to fake the suicide—death by carbon monoxide poisoning, or death by hanging."

Strawn nodded. "Anybody living in Hamilton would have known there wasn't enough water in the river for her to drown in, though he could have taken a chance on her breaking her neck if he'd simply pitched her over the bridge."

"He chose hanging," Dundee took up the tale. "There was a rope in the tool chest, but no tube to connect with the exhaust pipe, so carbon monoxide poisoning wasn't feasible. He worked thoughtfully, and with extraordinary caution. Removing the dead girl's gloves he put them on—"

Strawn interrupted with a snort of mirth. "Kind of a little-fisted guy, wasn't he? Looks to me like you'd better begin callin' that murderer 'she' instead of 'he'."

"Not necessarily," Dundee contended. "Not only were the gloves large, but I found them split at the seams in three places. Now, if Miss Conova herself had tied those knots, it is almost certain the gloves, being too large for her, would have stood the strain easily. Therefore we can take it for granted that the one who did wear them while tying the rope was either a woman with a considerably larger hand than Yola Conova's, or a man. My hand is larger than the average man's, but I'll wager I could get those gloves on and still be able to tie loose knots in a rope without bursting them any worse than the murderer did."

"O.K.," Strawn conceded grudgingly. "How near was the sedan to the wall of the bridge?"

"You're wondering," Dundee guessed, "how much of a chance the murderer took of being observed. As a matter of fact, none at all. The car was parked at an angle, the rear wheel almost touching the wall, the front of the car being about two feet away from it. That is, the front left door of the sedan, when closed, was little more than two feet from the wall. And, directly opposite that door, on top of the wall, was the spike to which the rope was tied."

"I see," Strawn agreed, with lips puckered grimly. "Pretty smart. Even if anyone was passing along the street below the bridge, he couldn't a-seen nothing till the body had beer drug out of the front seat of the car and propped against the wall, ready to be hoisted over."

"Even then the open door of the car, almost bumping this wall as it must have been, would have acted as a very effective screen," Dundee reminded him. "Yola Conova was not a tall woman—not more than five feet two. Her head, ever if she was braced upright against the wall, would not have reached much above the top of the door, and the glass window was undoubtedly clouded with steam at that time. All the murderer had to do to play safe, if he heard footsteps, was to crouch and wait until they had died away in the distance. If McGurk had been less indulgent toward romance and had investigated an hour before he did, he might have caught our clever murderer in the act of faking the suicide—might even have saved Yola Conova's life."

"I wouldn't like to be in McGurk's Number Elevens when Kelly gets through with him," Strawn commented. "By the way, would it have been possible for Miss Conova to get up on top of that wall unaided? If it wouldn't, there's your proof of murder, with no ifs and ands about it."

But Dundee shook his head. "The murderer visualized the 'suicide' perfectly, Captain. Not only was the car so placed as to aid him in his work, but so as to make the suicide theory entirely plausible. Miss Conova could have stepped from the running-board of the sedan, up onto the rear fender, and thence to the top of the wall, which is only about four feet high. The murderer took pains to provide evidence that she did exactly that, before he hanged her. For, on the highly polished surface of the fender I found footprints. They were slightly obscured by dust—there was a high wind, you know—but they were obviously made by a woman's shoes—Conova's shoes, I think Carraway will tell us. It's pretty revolting to think of his doing that—taking off a helpless woman's shoes and, with them, carefully faking her 'footprints.' But it is even more sickening to picture him trying to replace the poor thing's gloves, after he had finished with them. Fortunately for us, it is almost impossible to put even a loose pair of gloves on limp hands—dead hands. And the murderer was undoubtedly in a hurry. Hence the empty glove tip clue, which first put me onto the track of murder."

Strawn heaved a deep sigh. "Sounds pretty conclusive," he admitted.

"Glad you think so. Now for a little chat with Dr. Price."

After considerable delay the high-pitched, querulous voice of the police surgeon, who also held the post of coroner, came over the wire.

"Dundee speaking, Doc. What's the diagnosis? 'Death by strangulation,' you say? Then, in your opinion, was the tow rope the agency of death? Sure, I know that, Doc, but at least you can say whether there is any indication that the victim was first strangled by human hands? ...None at all? Thanks! Now, from a superficial examination, can you tell me whether the deceased has ever given birth to a child? You think so? When? Not within the last year? . . . Yes, of course! By the way, has the body been formally identified?"

"A couple of men were waiting here when we brought the body in," came the answer. "Chap by the name of Weinberg, and an Englishman whose moniker I didn't catch. Said he was the dead woman's husband."

"That would be Arundel," Dundee told him. "Did you get permission from the husband to make a post-mortem? Good! Now, Doc, speaking for Captain Strawn as well as myself. I suggest you make an autopsy of the brain, giving us your report as soon as you can. Specifically, we are interested to know if the deceased, *before death*, suffered a concussion of the brain sufficient to result in unconsciousness. Yes, I know that. The wind banged the body about quite a bit, causing the head and face to strike against one of the concrete supports of the bridge. But you will be able, won't you, to differentiate between those bruises and abrasions sustained *after death,* and a concussion or a severe blow sustained *before death?* . . . Fine! Just one thing more. Have you removed the gloves from the hands of the deceased?"

The crusty-tempered surgeon's affirmative was barked at the detective.

"Don't snap my head off, Doc," Dundee pleaded. "I haven't been to bed all night. . . . O.K.! What I want to know is, have you observed any stains, scratches or broken nails on the hands of the corpse? . . . Nothing of the sort, you say? Yes, I know about the condition of the gloves. Thanks a million, Doc! And by the way, when you turn over the deceased's clothes to Carraway, tell him I said to watch out for her beret—that's a cap, Doc!—guard it with his life. It's important that not a grain of cement be shaken off it. Thanks again. We'll be waiting for your report. Call us at the Randolph Hotel, Suite 2-A. . . . Sure! We're plutes now. Never heard of a recession."

"What's all that about a berry?" Strawn wanted to know.

"Just a hunch of mine that it will convict the murderer—when or if we find him. Well, looks like we've got our work cut out for us. Guess we'd better begin by rounding up the Conova party. It suited my book to let the newspapers take over the dirty work of notifying the bereaved husband and friends and plaster the suicide theory all over these extras. The longer we can keep everyone thinking it was suicide, the freer our hands will be and the less likely our murderer will be to bolt. Give him enough rope, you know, since he's partial to rope—"

Strawn heaved his big body out of his chair with a grunt and a groan. "Ho hum!" he sighed gloomily. "Another blasted murder case with a De Russey's Lane crowded with suspects. It may be fun for you, boy, but it's plain drudgery for me. Guess you realize we're both on the spot. This Conova dame being a famous movie star, the whole world will be watchin' us after it gets out, that she was bumped off—if she was."

"I dread the flood of reporters worse than anything else," Dundee admitted. "There'll be a locust plague of them within twenty-four hours, but it would be ten times worse if we'd given one hint of murder to the local papers."

"Well, gimme that 'phone. My squad oughta be rounded up by this time, if Kelly hasn't been soldierin' on the job. I'll assign a couple of the boys to keep an eye on the Kenyons until we're ready to haul 'em in for questionin', and another pair to round up Dink Garnet. . . . Any other suggestions?"

"Can't think of anything at the moment, except that it would be a good idea to have the rest of your squad hotfoot it over here to be on hand as we need them," Dundee answered. "They can hang out in the bedroom of this suite, and God save the carpet! . . . Come in!"

The young detective, expecting a waiter to remove the breakfast table, did not turn toward the door as it opened. "Good morning, Jimmy!" a trembling voice called faintly. Dundee whirled, then ran toward the small girl leaning weakly against the closed door.

"Ginger! I was just going to call your apartment—"

Her cold hands lay limp in his. "The newsboys yelling 'Extra!' woke me, up, and half an hour ago my city editor 'phoned for me to come down early."

"But you're not able to work today!" Dundee protested. "You look as if you'd collapse any minute."

"I'm all right," she smiled. "But I had to see you first, to beg you not to—" She paused uncertainly, her eyes flicking a questioning glance toward the old man at the telephone.

"Captain Strawn—Miss Loring," Dundee introduced the two, and the old detective nodded, without interrupting his   conversation with Headquarters.

"Captain—*Strawn*?" Kay Loring whispered. "Why, Jimmy, he's chief of the Homicide, Squad, isn't he? What's *he* doing here? Suicide isn't—homicide!"

"No," Dundee agreed gravely.

"Then you mean—Oh!" and she pressed a clenched fist hard against her pale lips. Then: "May I use the telephone when Captain Strawn has finished?"

"No, not to give a tip to your paper, Ginger. Sorry, but—"

"You're being stupid," she accused. "I want to call my city editor to give him my resignation, effective immediately. He's always telling us that reporters can't have personal loyal ties, so I won't be a reporter again until—until—"

"I understand," Dundee assured her gently. "And I'm glad you'll be free to help us."

"No, no!" she cried. "That's not it. She's dead. Let her rest in peace."

"You don't really mean that, Ginger. I'm sure that you as much as anyone in the world, want this business cleared up. And I honestly believe that if the murderer is caught, you will be largely responsible. Now listen, Funny Face! Whether you like it or not, you're in this thing with me—right up to your short little neck. Shut up. And listen. By this time tomorrow this town is going to be lousy with reporters from all over the United States. I can't be bothered with them, and Captain Strawn ,doesn't want to be, either. . . . Right Captain?"

The older detective had finished his conference with Police Headquarters, and was listening.

"Damned nuisances—begging your pardon, miss!" he said now.

"How about taking over the job of press representative of this investigation, Miss Kay Loring?" Dundee put it to her abruptly.

"You—you mean you'd let me decide what the reporters would be told?" the girl asked incredulously. "Then I could—protect her?"

"As long as possible, and forever if that is possible," Dundee assured her solemnly. "Will you take the job, Ginger?"

As the girl was nodding, too tearful to speak, the door into the corridor was torn open and a man plunged into the room, closely followed by another, who was ineffectually trying to restrain him.

The determined intruder was Clinton Risher. His wild eyes swept the room, then fastened on Captain Strawn, who was in uniform.

"Are you investigating this suicide?" he panted. "Then listen to me! . . . Let me alone, Mr. Weinberg! You can't stop me! . . . *I* say it wasn't suicide! I say it was *murder*!"

VI

OH, THESE ACTORS! These actors—" moaned Max Weinberg wringing his hands. "Before I should manage another personal appearance tour I should starve, and be thankful for an easy death—"

Strawn ruthlessly interrupted the little man's lament. "Do you write shorthand, Miss Loring? . . . Fine! You'll find paper in that desk. Here's a pencil. You'll oblige me by taking my stenographer's place until he arrives. . . . Now, young man," and he turned to Risher, "take it easy. What's your name?"

The extraordinarily handsome young actor stood for a moment longer, clenching and unclenching his fists, then dropped into a chair.

"Sorry I busted in like that," he apologized. "But Lord! I'm nearly off my head. . . . My name is Clinton Risher. I am—I was a member of Miss Conova's party," he added, his soft Texas voice breaking as it pronounced the star's name

"Are you an actor?"

The boy did not seem to resent the old detective's apparent ignorance of his sudden fame, though Weinberg shrugged and wailed: "Is he an actor? Ach! Mein Gott!"

"Yes, sir. Not much of one," Risher answered humbly. "Just in the movies. But it ain't me that matters, Sergeant—"

"*Captain* Strawn," the detective corrected sourly. "And don't butt in. I'll decide what matters and what don't matter. Now, young man, where were you last night between one o'clock and half past two?"

Under the matter-of-factness of Strawn's questions the boy lost some of his wildness, but he continued to run distracted fingers through his curling, bright brown hair.

"I was in bed asleep, of course," he asserted. "But—"

"Got anybody to prove that?" Strawn interrupted menacingly.

"Prove—?" Clinton Risher stared at him blankly. "Sure I haven't! I've got a room to myself in a suite. Weinberg here has the other bedroom. But what do you mean? Gosh! You don't think *I*—"

"It was you, not me, that said anything about murder," Strawn pointed out acidly. "Does your bedroom adjoin this man Weinberg's?"

"Sure he was in bed," the tour manager contributed. "With my own eyes I saw him in his pajamas—"

"Pipe down till you're spoken to," Strawn commanded. "Answer my question, Risher."

"No, sir. There's a sitting room between our bedrooms."

"Then Weinberg couldn't have heard you if you'd sneaked out after you were supposed to be in bed?"

"Sure he couldn't, but I didn't sneak out." The boy was on the edge of tears. "I come here to tell you something, and you light in on me, like I was a criminal—"

"A fine boy!" Weinberg assured Strawn. "A credit to the industry—"

"May I ask Mr. Risher a question, Captain Strawn?" Dundee interrupted deferentially. "Thank you. Now, Mr. Risher, I am going to ask you an embarrassing question, which you may refuse to answer, if you like: Were you more than a friend to Yola Conova?"

"Such an idea!" Weinberg moaned.

But the boy flushed scarlet. "If you mean to say, was I in love with Yola Conova, I'm proud to say I was," he answered with fierce eagerness. "That's part of what I come here to tell you all. But if you mean was there anything wrong between us, I've got two fists that say you've got to apologize tight here and now."

"Oi, oi!" wailed Max Weinberg. "First a scandal, then a fight! Haven't you ever heard yet of Mr. Will Hays, Clinton, l ask you?"

"I assure you that I meant to imply nothing immoral in your relationship," Dundee smiled.

"You're mighty right there wasn't nothing immoral!" the boy assured him violently. "I was in love with her, and Yola was in love with me! And you needn't remind me she was a married woman. If she hadn't told me with her own lips that she and Arundel meant less than nothing to each other, and that she hoped she'd never set eyes on him again, I'd have cut my tongue out before I'd have said one word to her about how I felt."

"You see?" Weinberg beamed. "No scandal!"

"I see," said Dundee "Now, Mr. Risher, when you came charging in here you made the flat assertion that Miss Conova had been murdered. Will you explain that statement?"

"Who are you, anyway?"

"My name is James F. Dundee, and I am a special investigator attached to the district attorney's office."

"O .K. I thought maybe you was—I mean were—a reporter. Yola was trying her best to learn me to talk proper," he confided miserably. "Well sir, I said it was murder, because I know good and well she wouldn't have committed suicide last night. Not after what passed between us after the show."

"Yes?" Dundee prompted.

"I went up to her suite with her," the boy explained, twisting his hands until the knuckles cracked. "We'd sort of got into the habit of rehearsing our one-act play after the show every night, instead of in the mornings. Mr. Weinberg—he was our stage manager and director, as well as the manager of the tour—always had a lot of new ideas after each performance—"

"How long did you rehearse last night?"

"We didn't rehearse at all. Yola begged off, so Mr. Weinberg went on to his room, and Miss Patton—that was Miss Conova's companion—went to hers. So Yola and I were alone. She was upset over something—"

"You mean Arundel's unexpected arrival?"

"That's it. I wanted Yola to let him come up to her suite so she could tell him right in front of me that she was through with him for good and all."

"How long had you known Miss Conova?" Strawn cut in.

The boy reddened. "It would have been one whole week today. I joined the tour in Chicago. Miss Conova appeared alone in New York, because I hadn't finished a picture I was making in Hollywood. As it was, I had to take a plane to Chicago—"

"Just a moment. . . . How long had you known Miss Conova, Mr. Weinberg?"

The little man spread his hands. "One week. I met the train on Thursday when Miss Conova and Miss Patton arrived in Chicago. The New York office had sent me on a week in advance of the Chicago opening, to make all arrangements. I didn't have anything to do with Yola's New York appearance. All she had to do in New York was to show herself and make a little speech—"

"Thank you, Mr. Weinberg," Dundee cut him short. "Go on, Mr. Risher. You arrived in Chicago on Friday?"

"Friday morning, yes, sir. We rehearsed the one-act play Friday, Saturday and Sunday, and opened in the Empire Theater Sunday night, closing Wednesday night. But it don't take a week to fall in love. Anyway, I'd had a fan crush on her for years. I thought she was the greatest actress on the screen—"

"How old are you, Mr. Risher?" Dundee interrupted, smiling slightly.

Again that painful flush. "Going on twenty-three. Plenty old enough to know when I'm in love, if that's what you mean!"

"And last night?" Dundee prompted.

"Well, sir, it seemed to upset her something dreadful when I tried to make her have a plain talk with Arundel," the boy continued. "I ain't acquainted with him personally, and don't care if I never am. He must have been doggone mean to that poor girl, the way she was scared of the very mention of his name. She just trembled all over when she told me that the one thing I mustn't ask of her was to see him again. But she promised me, and crossed her heart," he assured Dundee solemnly, "that she'd be free to marry me within a month after the tour was over—if I still wanted her then, she kept saying over and over. As if I'd change—"

"A month?" Dundee repeated.

"Reckon she had a Mexican divorce in mind," Strawn suggested. "These picture stars are in too big a hurry to unmarry and remarry to waste time on Reno and Paris these days."

The boy started up, fists clenched, then subsided with groan, as Weinberg crossed to pat his shoulder.

"Was Miss Conova in a happy frame of mind when you left her?"

"Happy?" the actor repeated. "Happy is no name for it. She was as tickled as a kid let out of school. Why, sir, she told me she was happy for the first time in ten years! Gee! Was I proud?" And his beautifully cut mouth quivered like a grieved child's. "We'd talked and talked, making plans. She was going to retire from pictures, and have a baby—"

"Just a moment, Mr. Risher," Dundee interrupted softly. "Did Miss Conova tell you whether she'd ever had a child?

"Of course not! The whole world knows she never had any children!"

"Sorry," Dundee murmured. "Now, Mr. Risher, I wish you'd tell us anything you can about Miss Conova's mental condition during the week you knew her. In other words, was she depressed, nervous, worried—anything of that sort?"

The boy answered reluctantly: "Well, I wouldn't say she was depressed, but she *was* nervous—and worried, too, I guess. And seemed like she was scared of crowds and reporters. I guess she was afraid the reporters would ask her a lot of questions about her and her husband, because they were printing rumors about a divorce, and all. Another thing, she wasn't used to acting on the stage and every night she nearly passed out with stage fright."

"Did you suspect, from her manner or anything she said, that she was contemplating suicide?"

"Absolutely not!" the young actor denied vehemently. "And," he added, "she had a fine appetite. She was on a diet to keep thin, like most screen stars are, but she was always hungry, and I've seen her eat nearly half a pound of chocolates at a time."

Dundee was startled and showed it. "That's odd!" he commented, frowning. "Now, Mr. Risher, did Miss Conova realize—please don't get sore—that her day as a picture star was almost over?"

"Of course we all know the public is fickle," the boy answered sadly. "I hope to God she didn't realize it. If she did, she never let on to me. I did everything I could—"

"I'm sure you did. In fact, I can testify to your efforts in Miss Conova's behalf," Dundee assured him. "By the way, did the audience last night hurt her badly?"

"Now, that's a funny thing," the actor brooded. "She didn't seem to care a Continental. Looked like all she thought of was me! I was afraid those fool women had made her feel terrible, but when we went backstage she just grabbed me and kissed me and said how proud of me she was. And I vow she wasn't kidding, or smiling to hide an aching heart, as the saying goes, or anything like that. She wasn't a bit proud or stuck-up, or conceited," the boy digressed, in a desolate voice. "She was just wonderful. I—I wish to God I was dead, too!"

The detective gave him a moment to control himself, before he asked: "How long were you with Miss Conova in her rooms after the theater last night?"

"Until half past twelve," Risher answered, licking at a tear that had run to the corner of his mouth. "She said she had something to do before she went to bed, and that after she'd done it, she'd sleep like a baby."

"Ah" Dundee caught his breath sharply. "Did she tell you what it was she had to do?"

"No, sir, but I kind of thought she meant she was going to write Arundel a letter, or telephone him or something, because it was him that we talked about mostly, and it was only him that stood between us being happy?"

"Are you *sure* of that?" Dundee asked.

"Of course I am!" the boy answered, with belligerent surprise. Then his frank young face clouded. "Well, she did say some foolish things, like girls will—"

"For instance?" Dundee prompted.

"Well, every once in a while she'd say there was something in her past she ought to tell me," Risher explained miserably. "But you know how girls are. They get a big kick out of confessing old love affairs and things like that. I told her I didn't give a hoot what she'd done before I met her and I didn't want her upsetting herself telling me a lot of stuff. And once she asked me if I'd love her just the same if she wasn't a famous movie star, and I told her—mind you, I meant every word of it, too—that I'd rather she was a nobody, so's I could prove I loved her for herself alone. It breaks my heart now to remember how she broke down and cried when I said I'd have fallen in love with her at first sight if she'd been the hotel chambermaid come to clean my room."

There came a choking cry from the desk where Kay Loring sat, and Dundee saw her groping blindly for a handkerchief. Little Weinberg moaned, wringing his hands, and Dundee had to clear his own throat before he could put the next question:

"To your knowledge, Mr. Risher, did anything unusual occur yesterday after your party reached Hamilton, to worry or frighten Miss Conova?"

"Outside the fact that Arundel turned up unexpectedly, you mean?" the actor asked. "Well, there *was* something funny, though I didn't think much about it at the time. I know from my own short experience in the movies what crazy letters you get from fans and cranks."

"You mean that Miss Conova received a letter which upset her?"

"Yes, sir. It was after we'd been on our drive to see the city—"

"Just a minute, Risher. Sorry to interrupt so much," Dundee apologized. "But I wish you'd tell me whether you gathered from her manner, or whether Miss Conova told you, that she was, familiar with Hamilton?"

"She didn't say anything, but I couldn't help noticing that she seemed to know the town. She acted almost like it was her home town, and she was looking for landmarks. She was kind of sad and absent-minded all during the drive, but she didn't say anything and I didn't ask any questions."

"Now about the letter, that upset her," Dundee urged.

"We stopped at the desk when we came in. That is, Mr. Weinberg and I did, and the girls—Miss Conova and Miss Patton—waited for us at the elevator," the actor explained "There was a bunch of mail for Yola, and a lot for me, too, and some for Mr. Weinberg, and one letter for Miss Patton. I gave Yola her mail but she didn't open it until we were alone together in the parlor of her suite. We began to read our fan mail together and laugh at some of the silly things the fans wrote. Then all at once Yola was tearing up a letter, like she was hopping mad. She was white as chalk and her eyes were blazing. I was scared, I tell you—"

"Was Miss Conova frightened also, or only angry?"

"Both, I reckon," the boy answered. "Her hands were shaking so she dropped some of the scraps of the letter when she was stuffing them into that pottery bowl on the coffee table there. I picked them up for her and put a match to the scraps to burn 'em, like she told me to—"

"Can you tell us anything about the paper the letter was written on, or the handwriting?" Strawn cut in.

"Yes, sir. I couldn't help noticing," the actor confessed. "It wasn't handwritten. The letter had been done on a typewriter, but what struck me as funny was that whoever wrote it had sent Yola the carbon copy. It was ordinary 'second sheet' paper—you know, kind of flimsy and pretty thin an cheap. The writer had used purple carbon and some of the words were smudged, but I didn't try to read any of 'em."

"Did Miss Conova make any comments on the letter?"

"Not exactly, but while it was burning she kept whispering to herself, 'Just deny everything! Say it's lies! Lies!' Of course I asked her what was the matter, but she just said to forget about it. I thought it was some one pestering her like they do me. Why, you wouldn't believe it, but there's an old lady in Texas writes me every week. She claims she's my mam and I got to support her or she'll expose me in the newspapers. Sometimes it ain't much fun being famous," He told them sadly. "Lots of times I wish I was back in Waco, Texas, working on the old Katy railroad."

"How did you get into pictures, Mr. Risher?" Dundee digressed.

"Just by accident. I was assistant ticket agent for the Katy down in Waco, Texas. One night I sold a ticket to a gentleman who kept hanging around my window, while he was waiting for his train. Finally he told me he was a director and that he thought I was just the type for a movie he was going to make. The upshot was he laid over for a day and made me take a screen test, then he offered me a contract for that one picture. So I went to Hollywood with him, and the studio hired a lady to give me some lessons in diction and grammar and things like that. I can talk pretty good now when I put my mind to it."

"Ever been mixed up with a woman?" Strawn shot at him. "Before you fell for the Conova woman?"

The boy sprang to his feet, his face scarlet and his hazel eyes blazing.

"You're an old man, mister, and I don't want to fight you," he panted, "but you can't get away with insulting Miss Conova!"

"I apologize," Strawn growled. "Didn't mean any harm. Now answer my question, and don't be so touchy."

The actor sank back into his chair. "I used to go with a girl in Waco, but she broke it off before I got into the movies. She said I didn't have any ambition, and wasn't making enough money to support her right."

Strawn chuckled. "Been gettin' quite a few letters from her lately, haven't you, kid? . . . What's her name?"

"That's none of your damned business, sir!"

Dundee smiled. "Suppose we go back to Miss Conova's last hour with you, Mr. Risher," he suggested. "You say you left her at twelve-thirty?"

"Yes, sir. I know, because the radio was on, and a station announced the time. Yola said she hadn't realized it was so late, and she hurried me off."

"Will you tell us whether Miss Conova had any telephone calls while you were with her after the theater?"

"Yes, sir. Seemed like the 'phone was ringing all the time. We'd hardly got into the parlor when it rang. Miss Patton answered it from her bedroom, and she come to tell Yola that Arundel was on the wire, wanting to know if he could see her. Yola said no. Before she left the room Miss Patton told Yola she'd be taking a bath for the next few minutes, and for her to let the 'phone ring without answering it. Well, in a minute or two it did ring, and I offered to answer it, but Yola said let it ring. It seemed to make her nervous, though, and pretty soon she answered it herself. I thought she'd faint!"

"What!" Dundee exclaimed, with a quick glance toward Strawn. He heard Kay Loring gasp. . . . "Please repeat as exactly as you can remember it Miss Conova's part in that conversation, Mr. Risher."

The boy shifted uneasily in his chair, his hands again busy at their maddening knuckle-cracking. "She didn't hardly talk at all. She just listened mostly, her face white as death. And she pushed me away when I put my arm around her, to hold her steady, because I thought she was going to faint. Well, first she said, '*Who*?,' as if, she couldn't believe her cars. Then she said, 'You're mistaken—absurdly mistaken.' Then she listened for a long time, instead of hanging up like I thought she would. Suddenly she got all flushed up, and I saw tears in her eyes, but somehow, she didn't seem—well, either scared or sore Honest! I almost got jealous, thinking it was some man she used to know here, and kind of—like. After she'd listened some more she said, 'Maybe I will—just to convince you you're wrong.' Then she listened for another minute, and after that she said, 'Wait and see,' and hung up the receiver quick. She was smiling and seemed like she'd forgot I was there. Then, all of a sudden, she threw her arms around my neck and said, 'Isn't life funny, darling? Funny and wonderful?'"

"Did you ask her about the call?" Dundee demanded tensely.

The boy squirmed. "No, sir. I—well, I guess I didn't want to know too much, lest I wouldn't feel good about it. And it was after that call that Yola said she'd marry me within a month after the tour was over, so I almost forgot about it.

"But say!" he cried, springing to his feet in sudden impatience. "We're wasting time! My girl's *dead*! She's been murdered, I tell you, and here we sit chewing the rag—"

"Sit down, Mr. Risher!" Dundee ordered, not unkindly. "I assure you that we have wasted no time. You say Miss Conova was murdered. Have you a definite charge to make?"

"You bet your life I have!" the actor shouted, but he took his seat obediently. "I *know*—"

"Na, na!" moaned little Mr. Weinberg. "To him you shouldn't pay any attention, Mr. Dundee. A boy off his head with grief—"

"You shut up!" Risher ordered his manager roughly. "Can't you forget the damned movies for a minute? To hell with the movies! Yola Conova is dead, and Geoffrey Arundel killed her!"

In the silence that followed the explosion of that bomb. The only sound was Weinberg's low wail of despair, as he rocked his gray head.

"You're making a very serious charge, Mr. Risher," Dundee said at last. "What facts have you to back it up?"

"Plenty!" the boy assured him grimly. "You're a detective. Mr. Hepburn says you're a hell of a good one. Well, when you're looking for a likely suspect, what's your first concern?"

"Motive, of course," Dundee answered obediently but with a smile. "Naturally we look first for the person who would benefit most by the death of the victim—"

"In this case, that person is Geoffrey Arundel. Yola Conova was insured for *one million dollars*. And, although they had separated and she was going to divorce him, Geoffrey Arundel's name is still on that policy as beneficiary. Alive, she was nearly broke. Dead, she was worth *one million dollars*—to Geoffrey Arundel!"

Dundee whistled, long and loud. Then he turned toward the desk at which Kay Loring was making shorthand notes of the entire conversation. "Do you happen to know if that's true, Miss Loring?"

"Yes, Mr. Dundee. She took out the policy about three years ago. I remember quite well. Several of the big stars have million dollar policies. It's considered good publicity, as well as good business—"

She was interrupted by the ringing of the telephone, which Strawn answered.

"It's for you, Weinberg. New York's calling."

The manager clasped his head with both hands. "In these times I should lose my job and walk the streets!" he moaned. "Tell the young lady I'll take the call in a booth downstairs."

When he had rushed out, like a distracted woman, Dundee turned to the actor again. "It is your theory, I presume, Mr. Risher, that Arundel, sure that his wife contemplated divorce action against him, and fearing that she would lose no time in changing the beneficiary of her policy, murdered her before she could take such action?"

"You're damned right!" Risher agreed violently. "But he waited one week too long! Just one little week! Arundel don't know it yet, but he'll never collect one red cent of that million dollars!"

VII

CAPTAIN STRAWN WAS SUDDENLY the typical police bully as he towered over the boy in the chair.

"Pretty sure of what you're sayin', ain't you, Risher?" he thundered. "Didn't waste no time persuadin' your sweetie to write the insurance company to change the name of the beneficiary on her million dollar policy from Geoffrey Arundel to Clinton Risher, did you?"

From the desk where Kay Loring was taking it all down in shorthand there came a choked cry of protest, and if Dundee had not moved quickly the young actor's fist would have crashed against the old man's jaw.

"You dirty liar!" the boy sobbed, as he fell back into his chair. "I come here to help you-all, and a big stiff of a cop don't do anything but insult—"

"Quit blubberin'!" Strawn commanded sourly. "You handle this crybaby, Dundee. I left my kid gloves in my overcoat pocket."

As Dundee obeyed, his voice was brisk, though kind. "Will you explain, Mr. Risher, just what you meant by saying that Mr. Arundel would not be able to collect Miss Conova's insurance?"

All the fight seemed to have gone out of the boy. "Because the policy has lapsed," he said dully.

"Lapsed?" Dundee repeated. "How do you know?"

"There was an air mail letter from the insurance company, in that bunch of mail Yola got yesterday afternoon," Risher explained wearily. "She showed it to me. There was a check of hers pinned to the letter. The Reliance Life Insurance Company—the Los Angeles branch—had written her that the check had been returned to them marked 'Account Closed,' and the letter went on to say that evidently Yola had made a mistake

and given 'em a check on the wrong bank, because this
bank the worthless check was on had told the insurance
company that Yola had changed her account from that
bank to another one more conveniently located. So the
insurance man wrote Yola that it would be necessary for
her to send another check on the right bank immediately.
Otherwise, the policy would lapse, since the thirty day
period, of grace had already expired; and she didn't have
the kind of insurance that carries itself, for a long time. I
forget what they call that kind. . . . So now the policy has
lapsed," the boy concluded his clumsy explanation.

Dundee considered for a moment, frowning. Then:
"Not if Miss Conova mailed a check to cover before she
died."

"But she didn't!" Risher told him. "She acted like she
didn't care a hoot whether the policy lapsed or not, and I
didn't blame her, knowing who the beneficiary was—"

"Did she tell you that Arundel was the beneficiary?"

"No. I read it in the papers, same as Miss Loring did."

"What comment did Miss Conova make when she
showed you the letter?"

"She said something kind of funny," the actor
remembered. "She said, 'Imagine, Clint, being worth a
million dollars dead, and nothing much alive! What a
horrible temptation!' And then she shivered, and looked
scared to death. I told her to cancel the policy, and notify
Arundel what she'd done, but she said, 'I can't, Clint! I
wish I could!' Then all at once she brightened up and even
laughed a little as she handed me the letter again. 'Send
that on to Mr. Arundel for me, Clint,' she said, so I
addressed one of the hotel envelopes to Geoffrey Arundel,
in care of, the Friars' Club, New York City, like she told
me, and—" Suddenly the boy stopped speaking and
clapped a hand to his breast pocket.

"And forgot to mail it?" Dundee guessed.

"I sure did!" Risher confessed ruefully, then laughed
with bitter mirth. "It wouldn't have done any good if I'd
mailed it, but I sure thank the Lord I didn't remember it

last night after I knew Arundel was in town. If I had, I'd have sent the letter over to his hotel, and he'd have got a check into the mail before he killed her." His voice broke, and he gulped twice before he could continue. "Well, I got one consolation! Yola ain't worth a million dollars to him dead! I wish she knew, too."

"Even though the policy has lapsed," Dundee remarked thoughtfully, "Miss Conova must have left a very large estate."

"Large?" the actor repeated. "Say! She was nearly bankrupt! Mr. Weinberg was telling me all about it. Said it was common talk how much it would mean to Yola to make good in this new picture and on this personal appearance tour, so's World Wide would sign her on a contract. He says he knows for a fact that she was cleaned out in the stock market and that her real estate holdings in Hollywood are mortgaged for more'n they're worth now."

"I see. . . . May I have that letter now?"

Risher surrendered it dubiously. "I guess it's all right, since it ain't even stamped."

But Dundee seemed to have no worries about committing a Federal offense as he loosened the flap of the envelope. The two detectives bent over the astonishingly important document and its enclosure—the worthless check for $3,930.

"Hmm. Million dollar life insurance don't come as high as I figgered it would," Strawn commented. "But I reckon that's only a quarterly premium. . . .'Funny thing—her not sendin' a new check herself, but passin' the buck to her hubby."

Kay Loring cleared her throat nervously. The three men looked at her.

"Forgive me for interrupting," she said meekly, "but don't you all realize that everything Mr. Risher has told us points to the conclusion that Miss Conova did commit suicide? Please, Mr. Risher! I'm terribly sorry for you. I know how you must feel. But won't you listen a minute, if the other gentlemen are willing for me to speak?"

"Go ahead, Ginger," Dundee encouraged her.

She spread her small hands with a helpless gesture. "It's awfully hard to put into words, but it seems to me that everything Yola said and did yesterday indicates that she had made up her mind she couldn't go on. . . . Jimmy, I'm sure you can guess my reasons for thinking that telephone call was the last straw. She did have a past, Mr. Risher, that she felt was hopeless to try to live down. She knew that the life she was planning with you was a dream too sweet ever to come true, for to ally herself with you, as your wife, would hurt your career too seriously. Night after night, for a whole week, that one-act play of yours suggested the only solution to her. And remember her own words to you—that after she had done something she had to do, she would 'sleep like a baby.' *The dead sleep very soundly, Mr. Risher!* . . . Please! Just a moment more! I think it gave her a sort of bitter, mischievous joy to know that the husband she did not love and who had made her life miserable would not profit by her death. I think that is why she laughed when she told you to mail him the insurance company's letter. She knew he would receive it too late to rectify her error in paying the premium with the wrong check, even if he had the money to do so, which is unlikely."

"But she was much too happy when I left her last night to dream of dying!" Risher protested, his head bowed on his hands.

Outside the door there was the sound of many feet walking heavily and a rumble of male voices, followed by an unmistakable knock.

"Your boys are on the job, Captain," Dundee informed his old chief unnecessarily. "You may go now, Mr. Risher, but please remain within call; that is, we'd rather you did not leave the hotel until—"

"Yes, sir," the actor agreed without resentment, but with the docility of despair.

A minute later Dundee was alone with Kay Loring, Captain Strawn having left the parlor to shepherd his squad into the bedroom of the suite and there to assign them their duties.

The girl rose from the ornate little desk and stood rubbing her frail wrist ruefully. "I didn't know I could write shorthand so fast," she remarked, without meeting Dundee's compassionate eyes. "Guess I'll try for a job as court stenographer, now that I've cooked my goose as a newspaperman."

"You shan't have to take down any more evidence," the detective assured her. "Brede, Strawn's stenographer, has arrived. It was wonderful the way you filled the breach, Ginger. But then, I wasn't surprised. You're wonderful in so many ways."

"Don't!" she protested. "I don't deserve—But tell me what I'm to say to the reporters, if you were serious about wanting me to be the press representative of the investigation."

"That can wait," Dundee told her gently. "Sit down again, girl. You look exhausted. . . . Now, Ginger, you must show me that letter you should have given me last night."

"I can't," she confessed. "I—I destroyed it."

"Why?" It was the detective, not the man, who asked the question, and who was angry.

"To protect—her," Kay Loring answered faintly, without meeting his eyes.

"And while you were 'protecting' her, she was losing her life," Dundee pointed out cruelly. "I must ask you to explain your amazing behavior."

She flushed painfully. "I suppose you must, but please don't use that tone, Jimmy. . . . When I was about to show you the letter last night a plan came to me suddenly, one that seemed better than calling in an—an outsider. I realized I didn't have a right to betray her secret. After you'd gone I tried to get Yola Conova on the telephone. The hotel operator told me she had left orders not to be disturbed, and that she had left her telephone receiver off the hook. I planned to see her as early as possible this morning, and to try to persuade her to agree to—"

"To let you write a sympathetic and laudatory account of her life in Hamilton?" Dundee suggested. "In other words, to remove the fangs of the snake who was blackmailing her. Is that correct, Ginger?"

"Yes. But how did you know?"

"I thought of the same scheme," Dundee told her. "What was her real name?"

"I don't know."

"This is no time for evasions, Ginger," he reminded her coldly.

"That's unfair!" she accused him, with sudden anger. "I don't know her real name. It was something long and foreign, but if I ever heard it I've forgot it. Pauline changed her name to Madge Smith the very first day she was with us as Chris's nurse, and she was known as Madge Smith all the time she lived in Hamilton."

"Rather highhanded of your stepmother, wasn't it? Madge Smith! . . . How long did she live here?"

"About two years," Kay answered. "Madge wasn't a qualified teacher—with a state certificate, I mean. I believe she was just a high-school graduate, from Chicago. Anyway, she was quite competent to teach Chris and me, and to help Pauline and our one other servant with the housework. . . . Chris and I fairly worshiped her. I tried to imitate her in every way —even to her accent—"

"She had an accent then, did she?"

"Yes. That was one reason I couldn't be sure last night, even after I'd heard her talk. And the chief reason why, before last night, I could never make up my mind whether Yola Conova was our own darling Madge or not. But her accent when she was sixteen was the merest suggestion of foreignness—a sort of flavor, and an occasional awkward construction. I remember she told us she was American-born. I suppose her parents talked Polish or Russian in the home—"

"What did she look like at sixteen?" Dundee interrupted again.

"Utterly beautiful," she answered. "I was only ten, you know, and quite tiny, so Madge seemed big to me then. She was plump and firm-fleshed—strong, and a little slow in her movements. Sort of quiet and serene and sure. I remember hearing Pauline describe her as 'stocky' and 'bovine,' but she wasn't really."

"I gather your stepmother didn't like your peasant goddess."

"Peasant goddess," Kay repeated softly. "That really describes her exactly—as she was then, I mean. No, Pauline didn't appreciate Madge, as Chris and I did. And Madge was afraid of Pauline, of her sharp tongue. She used to shrink from her scoldings, with exactly the same gesture she used on the stage last night? You remember? Her hand up, palm outward, as if to shield her face from a blow."

"I remember," Dundee agreed soberly. "Why didn't your stepmother dismiss her if she didn't like her?"

"Because Madge never gave her any real excuse, and because Dad wouldn't stand for it," Kay explained. "Besides, she was wonderful with Chris. He'd never been so well or so happy in all his poor little life, and after Madge left he was never well or happy again. . . . He died when he was eight, just six months after Madge left us."

"Then how did Madge happen to leave?" Dundee asked hastily, turning his eyes away from that grief-twisted little face.

"I—don't know," the girl faltered, her eyes downcast and her hands twisting together in her lap. "She was with us about a year."

"She stayed on in Hamilton?"

"Oh, yes. For, another year, or so. First she got a job as housekeeper for Professor and Mrs. Martin, who both teach in our junior college. But it didn't last long. Madge was too beautiful, too—too—"

"Was she a flirt?"

"Oh, no, no!" Kay denied vehemently. "She didn't have to be. No man could help admiring her. She made nearly all other women look silly and trivial. . . . Wives didn't like that, of course. After she left the Martins she became a maid in the Kenyon home. The wholesale produce people, you know—awfully rich. Bruce Kenyon was one of the most popular young men in Hamilton at that time. Terribly good looking, cordial and jolly with everybody. Really charming. He's changed awfully since then."

"He must have," Dundee commented drily. "The Bruce Kenyon I've met around town is anything but cordial and jolly. His mother seems to have been curiously indiscreet in her choice of servants."

"Bruce was away at college," Kay explained, "but he broke his ankle in a football game that Thanksgiving and had to come home for three weeks. I suppose even then Mrs. Kenyon thought he was safe enough, because Bruce had just got engaged to Helen Winter. But he wasn't safe. Or rather Madge wasn't safe."

"What happened?" Dundee asked bruskly.

"A baby, I think," Kay confessed, flushing, "but whether it was born alive or dead none of us ever knew. I'll never forget how sick at my stomach I felt when I heard Pauline telling Dad about it. The following May, that was. Pauline told Dad that Madge wouldn't name the man. I guess she loved Bruce too much to want to get him into trouble. Anyway, it must have been Bruce, because everyone said the Kenyons paid Dink Garnet to marry her."

"Poor girl," Dundee sighed.

"She didn't live with him at all, I understand. Just married him and disappeared. Dink stayed here and bought a pool hall—with the Kenyon money, gossip said."

"And your hunch, of course, was that it was Dink Garnet, her former husband, who had written Yola Conova the blackmail letter?"

"Yes, of course!" Kay answered with hasty emphasis.

"But why," puzzled the detective, "has a low-life like Dink Garnet waited all these years to blackmail so rich a victim?"

"I don't know," admitted the girl, in a low voice, "unless it was because Dink simply couldn't believe the maid servant he'd been paid to marry had turned into a famous screen star. You see, he scarcely knew her. And even if he'd known her quite well, as she was at seventeen or eighteen, he could not have been absolutely sure that Yola Conova was really Madge Smith. Even I was never sure—until I saw her last night in person."

"And last night *he* made sure, too," Dundee said, his nostrils flaring at the memory of that scene in the alley. "A scar or a birthmark on her arm, I suppose."

Kay shook her head. "Madge had no birthmark on her arm. But she might have got a scar, after she left us. At any rate, he satisfied himself that his suspicion was correct."

"And then dared her to have him arrested for annoying her," Dundee remembered with angry disgust. "It will be a pity, Ginger, if your zeal to protect Yola Conova proves to have protected her murderer instead."

All color was wiped out Of her cheeks. Her brown eyes were pools of terror. "No, no! You're terribly wrong!" she gasped.

"Tell me what the letter said, Ginger," he commanded, more gently. "I'm sure you remember it almost word for word."

She shivered and clasped her hands tightly. "I—let me think," she pleaded. "My head aches. I'll try to reproduce it on paper. I think I can. I read it several times, of course, and I have a visual memory," she added, with a forlorn touch of pride.

She returned to the desk, and Dundee paced restlessly up and down the room while she labored with pencil and paper.

"I think this is almost verbatim," she said at last, offering a sheet of paper over her shoulder without turning to look at him. And while he read she sat at the desk with her head bowed upon her crossed arms.

The blackmail letter began without salutation:

"Don't you think all your readers would be interested in know that the famous Yola Conova is none other than our own Madge Smith? I have written out the story of Yola Conova's life in Hamilton, giving the dates and the names of her employers here and a lot of other very interesting information. I can also furnish proofs to back up all my statements. I am sure the complete story of this great star's humble life in Hamilton will be a real inspiration to all who read it.

"I am addressing this note to you, Miss Loring, because it will not take you by surprise, and because you can assure your editor that the story I am offering is a true story. Please tell him that I will call on him with the manuscript tomorrow morning, Friday, at ten o'clock sharp."

The note was signed, ONE WHO KNEW YOLA CONOVA WHEN.

"Of all the damnable things!" Dundee exploded. "Clever as hell, too, blast his hide! I must say Mr. Garnet's appearance is deceptive. I should never have credited him with—Oh, there you are, Captain! Take a look at this!"

Captain Strawn listened silently as Dundee explained, and as silently read the proffered sheet.

"Humph!" he grunted at last. "It's not evidence. And I don't believe Dink Garnet wrote it in the first place. Sounds more like a woman than a man, to me. . . . You're a reporter, I understand, Miss Loring?"

"I—was," Kay answered.

"I never saw a reporter yet that would stick at anything to get a scoop for his paper," Strawn generalized, but his narrowed eyes were fixed upon the girl.

She sprang to her feet. "What do you mean?" she blazed.

"Nothing. Nothing *a*-tall," the old detective denied grimly. "But I was just thinkin' what a pity it was you destroyed the original of this interestin' document. Typewritin' is a heap easier to identify than disguised handwritin'. . . . Well, boy, we gotta get busy. Garnet and the Kenyons'll be along soon, and I guess we'd better have a look at the Conova woman's rooms before we tackle them."

"Right you are, chief," Dundee agreed. "Ginger, will you take on the newspaper boys while we're away? Stall 'em along. Keep 'em happy with the suicide theory, but don't let 'em get at either the nurse or Risher for interviews. If Arundel and Weinberg want to talk, that'll be O.K., but be sure to tip off Weinberg—not that he'll need the tip, I suppose—that he's not to spill any of Risher's suspicions. For Pete's sake, child, don't let any hint of murder or of this Madge Smith business get out. And don't slip anyone the news of the lapsed insurance policy until we've had a chance to spring it on Arundel."

She nodded mutely, but her eyes were so full of distress that Dundee found it hard to turn his back upon her.

"That youngun knows a heap she ain't puttin' out," Strawn rumbled, after he and Dundee, with Brede, the stenographer, in tow, had pushed their way through a small but importunate crowd of local newspapermen outside the door and were headed for the stairs. "That's the big trouble with a murder investigation. Everybody concerned has a pet secret they're scared will be found out, even if it hasn't any bearing on the case, so they he and mess things up for all of us. . . . Hello! What's all this? . . . Shh!"

They had reached the head of the stairs and Strawn had just opened the door onto a third floor corridor. Now he released the door and let it close silently against his foot, so that he, Dundee and Brede, from behind the door, could see and hear without being seen.

Geoffrey Arundel, whom Strawn had not seen before but whom he recognized from Dundee's description, was standing in the doorway of Room 316, obviously on the point of leaving.

Arundel was speaking, with cold fury but in a low voice: "I repeat—gross negligence! I hired you to safeguard her, paid you a trained nurse's exorbitant salary, to do nothing but watch her, and you—*you*—" The man choked on a vile epithet. "I warn you, Miss Patton, I'll exert every ounce of influence I possess to get your name struck from the nurses' register!"

And on that threat the actor banged the door behind which a woman had begun to weep hysterically.

VIII

"WHAT ARE you doing here, Arundel?" Dundee asked in a low voice, blocking the path of the hurrying actor.

The dapper figure stiffened haughtily, but the hand which reached for the monocle dangling from a black ribbon was shaking like a very old man's.

"I beg your pardon!" Yola Conova's bereaved husband protested with icy politeness, a pale gray eye glaring from behind its shield of glass.

"Sorry," Dundee apologized with a grin. "I quite forgot that we haven't been introduced. This is Captain Strawn of the Hamilton police, and I'm Dundee, acting as special deputy under Captain Strawn for the present. And now that the formalities have been duly observed, perhaps you will answer my question, Mr. Arundel."

"I'm on my way to my rooms, sir," the actor answered stiffly.

"Your rooms?" Strawn cut in. "I thought you were stopping at the Hamilton."

"I was—until half, an hour ago," Arundel told him crisply. "I thought it best, under the circumstances, to be in close touch with my wife's party."

"Quite!" Dundee agreed, borrowing the actor's favorite word, to Arundel's obvious annoyance "Your room number?"

"I'm in *Suite* 3-A," the Englishman retorted arrogantly.

"Its nice to be rich in times like these, isn't it?" Dundee reflected aloud cheerily. Then, with sudden authority "Go to your *suite* please, and remain there until we have time to talk things over with you. And by the way," he added, forcing the difficult words with as good grace as possible, "Captain Strawn and I offer our sympathy in your bereavement."

The pale eyes remained cold. "Thank you—*very* much!" said Geoffrey Arundel, and marched swiftly away.

"Brede," Strawn Ordered, "run downstairs and tell Harmon I want him to keep an eye on that baby—Suite 3-A. We'll wait right here for you. Gosh, boy!" he added to Dundee, after Brede had left on a run, "You were kinda rough on the poor ham. After all he *has* lost his wife in a fair-to-middlin' nasty way, and he *has* got what looks like an ironclad alibi—"

"I know," Dundee admitted irritably. "But I don't like that guy. He annoys me. . . . Shall we barge in on the nurse as soon as Brede gets back, while she's all upset from the tongue-lashing that British blight has been giving her, and likely to be talkative?"

The three men found Louise Patton in bed, in one of the smallest and cheapest rooms available at the smart Randolph Hotel. Pungent, aromatic odors of medicines hung heavy over the narrow bed. The blonde nurse was propped high against four pillows, but even so her breathing was difficult and noisy.

"Pneumonia, if they're not careful," Dundee diagnosed to himself, his eyes taking in the round patches of scarlet on the thin cheeks, and the feverish glitter behind the tears in her big, round blue eyes. But the fire in her blood made her look very pretty.

"Oh, it's you!" she gasped, looking at Dundee with almost hysterical relief. "I was afraid—Oh, please don't let that dreadful man come near me again, Mr. Dundee! I can't stand it! I'm scared to death of him."

"Of Geoffrey Arundel?" Dundee asked gently, swinging two chairs to the bedside and signaling Brede to take his Place at the small writing desk. "Why are you afraid of him, Miss Patton?"

The girl beat upon the blankets with frantic hands. "He blames me for everything!" she cried, her hoarse voice cracking. "I know I did wrong, but it's not fair to treat me like a murderess—"

"Now, now, girlie," Strawn cut in, with rough kindliness. "You'll get yourself all worked up, and run your temperature higher'n a kite—"

The girl relaxed against her, pillows with a sigh and closed her too-bright blue eyes. "I wish to God I could get sick enough to die of pneumonia," she moaned, and tears began to slide down her fever-red cheeks. "Nobody has to tell me it's all my fault that Yola Conova is—dead. I was the first to admit it, wasn't I, Mr. Dundee? But anybody would have done just what I did—"

"Please try to control yourself, Miss Patton," Dundee interrupted, his voice stern, since kindness only aggravated the girl's hysteria. "There's no use blaming yourself now. What Captain Strawn and I want are facts—not tears. By the way, have you seen a doctor?"

"Yes, sir," she answered meekly. "Mr. Hepburn called a doctor last night. Dr. Wayne, from the Hamilton Hotel. The house doctor for the Randolph is sick in the hospital himself. Dr. Wayne says I'm threatened with pneumonia, and I hope to God—"

"Stop that, Miss Patton!" Dundee commanded, seizing one of the hands which was beating at the covers. I am surprised at you—a nurse! I thought trained nurses were of tougher fiber, more fatalistic about death. You *are* a registered nurse, I believe?"

"Yes, sir. I graduated from St. Paul's, in New York, in 1931."

"How old are you, Miss Patton?"

Her eyelids twitched, "Twenty-four," she said faintly.

"How old are you really, Miss Patton—not for publication?"

"I'm twenty-eight," the girl admitted. "But I want to get into the movies, or I did before—before—and you've got to be young—"

"So that's why you joined up with Yola Conova?" Dundee asked curiously. "Using a patient as a stepping-stone?"

The scarlet spread over the girl's whole face. "You make the sound so mean," she protested piteously. "But I don't see any harm in a girl's using all the pull she can—"

"Neither do I," Dundee assured her, smiling. "So you didn't like nursing—wanted to change professions?"

The girl stirred restlessly on her pillows. "There's no money in nursing these days, and the field is terribly overcrowded, but I like it well enough, or I did before—before—"

"Before, as Arundel puts it, your negligence resulted in a patient's death?" Dundee cut in sharply.

"You, too!" Louise Patton cried hoarsely, and covered her face with her hands "I'll never live it down! Nobody'll ever trust me again with a 'mental' case or any other kind! I'd be better off dead—"

"In your opinion, Miss Patton, was Yola Conova what is professionally known as a 'mental' case?"

"Of course!" The girl opened her eyes wide, as if astonished at the question 'She was what we call a 'manic-depressive.' She was obsessed with a desire to commit suicide—"

"Do you know that to be true from personal observation of Miss Conova while she was under your care?" Dundee cut in.

"I do, because I saw her attempt suicide on two different occasions," the nurse said firmly.

"Two? Really?" Dundee ejaculated. "Tell me about those attempts, Miss Patton."

"The first time was in Chicago," the girl began, her voice coming in hoarse gasps. "We had a suite in the Drake Hotel, on the twelfth floor. There was a little balcony outside the parlor windows. Miss Conova and Mr. Risher had been rehearsing their one act play, when suddenly Miss Conova stepped out of one of the French windows onto the balcony. I was watching her, as I always did, without letting her suspect what I was doing, but it was Mr. Risher, who sprang out and grabbed her just as she was about to jump. She'd climbed up onto the stone balustrade and was poised to leap when he caught her skirt. I could not possibly have reached her in time myself—"

"And what did Miss Conova say after she had been rescued?"

"She was shaking all over, but even then she did not admit she was determined to kill herself. She explained that looking down from a great height always affected her like that—gave her an irresistible impulse to jump."

"A common enough disease of the nerves—height phobia," Dundee contributed thoughtfully. "Did Mr. Risher believe her?"

"Oh, yes! And I pretended to believe her, too," the girl answered eagerly. "But both Mr. Risher and I insisted that she change to a suite on the second floor. We were on the fourth floor here, but she said that didn't seem high at all; and there was no balcony outside her rooms here, so we felt safe enough."

"And the second time?" Dundee urged.

"Well, as soon as I took on the job I went through her bags and trunks thoroughly—looking for hidden poisons, you know," the girl explained feverishly. "Depressives are terribly clever about hiding them. I found two bottles labeled 'Poison,' with skull and crossbones. One of the labels had 'Carbolic Acid' written on it in ink, and the other had 'Hydrochloric Acid' written on a typewriter. I knew she could kill herself with either one, of course. I took them both, and she didn't seem to miss the carbolic acid, but at lunch that day she asked for the other bottle. She said she had to take fifteen drops of hydrochloric acid in half a glass of water with her meals. I knew fifteen drops in that much water couldn't hurt her, if she had a hypoacidity, so of course I gave it to her. Before each meal I fixed the dose for her, but kept the bottle."

"Did she seem to resent your having abstracted the medicine?"

"Oh, no! I explained that I'd found it while unpacking for her and had been afraid the bottle would break and spoil some of her things. I poured out the last of the acid this morning when I was packing to move to this room, and left the empty bottle in the waste-basket in my room in Miss Conova's suite."

"She made a second attempt at suicide, you say?" Dundee prodded.

"Something made me suspicious one day—last Tuesday it was, I believe," the nurse continued, her breath coming rapidly and unevenly. "I followed her into the bathroom and saw her standing at the basin, with a little glass tube in one hand and looking at eight or ten tiny tablets in the palm of the other hand. When she saw me she gave them up without a struggle. She seemed dazed, strange. I was terribly afraid she had already swallowed some of the pellets, although she protested she hadn't; so, on the pretext of giving her some aromatic spirits of ammonia, because she looked so faint, I gave her a whopping big dose of ipecac, which I had on hand in case of just such an emergency. If she *had* taken any of the strychnine, she lost it then!"

"Strychnine?" Dundee echoed. Strawn whistled. "How did you know it was strychnine, Miss Patton?"

"Because I'd been warned to look for it," she told them dramatically. "That very morning I'd had an air-mail letter from Mr. Arundel, telling me he'd missed a tube of strychnine tablets which he takes for his heart. He wrote that he was afraid his wife had stolen the poison and that I must search her luggage for it. I had already searched for poisons, as I told you, but I went through everything again without finding it—but she had it, all right—"

"What became of the tube of strychnine, Miss Patton?" Dundee interrupted.

"I washed the tablets down the drain of the basin and threw the glass tube out of the bathroom window. I was so upset I did the first thing that occurred to me."

"Have you the letter from Mr. Arundel, Miss Patton? The letter warning you to look for strychnine?"

The girl hesitated. Then, in a burst of confidence: "Yes, I have! I kept all of the three letters I received from him, just in case—in spite of my vigilance, anything *did* happen—"

"I see," Dundee said, very slowly. "I presume Mr. Arundel tacitly or plainly suggested that you keep them— for the same reason?"

"Oh, no!" she denied. "He put a postscript on each letter, telling me to destroy it, for fear Yola—I mean, Miss Conova—should find it and get onto the fact that I'd been hired to watch her. He was afraid she would discharge me if she knew I was a nurse hired to prevent her committing suicide."

"You mean to tell me she never suspected?" Dundee was frankly incredulous.

"I'm sure she didn't. I'm really a very good ladies' maid, because I've always been poor and had to take care of my own nails and hair and clothes. A nurse has to do a lot of personal services for her women patients, too, you know, so it was easy to get by as a maid. She was not at all exacting, either—not a bit critical or overbearing. She treated me almost like an equal, was so kind and considerate—"

At the sight of fresh tears Dundee patted the girl's hand, but hastened to put his next question.

"Then you liked Miss Conova?"

"An awful lot," the girl sobbed. "Of course, a nurse gets sort of hard-boiled, and it's so easy to get into the habit of thinking of a patient as just another case, instead of as a real person; but nobody could have helped liking Yola Conova. It was sort of pathetic to see how hard she tried to please everybody, to make everybody like her. There was only one thing I had against her—"

"Yes, Miss Patton?" Dundee urged, as the girl stopped, with a little gasp of dismay.

"That just popped out," the nurse stammered. "I didn't mean to say it. But—well, after we'd got pretty well acquainted, being together so constantly, you know, I told her how terribly I wanted to get into the movies. I didn't ask her in so many words to introduce me to a director when we got to Hollywood, but I did hint, and she froze right up. Said she was sorry, but it would be utterly impossible for her to be of any assistance. Of course I knew she could help me if she really wanted to, and it wouldn't have cost her anything, either—"

"So you got good and sore at her, didn't you?" Strawn pounced.

"No, sir! I did not!" the nurse denied furiously. "Of course, I was disappointed, but I wasn't sore! I told myself that everybody she met must be at her to help them get into the movies, and she must be terribly fed up. I knew— or I thought then—that I'd get to Hollywood anyhow, expenses all paid, and that I'd have made other friends in the business—like Mr. Risher and Mr. Weinberg and Mr. Arundel—"

"How did you happen to get the job, Miss Patton?" Dundee interrupted.

"Through an ad in the paper. But I wish to God I'd never seen it or that somebody else had beat me to it! It was just a three-line ad in the classified, under 'Help Wanted—Female.' In *The World-Telegram*, I think it was."

"How was the advertisement worded, Miss Patton?"

The girl knit her plucked, light-brown eyebrows. "I think I can remember it almost word for word, except the telephone number, which, turned out to be the number of the Friars' Club, where Mr. Arundel was waiting for answers. it said, 'NURSE, to travel California with nervous lady. Must be young, pleasing personality, discreet, competent to act as personal maid.' Then it gave a telephone number and said to ask for Mr. G. A. As soon as I read the ad—"

"Were you out of work, Miss Patton?" Dundee interrupted.

"No. I was employed as office nurse and receptionist by Dr. Hugo Alexander, a well-known heart specialist on Park Avenue," the girl told him. "He has a lot of movie people among his patients, as well as society people, and all the time I worked for him they kept on telling me how—how pretty I was, and that with my looks and personality I'd make a hit in the movies. Maybe they were just kidding," she conceded forlornly, "but I saw a lot of stars who weren't as good-looking as I am, off the screen, so I did get ideas into my head. For a long time I'd been going through the classified ads, in the hope of finding a chance to go to California with some rich patient. So I telephoned 'Mr. G. A.' and he said I was the first to answer his ad, and he liked my telephone personality, so he'd take me to lunch and talk it over."

"Just what day was that?" Dundee interrupted.

"That was Tuesday, November 9th," Miss Patton answered promptly. "I met Mr. Arundel at a little tearoom on Madison Avenue, and there he told me all about the case—Miss Conova, I mean—how she wasn't really well enough to undertake this personal appearance tour, and about how she'd tried to commit suicide in Hollywood. He said he'd tried to persuade her to give up the tour, regardless of how important it was to her future, but she'd refused. And he said he would insist on going with her himself, to watch over her, but he couldn't, because he was rehearsing for a stage play, and it was his big chance of a Broadway comeback. Of course, I was thrilled to death at the prospect of meeting and actually traveling with the 'Incomparable Conova,' as the movie magazines used to call her—"

"Then you had never met Miss Conova before?"

Again the blue eyes flew wide with surprise. "Of course not! My only chance would have been if she'd been a patient of Dr. Alexander's, and she wasn't. I never saw her in my life—except in pictures, of course—until just before the train pulled out for Chicago Wednesday noon."

"You mean that Mr. Arundel engaged you, without his wife's consent?"

"Not exactly," Louise Patton answered, moistening her parched lips. "She had agreed to have a personal maid, sort of a companion, he told me, and had left the job of finding one up to him. But she wasn't to have the least suspicion that I'm a nurse, Mr. Arundel said— otherwise she'd hit the ceiling and fire me. After lunch he telephoned her in my presence, and told her he'd found a nice, pleasant, competent girl—that's the way he described me. Then he asked her if I could call at the hotel to see her, but she said there was no need of that— she was so awfully busy, and there was a big party she was supposed to go to that night. Of course I was going to be terribly busy too, so that suited me fine. I had to finish out the day at Dr. Alexander's—I really felt awful leaving him flat like that, but a girl has to look out for herself when it comes to a big chance—" A violent fit of coughing choked off her words.

"Here! Drink this!" Dundee commanded sharply, as he filled a glass of water from the bedside thermos pitcher.

"Thanks!" she gasped, and lay back, panting, her eyes closed for a long moment. "That afternoon, late, Mr. Arundel sent a messenger to my office with an envelope containing my ticket and Pullman reservation to Chicago, some expense money, and a note of introduction to Miss Conova, to identify me by, of course. I got my things ready that night, and did some shopping Wednesday morning, and then went to the Grand Central to catch the train. It wasn't the Twentieth Century, though the papers said that was the one she was going to take, so there wasn't anybody there to see her off—not even Mr. Arundel, because he was busy rehearsing. I showed her Mr. Arundel's note, and she was very cordial and kind. I could tell she really preferred to be alone—"

"Was she noticeably depressed?"

"Not depressed, exactly, but—strange, somehow," Miss Patton answered painstakingly. "She hardly spoke, and for hours she stayed shut up in her drawing room. She said she was studying the play script. Depressives act like that. Sometimes they just sit—for days and days—"

"How about Mr. Arundel," Dundee interrupted bruskly. "Had you known him previously, as a patient of Dr. Alexander's, or otherwise?"

"I don't think he was ever a patient of Dr. Alexander's," the girl answered, her voice strained and hoarse. "If he was I never saw him there. He seemed to know the doctor by reputation, and he said the fact that l worked for Dr. Alexander was more than recommendation enough. While we lunched together Mr. Arundel gave me instructions to watch his wife very carefully, to do my best to keep her in good spirits, to flatter her about her work in the movies, to keep any bad notices in the newspapers from her, if possible, and to write him every day as to how she seemed. I filled my job to the very best of my ability—"

"Until last night," Dundee finished the sentence for her, his voice grim. "Now, Miss Patton, we want you to tell us about last night. Beginning with your return to the hotel from the theater, I mean."

The girl drew a deep breath, which ended in a bronchial wheeze. Before beginning to speak she reached to the little bedside table for a throat spray. When she had finished with the atomizer she selected a red menthol lozenge from a box that was already half empty.

"Have you a nurse?" Dundee asked, with sudden solicitude, for the girl was looking very ill indeed.

"I refused to have one," she told him. "If I get any worse I'll have to go to the hospital, I suppose, but I can't bear the thought of being cooped up in this little room with a nurse. Every registered nurse in town knows by this time that I fell down on my job—"

"I think you're hypersensitive, Miss Patton," Dundee assured her gently. "Now tell us exactly what happened last night."

'Well, it was about half past eleven when we reached the hotel after the theater," the girl began slowly. "Miss Conova was nervous and obviously under a terrific strain, because of a man who had accosted her at the stage door—"

"Yes, yes? We know about that," Dundee interrupted "Did she discuss the man or his actions with you?"

"No. She made no reference to him at all, but she kept trembling, and rubbing her arm where he had caught hold of it."

"Did you notice anything out of the ordinary about that arm, Miss Patton?—a scar or a mole, or any sort of birthmark?"

"There was nothing—no blemish of any kind," the nurse assure, him. "I've helped her dress often enough to be sure of that. Her arms were both perfect."

"Go on, please."

"I was worried about her, so I ordered up some hot milk, which I persuaded her to drink. She wouldn't let me put a mild sedative in the milk, although she had been taking one every night before retiring. It was because I was afraid she wasn't sleeping that I went into her room for a look at her about half past two—"

"We'll get to that later, Miss Patton. What happened after she drank the milk?"

"She seemed to feel better, and turned on the radio. There's one in every room here, you know. She even hummed a song that was being sung over the radio— 'When My Dream Boat Comes Home,' I think it was. And she smiled sort of queer while she was singing it under her breath. She had just changed from her theater dress into lounging pajamas when Mr. Risher arrived with Mr. Weinberg. All four of us talked together for about ten minutes, then Mr. Weinberg left, saying he was tired out and was going to bed. I stayed in the parlor for about ten minutes more, to answer the telephone, which was ringing almost constantly—"

"About those telephone calls, Miss Patton," Dundee stopped her. "Whom were they from?"

"At least three were from movie fans, or so they claimed," the nurse explained. "We were driven nearly crazy the whole week by fans trying to speak to her over the 'phone or to get her autograph in their everlasting albums."

"And did Miss Conova oblige?"

"Never! If she'd once started there'd have been no end to the nuisance. I always had to explain that Miss Conova was resting, and that she was not well enough to give personal interviews, even to the press."

"And the other calls?"

"Well, one was from Mr. Arundel. He said he was wanted to make a fourth at bridge, but that he would refuse to play if there was any chance that his wife would see him. I took her the message—I'd just gone to my bedroom when that call came—and she refused to speak to him."

"Was Arundel pretty sore?" Strawn wanted to know.

"No. He seemed to expect nothing else, but I heard him sigh before he said, 'Well, that's that!' and hung up the receiver."

"Did he ask if Miss Conova was alone?" Dundee wanted to know;

"No. And I did not volunteer any information—"

"Although you were in Arundel's employ?" the younger detective demanded sharply.

The girl's eyes flashed with anger. "He did not employ me to spy on his wife!" she retorted. "I'm not a private detective, I'm a nurse, or—was." Her voice dropped on the last word.

"Just a moment, Miss Patton. What, to your knowledge, was the relationship existing between Miss Conova and Clinton Risher?"

"Crazy about each other, weren't they?" Strawn suggested

"If you mean was there anything *wrong*—" the girl flared. "Clinton Risher is what I'd call a perfect gentleman, and Miss Conova seemed to me to be the soul of honor. And I may as well tell you right now that so far as she and her husband were concerned, my sympathies were with Yola Conova, regardless of the fact that it was Mr. Arundel who gave me the job!"

"O.K.!" Strawn grinned, with a sidelong glance at Dundee.

"Were there other telephone calls, except those from movie fans and the one from Mr. Arundel?" Dundee prodded.

"Yes, there was a woman calling. The same one called twice. I remember the voice because my first thought was that it was disguised—sort of low and deep and monotonous, if you know what I mean. Each time she said, 'Tell Yola Conova I want to speak to her in regard to Madge Smith'."

"What!" Dundee exclaimed, hitching his chair a little closer to the bed. His blue eyes blazed. "And what did Miss Conova say?"

The nurse looked at him blankly. "Why, I didn't tell her about those calls," she confessed. "Do you think they were important?"

"Important!" the detective groaned. "Just when did those calls come?"

"I couldn't say to the minute, but they came before Mr. Arundel's call—sometime around midnight, I think. I just pretended to speak to Miss Conova, and then told the woman at the other end of the wire that I was sorry, but Miss Conova could not speak to anyone, but wished me to take the message."

"And what did the person on the 'phone say to that, Miss Patton?" Dundee asked tensely.

"I did think it was odd, but I concluded the woman was just another crank," Louise Patton admitted. "She said, the first time, 'Remind the great Conova that the dead past does not always bury its dead'. . . . Kind of gave me the shivers, the way she said it." And the nurse shuddered, drawing a scarf more closely about her thin shoulders.

"Did the caller say the same thing both times?"

"No. The second time when I told her Miss Conova did not care to speak to her, she said, 'Then on her own head be it!' and slammed up the receiver.... Honest! I thought it was only a nut, like the woman who kept pestering us over the 'phone in Chicago—"

But cranks in Chicago did not interest Dundee. "And after Arundel's call, Miss Patton?"

"I took a bath. Mr. Risher was still with Miss Conova, and I knew she was safe as long as he was there. I told her just to let the 'phone ring. After I finished my bath I got into pajamas and dressing-gown and read until half past twelve. Mr. Risher left at that time and Miss Conova came to my room. She seemed to be all wrought-up, so nervous she couldn't stand still—"

"Unhappy?" Dundee suggested.

"No. On the contrary, she seemed to be elated. She was talking about Mr. Risher, saying what a darling he was, and asking me if I thought she was too old for him, when the 'phone rang again. I started to answer it but she said she would, and ran out of the room, shutting my door behind her. All the telephones in the suite are on one line, and are fixed so that they ring at each extension. I think she answered from her own bedroom, but she may have taken the call in the parlor. I don't know."

"Did you listen in on your own extension?"

"Certainly not!" the nurse denied angrily. "I've told you I'm not a spy! I thought it was a call she was expecting, and so I went on with my reading. It was about five minutes before I heard a little tingle of the bell, the kind of sound the telephone makes when the receiver is hung up. But it was at least five minutes more before Miss Conova returned to my room. She was a changed woman. At first she looked so bad. I thought she might have taken poison, and I was ready to get out my stomach pump and call a doctor, but she assured me she wasn't ill—was just terribly upset by something that had happened. I was sure it was the telephone call that had upset her, but she didn't say so. She just dropped down on her knees beside my chair and began to implore me to do her a great kindness. I told her that of course I'd do anything I could for her. 'There are only two people in the world I can trust to help me now, Louise,' she said. 'You and Clint. But I can't have him mixed up in this. I'd have to explain to *him*.' And she cried terribly, and held onto my hands as if she were drowning. I kept trying to soothe her, but nothing I could say had any effect on her until I gave her my promise to do whatever she wanted me to do. Then she sprang to her feet and kissed me and hugged me hard, and said I was—a—a darling, that I'd never regret helping her. I thought she meant she'd pull wires to get me into the movies," the girl confessed, in a low, miserable voice.

Dundee cleared his throat noisily. "And what did she ask you to do, Miss Patton?"

"She swore she'd kill herself if I didn't do it," the girl sobbed heartbrokenly. "And she said if I did do it for her she'd be the happiest woman in the world, that she'd have a new lease on life. Honest! I thought if I did what she begged me to do, that she'd never try to commit suicide again. Can YOU blame me terribly?" she pleaded, her blue eyes swimming in tears.

"Just what did she ask you to do?" Dundee again demanded.

"She had a big envelope already filled and sealed," the girl answered. "There was no address, but she told me to take it to Riverside Park, and wait there until a person called for—"

"A *person*?" Dundee echoed. "Did she not say, whether the envelope was for a man or a woman?"

"No. I'm positive she didn't. While I was waiting there in the park and freezing to death I racked my brains to remember whether she'd even once said 'he' or 'she,' in referring to, the person who would call," the nurse assured him earnestly. "She told me to sit on a bench in the middle of the park—a bench beside a cedar tree clipped in the shape of a big basket, on the edge of the main drive. I knew it was terribly cold out, so I asked her how long I'd have to wait. She said she didn't know, that the 'person' had just said the messenger was to wait there until the envelope was called for. I asked her how I'd know this person—I remember I said 'person,' too, because she was saying it—and she said the 'person' would know me, that she had been so sure I'd help her that she'd described me I was just to wait there on the bench until some person came up to me and said, 'Pretty hot for this time of the year, isn't it?'—that being what no one else would say, the weather, being what it was last night, you know. So, after this password I was to hand over the envelope, without asking any questions, and return to the hotel, taking care not to be seen either going out or coming back in. She was very emphatic about that, so I used the stairs both trips. I'm sure no one saw me either going or returning. I used that side entrance by the florist's shop. There was no doorman on duty, and no cars arriving or leaving either time, as it happened."

Dundee nodded. "I see. And at the park?"

The girl shivered and huddled deeper into her pillows. "I sat there on that damned, hard old bench from a little after one o'clock until ten minutes past two, by my wrist watch, which has a radium dial. It was horribly cold and windy. The nearest light was much too far away for me to read, and I didn't have a book with me anyway. At last I simply couldn't stand it any longer. I was taking cold and my feet were clumps of ice. Suddenly it popped into my head that I'd been tricked, that Miss Conova had simply cooked up a tall yarn to get rid of me. But just in case I'd got the wrong bench I took a quick turn through the park, which seemed to be as deserted as a cemetery—"

"Did you see anyone at all during your hour's wait?" Dundee interrupted.

"Yes. A policeman in uniform walked through once, but I saw him coming when he passed under a lamp post, so I ducked down between the bench and the cedar tree till he was gone," the girl told him. "I was afraid he'd see me and ask a lot of questions, because it would seem awfully funny for a girl to be sitting all alone on a park bench at that time of night, in that kind of weather. I was afraid too that he would pull a flashlight on me and maybe recognize me as one of Miss Conova's party. There were a lot of policemen at the station and around the hotel lobby when we arrived."

"So you spoke to no one?"

"Not to a soul, and no one tried to speak to me. There may have been other people in the park, but if there were they didn't come near my bench, and I didn't see them. When I was leaving the park I broke into a run, I, was so scared all of a sudden, and so terribly cold. I'd have run every step of the way back to the hotel if I hadn't been afraid of being stopped by a policeman or somebody. Miss Conova had cautioned me not to use a taxi, but it wasn't a long walk."

"How did you know where the park is?"

"I knew the location in a general way, because we'd driven through it on our sightseeing trip this afternoon; but Miss Conova herself told me how to get there the shortest way, giving me the names of all three of the streets I had to cross."

"I see. And when you returned to the hotel?" Dundee prompted.

"It must have been nearly half past two. I had left my door unlocked so I could slip in without wasting a second, if necessary. Well, I got in without seeing a soul, and took of my hat and coat and gloves. Then I took time to warm myself at the radiator. The steam was still coming up. As soon as I'd thawed out a bit I screwed up my courage to report to Miss Conova. I was in an awful quandary. Through no fault of my own I'd failed to deliver the envelope. If she had not done it to trick me for some reason or other, then she wouldn't know I hadn't delivered it, and I really needn't tell her till she had had some sleep—"

"What reasons could you think of that she might have sent you away deliberately on a wild goose chase?" Dundee asked.

"I couldn't help thinking maybe she'd wanted me out of the way so she could keep some private date she had made over the telephone—"

"Or with Risher?" Strawn cut in.

The sick girl looked startled, then slowly shook her head. "No. I never thought of *that*! If she had wanted to be with Mr. Risher later than she was, she knew I was in sympathy with them and that I wouldn't have gossiped—"

"But you *might* have slipped into her bedroom to see if she was resting comfortably, or needed anything—in I your capacity as nurse. Isn't that true?"

"Yes. I always looked in on her two or three times a night," the girl admitted. "On that kind of case it's a nurse's duty—"

"Of course!" Dundee interrupted impatiently. "Now, tell me if you seriously entertained the idea last night that she had got rid of you in order to be free to commit suicide?"

"Naturally the thought crossed my mind, but since she and Mr. Risher had come to an understanding—and it was plain to see that they had—I believed she had been cured of any wish to destroy herself. She was like a new woman the last two days of her life—Oh, I can't realize—"

"Please, Miss Patton," Dundee begged, taking her frantic hands in his and holding them firmly.

"I can't bear it!" she sobbed. "If she wanted to kill herself, why in God's name didn't she do it in her own room, after I was safely out of the way? Listen, Mr. Dundee! You're a clever man. Don't you see that something is strange about all this? I've thought about it until I'm nearly crazy, but it always comes back to this— she would have done it in her own room *if something had not caused her to go out*! A secret meeting, which ended so terribly and hopelessly for her that she could see no other way out but suicide—"

"Probably," Dundee soothed her, for he had no intention, of bringing the word murder into the interview. "But you really must not cry like that. Tears can do her no good now, but can do you a lot of harm in the condition you are in. Now, where is that envelope that she gave you?"

The nurse raised herself in bed and pointed with a trembling forefinger. "In my suitcase, on the floor of the closet. I put it right on top of my things when I packed this morning, after Mr. Hepburn told me you wanted to close up Miss Conova's suite."

Strawn and Dundee both knelt over the suitcase. Atop a jumble of clothing and toilet articles lay the envelope— one of the rather large square envelopes furnished its guests by the Randolph Hotel.

"I opened it this morning," the girl confessed, in a frightened whisper. "I thought maybe there was a letter in it, which the poor darling would not want to fall into the hands of the newspapers or the police. I know. I shouldn't have done it, but—I'd failed her while she was alive and needed me, and the least I could do was to serve her—in death—" Suddenly her voice was quiet and steady: "Naturally you won't believe me, but there wasn't even a note—not a single word! Just that money. I didn't know what to think when I found the money. It looked as if she hadn't been trying to trick me, after all, but was really being blackmailed. But—I don't know. Maybe the poor thing was in such a state she couldn't trust anyone— was afraid I'd open the envelope out of curiosity, and come back to the hotel immediately if I found it contained nothing but blank paper. Anyway," and she began to weep again, "there it is—exactly as I found it. I didn't count the bills."

But Dundee had no such scruples. "Four hundred dollars," he announced to Strawn, in a low voice. "Rather an odd sum with which to try to silence a blackmailer, if that is what it was really intended for. Certainly an insignificant sum, all things considered."

"Reckon that's nearly all she had in cash," Strawn reasoned. "Outside of the sixty five dollars you found in her purse. You gotta remember she wasn't dealin' with big-time crooks—just amateurs, and a down payment of four hundred bucks would make her blackmailer hold his horses till she could ante over with a bigger wad."

"Perhaps," Dundee conceded. Then, turning on his heels he directed a rather strange remark to the woman in bed: "Got any money saved up, Miss Patton?"

She stopped sobbing to stare at him. "Money? Why, yes. About a hundred dollars. But I don't see—" Then she flushed painfully. "I'm not a thief, Mr. Dundee. If I were starving, I wouldn't touch a penny of a dead woman's money!"

Dundee nodded approvingly. "Not every woman in your circumstances could have resisted the temptation to fill this envelope with blank paper"

"Thank you," said Louise Patton, in a choked voice.

"I shall have to ask you to let us have all the letters you received from Mr. Arundel since you've been in his employ, Miss Patton."

"I told you I only got three," said the girl, wearily. "They're in the right hand pocket of my suitcase. I kept it locked, so I'm sure Miss Conova, even if she had been suspicious, never saw them."

Dundee rummaged in the hastily packed suitcase, the nurse watching him. "You don't blame me too much?" she asked. "You don't think—"

"It is not my province to judge anyone, Miss Patton," Dundee told her gravely. "Our sole duty is to learn the truth—how and why Yola Conova met her death. You have been of great help and I hope the strain we have subjected you to has not made you more ill." Transferring the thin packet of letters from his right to his left hand, the detective took the sick woman's hot fingers and held them for a few seconds. "Take care of yourself, Miss Patton."

The three men closed the door upon the dreary sound of the girl's weeping.

Dundee shook his head. "I don't like the looks of that girl," he worried. "Damned sick. . . . Whoever killed Yola Conova may yet be responsible for another death. . . . Brede, chase up to the Conova suite and get that poison bottle Miss Patton said she emptied and discarded in her wastebasket."

"And Brede," Strawn added, a little sourly, since he did not relish having a district attorney's man giving orders to his boys, "tell Branagan I'll have a copper up there to relieve him in a few minutes, but that he's to stick closer'n a kidney plaster until he is relieved. Nobody except the police, or Mr. Dundee, is to be allowed inside the Conova suite—not even his boss, Hepburn."

"Poor Branagan!" Dundee laughed, as Brede bounded up the stairs on his errand. "He'll never get through trying to explain to Hepburn that even a hotel detective has to eat. And the unfortunate Mr. Hepburn may be forgiven if he fails to understand why even a hotel detective needs to take an hour and a half for his midnight luncheon. To be exact, Branagan was in the kitchen from half past twelve until a bit after two. He says, naively enough, that it was too early for burglars, and that all the curiosity seekers, hanging around for a glimpse of the movie stars, had been cleared out. He was really pathetically glad to stand guard over the Conova suite until you could get organized. Any luck, Brede? Good!" And he took the carefully wrapped bottle from the panting messenger, to put it in his pocket.

"What next, Bonnie?" Strawn asked. "Shall we have a crack at Arundel?"

"Not just yet," Dundee decided. "You'll want to check his alibi first, over at the Hamilton Hotel. But I want to get these Arundel letters, the blank envelope that had the money in it, and this poison bottle into Ferber's hands for fingerprinting and photographing. They're prize exhibits in more ways than one, or I'm a bum guesser. I'll take them over to City Hall myself. Feel the need of exercise. Probably a stroll through Riverside Park is indicated. When I return, glowing with health and boyish spirits, I'd like to take a crack at little Dinkie Garnet—preferably a crack at his jaw; that is, if the boys have rounded him up by then."

"He'll be here," Strawn predicted confidently. "Well, I guess it's the dirty work for me. Hotel crew that was working last night—elevator operators, night clerk, bellhops, switchboard operators, maids, and so on. It's a damned shame to have to roust 'em out of bed after a long night's work."

IX

AS TO WHAT HE EXPECTED to learn from his visit to the park Dundee himself was not quite clear, but if he was to make any effort at all to check up on the nurse's story of her ill-fated errand now was most decidedly the time. It was just on the stroke of eight when he passed between the tall marble pillars that marked the southern entrance to Riverside Park. The name was slightly inaccurate, since a busy street and a long row of warehouses and factories separated the stretch of carefully kept public ground from the sluggish river. The winding drive, bordered by trees, shrubs and flower beds, was a favorite thoroughfare between East Hamilton, beyond the river, and West Hamilton, which was Hamilton proper. At noon the park benches were filled with clerks and stenographers from Hamilton's crowded business section. Afternoons it was a children's and nursemaids' Paradise. Evenings, it was a trysting place for sweethearts. And nearly all who used it left behind them some evidence of their use and abuse of the city's hospitality.

"Morning, Tom," Dundee greeted the stooped old man who was spearing bits of paper and refuse; to stuff them into a burlap sack. And, "Morning, Flynn," he nodded to the policeman who had stopped for a word with the grumpy keeper.

"Morning to you, Mr. Dundee," Flynn replied heartily. "Guess this Conova suicide is what got you up and around so early...I'm on me way home now, but it's lucky I'll be if I snatch a wink o' sleep this day, the wife bein' what she is. She'll think, jis' because I'm a cop, I oughta know the inside dope on the whole bloomin' case, when the truth is, any man in the streets knows more about it than I do, me trampin' my beat from midnight till this very minute. No question about it bein' suicide, I guess?"

"It certainly looks like suicide, Flynn," Dundee evaded. "How often do you make the park on your rounds?"

"Once every hour, sir," the patrolman answered, his shrewd eyes beginning to gleam with interest. "And a waste of time it is, on a night like last night. Outside of a few cars whizzin' home this-here park mighta been a desert island."

"Then you saw no one at all?"

The policeman tilted his cap to scratch his head. "Lemme think. . . . Sure, but I was forgettin'! Curious thing, too. Some dame, all by herself, come' streakin' through the park and out this entrance, runnin' like a ghost was at her heels. Heard her first, then seen her when she passed under the lights, but I wasn't close enough to stop her. I kinda doped it out she'd been neckin' with a guy that maybe got too fresh, but I had a good look around and couldn't find a soul!"

"What time was that, Flynn?"

Again the patrolman scratched his head. "Now, lemme figger. . . ." His lips moved silently, as he conferred with his own, memory. Then, triumphantly: "Long about a quarter past two that musta been, Mr. Dundee. I start through the park from the north entrance on the hour every, hour, and it usually takes me about fifteen minutes to make the round of all the benches. Lookin' for vags, mostly, and—"

"Did you get a good look at the running woman?" Dundee' interrupted.

"Not what you'd call a real good look," Flynn denied, conscientiously. "A smallish or medium-sized woman, I'd say, real spry, like a girl. Had on some sort of a dark coat with fur around the neck, and one of them close fittin' hats—black, I'd say."

Dundee, who had seen just such garments on the nurse's bed the night before, was satisfied.

"Except this woman, Flynn," he persisted, "did you see anyone else hanging around the park last night? A man alone, for instance?"

"No, sir. I didn't see anybody else on foot at all, from midnight till six this mornin'."

"Thanks, Flynn. Hope you get some sleep. Well, Tom, what are you muttering about?"

The old man straightened, a hand to his lower back. "And ye'd mutter, too, I'll be bound, if ye had to do another man's work, on top o' yore own, and no extry pay, not even a thanky. If you ain't deef you heard what Officer Flynn said. Not a soul, sez he, outside one lorn woman, was afoot in this-here park after midnight last night. That bein' the case, I ask you fair, as man to man, where in tarnation did all this trash come from? Jis' left layin' around for me to break my back pickin' it up—"

"Let's have a look, Tom," Dundee suggested amiably, as he knelt before the almost empty burlap sack. "Not much here to grumble about, I'd say."

"Mind ye don't scatter it agin for me to gether up—me with my lumbago—"

"Don't worry. The wind's down now, Tom," the detective soothed him. "Hullo! Where did you find this?—and this?—and this?"

The old man groaned as he stooped over the penciled sheets of paper which had awakened such intense interest.

"Them there?" he asked scornfully. "School kids throwed 'em away, I'll be bound. Young devils! No more respect fer a public park—'

"But these," Dundee marveled aloud, "are test papers—*uncorrected*! No, Tom, I don't think you can blame this on children. Now I wonder who teaches 'Algebra III' in the Hamilton Junior College."

"Professor Martin that'd be," the old man volunteered. "Gives tests and throws the papers away without correcting 'em, does he? The taxpayers ought to hear about this! Just wait till that schoolmarm in pants comes along this morning and I'll give him a piece of my mind he won't forget in a hurry—"

"Martin . . . Martin? . . . *Martin!*" Dundee sprang erect as a bell rang in his memory. "Good old Tom! Here's a dollar! Buy yourself some liniment for that lumbago. Now show me where you found those papers."

The dollar bill acted as a magic plaster upon the old mans back, for he straightened and set off with spry alacrity along the winding driveway through the park.

"Right in here they was, Mr. Dundee," he triumphed. "Twixt that bench there, and this hedge. Two-three papers was blowed agin the legs of the bench and two-three more had got stuck in the hedge."

"I see," said Dundee quietly, but his blood pressure was at least ten points higher. For the bench at which the old man was pointing an arthritic forefinger was most certainly the bench on which Louise Patton, according to her story, had awaited a blackmailer who had never come. Or *had* he come—*too early or too late* to meet Yola Conova's messenger?

"Does Professor Martin visit the park frequently?" he asked.

"Him and his wife, the lady perfessor, passes through the park ever' morning and evening, on their way to and from school," Tom told him "They ought to be along any minute now. Reg'lar as the clock, they are—And here they come. Are you aimin' to arrest him fer violatm' the ord'nance about clutterin' up the park with trash? Make an example of him, says I! Mornin', Perfessor! Mornin', Miz Martin. Cold enough fer ye?"

Dundee wheeled and was astonished to find that the wife of the mathematics professor was the stout and bad-tempered matron who had been his neighbor at the theater the night before. Then he had thought her a typical society dowager. Now she looked even more typically the female educator. He could imagine her laying down the law on whatever subject it was that she taught, and fixing her pupils with a stern eye, that dared even the most empty-headed to waver in attention.

He stepped forward, blocking the progress of the couple "Professor Martin? Mrs. Martin? . . . I'm Dundee, of the district attorney's office—"

"Interesting, I'm sure," snapped the woman "But my husband and I are in rather a hurry—"

"So am I. Get along with your work, Tom. As I was saying," Dundee continued, after the old man had hobbled away, "I am connected with the district attorney's office, and I am investigating the death of Yola Conova. Now, Professor Martin, are these yours?" and he extended the sheaf of uncorrected test papers.

The teacher drew back slightly, throwing a sidelong, fearful glance at his wife, then, with a forced smile, he accepted the papers. Somehow he looked a bit less distinguished in the morning sunshine. His black hair was a trifle too long, his waxed mustache was almost certainly dyed. And his thin, esthetic face was sallow. Behind his *pince nez* his dull black eyes were bloodshot and given to quick, nervous shifting.

"What luck!" he said, with assumed heartiness, stuffing the sheets into a coat pocket after a hasty glance. "I thought they were hopelessly lost and that I'd have to give the test all over again."

"When did you lose those papers, Wesley?" Mrs. Martin demanded.

Her husband flushed like a delinquent schoolboy. "Last night," he admitted. "I walked home through the park—"

"After the theater" Dundee interrupted "I remember bumping into you just as the show was ending at the Egyptian; or, rather, I was with Miss Loring, whom you bumped into."

"So you did go, after all, Wesley!" his wife commented grimly. "I presume the fact slipped your mind. Just another absent-minded professor, Mr. Dundee," she added, her nostrils flaring and contracting. "I'm sure Mr. Martin thanks you—and so do I! Good morning!"

"May I detain you a moment longer, please?" Dundee suggested pleasantly. "Professor Martin, it is quite necessary that I know the exact time, or as exactly as you can fix the time, that you passed through this park last night."

"I fail to see—" the teacher began to bluster, darting uneasy glances at his formidable wife.

"Please answer the question, Mr. Martin!"

"You saw me leaving the theater," the man pointed out sourly. "I set out for home then, walking through the park. The show was over about half-past eleven, I believe. I must have entered the park by a quarter to twelve, since I stopped at a drugstore for a cup of hot chocolate. I was carrying a sheaf of test papers in a textbook. I dropped the book and the wind scattered the sheets. I picked up all I could find in the poor light."

"Do you make a practice of taking your home work to the theater?"

The sallow cheeks of the professor turned red. "Not as a rule! It merely happens that I had not been home after my school work was finished yesterday. I did some research work at the public library and had a bite of dinner downtown, intending to do further reading at the library, since I knew my wife was going to the theater."

"Since you saw the show yourself later, Mr. Martin, may I ask why you did not choose to accompany your wife?"

"Damn your impertinence, sir!" the professor exploded.

"Now, now!" Dundee protested, smiling. "I'm not in one your math classes, you know. . . . Shall I repeat the question?"

The mathematics teacher glared. "There was no question of 'choosing' to accompany my wife—at the time I decide to go to the theater. She was undoubtedly there ahead since I purchased a ticket after the performance had begun."

"Really?" Dundee murmured. "I was under the impression that the house was sold out hours before the show went on."

"It was," Professor Martin agreed snappishly. "By luck, I secured a ticket which had been reserved and not called for."

"What caused you to decide to attend this particular performance, Mr. Martin?"

The professor drew in his breath, and for a moment Dundee was sure he was going to be told in no uncertain tern that it was none of his business. Then a wry, but rather engaging smile twisted the older, man's lips. "To be perfectly frank, Mr. Dundee, I wanted to see the star, Yola Conova, in person, in order to convince myself absolutely that I had been right and my wife wrong in an argument that has—er—made ours a house divided—but in that one particular only, needless to say. On all other subjects Mrs. Martin and I are in remarkable accord for a pair of old married folk."

Dundee cut an interested and amused eye at the professor's partner in marital bliss. Then he looked away hastily, for if the woman was going to burst, or have a stroke, he preferred not to watch her.

"And that argument, Professor?"

Martin tapped Dundee's chest with a gloved forefinger confidentially and in a man-to-man fashion. "You are a gentleman, Dundee, and I am sure I can depend upon your discretion. And, after all, the poor girl is dead now. But even so, her reputation should be preserved and her memory honored. For she deserves the greatest credit—"

"You're hinting, of course, that you and Mrs. Martin disagreed as to whether Yola Conova was Madge Smith," Dundee said bluntly.

Both Martins gasped. The woman was the first to recover her voice.

"There, Wesley! What did I always say? Mr. Dundee, the 'Incomparable Conova,' as they used to call her before she became a back number—if I may be pardoned the vulgar expression—used to work for me as a common housemaid!"

Dundee felt an unreasoning irritation. "As a housemaid, yes. I know that, Mrs. Martin. At least, I know that Madge Smith was in your employ about ten years ago, and I know that several people in Hamilton are convinced that Madge Smith became Yola Conova."

Watching the two of them keenly, Dundee was sure that relief was responsible for the quick expulsion of breath which momentarily reduced the circumference of Mrs. Maxim's truly magnificent bosom. And he was equally sure that Professor Martin's smile bore a trace of pride.

"I understand that you discharged Madge Smith, Mrs. Martin," Dundee continued curtly, for it was cold and a public park was hardly the place for extended questioning. "May I Ask why?"

"You have been misinformed, sir," the woman answered. "It was my husband who discharged our housemaid, Madge Smith—without consulting me first, I may add; but naturally I abided by his decision."

Dundee was astonished, but Martin forestalled the obvious question. "Yes, it was I who dismissed the girl. Not for incompetence or impertinence, but for returning home, after her half day off, at one o'clock in the morning. I happened to be working late over some examination papers and heard her come in. It is an inflexible rule of our house that a maid be in her room not later than eleven o'clock in the evening on her Thursday off. Since she had no excuse whatsoever to offer for her conduct I gave her notice summarily."

Dundee regarded the teacher a moment, silently. Not nice person at all, he thought. Still vindictive. Still meanly futilely jealous of that other man, either known or unknown to him, with whom Madge Smith had "consorted."

"Do you know—either of you—with whom Miss Smith spent that evening?"

"Certainly not!" Mrs. Martin answered emphatically.

"I have told you she refused any explanation whatever on her late return," the man pointed out, his sallow face flushing slightly.

"As I understand it," Dundee went on, "you, Mrs. Martin, believed that your former housemaid became Yola Conova and, you, Mr. Martin, refused to credit the idea. Am I also to understand, Mrs. Martin, that you were confirmed in you belief after seeing Miss Conova last night in person?"

"I was! Absolutely!"

"And you, Mr. Martin—"

"I had to admit to myself that my wife had been right all along. I was half convinced when she made her first appearance on the stage, for the introduction, you know, before the screening of the picture, but after watching her performance in the one-act play I was absolutely certain that Yola Conova, was Madge Smith. Don't ask me to tell you how I knew, for I could not possibly tell you. Of course I had always conceded the resemblance between the screen star and the girl we had known, but last night I learned how the camera can lie."

Dundee was enormously interested. Perhaps here was a clue to the strange controversy which undoubtedly had raged in Hamilton for years, ever since Yola Conova had skyrocketed into fame as a movie star. "Just what do you mean, Mr. Martin?"

The teacher's eyes shifted from Dundee's to his wife's forbiddingly grim face, then concentrated upon the toes of his well-polished boots "I'm afraid it will be impossible for me to explain myself precisely," he admitted nervously. "The Conova of the screen and the Conova of the—personal appearance, I believe they call it—are—were—two distinctly different personalities. The screen actress seemed to me to be a highly complex, even mysterious woman. The stage actress, if one could call her that, seemed, to have almost the exact personality, allowing for the passing of the years, of course, that I had associated with the girl 'we knew as Madge Smith."

"And that personality was—" Dundee prompted, trying not to sound impatient.

The professor cleared his throat, and swallowed convulsively. "Madge Smith was—or *seemed* to be," he amended with a return of that early venom, "a curiously simple creature. To borrow a phrase from one of Eugene O'Neill's plays, she typified the, 'earth mother'—the sort of unthinking, fundamentally female creature to whom all men turn instinctively. She seemed to be gentle and strong; not quick-witted, not even a thinking creature, as the intelligentsia use the word. She seemed to have no guile, no awareness of her own peculiar quality—"

"That will do, Wesley!" Mrs. Martin interrupted acidly. "I am sure Mr. Dundee is too busy to listen to an analytical rhapsody, however *impersonal* it may be. The truth is, Mr. Dundee," she continued emphatically, turning to the keenly interested detective, "that Madge Smith was not at all extraordinary. She was good-looking, in a healthy, European peasant sort of way; a good enough worker, but not ambitious, and rather stupid. So far as being different on the screen is concerned, it is a well-known fact that a motion picture player is merely a puppet. To the director, I am sure, should go the credit for Yola Conova's 'acting' and to the cameraman credit for her 'exotic beauty' I've said as much to my husband all along."

"And you were undoubtedly right, Mrs. Martin," Dundee assured her amiably. "By the way, did Madge Smith tell you her real name, or anything concerning her ancestry, and former home or homes?"

"No. She came to me as Madge Smith, and I was not sufficiently interested in a maid's pedigree to question her. Her references, from Mr. and Mrs. Christopher

Loring, were entirely satisfactory. And, in spite of the fact that my husband thought best to discharge her, I gave her an unqualified letter of recommendation, which, I am sorry to say, in view of later developments, helped her to secure employment in the Kenyon home."

"And those developments were?"

"A typical son-of-the-house and servant-girl romance between Madge Smith and young Bruce Kenyon," Mrs. Martin answered promptly. "Ordinarily I lend no ear to scandal mongering, but since the late Mr. Kenyon took it upon himself to question Professor Martin and me at some length as to our knowledge of the girl's morals—or lack of them—when she was in our employ, I could not escape hearing some details of the unsavory story."

"And you told him—" Dundee prodded.

"That so far as we knew the girl was above reproach," Professor Martin answered for the pair. "Quite absurdly, Kenyon seemed to be bent upon fastening the blame for the girl's—er—condition—upon one of her former employers, rather than upon his own son, where it undoubtedly belonged."

Dundee smiled slightly. He could well imagine that this frustrated little pedagogue had been more flattered than angry when taxed with seduction. "I take it, then, that Kay Loring's father was also a suspect as the father of the unborn child?"

"Unfortunately he was," Professor Martin answered. "Pauline—Mrs. Loring—was always a difficult woman. She was a teacher in one of our elementary schools before Chris Loring married her, for reasons mysterious to everyone but himself. And I understand that she led poor Chris the very devil of a life after old Kenyon put him through the third degree. One can scarcely blame Kenyon for wanting to fasten the blame anywhere but on his own son, but his parental zeal had most deplorable consequences."

"Really?" Dundee frowned.

"My husband, in his best platform manner, is leading up to the fact that Christopher Loring committed suicide," Mrs. Martin cut in.

"Is that so?" Dundee said, careful to show no undue interest. "When did that happen?"

"Less than a year after Kenyon trumped up a marriage between Madge Smith and Dink Garnet," the professor answered. "Drowned himself. Set out in a rowboat when the river was almost over its bank, due to the spring floods. The overturned boat was recovered, but his body was never found, or, if it was, it was never identified. More than a hundred lives were lost that spring—not here, but down the river a few miles. But Chris was declared legally dead after the required lapse of time. And there's small doubt in anyone's mind that Pauline Loring's suspicions and nagging sent him to his wilful death."

Dundee's eyes narrowed thoughtfully. It was a long moment before he spoke again, although it was very cold and his unwilling companions were obviously resentful.

When he did speak, his question was apparently so irrelevant that the Martins stared at him blankly.

"Does either of you own a typewriter?" Dundee asked.

"I do," Mrs. Martin answered.

"And you, Professor Martin?"

"The machine is community property," the teacher snapped. "My wife is more adept at its use than I. Typing is one of the subjects she teaches, but unfortunately, I have never availed myself of her instruction in the art. I am a hunt-and-peck amateur."

"What else do you teach, Mrs. Martin?"

"Shorthand and business correspondence," the woman tok him curtly. "May I ask why you are interested in my owning a typewriter?"

"I was just wondering," Dundee drawled, "if you were the author of a—friendly note typewritten and mailed to Yola Conova, reminding her of an old acquaintance."

"Certainly not!"

"The idea is absurd!" snapped the professor.

"Since you telephoned her late last evening, Mrs. Martin, I naturally inferred—" Dundee began, with charming diffidence, his candid eyes giving no hint that he was guessing wildly.

"How do you know I telephoned her?" Mrs. Martin demanded. "What I mean is, of course I did no such thing!"

"Oh, yes, you did, Mrs. Martin!" Dundee contradicted her blithely. "Have you never heard of the very ordinary police procedure of tracing telephone calls?" And he had hard won to keep a straight face at his own audacity. The amazing credulity of the public where the mysterious powers of the police were concerned had stood him in good stead many times before.

"I did call," Mrs. Martin admitted, "but the switchboard operator at the Randolph Hotel told me that Miss Conova had left orders that she was not to be disturbed. So I did not speak to her, and I did not leave any message. I merely called to show a friendly spirit. After all, I had known the girl quite well—"

"Very commendable, Mrs. Martin," Dundee soothed hei smiling. "And *your* call, Martin—made from the drugstore—you know, while you were waiting for your hot chocolate—"

"I made no call, from the drugstore or anywhere else. And I am not quite so gullible as my wife. I happen to know that it is impossible to trace any ordinary telephone call, either from a private line or from a coin box, unless the police are listening in at the time the call is being made."

"You are admirably well informed, professor," Dundee said. "But what if I should tell you that, for certain well-founded reasons, the police *were* listening in on every telephone call that came into the Randolph switchboard for Yola Conova last night?" And to himself the detective added, grimly: "I wish to the Lord they had been! And if

Kay Loring had been frank with me from the beginning of
the evening, they damned well would have been."

His eyes darted keenly from one teacher, to the other.
And were well rewarded. Although the Martins were as
different physically and temperamentally as two people
well could be, they looked curiously alike now, with their
faces blanched into masks of fear.

Dundee regarded them with peculiar satisfaction.
Ordinarily a kindly person, he felt no pity now, no
compunction for the tacit lie which had terrified these two
people. For if they had had any part, however small, in
Madge Smith's bitter homecoming as Yola Conova, they
deserved whatever torment might now be racking them.

"That will be all for the present," he said his blue eyes
icy, his mobile mouth closing in a grim line, which, if he
had caught a glimpse of himself in a mirror, would have
reminded him startlingly of Captain Strawn. "But hold
yourselves ready for questioning at any time."

Professor Martin thrust out his lower lip belligerently.
"Since Madge, or rather Yola Conova, committed suicide,
I fail to see, sir—"

"When the coroner holds an inquest upon her body,"
Dundee interrupted, "he will be enormously interested
not only in how she met her death, but *why*. Blackmail
and malicious persecution are still crimes in this state—
very serious crimes indeed, when the victim dies. . . .
Good morning!"

As he watched them walk away—falteringly and as
widely separated as the graveled path through the park
allowed, not speaking, as if they feared and distrusted
each other—Dundee congratulated himself on his
restraint in keeping them in ignorance of his own
conviction that the girl who had worked in their home
had not killed herself, but had been diabolically
murdered. Let them recuperate somewhat from the state
into which he had already plunged them before he sprung
his news upon them. Of one thing he was morally sure:

either of that unpleasant pair was capable of murder, but from entirely different motives.

X

"HELLO! CAPTAIN STRAWN? Dundee speaking. I'm in the Conova suite. No, just got here. Well, join me when you've finished. In the meantime, ask Miss Loring to come up, if she's managed to get rid of the reporters. She has? Fine! Tell her to hurry, will you? And say, the D.A. is absolutely convinced we're on the right track. Oh, sure! He's giving me a free hand, with his blessing—and his thanks to you. Yeah! Exactly! By the way, have your boys found Dink Garnet yet? Didn't come home all night? Hmmm. Not so good. Well, be seeing you."

As he replaced the ivory-white French telephone in the cradle which stood on a beautiful little rosewood desk between two wide windows in the parlor of Suite 4-B, Dundee yawned so widely that his jaws cracked.

"Holy jeepers, but I'm sleepy!" he muttered. His heavy head began to nod and gradually sank until his crisp, wind-tousled black hair touched the blotter with which the flat top of the desk was protected. He yawned again, tried to lift his head, and let it drop. He'd relax for just one little minute.

His long legs and arms went limp.

"Jimmy! Jimmy Dundee! . . . Bonnie! Oh, dear God! He's dead!"

With a mighty effort Dundee swam up out of the fathomless depths of sleep. One of his weakly flailing hands struck something soft—

"'Hey! No fair slapping me! I'm half dead with fright anyway!" Ginger Loring laughed. "I thought you'd been murdered, you sleepy pig! The second victim in one of those ghastly murder mysteries in which the whole landscape gets cluttered up with corpses."

"Sorry!" the embarrassed detective apologized, then further disgraced himself with another jaw-splitting yawn. "Gosh! What's the matter with me? Nobody could get this sleepy without being doped—"

"For heaven's sake, quit that yawning!" Ginger scolded. "You'll have me doing it, too. You're doped, all right, but it's with stale air, heat, and perfume from the flowers the rooms are smothered in. Phew! The heat is pouring out the radiators in visible waves! Open a window before we both pass out."

When he had thrown wide the two windows of the room Dundee leaned out to drink in great gulps of cold November air. Then, feeling almost as vigorous and alert as if he had enjoyed eight hours sleep, he turned to face Ginger, and found that small person nearly concealed behind huge baskets of flowers, with which her arms and hands were loaded. One beribboned basket swung from her neck.

"What are you going to do?" he asked.

"Now that I've lost my job, maybe I can make a new start in life as a street-corner flower pedlar," Ginger laughed. "But for the moment I'm going to set these pretties outside. There just isn't enough oxygen for them and us, too."

Without a word Dundee removed the basket from around her neck, set it on the desk, and then began to unload her arms.

"I *am* a dimwit," she admitted meekly, when she saw him search swiftly through the hothouse treasures for the sender cards. "But, frankly, it never occurred to me that the murderer might send pre-mortem—or should the word be ante-mortem?—flowers, with his card."

"Nothing about this case would surprise me," Dundee assured her, as he made a little stack of the cards. "Let's see, now: nineteen floral tributes, and only fifteen cards. Waste baskets empty, though that is not surprising. The maid, when she came in to turn down the beds last night while Conova and the Patton girl were at the theater, would normally have emptied wastebaskets and ash trays, and replaced all soiled towels. Now here," and he separated the stack into two neat piles, "are what we might call the duty offerings: from Gordon, the manager of the Egyptian Theater; from Hepburn, the Randolph Hotel manager; from the New York offices of World-Wide Pictures; from Weinberg; from the city ticket agent of the Southern Pacific; from the director of the Hamilton Little Theater group; from the president of the Chamber of Commerce; from—" He hesitated and frowned, squinting at the card.

"Let's see," Ginger begged eagerly, and reached for the bit of white pasteboard. "Yes, I thought I recognized it. I—I printed the letters, in the way I used to write when Madge was our governess. I—well, I thought she might recognize it—"

"But doesn't it say, 'The Yola Conova Fan Club'?"

"Well." Ginger bit her trembling lips. "You see, Jimmy, there used to be a Yola Conova Fan Club, with the largest membership in the United States. I organized it myself, and hounded all the high-school kids into joining. Everyone has forgotten about it now—but me. I thought she would be proud and pleased if she believed there was an active club here now."

Dundee sat back on his haunches, among the confusion of wilting flowers, and looked up at the girl with deep sincerity in his blue eyes. "You're a grand girl, Ginger."

She smiled at him, but her smile was more serious and more touching than tears. "Thank you, Jimmy Dundee. But what I really am is a hopeless sentimentalist. Now what about the other cards?"

"Here's one from Arundel," Dundee continued rather absent-mindedly, for he was repeating Ginger's words silently, trying to use them as a key to open the mystery of her behavior of the night before, "I took it from that over-size sheaf of blood-red roses, which he must have wired her from New York. It says simply, 'You're wonderful!' and signed 'Geoffrey.' Just another bit of evidence that he was exerting himself to buck up her morale—"

"When it would have been vastly to his interest, from mercenary standpoint," Ginger interrupted, "for her to commit suicide, since he undoubtedly did not know that she had issued a check on the wrong bank."

Dundee stared at the girl, his eyes widening. "That gives me an idea, my girl. Suppose the insurance company notified him, as beneficiary, that the policy would lapse if a covering check were not mailed immediately. On the chance, of course, that their letter might not reach her promptly, and that he as beneficiary, might want to pay the premium himself. That would explain his dashing here from New York, and trying so urgently to see her or speak to her. At any rate, I shall enjoy watching Mr. Geoffrey Arundel's face when the new is broken to him that he has not become a millionaire over night. Here's a card from some man who is almost criminally lavish with sweet talk. Listen: 'For a superb artiste, swell little trouper, and the most beautiful woman in this world.' And it is signed, 'Hank.'"

Ginger knitted her brows, then laughed. "Hank!' That's the director of 'Magnificent Sin'—Henri Monel, whom every one in Hollywood calls Hank, because the nickname is inappropriate. His extravagant praise is quite understandable. This is his first American picture, and quite likely to be his last. If Conova and the picture had made a big success he would have been sitting very pretty on a long-term contract. Naturally he was sparing no expense—either in words or flowers."

"Too bad!" Dundee laid the card aside. "There goes a firm suspect for a *crime passionel*. And here's another card that really belongs among the 'duty' offerings—or rather, among those who 'ask it with flowers.' I took it off an enormous basket of bright but I don't think very expensive flowers." He held out a card.

Ginger Loring accepted it. "Why, Jimmy, I think this is rather touching," she said. "From your devoted fan, Louise Patton,'" she read softly. "Even if Miss Patton was a nurse paid to watch Yola--or Madge—to keep her from committing suicide, she did more than her duty when she sent her flowers to flatter her and to help keep her pepped up. And no one could have helped loving Madge, even in the state of depression or despair she seems to have sunk into. You can't know how glad I am she had someone with her who admired her and was fond of her."

"Yes, you *are* a sentimentalist," Dundee reflected, but with obvious approval. "The cold fact, my innocent, is that Louise Patton has confessed that she was trying to get in good with Yola, in order to land a job in the movies. On the other hand, she seems to have been genuinely fond of Yola, and to be crushed by the tragedy. Well, let's get on with it. Here are three cards, all inscribed with the same handwriting, and all unsigned. Listen. 'For the Only Girl in the World,' 'For Yola Conova, from a Fan who loves her;' 'For the Incomparable Conova, from 'a Humble Admirer.' . . . Three guesses, Ginger?"

"One will do—Clinton Risher," the girl answered promptly. "The sweet thing. You know, Jimmy, I honestly think he meant it when he said he wished she had been a nobody. If she had only had faith enough in his love, there would have been no earthly reason for her to go out to her death last night."

"She didn't kill herself, Ginger," Dundee told her firmly. "Get that idea out of your head, so it won't hamper you in helping me. I had Strawn send you up, so that I could tell you everything I know so far. I need your help badly."

She caught her lower lip between her teeth to stop it trembling. "I'll do—anything I can—"

"Then listen!"

After Dundee had spoken, almost without interruption, for a full quarter hour, Kay Loring remained silent, huddled against one arm of the big down-cushioned sofa. She was very white.

"Well, I think that brings the story up to the minute," Dundee concluded cheerfully, as if he were unaware of hid listener's distress. "Except for one detail which you can supply. Last night you were going to tell me how you knew there was a carbon copy of the so-called blackmail letter."

Ginger smiled slightly, but still did not look up. "It wasn't a very brilliant deduction. You see, the typewriter ribbon that had been used was a black record, and there was a thumb print or fingerprint in the lower right hand corner of the sheet of paper, that was a bright purple— the shade that is so common in carbon paper. The cheap carbon paper smudge terribly. I know, because when I'm typing a final draft of short story, trying to make it fair and beautiful to behold: I'm almost dead sure to leave a thumb smudge of purple on the margin."

"I see," Dundee replied. Then, more briskly: "Kay, there are a number of inevitable suspects in this case. You know that as well as I do, and even better than I, you know that your stepmother belongs in that category. I don't want to send for her just yet if you can give her an ironclad alibi. Can you?"

At that, the girl got to her feet, and stood very erect before the detective, her hands clasped tightly. "I won't pretend to be surprised, after what I told you about Pauline and Madge last night," she said steadily. "And thank you for giving me a chance to speak for her. You know she was at home when you left the apartment last night. I did not go to sleep until nearly four o'clock. I'm positive I should have heard her, no matter how quiet she might have been, if she had left the apartment and returned between the time you left and four o'clock. There is only the bathroom between my bedroom and hers, and my door into the hall was open all night. She would have had to pass my door, you know, to reach the outside door in the hall."

Dundee was silent for a while, then asked reluctantly: "You've said that you tried to get Conova on the telephone after I left, and failed. Then, I take it, you got ready for bed?"

"Oh—I forgot! I was in the bathroom going through my usual bedtime routine, for at least ten minutes. The bathroom door was closed, of course, and water was running most of that time."

"Then your stepmother could have dressed hastily and left the apartment while you were shut in the bathroom?"

"It was physically possible for her to do so—yes," Ginger answered cautiously. "But as I told you, I was awake until nearly four o'clock, with the door of my bedroom open. Pauline could not have returned, provided she had gone out, without my seeing and hearing her."

Dundee shook his head. "I'm afraid that is not strictly true, child. Let's suppose, for argument's sake, that your stepmother did leave the apartment, and that, as she neared the building on her return home she saw that a light was burning in your bedroom. It is quite possible that she could let herself into the hall without making enough noise for you to hear from your bedroom. Once inside the apartment, the living room would furnish a refuge for her until your light went out, and you were asleep. Right?"

"All I can say is that it would be physically possible," ' Ginger repeated wearily. "I'm sure Pauline did nothing of the sort, but I have no proof she didn't."

Dundee rose from the big armchair and gently pushed the girl down into its soft embrace, himself taking the big overstuffed ottoman.

"Relax, Ginger!" he pleaded with real concern. "This isn't any third degree, you know. You're merely answering a few questions to help me out and to save time and bother for all of us, including your stepmother. Now, tell me, does Mrs. Loring use a typewriter?"

The girl's brown eyes widened and her cheeks went a little whiter. "No. So far as I know she has never touched a key."

Dundee kept his eyes fixed upon his loosely clasped hands "I see. How long have you had a typewriter in your apartment?"

"About three years. Pauline hates typewritten letters," she vouchsafed suddenly. "Among other things she taught penmanship when she was a schoolteacher. She blames the typewriter for having spoiled the ancient art of penmanship."

"Did your stepmother recognize Madge Smith in Yola Conova?"

Ginger considered the question, then slowly shook her head "I honestly believe she did not. You see, to Pauline, Madge was an ignorant, foreign servant girl. She didn't even think Madge was pretty. It would have been impossible for Pauline to imagine Madge's becoming an internationally famous movie star."

"Do you mean to say," Dundee demanded incredulously "that you never discussed the matter with your stepmother?"

"After Chris died," she answered, her lips trembling, "Pauline forbade me ever to mention Madge's name again. She never forgave us—Chris and me—for loving Madge better than we loved her. She was terribly jealous. Then after Dad—died—"

"I'm afraid I've already heard a little bit about that Ginger," Dundee interrupted unhappily. "Mrs. Martin told me that he was lost in a flood."

"Mrs. Martin!" Ginger's small face flamed, her eyes shot sparks of fire. "I'll bet she never told you that Dad saved at least a score of lives before his rowboat overturned, and he was—lost," she challenged fiercely. "That woman never had a good word to say about anybody in her life!"

"Somehow my heart didn't exactly rush out to either Martin—male or female. Apparently, however, your stepmother tolerates Mrs. Martin, at least."

"Pauline?" Ginger gasped. "Hunh! 'Big Bertha,' as the female Martin is called by her loving pupils, is one of Pauline's pet aversions. What? No, I didn't look at those pictures closely," she admitted, as she accepted the newspaper extra which Dundee was offering. "Ye-es, that is Pauline, right next to Mrs. Martin. But that doesn't necessarily mean that they went to the station *together.* Look! Isn't that Dink Garnet crouching against the ropes? The nasty little beast! Judging by the expression on poor Madge's face, she was looking right at him."

"Yes," Dundee agreed. "She looks both disgusted and frightened—an emotional combination that does not emphasize girlish beauty. A good snap of Risher, isn't it? By the way, I think you're quite right—as a movie critic, I mean. He seems to be pretty swell. So you didn't know your stepmother went to the station to see the celebrities arrive?"

"No. I wasn't there myself. I had to catch an advance showing of the Conova picture in order to get my review in for the afternoon paper. I was rather glad, in a way. I didn't want to be one of a mob surging around her. I wanted to see her alone, where she could be herself with me, and trust me not to betray her—if she was our Madge, I mean. You remember I wasn't at all sure until I saw her 'in person' last night. And I had not yet received that abominable letter, proving that someone else recognized Madge Smith in Yola Conova."

"The letter was written *after* she arrived, I have no doubt,"

Dundee contributed confidently. "Probably by someone in this very picture. Someone who, like you and the Martins and Dink Garnet, couldn't be *sure* until his eyes rested on the flesh-and-blood girl."

Slowly his eyes closed as he began to tap an extremely white and sound front tooth with the nail of his right forefinger.

At last Ginger cried: "Oh, do stop that awful tapping! feel as if you're tapping a Morse code on every nerve in my body."

"Sorry!" Dundee's blue eyes flew wide, to stare at her long and thoughtfully. "Morse code? That's an idea! Maybe my unconscious mind was trying to get a message through to my conscious mind. At any rate, there's something bothering me about this case—something I ought to *see*, and don't. Of course, the temptation will be to pin the murder on the writer of that letter, or to try to hook up the two. And I seriously doubt that the two are connected—What's that?" he interrupted himself to demand, for the girl had uttered a sort of strangled cry.

"Sorry!" she gasped. "I—it's just that I've been feeling horribly guilty about the whole business of the letter. I'd be tremendously relieved if I could hope there was no connection—"

Dundee's eyes were slightly puzzled as they searched her face. "It must be rotten for you to be tormented with the thought that you might have saved her. But don't you go of the deep end as Louise Patton has done. It's my opinion she sicker with remorse than with chills and fever. As matter of fact, Ginger, I can't conceive of the murderer as the blackmailer in this case being one and the same person. It takes a fair amount of courage to commit murder—almost any kind of murder. A murderer is a desperate gambler, with the odds terribly against him. A blackmailer takes almost no chances; in his own mind, he is convinced that he takes no chance whatever—his victim will not dare squeal."

"But what if a blackmailer became terrified that his game would be—exposed?" the girl asked. "Oh, I was such a fool, Jimmy Dundee! Can't you see how horribly I bungled? I, the recipient of that letter, appeared publicly with you—famous in Hamilton as the brilliant special investigator for the district attorney—just a few hours after the letter reached me! Appeared with you in the one place where the writer of that letter was sure to be—at the theater! My only excuse is that I wanted the letter-writer to be warned against doing anything else to frighten or annoy Yola Conova. As it was, maybe I frightened the blackmailer so badly that—he—"

"Stop a second," Dundee commanded. "You hesitated before that pronoun 'he.' Why?"

"Because the letter sounds like the work of a woman," she answered. "'Captain Strawn thought so, too."

"Or like the work of a womanish man," Dundee offered grimly, thinking with lip-curling distaste of Professor Wesley Martin. "But man or woman, the writer of that letter was a clever coward—not a gambler. He or she was taking no chances whatsoever; that letter could have been turned over to the police or the district attorney by its victim, if Yola Conova had felt inclined to prosecute, and the law would have been helpless to punish the writer. It is no crime to write anonymous letters, if the letters themselves make no attempt at extortion, convey no threat of bodily or mental harm—"

"You're right!" Ginger Loring interrupted exultantly. "The writer of that letter had nothing to fear. Remember, I am sure the complete story of this great star's humble life in Hamilton will be a real inspiration to all who read it. Clever, malicious, cowardly," she concluded, with fierce contempt.

"Not by any stretch of the imagination can I visualize the writer of that carefully 'within-the-law' letter being stampeded into murder in order to recover it and to escape prosecution for having written it,' Dundee assured her. "What puzzles me, and *has* baffled me all along, is why on earth the letter was ever sent to you in the first place. We know, from your deduction and from Clinton Risher's story, that a carbon copy was made and that that copy was received by Yola Conova, and destroyed. Why did the writer take even that much chance of being exposed as a malicious persecutor?"

"I—don't know," the girl confessed, then: "It was really more—fiendish, Jimmy, to send the original to a newspaper. Don't you see? When she received the carbon copy of a letter written to a newspaper, Yola Conova would have known absolutely that she could not buy the silence of the writer; that it was not a case of ordinary blackmail—for money, I mean; but a subtle sort of persecution from which she could not possibly escape. The writer, also, must have counted on Conova's familiarity, as a movie star, with sensational yellow journalism. Such a tip to a newspaper—that a famous 'foreign' movie star was once a humble working-girl of Hamilton—could be expected to result in a tremendous scoop for that newspaper, and not a chance in the world for the story to be soft-pedaled. If the writer merely wanted to torment her, he —or she—could have chosen no surer way!"

Dundee nodded slowly. "Yes. Yes. Subtle and hellish torture." His head kept nodding, slowly, regularly, as if once started it could not stop itself. "Whoever wrote that letter must have known her very well indeed—and must have known you! For it was part of the persecution to address the letter to you—the one person in all of Hamilton that Madge Smith might have dreamed of seeing again, after all these years. If she had seen your name on press clippings, heading your reviews of her pictures, she must have been both afraid that you would want to interview her, and hopeful that, if you did, you would spare her the shame of exposure —because you had loved her when you were a child."

Tears filled Kay Loring's eyes. "I would have done anything in the world to protect her. And she had to die, believing that I was trying to track her down, to expose her before all Hamilton."

"Having known you so well, she should have had more faith in you," Dundee declared sternly. "She must have known herself to be guilty of more than you have suspected—to fear you. I suppose she refused to give interviews in Chicago, to set a precedent for her necessary exclusiveness in Hamilton. Probably if everything had gone off well here, and she had played her engagement without being recognized and exposed, she would have reverted to a movie star's normal appetite for reporters, cameramen, and autograph albums."

The tears had dried in Ginger's eyes, which were fixed on Dundee in a wide, strange stare. "Jimmy, you said something that sounded odd—and your voice was odd," she challenged him. "You said Madge must have been guilty of worse than I knew—"

"Not 'worse.' More," Dundee corrected her gently. "Tell me, child, do you honestly believe that your father died in that flood?"

XI

KAY LORING, trying to speak, could only gasp; but her brown eyes blazed out of a face that was paper-white. Her angry amazement was so genuine that Dundee could hardly force himself to continue.

"I understand that his body was never identified among the flood casualties; that is, not absolutely identified. Forgive me, Kay, but was your father—happy? I mean, did he want to live?"

Before the detective's pitying eyes tiny beads of sweat formed in a ring about the girl's bluish white lips. She looked as if she might faint, and her voice came thin, and as if from a great distance:

"Not happy—after Chris died. He worshiped Chris. He was too big a man, though, to—to commit *suicide*. But," and she gasped again, "you didn't mean suicide, did you? Suicides have—bodies. You think he—deserted us— Pauline and me. No, no! Oh, *no*! Not my Dad! He wouldn't have deserted *me*! He'd have known how desolate I should be without him—without Chris—without Madge. *Without Madge*," she repeated strangely. "Oh!"

The last word was wrung from her, and the pain of that wrenching doubled her small body.

Dundee wanted, with all the kindness of his young heart, to comfort her, to erase from her mind the thought that he had put into it—a suspicion, he knew, from which she would never be free again. But more than man, he was a detective.

"You must have guessed why your stepmother hated Madge Smith so bitterly, since she forbade you ever to mention her name again after she was gone."

The wide brown eyes stared blindly, seeing nothing in the Yola Conova suite in the Randolph Hotel. And slowly, after a bit, a red stain crept from her breast to her throat, and up over her childishly freckled cheeks, and then ran into the roots of her fiery curls. Dundee had never before seen anyone blush so extravagantly. But at least she would not faint now.

"I didn't—guess—I—" she faltered at last, in a thin whisper. "You must think I'm stupid. But a little girl—doesn't think things—like that—about her father." She shivered, then suddenly anger poured its heat and its strength into her. "It's not true! You've been listening to that horrible Martin woman! . . . Don't you know a red herring when you see one? A fine detective you are!"

Dundee grinned, immensely relieved. Far, far better for her to be furious with him, than for her heart to break before his eyes. "Oh, I detect a bit here and there, now and then, and sort of by the way. For instance," he almost babbled, "I detected—what a bright lad am I—that Mrs. Martin had had good cause about eleven years ago to be more than a little jealous. I also detected that Professor Martin had been completely frustrated in his guilty love—a frustration that made him hate Madge Smith more than he loved her. Not, of course, that Mrs. Martin believed her lady-killing husband was frustrated! I also detected on Mrs. Martin's part an aching desire to acquaint me with all the scandal against a pretty woman, now dead. A more charitable obituary would have been indicated, I thought—if the lady's conscience were entirely clear."

Ginger laid a timid hand upon his arm "I'm sorry. I have a vile temper, and—my heart hurts. But I didn't mean to suggest that Mrs. Martin *murdered* Madge."

"But you do think she might very well be guilty of having written that abominable letter," Dundee guessed confidently.

"You know, Ginger, it's strange how deeply one lowly, humble servant girl affected the lives of so many of her 'betters.'"

"You wouldn't think it strange if you had known her," Ginger assured him gravely, eyes again brimming with tears. "If my father did love her, he could not help himself. She was so lovely—and lovable. So gentle. So—heavenly kind and sweet. But Jimmy, don't make any absurd mistake. My father did not go away to join Madge somewhere. For that's what you were thinking. He just couldn't have done that—and be Christopher Loring. It may be—" and she drew a sharp, painful breath, "that he chose to die in the flood, or was glad to risk his life that way. If I knew that to be the truth—" She choked on a sob before she could finish her sentence: "I would not love my father less, or love Madge less."

Dundee's pitying blue eyes turned away from her white, working face. There were limits to his duty as an investigator. There was certainly no duty laid upon him to say, "But if Madge Smith loved your father as much as he loved her, and if there was a child of that love, don't you believe your father would have followed wherever she went?"

Dundee shook himself impatiently. All the evidence so far pointed to Bruce Kenyon as the successful lover, as the father of Madge Smith's child, born somewhere under the purchased name of Garnet. Had Bruce Kenyon loved her? Had every man who met her succumbed to the magic of her?

"How are you making out with the reporters?" he asked abruptly.

"Fine," she answered, obviously grateful for the change of subject. "There's no suspicion of murder. I've explained, as cagily and vaguely as possible, that, while Conova was known to be in an abnormally depressed mood for several months, there is some reason to think that something may have happened in Hamilton to aggravate that depression into despair, which resulted in suicide. Therefore, I point out, a very exhaustive investigation into every detail of her fourteen or fifteen hours in Hamilton seems to be indicated. Either the fair city of Hamilton and all its citizens must be completely absolved of blame, or the guilt—whether punishable by law or not—must be laid at the right door. To account for the presence of some of our witnesses, I've hinted that a number of Hamiltonians saw Yola Conova on her last journey—saw her quite by accident, of course."

Dundee nodded his approval. "Good! We've got to stick to the suicide theory as long as possible. And I hope to God nobody blabs to a reporter about the Madge Smith business—not for a day or two at least, or we shall be badly handicapped. By the way, Ginger, does *The Sun* keep a separate 'morgue' for movie people?"

"Yes, a huge one," Kay Loring assured him. "But you don't need to ask me to steal the file on Yola Conova. I've been keeping a private scrapbook on her ever since she first appeared in pictures, eight years ago. She was one of those star-overnight sensations, you may remember. Did you see her in Chekhov's 'The Cherry Orchard'?"

"It's one picture I'll never forget," Dundee admitted.

"Nor I. Well, she was ballyhooed as a foreign discovery, and she had a trace of accent, as well as a markedly foreign and exotic flavor. They called her the Russian Garbo—remember? The story went that her mother was a Polish countess, and her father a White Russian army officer. She was born before the war, of course, and there were a lot of stories built around the assassination of both her father and her mother in the 1917 Bolshevik revolution. Yola was raised in a French convent, where she had been smuggled after a faithful old nurse had escaped with her by way of Finland."

"Melodramatic, but plausible enough," Dundee remarked.

"Of course it may be true—in moderation," Ginger conceded "We knew next to nothing about Madge, as I told you. As a matter of fact, I'm quite sure Madge had had convent training, and she did speak French. Whether she spoke it 'like a native' or not, I don't know, but she taught both Chris and me to speak French with her. But it wasn't of Russia that Madge talked. It was of Poland, which she loved fanatically. But as I told you before, Madge gave us the impression, without exactly saying so, that she herself was born in America, of Polish parents, and that she spent her childhood in Chicago. Yola Conova married Geoffrey Arundel six years ago, just before she took out that million dollar life insurance policy. Her life as a star has been remarkably free from scandal. The publicity department of her studio and the newspaper and radio gossip writers had her engaged half a dozen times before her marriage, but there was no faintest breath of scandal—just the normal romances of a glamour girl. For five years she was a top rank star, and for nearly three years she has been going slowly but surely downhill."

"Why?" Dundee was keenly interested.

Ginger shrugged. "Who knows? Changing fashions, fickle public, younger, fresher faces. The usual reasons. But, no! I think *she* changed herself, before the public stopped worshiping her. She seemed, suddenly to have lost something—the quality of splendor. On the screen she had always seemed a queen by birth. She seemed happily sure of herself—not arrogant, you understand, but endearingly confident. Sure-footed, strong, but with a delicate tread—as if," and Kay Loring drew a sharp breath, "she could walk on flowers without hurting them. Then, for some reason, she began to stumble. She seemed to *lose herself*, if you can believe me—"

"I know." Dundee nodded. "I've seen all of her pictures, I think, except the last two or three perhaps. It became rather painful. I didn't know why. But you put it correctly. She had lost her essential quality—whatever that was."

"She began to look ill," Ginger continued. "And strained. Of course the whole trouble may have been physical, but when we saw her so close last night she didn't look as if she had been physically ill, did she?"

"No. But nervous breakdowns don't always express themselves in wrecked bodies."

"Well. . . . Her acting became uncertain, uneven. Sometimes her eyes would look feverishly bright and intense, and again—perhaps the next scene, when animation was really needed—they would be as dull as burned out coals. I grieved for her, and was frightened."

"Did you ever write to her?" Dundee asked.

"Write? Oh, no!" Ginger shook her head. "You know, I didn't want to write her. I was never more than half convinced that she was Madge Smith, and I never dared put it to the test. If she had failed to answer, or if she had proved not to be Madge, I should have felt bad. The only gesture I ever made toward her was to put her name on the subscription mailing list—as a deadhead, of course— for *The Sun*, after I was made dramatic editor, with a by- line. It was addressed to her Beverly Hills home, and I've hoped that she saw it personally, and read it occasionally, both because it is in a sense her 'home town' paper, and because my name heads a department in it."

Dundee frowned, and began to tap with his fingernail against his teeth again, in a spasmodic, maddening tattoo. Ginger winced, but heroically kept silent. Finally he desisted, with a gesture of angry bafflement.

"I'd like to see that scrapbook, Ginger. Also I want copies of all the pictures taken by the news cameramen— crowd pictures, as well as close-ups of the whole Conova party. As press representative for the investigation you ought to be able to wangle them for me, even if you have chucked your job on *The Sun*."

"Can do," the girl promised, almost cheerful again at the prospect of definite work. "Also I've got an envelope full of crowd pictures and close-ups, taken in Chicago, and sent on to us by the news picture service we subscribe to. It's tucked into my scrapbook, which I keep at the office. I'll send a messenger—"

The outside door of the parlor of Suite 4-B was flung open and Captain Strawn, followed by Detective Brede, carrying his stenographic notebook, strode into the room.

"Well, Bonnie lad!" he boomed. "Here I am at last. Thought I'd never get through with that gang of hotel hired hands. But I warrant you didn't miss me. I ought to warn ye, lass," he addressed Kay Loring solemnly, "yon's a great lad for the lassies."

"Lay off the Scotch brogue, you big Irish palooka!" Scotch-Irish Dundee advised, grinning broadly, much pleased that his temporary chief had relented and accepted the girl. "Any luck?"

"Luck!" Strawn snorted with disgust, and dropped heavily upon the down cushions of the big sofa. "Ho hum! A policeman's lot is not a happy one. I figured the switchboard operators would be a gold mine, but Branagan, the house detective, told me, after I'd tussled with the girls for upwards of an hour, that a telephone operator had been canned last week for listening in on a guest's call, so that explained why the whole lot of them seemed to be ailing with lockjaw and deafness."

"But surely," Dundee protested, "it was possible to get some sort of confirmation or denial of Risher's and Miss Patton's stories of the telephone calls to this suite. After all, on a hotel switchboard the operator has to hang on until the call is actually completed."

"Correct," agreed Strawn. "And between the two sets of operators—they change shifts at midnight here—I did manage to get a fair amount of corroboration of the evidence already in hand, but not complete corroboration, and almost nothing new turned up. Seems to me like the girls have been primed. They'll cautiously admit something we've already got hold of, but—"

"Hepburn, of course," Dundee interrupted. "Thinking of his precious hotel's reputation. Can't blame him. A death in a hotel is bad enough, but an investigation into—"

"Suicide," Strawn cut in. "They all think it's nothing more than suicide, and can't see why the police and the district attorney's office should get so het up about it. Anyhow, it was like pulling eyeteeth, trying to get information out of those girls. One thing turned up that'll please you, Jimmy. That call that Risher told us about— the time when Conova herself answered the 'phone—"

"Yeah?" Dundee jumped to his feet in his eagerness. "Did the operator recognize the voice?" He thrust a hand into his pocket and pulled out a silver dollar. "Here's a buck that says she did, and that it was Bruce Kenyon!"

"Put your talking money back in your jeans," Strawn commanded, his pale gray eyes glinting with affectionate amusement. "But I might as well admit that if I'd been betting against you, you'd a-won. Kenyon it was. Seems that all the girls know Bruce Kenyon's voice. And his wife's. Bruce's mother lives in the hotel, when she's not in California or Florida, since old man Kenyon died, and the young couple talk with her on the 'phone every day, as well as spend a lot of time in the hotel with her."

"Is the dowager Mrs. Kenyon staying in the hotel now?"

It was Ginger who answered: "No. She left about two weeks ago for Pasadena. I saw the item in our society column."

Dundee whistled with relief. "Thank God for that small favor! For one dreadful minute I could see a frail, white-haired old lady achieving the honor of being our pet suspect. Naturally the operator wouldn't admit to listening-in?"

"Oh, no! 'How dare you, sir?' Strawn mocked in high falsetto. "But she did break down and own up to hanging on long enough to know that it was Conova herself who answered the call, after the bell had rung three or four times. She swears she got off the line just as soon as she heard a voice say, 'Hello! Yes, this is Miss Conova speaking.' All who believe her can stand on their heads— but there you are—"

"Yes, here I am, standing on my head," Dundee said gravely. He was highly amused at Strawn's unusual spin. Was the old flatfoot showing off for Ginger's benefit? "I suppose you asked her more than once if she got the impression, before she so commendably got off the line, that someone lifted a receiver of an extension telephone and listened in?"

"If I asked her once I asked her a round dozen time." Strawn assured him bitterly. "I do happen to know the A.B.C.'s of my job, young squirt! But the answer was no, a dozen times no."

Dundee grinned briefly to show his appreciation. "It just possible, of course, that she didn't stay on the line too afraid of losing her job, or too busy. But Kenyon was a fool to take such a chance—making a midnight date with a famous movie star, over a hotel telephone line. Only a very desperate man, or a man entirely innocent of any wrong intent, would take such a chance of involving himself in scandal, unless he was a born fool, of course. And Kenyon has the reputation of being one of Hamilton's most brilliant young business men. Get anything on those telephone calls Miss Patton spoke of—the two made by the same woman apparently with a disguised voice?"

Strawn shook his head. "The girls didn't notice anything specially funny about a woman's voice, but it seems certain that most of the calls came from women— calls for Conova I mean." He broke off to laugh sarcastically, contemptuous. "That Risher kid sure has 'em going—the telephone girls and the rest of Hamilton's female population—judging by the avalanche of telephone calls that swamped the Randolph switchboard all day yesterday and last night, and today, too. He's sure a humdinger for sex appeal! Won't surprise me a mite if our murderer turns out to be a she-killer, jealous as all git out of this Yola Conova. Think of that angle, son?"

"Naturally," Dundee smiled. "Funny thing about the love between Yola Conova and Clinton Risher. It was something so plain you could almost swear it was both visible and tangible. I'll bet hundreds of people in that theater last night saw that they were madly in love. Rose Berman, Sanderson's secretary, jumped me about it as soon as I stuck my head in the D.A.'s office an hour ago. Comically enough, she was jealous of Conova! Not only jealous, but fighting mad, and sarcastic as all get out! Actually! I'm really not kidding! If that gold-and-amber young god from a railroad station in Waco, Texas, has the power—at a considerable distance, mind you!—to turn the head of our Rose Berman so completely, God only knows what tragic forces he has set in motion. Murder? Why not? But—to be matter-of-fact again, did you manage to get any dope at all on that last telephone call that Conova answered, before she left word that she was not to be disturbed? The one that came at about twenty minutes to one, according to Louise Patton's story."

Strawn shook his head. "I drew a blank there. Maybe I acted too damned anxious, and the girls got scared— thought it would be smarter and safer to play dumb. One of the girls that's on from midnight till six seemed anxious to help out, or maybe she just liked to be the center of attention. What was her name, Brede?"

The young police detective grinned guiltily, as he answered without consulting his notebook: "Simpson, chief. Phyllis Simpson."

"A neat little job, streamlined and fresh as new paint, eh, Brede?" Strawn chuckled. "She talked a lot, but didn't say much. Seems that she took the last call that was answered in Suite 4-B, but Phyllis says she couldn't say for sure whether it was a man or a woman calling, and whether it was Conova or the Patton woman who answered. As for the calls after twelve forty-five, there were at least half a dozen of them."

"Did you get a confirmation of the fact that it was Conova herself who gave the order for no more calls to be put through, saying that she was going to leave the receiver of the hook?" Dundee asked. "I gathered from what the operator said when I tried to reach Conova around one o'clock this morning that it was the star herself who'd given the order.

"The operator you talked to was Phyllis Simpson," Strawn told him. "But she says she doesn't really know whether it was Conova or Patton who gave the order. She says some female voice from a telephone in this suite said: 'Please do not put through any more calls for Suite 4-B tonight *under any circumstances.* Say that Miss Conova has given orders that she is not to be disturbed.' And the Simpson girl says nothing was said about leaving the receiver off the hook But it was taken off and left off, a minute or two after the 'don't disturb' order had come through. The girl had to plug out the line, to keep the red light from showing continually. Of course, soon as the receiver was replaced, the girl knew it, because what she calls a 'supervisory' signal flashed on. Same as when anyone gets through talking and hangs up."

"When did that signal flash?"

"About half past two, when the Patton girl gave the alarm," Strawn answered. "Phyllis says she jerked out the plug as soon as the supervisory signal flashed on, then the red light began to flash like all get out, off and on, you know, showing somebody was jiggling the hook in a tearing hurry to be answered. It was the Patton woman, half out of her head, Phyllis says."

"Well, that's that," Dundee observed gloomily. "Did you—yes, Miss Loring?"

"If you don't need me just now I think I'll run over to the newspaper office and get my Conova scrapbook and those news pictures myself, instead of sending a messenger. It's only three blocks each way," Ginger told him. "There are a few personal things in my desk that I'd like to gather up, now that I've quit the job, and—" But she could not finish the sentence.

Dundee laid a comforting hand on her shoulder as she turned sharply toward the door. "Don't you worry, child. All three papers will be bidding against each other to get your services, and you'll take your pick soon as this bad business is cleared up or—the cat's out of the bag."

The girl dashed at sudden tears with the back of a hand, like a child. "I've been wanting to say," she confessed, "that if, for any reason, the newspapers get hold of the story of Madge Smith, I want to get back on my newspaper job, if they'll have me. I could do more for—her—by writing about her as I knew her, than in any other way."

The three men watched her go. It was Strawn who spoke, shaking his massive gray head. "That Madge Smith of hers must have been some gal! Makes me kinda sorry I didn't meet up with her myself, when she was making Hamilton lively a dozen years ago."

Dundee laughed. "If you had known her, Captain, maybe Mrs. Strawn would be among our choicest suspects now. By the way, did you check Arundel's alibi? We mustn't forget that he's the baby that has the good old standard motive—one million cool, hard smackers of insurance money. And that he couldn't possibly know that the policy has lapsed."

Strawn twitched his thin lips into what passed for a smile on his granite face. "If I had that much motive for murdering my wife, I'd take pains to insure myself an iron-clad alibi for every hour of the twenty-four, every day of my life, on the off-chance of something happening to her, and me getting booked for the rap. No wonder Arundel was so scared she'd bump herself off, and not be obliging enough to leave a suicide note. By the way, I told your Loring girl to tip off the papers that there wasn't any suicide note, which was one reason we have to be so damned thorough in investigating her death."

Dundee nodded. "I take it then that Arundel's alibi is airtight?"

"'Fraid so," Strawn grunted. "Colvin and Bowen—and I haven't got two better men—worked that angle from the Hamilton Hotel. He's my pick for the murderer, first, because of that whopping big motive, and second, because

I don't like anything about him. But he didn't do no personal murdering last night—leastways, not on or near Old Bridge, twenty blocks or more from the hotel room in which he was playing bridge. Matter of fact, according to the stories of the other three men that he played with, Arundel sat down at the bridge table on the stroke of twelve exactly, to take the place of a guy that had to drop out, and wasn't out of the room, except to step into the bathroom possibly while he was dummy, until the game broke up this morning, about six o'clock."

"Six" Dundee repeated "Before or after the first extras on the Conova suicide woke up the, town?

"Before," Strawn answered "Colvin and Bowen said the other three bridge players were asleep when they got over to the Hamilton, and the manager gave 'em hell for disturbing his good cash customers. Not one of the three men had an idea what all the shoutin' was about, but they all told the same story. Arundel wasn't out of their sight for more than ten minutes at a 'time, if that long, and they all insisted that he hadn't left the suite, even to step into the hall."

Dundee considered, frowning. "How did he happen to play bridge, last night? Looks like a damned well planned alibi to me!"

Strawn shrugged his broad, gaunt shoulders, but there was a gleam in his pale eyes. "Wrong again, Bonnie lad. It seems that Arundel was having a little good-night chat with the room clerk when a couple of these bridge fiends come downstairs looking for a fourth, to take the place of their early-to-bed playmate. They stopped at the desk—both guys are well known at the Hamilton, traveling men—to ask the clerk if he could make any suggestions. This night clerk—Cruze, I believe his name is—introduced Arundel, and in two shakes of a sheep's tail the three were on their way up to their game. Arundel said he would play a couple of hours only; but one rubber led to another, and finally he agreed it didn't seem worth while to go to bed at all, seeing as how he was going to take a train out for New York at seven-thirty this morning. So—"

"So—did he hire the job done?" Dundee put the question brutally. He did not wait for the older man's answer. "Somehow, I can't see Arundel sticking his neck out to that extent—hiring an assassin. Too risky—for Arundel, with that walloping big motive—the million bucks—ready to put the finger on him. Besides, if he was hiring someone to hang her last night, he'd have wanted to be as far away as possible. No sense in coming to the party."

Strawn stripped the tinfoil from a stick of chewing gum, sniffed the fruity odor appreciatively, opened his mouth just enough to permit the insertion of the wafer, then began to chew slowly and thoroughly. Dundee curbed his impatience. The gray-haired old chief of the homicide squad used chewing gum, not as an aid to digestion, but as a mental stimulant.

The gum was taking effect. Strawn was thinking out loud, chewing between words. "Arundel comes to Hamilton. Leaves New York, where he's rehearsing for show. Makes long trip to be here only few hours. Why?"

Although Dundee knew he was interrupting, that Strawn was asking the question of himself, rather than of his colleague, he broke in: "He will say, of course, that he was so worried about his wife's health and spirits that he could not let her get farther away without seeing her and trying to patch things up between them. And, from all accounts he has had good cause to worry—"

"Or to *hope* to God she'd go ahead and do it," Strawn corrected. "It sure must not've been any fun to have a million dollars dangled in front of your nose that way—then jerked out of reach."

"Well, that million's gone bye-bye most definitely now,' Dundee agreed."If Arundel is innocent of even so much a wish that she'd die naturally or kill herself to get out of her mental misery, I'm inclined to feel a bit sorry for the pasty-faced blighter."

"Want my crying rag?" Strawn proffered a handkerchief. "So Arundel hotfoots it here. Why? Because he's been tipped off that Conova and Risher have gone nuts about each other. How? Maybe the Patton girl spilled the beans in one of her written reports to her boss Arundel, whether she denies it or not—"

"If she did think it was only fair to tip him off, since he had hired her," Dundee put in, speaking slowly, fumblingly, "that would account for her exaggerated feeling of responsibility and remorse. She, of course, has had no way of finding out that Arundel played bridge all night, and could not have committed the murder 'in person.' If she thinks she aroused his jealousy to the point that he'd come rushing out hen and—"

"Shucks!" Strawn exclaimed. "You got a mess of ifs and ands there, but they don't add up to nothing. A jealous husband all primed to kill his wife don't look around a strange town and pick out a murderer from the 'Help Wanted—Male,' then play bridge while the dirty work's being done. But there's *one* fair-haired boy that didn't play bridge, that hasn't any more alibi than a silverfish, but that *did* have plenty of reason to be jealous of Yola Conova last night."

"I see your point," said Dundee. "And of course you may be right. But personally I very much wish that Clinton Risher became violently suspicious and jealous last night, enough at least, that he would have kept an eye on this end of the hall and followed Yola Conova when she left to keep her date. I believe, if he had, she would be safe and well now. Happy, too, with a load off her conscience."

"Sure your name ain't Bonnie *Lassie*?" Strawn sneered inelegantly. "Looks to me like you've fallen as hard for that Texas Romeo as any of the girls. My daughter-in-law Joan had the gall to call me up and ask me to fix it up for her to meet America's Number One Heart Throb. Fact! That's what she called him—to me! Hunh! If we got a signed confession and tried him for the murder, he'd get acquitted with a vote of thanks—if there was as much as one woman on the jury!"

"Then let's not worry about him now," Dundee suggested amiably. "We could spin half a dozen plausible theories, but what we need now are a few facts. By the way, while I was wising up Sanderson, I had his secretary call both the Kenyon home and Bruce's office on pretexts, just to make sure they were both safely where we could find them when we were ready. Which ought to be soon now, don't you think? As soon as we can give this suite the once-over. I had a casual look around before I sent for Miss Loring, but—"

"So did I—while you were gone to City Hall," Strawn admitted. "Thought it was kinda foolish to go ahead before we made sure there wasn't a suicide note, or some outstanding clue, waiting for us here."

"O.K.," Dundee said curtly. He knew very well that Strawn had hoped to get ahead of his young colleague, but he was also comfortably sure, from long knowledge of his former chief, that Strawn would not have concealed any important information from him, if he had found it. "Any luck? Of course I had a look around myself while I was waiting for you to get on the job this morning about daybreak, but only a casual sort of look."

Strawn shook his head. "Pretty bare. Almost nothing of a personal nature, outside of her clothes. I did hit on something that struck me as kinda odd, though. Gimme, Brede."

The police stenographer laid aside his notebook and opened a brown paper portfolio, from which he extracted a thick sheaf of legal-sized envelopes, fastened together with a rubber band. Strawn handed the lot to Dundee, who flipped through the bunch incredulously.

"I'll say it's odd!" he ejaculated. "Every envelope addressed in handwriting to Mr. Geoffrey Arundel, c/o The Friars Club, New York City. What do you make of it, chief?"

That title never failed to please the hard-bitten old captain of the homicide squad. Now, he expanded his chest and hooked a thumb in the Sam Browne belt of his handsome uniform. "I didn't waste my time guessing, lad," he boasted. "I went right to headquarters for the what-for and how-come—Mr. Geoffrey Arundel himself."

"No!" Dundee ejaculated, unable to conceal his annoyance.

"Oh, yeah, I did!" Strawn chuckled. "And no applecarts upset, my boy. I'm not quite the blundering ox that you may think I am. I simply asked the gentleman if that was his wife's handwriting, and when he said it most certainly was, and what the hell of it, I asked him why, if the lady and him wasn't on speaking terms *last night*, she'd planned to write him so many fat letters that she'd taken the trouble to address a whole package of long envelopes at once."

"Well?" Dundee was impatient, as Strawn studied his boot toe complacently.

"Nothing mysterious about it," Strawn admitted. "Seems that Arundel was her business manager. Of course, like Arundel says, she had an agent, too, out in Hollywood, but Arundel even managed her affairs with the agent. These envelopes was being used to send all correspondence—fan mail and any other kind, except letters from personal friends, of course—on to Arundel, for him to attend to."

"Is that so?" Dundee marveled. "Then why in hell didn't Arundel have charge of paying the insurance premiums? That check on the wrong bank was signed 'Yola Conova Arundel'—not Geoffrey Arundel."

"I asked him that—without giving it away about the insurance check, and the lapsed policy and all," Strawn confessed. "Just asked him if he had charge of all her earnings, as her manager. He said he did, but claims he banks all her money in her name, and she has to sign the checks for all bills and expenses. Reckon she was afraid to trust him too far," Strawn concluded sagely, "but wanted an excuse to pay him a salary as a manager, instead of making a kept man out of him. This play he's rehearsing in New York is the first job of work he's had in a couple of years, I gathered."

Dundee slapped his knee suddenly and laughed. "One less mystery to solve!" he gloated. "No wonder Arundel came hurrying out to Hamilton to see his dear wife! To cheer her up? To protect her from evil in a city she had feared, for some strange reason? Oh, no, no! Simply and merely to get a check signed, because she held the purse strings and he was all out of cash. It must be hell to be married to a woman who makes all the money."

"Reckon it's a damned sight worse when she gets sore at you and won't shell out," Strawn contributed grimly. "Anyway—"

"Let's see her checkbook!" Dundee demanded, with sudden excitement.

"Checkbook?" Strawn echoed. "Wasn't it in that handbag of hers you found in the sedan?"

"No, it wasn't," Dundee told him. "You're sure you didn't find one among her things?"

"Sure I'm sure!" Strawn sputtered "And no use looking again," he tried to stop Dundee, who had jumped to his feet and begun to pull open the drawers of the ornate little rosewood desk.

But Dundee was not to be stopped. He sped from room to room, opening and searching drawers with immense speed and efficiency, not neglecting the pockets of suits, coats, pajamas, and bathrobes. He even scrabbled among the shoes in the closet, thrusting a hand into each small piece of expensive footwear. The wardrobe trunk stood wide open in the deep closet of the bedroom, and someone—probably Louise Patton—had unpacked it completely. The three pieces of hand luggage were as empty of the object that Dundee sought with so much excitement.

"What did I tell you?" Strawn triumphed. "I didn't go into this work yesterday, son."

Dundee made a gesture as if to brush off an annoying mosquito. "No checkbook!" he said, speaking more to himself than to Strawn. "No checkbook. Which accounts for her having four hundred and sixty-five dollars on hand in cash."

"A mere penny for a movie star," Strawn suggested.

"Not for a star that was on the verge of bankruptcy," Dundee retorted. "Of course it's possible that Louise Patton had charge of the checkbook, since she probably filled the job of private secretary to Conova, in a small way, along with her other duties—"

"Hasn't got it and hasn't seen it," Strawn contributed bluntly. "Asked her myself. Like I told you, Bonnie, I ain't exactly an amateur in this here job. More'n likely, son," he added patronizingly, "the murderer could give us a line on the whereabouts of the missing checkbook—if he was a mind to, and if we knew just—"

The telephone's sudden jangle cut across the old homicide chief's heavy-handed sarcasm. Dundee swooped upon the instrument.

"Hello! . . . Yes, speaking! . . . *What? You've caught the blackmailer?* . . . Yes, yes! . . . Oh, fine! Don't say any more, and see that he doesn't, if you have to gag him yourself, Ginger! . . . Yeah! Within five minutes! Good girl!"

XII

"HOW DOES THE LORING GIRL KNOW that Garnet is the blackmailer?" Strawn demanded, but not before he had sent a couple of his squad racing to the offices of *The Sun.*

"I didn't give her a chance to tell all," Dundee replied, smiling. "But I imagine she jumped to a rather obvious conclusion. In the blackmail letter—so-called, for want of a better name—the writer announced his intention of calling at the offices of *The Sun* this morning at ten o'clock with the complete story of Yola Conova's life in Hamilton. Comes ten o'clock, and—comes Dink Garnet. Fortunately, since we don't want the beans spilled in the papers yet, Miss Loring had just arrived in the city room of the newspaper herself, when in marched Dink Garnet, demanding to see the publisher—no less. Said he had a story to sell to, the highest newspaper bidder, and wanted to see the man who could talk money—big money."

"Damn his sallow hide!" Strawn's thin lips curled slightly at one corner. "Matter of fact, the big city newspapers and the syndicates will all be after Garnet for his story, soon as it gets out that Yola Conova used to be Madge Smith of Hamilton, and that she married Garnet to give an illegitimate baby a name."

"You may be right," Dundee admitted. "Then again, newspapers and syndicates *may* be so unreasonable as to want proof—and plenty of it!—that Yola Conova used to be Madge Smith, servant girl, of Hamilton And there is no proof, you know. None whatsoever!"

A smile flickered across Strawn's grim old face. "By Hannah, you're right, Bonnie! The girl is dead, and can't confirm or deny. If Arundel wants to stick it out—as he will, of course, or he's crazy—that Conova was never in Hamilton and never heard of Madge Smith, he could collect fat damages from any newspaper or syndicate that libeled her with the story."

"And as for Dink Garnet," Dundee contributed with great satisfaction, "I've got a warrant for the arrest of the blackmailer which Sanderson issued to me this morning in blank, and I'll clap him in the cooler and keep him there until he loses his taste for publicity."

The telephone rang and Strawn caught it. After a grunted word or two he hung up.

"Got to get along downstairs to our headquarters. Two or three of the boys reporting in," he told Dundee. "Brede says Garnet'll be along in a couple of minutes. Holmes called back from the newspaper office; said the dirty little rat tried to give 'em an argument, but that Miss Loring threw the fear of the Lord into him by something she said. Coming?'

"Give me about five minutes up here alone, chief," Dundee begged with sudden, intense earnestness "There's something in this suite of rooms that I've got to 'get'— some message that my subconscious mind has taken in, but which I can't make come to the surface—something damned important, Strawn."

"You and your high-falutin' book talk! Maybe it's a poor little ghostie, trying to wigwag you for a private word or two—"

"Exactly what I think!" Dundee interrupted, almost pushing the older man out of the room. "If Garnet gets there before I do, keep him on ice till I get down, won't you, chief?"

The special investigator lost no time. Perhaps his subconscious mind decided suddenly to play ball, instead of hide-and-seek. At any rate, Dundee made straight for the large bedroom, which lay immediately behind the parlor of Suite 4-B. On each of his previous visits to the room he had been in a great hurry, searching at top speed for something entirely tangible and definite. In the small hours of the morning he had looked swiftly for a suicide note, before plunging through the cold and darkness toward Old Bridge and its gruesome burden. His second search had been just as unsuccessful, for, although he had gone through literally all of the star's personal possessions which the room held, he had found no checkbook.

On the bed, which had not been slept in, but whose covers had been turned back by the hotel chambermaid, lay, in a careless or hasty heap, the lovely wine-red evening gown in which Yola Conova had played her tragic role with Clinton Risher, in the one-act play. Half-hidden and badly crushed was the cluster of three white orchids pinned to the narrow shoulder strap of the gown. Haste, surely, not carelessness. For undoubtedly those orchids had been another token of Clinton Risher's extravagant devotion.

Tossed upon the bed, too, was a pair of evening slippers. Very small, very new, they were of gold kid, with rhinestone heels and bands of rhinestones for ankle straps. Absurd little shoes! Incredible that even a tiny thing like Yola Conova could actually walk in them! Not at all like those sturdy, rather scuffed, broad-toed Oxfords in which Hamilton's erstwhile Madge Smith had gone to meet her death. Of course these bits of jeweled footwear were deceptive in their looks. They were undoubtedly larger than they seemed, with their excessively high heels and their pointed toes.

The detective looked curiously at the inside of one shoe. Yes, there was the maker's name, and the size, as well as the stock number. "Duval Freres, Fine Footwear, Paris, New York, Hollywood"—a name that even a man as far removed from the world of fashion as Special Investigator Dundee recognized as synonymous with *chic* and expensiveness. But it was the size—indicated in tiny, indelible markings—that made Dundee whistle incredulously. Size three and a half! And he had been calling Madge Smith a "peasant goddess!" No peasant girl ever had a foot that could get into this scrap of a slipper.

And yet—and yet—those sensible, oldish little brown Oxfords hadn't looked exactly like Cinderella footgear—

Suddenly Dundee swung around the foot of the bed and snatched the telephone from the little night table. To his impatience it seemed like an hour before his connection was completed.

"Carraway? . . . Listen!" he snapped, so that the fingerprint expert at the other end of the wire almost failed to recognize his voice. "You've got the shoes taken from the feet of the corpse, haven't you? . . . Yes, yes! I know all that, but I'm not interested in fingerprints now. Are the shoes handy? . . . Fine! I'll hold on while you look to see what size they are. . . . No, size! *Size!* . . . Well, go ahead, you lunk! ... Yes? *What's that? Four* and a half? Are you sure, Carraway? . . . Sorry! What's the letter after the number? The width, I mean! . . ..*Four and a half B!* . . . No, no! That's all for the moment. And plenty, believe me! Thanks a lot, fellah!"

Dundee drew a deep breath and exhaled it slowly, with a feeling of intense relief. At the same time his brain seemed to become miraculously clear and—well, united; as if the conscious and unconscious had got together on a matter of vital importance. His fingers lost their restlessness, too; they no longer wanted to tap a crazy sort of Morse code invented by the desperate subconscious mind, to attract his full attention.

Now, whistling softly if rather heartlessly, considering that he was in the bedroom of a woman so newly dead and so fiendishly murdered, the special investigator went about checking his amazing discovery. It was easy to leap to an almost incredible conclusion; in fact, his unconscious mind taken that terrific leap many hours before, as soon as his trained eyes had rested on a small body that had stiffened in the bitter cold as it swung from the end of a tow rope.

"No! It was before that!" Dundee corrected himself. "I caught glimmers of the truth while I was watching her in one-act play last night. I wonder if Ginger has any suspicion?"

He himself felt so deeply sure of the truth that it rather irked him to have to check that truth painstakingly against the evidence that the room and its possessions could yield to his trained eyes. But old Strawn's lips were permanently twisted around a cynical, "Oh, yeah?" and District Attorney Sanderson had a competent and thorough mind, a bit antagonistic to brilliant mental acrobatics.

He picked up the pair of ridiculous gold kid slippers and studied them. Poor girl! No wonder she had seemed, awkward last night on the stage, had seemed to have a strange but quite distinct impediment in her walk.

For a foot that measures four and a half B for walking shoes cannot possibly feel happy in an evening slipper that is size three and a half A!

Tossing the telltale slippers upon the bed, Dundee lifted the long velvet evening dress, shook out its folds, and then, surprisingly, turned it wrong side out, just as a well-trained maid might have done before hanging it up. But the detective was not interested now in preserving the beauty of garment. His eyes and hands were exploring the seams—in partrticular, the underarm seams. And they found what were searching for.

The new and extremely expensive dress had been radically altered—and not by the meticulously neat and competent fingers of a modiste's alteration specialist. In fact, it was quite a clumsy piece of work by which the armholes had been enlarged, the "bust" made a full two inches *bigger*, and the waistline at least two inches *smaller*. The hip measure had been allowed to remain unchanged. Brown thread—coarse darning cotton—had been used for the amateurish job, and the stitches were uneven, as if they had been put in hastily. The dress, however, was not damaged; that is, the material had not been cut away. Fifteen minutes in the hands of a good ladies' maid or tailor and the evening dress would again be ready for the person for whom it had been originally designed or fitted.

Dundee was about to drop the dress carelessly back upon the bed when some impulse made him take it with him to the huge clothes closet, where the rest of Yola Conova's extensive wardrobe for her personal appearance tour was neatly arranged on hangers and shelves, and in drawers and shoe racks. Feeling somewhat foolish, and glad that he was unobserved, the young detective hung the evening dress upon a padded silk hanger. The gown was new; there was a lot of "wear" in it yet, and it was not the sort of thing to go quickly out of fashion. Better take good care of it, and the rest of these costly things, until—

But Dundee was not yet ready to deal with all the implications of his amazing discovery. His extraordinarily well disciplined mind closed itself to all alluring bypaths, and concentrated upon the matter of first importance— tangible proof. Dropping to his knees he began to sort the rather large collection of shoes, which his and Strawn's previous visit to the clothes closet had sadly disarranged. As he matched up slipper to slipper, pump to pump, Oxford to Oxford, Dundee checked the sizes. And all but two pairs of footgear bore the same markings in indelible ink—size three and a half A.

It was really not hard to separate those two larger pairs from the rest. A full size additional in length and in width makes a vast difference in shoes, but age and quality can make even more difference. For all of the tinier shoes—sandals, fur-trimmed and feather-decked mules, Oxfords, pumps, slippers—were either brand-new or only slightly worn.

The other two pairs were not only noticeably bigger and broader, but definitely older. And cheaper. Oh, much, much cheaper! Not examples of the art of the brothers Duval, these!

Dundee's handsome young face was very grave and his blue eyes dark with pity as he examined the two isolated pairs of small shoes. A pair of black patent leather pumps. Stiff patent leather that had begun to crack across the toes. A chain store shoe, sold from coast to coast, and from Canada to Key West, for five dollars or less. The size was four B. Dundee frowned. According to Carraway, the Oxfords were size four and a half B. The vanity of women was incomprehensible. But in this instance vanity had been more than adequately punished, for the girl who had worn that too short shoe had a small but definite corn on the third toe of her, left foot. But somehow he had not got the impression that Madge Smith was a vain and foolish girl. *Size four B.* He frowned. That number had some special significance, if he could only remember. Suddenly he snapped his fingers in triumph. For he recalled with peculiar vividness an adorable little "college widow" whom he had known and admired rather extravagantly in his student days at Yale. She had seemed to have dozens of pairs of shoes, but had cleared herself of Dundee's laughing charge of extravagance by explaining that an uncle was in the shoe business in New York and was able to give her all the "sample" shoes she wanted, since she had the good luck to wear the size on which all sample shoes are made—size four B.

But Madge Smith had not been quite so lucky. Actually a four and a half B, her foot had been squeezed almost habitually into the too short sample size. His hand closed on the cheap little patent leather pump. If the poor girl had been so hard up that she had had to buy her shoes off a bargain counter of manufacturers samples—

But his disciplined mind spoke sternly to his undisciplined Scotch Irish heart. The detective laid aside the betraying pumps and picked up the soft, dark-red leather bedroom slippers. Size five, and obviously too big for their owner, who undoubtedly had reveled in their roominess after the toe-cramping agony of sample shoes. But even in the soft leather toe of the left shoe there was the telltale mark of the third-toe corn. And Dundee's photographic memory had accurately registered the picture of an identical disfigurement in the leather toe of the scuffed brown Oxfords which the dead girl had been wearing. No need to check that particular item with Carraway! It was not even necessary for Dundee to close his eyes to conjure up every detail of the outward appearance of the corpse.

Gently he laid the shoes aside—the black patent leather pumps and the red kid bedroom slippers. "Kumfy Kuties" read the label stamped upon the inner sole of the slippers, and they, too, could be had from the chain-store racks. The smaller shoes, size three and a half A, were uniformly elegant and immaculate and fresh, not one little boot-toe in all that fine array disfigured by even the suggestion of a corn hump!

With swift but methodical thoroughness, the special investigator examined the dresses, suits, cloaks, wraps and negligees crowding the hanger pole down the center of the closet. He nodded with satisfaction as he scrutinized each garment and returned it to its place. Cloaks, wraps, robes, negligees, showed no signs of having been altered—at least not by a hasty amateur. But every dress, blouse or skirt that was intended to be form-fitting had been changed, and apparently, by the same hand, wielding a needle threaded with the same brown darning cotton. And always the alterations were toward the same end—to make the garments larger in certain measurements, smaller in others. Sometimes two or three snap fasteners had been set over or back, to give more bust room or shoulder room, and to nip in the waistline. Once, as Dundee examined a tweed skirt and measured its incredibly small waist with his accurate eye, he thought of the half a pound of chocolates that Clinton Risher had said he had seen the girl devour at one sitting. And he hoped that she had eaten a good dinner the night before she died, a superlatively good dinner, such a dinner as a movie star could well afford.

Dundee snapped his fingers with sudden elation, and turned toward the telephone.

"Cashier? Dundee speaking—of the district attorney's office. I'm in Suite 4 B now. Please send up to me immediately Miss Conova's meal checks. I understand she had her meals in her rooms—luncheon yesterday and dinner before the theater. Yes, please. As quickly as possible. Right. Thank you very much."

So swiftly had Dundee worked that less than ten minutes had elapsed since Strawn had left him alone in the Conova suite. Now, as he waited for the meal checks, he made a rapid but thorough search of dresser, dressing-table, night-table and desk drawers of the Conova bedroom and parlor. His findings were meager, but immensely satisfying. In one hand, as he finished, he held the sheaf of large envelopes, addressed in Yola Conova's handwriting to Geoffrey Arundel, care of the Friars' Club, New York City, and in the other he held three long typewritten pages, the paper being a Hollywood physician's expensive, engraved letterhead.

"Special Diet for Mrs. Arundel" was the typed caption across the first of the three sheets, which were clamped together. Closely typed, single-spaced, each sheet contained menus for one week, and under each menu was computed the total caloric content of the permitted foods. A rigid reducing diet, it was—and one which was designed to make up for a deficiency in hydrochloric acid. That is, no raw vegetables or fruits were included, except fruit juices, and only the most easily digested proteins were listed—no egg whites, no legumes. To supply easily handled protein, gelatine in some form was prescribed three times a day.

But it was not the restrictions of the diet which most interested Bonnie Dundee. It was a line written sideways across the margin —of the first page, in delicate penciling—the same handwriting as that which had addressed the envelopes to Geoffrey Arundel.

"Important!" ran the penciled line. "Maximum weight permitted by contract (the word was heavily underscored) is 105 pounds. Careful!"

Dundee sighed and shook his head ruefully. The motion picture world was a strange and fearsome place indeed, if grown women had to keep their figures down to the size of undernourished twelve-year-old children, or pay the penalty in canceled contracts and oblivion. Well, Yola Conova's fears had not been realized. For the dead girl had "weighed in" at the morgue at ninety-eight pounds. She could have dared a few more half-pounds of the chocolates she had craved, without endangering that infernal contract!

A knock at the door and the ringing of the telephone came together.

Into the telephone Dundee spoke curtly: "Fine, chief! I'll be down in a minute or two. Hold everything!" and the door opened to a solemn-faced young waiter who had brought the meal checks.

"I was assigned to Miss Conova's suite, sir, and it was I who served her luncheon and dinner yesterday, sir. Mr. Holloway, the cashier, thought you might like to ask me some questions."

"Quite likely," Dundee agreed. "I see Miss Conova did not sign the checks herself."

"True, sir," the waiter answered gravely, as if he were at a funeral and enjoying it. "Miss Patton signed Miss Conova's name and put her own initials underneath it, to make it legal, sir, not a forgery."

Dundee grinned. "I see. Now, waiter—"

"Bartholomew, sir," the waiter interrupted firmly, but with beautiful courtesy and a Continental bow. "No relation, so far as I know, sir, to the young motion-picture star of that name, although I too hail from England—"

"Indeed?" Dundee cut in with scant ceremony. "I see that Miss Conova and Miss Patton had quite a lunch yesterday. Salads, lamb chops, mushroom omelet, pineapple, angel cake, chocolate sundae, and coffee."

"And some of our special little butter rolls, with a double order of butter and honey, sir," Bartholomew contributed proudly. "Miss Conova had a wonderful appetite, sir. Ate as if she were half starved, the poor lady! To see her eat and enjoy it one would never dream that her poor head was full of plans for self-destruction, sir. Though they do say that a condemned man always eats a hearty breakfast—"

"How was Miss Patton's appetite, Bartholomew?"

"Her *appetite* was too good, as she said to me," the waiter told Dundee. "She's on what they call the Hollywood diet—an eighteen day diet, I believe, sir, to reduce. She had nothing but lean lamb chops, sliced pineapple and black coffee. Miss Conova said she sympathized with her, and advised her to try her own reducing diet. But she didn't say what that diet was, sir—in my presence, at least."

"And dinner?" Dundee prompted, his eyes running over the crowded meal check.

"Miss Conova ate nearly every crumb of the dishes she ordered, sir," the waiter assured him with melancholy pleasure. "Turtle soup, blue points on the half shell, a lovely little pair of broiled squabs, baked Idaho potato, French peas, romaine and water cress salad with celery hearts, ripe olives, and two pieces of French pastry. *With* a pot of coffee and a whole pitcher of cream, sir."

"Amazing!" commented Dundee, who was beginning to feel hungry. "And Miss Patton?"

The waiter's solemn lips twitched. "Lamb chop and pineapple, sir. She didn't seem very happy about it."

Dundee grinned. "Can't blame her." But to himself he said: "Ah! At last! A brand-new motive for murder! Would-be movie actress, fighting plumpness, on starvation diet, driven to homicidal fury by sight of successful star tucking in a man-sized banquet without even troubling to count her calories—for which an adding machine would be required, incidentally. Well, murder has been done for less valid excuses, I'll bet."

Aloud, to the waiter, he said "Did Miss Conova and Miss Patton lunch and dine together? That is, did you set up one table only?"

"Two tables, sir, adjoining each other. Mr. Risher and Mr. Weinberg had their waiter serve them in here. The whole party ate together."

"Did the two girls seem to like each other, to be on friendly, companionable terms?" Dundee asked, and experienced, not the first time in his career as a detective, a pang of distaste for his job.

"Oh, yes, indeed, sir!" Bartholomew was enthusiastic "Miss Conova had a wonderful way with her. She treated Miss Patton exactly as if she was her equal. You wouldn't have dreamed she was a world-famous movie star. Not a bit spoiled or high-hat, sir. And so appreciative of everything I did, and that Miss Patton or anyone else did for her—"

"Just what did Miss Patton have to do for her?" Dundee asked.

"Nothing much, sir, but little attentions, that Miss Conova didn't really seem to expect," Bartholomew answered. "Oh, yes! There *was* something special. She fixed a dose of medicine for Miss Conova, both at lunchtime and dinnertime. Drops of some clear liquid in a glass of water, to be drunk through a glass tube, sir. Miss Conova thanked her pretty and sweet—and then forgot all about the medicine, or pretended to. At any rate, she switched the glass tube from the glass of medicine to her glass of plain water and drank it, leaving the medicine untouched. I took a sip of the medicine, and it wasn't bad at all—just awfully sour, like unsweetened lemon juice. I fancy Miss Patton fussed over her quite a bit, making her do this and that for her health's sake, and worrying for fear she couldn't digest some of the meats she ordered. But little Miss Conova stood for it like a lamb, not wanting to hurt a kind, thoughtful person's feelings. A rare girl, sir. Not to mention a great actress. Her death is the world's loss, sir. Miss Conova was always a prime favorite of mine, sir; but not until I met her in person did I actually fall in love with her. Not meaning any disrespect, sir!" the waiter caught himself up hastily.

"But high and low, all movie patrons feel as if their favorites belong to them, sir, and as if it's no disrespect to fall in love with them."

And Dundee answered, in all seriousness: "You're right, Bartholomew. I'm sure Miss Conova would be enormously pleased to know that you are in love with her."

"You mean *was* in love with her, sir," the waiter corrected sadly. "You spoke as if she were still alive, sir."

"So I did. A slip of the tongue, Bartholomew," Dundee admitted.

"Anything else, sir?"

"No, and thank you, Bartholomew. . . . But wait! You say you served all four members of the party at both lunch and dinner. Were all four of your guests in good spirits?"

The waiter considered solemnly, his head on one side. Then: "All very jolly and friendly on the surface, sir. In fact, Miss Conova and Mr. Risher, the handsome young gentleman actor, were as gay and excited and happy as honeymooners. And Miss Patton seemed delighted with their high spirits, though she was quieter herself. But Mr. Weinberg—well, he was jolly and loud and affectionate to everyone, but he hardly ate a mouthful, and he was so nervous he kept dropping his fork. Once he spilled a glass of water, and—"

Dundee interrupted: "Had anything happened to cause him extra nervousness just then?"

"He was looking at Mr. Risher, and Mr. Risher was looking at Miss Conova, like he fairly worshiped her and didn't care if the whole world knew it," the waiter answered "I understand that Miss Conova was married, and that her husband was actually on the way here at that very, moment. When I read in the extras this morning about Mr. Arundel being here and trying to see her last night, to no avail," the waiter continued, "I said to myself that someone had tipped Mr. Arundel off about Mr. Risher and Miss Conova, though I'd wager my last penny, sir, that there was nothing immoral between those two young people—"

"Thank you, Bartholomew," Dundee interrupted curtly. "And don't talk for publication. The reporters will probably swarm all over you, but keep your mouth shut. And don't waste your time putting two and two together to make a dozen."

But when the waiter had gone, a bit richer than when he had come in, the special investigator, feeling like a man in a nightmare of trying to catch a train and never being able to get off, took time to cram into one of Yola Conova's suitcases a few of the garments from the dresser drawers and closet hangers, and shoes. A few samples, as it were. It would be dangerous, he decided, to leave what might eventually be evidence of the utmost importance in a court of law. The black patent leather pumps, size four B, and the red leather bedroom slippers, size five, were joined in the suitcase by an elegant assortment of shoes, size three and a half A.

As he was about to close the case on all the footwear it would hold, Dundee's trained eye flashed a stop signal to his brain. He obeyed that signal, and sat back on his haunches to study his loot. Ah! There it was! The "something wrong"—the "something" that didn't fit in. Two slippers that made a pair, but which didn't quite match! They were boudoir slippers, both of black satin, but one was trimmed with a narrow piping of silver kid and a silver bowknot buckle, while the other was finished in the same way in *gold* kid. Of course, he told himself impatiently, he had simply mixed the two pairs, and was about to snap the case shut. But that stop signal in his brain was still flashing. There was nothing for it but to dump out all the shoes, and to try, with those remaining in the closet, to match these two little strays with their true mates.

But that, it seemed, could not be done. There were no other slippers trimmed with silver kid or gold kid. Suddenly Dundee gave a whoop of uncontrollable exultation. Bless these little shoes! "Little Goody Two Shoes," indeed! For they spoke volumes. But in speaking they were only crying out the same message that he would have heard minutes ago, if he had not been in such a tearing hurry; if he had not been overwhelmed by his amazing discovery.

So great was his relief now that he knew why he had so dreaded the thought of considering that terrific discovery from every angle. Well, the one thing he had most feared to learn was obviously not true. These blessed shoes proved that. And other things backed them up. That dresser drawer, for instance, that held such a strangely meager supply of nightgowns and pajamas. And that other apparently odd inadequacy of wardrobe. But not odd now—not strange at all that there was only one negligee, foolishly elaborate and impractical; only one "housecoat"—and that of ivory white satin. No warm, comfortable, practical dressing gown. No bathrobe. No ever-useful lounging pajamas in which a girl could really relax. None of these necessities. And hooray for their absence! For now—he exulted—he was sure that *only one murder had been committed!*

But although he was sure of that now—just as sure in his own mind as he was of that other amazing truth—and although he was more eager than ever to join Strawn in a third-degree of Dink Garnet, the district attorney's special investigator conscientiously took time to find the answer to the one question both Strawn and Sanderson were sure to ask.

It was Dr. Wayne, resident physician of the Hamilton Hotel, who opened the door of the sick girl's room. The two men had met before. They shook hands cordially, but the doctor's manner was grave, even worried.

"I hope you haven't come to bother my patient with a lot of questions, Dundee," he said, in a falsely cheerful voice. "I've given this young lady a good stiff bromide and I want her to get some sleep."

"I shan't upset her, I promise you," Dundee answered, and stepped to the bed.

The girl's breath was coming in quick gasps, and her eyes looked alarmingly heavy, but whether with the stupor of fever or the effects of the bromide, the detective could not tell.

"What size shoe do you wear, Miss Patton?" he asked matter-of-factly.

The blue eyes flew open. "What size shoe?" she repeated. "Why, I wear a six B. Before I took up nursing I wore a five A, but being on my feet so much—"

"Yes, yes," Dundee interrupted. "I just wondered if by accident any of Miss Conova's shoes became mixed with yours, as could have happened if you had worn about the same size. There's a pair of her boudoir slippers missing—"

The sick girl smiled. "I'm flattered that you thought I was a Cinderella, too," she confessed. "And please don't think I'm being catty when I say that Miss Conova was not quite as much a Cinderella as she used to be. Most of her shoes were a size too small for her, and she suffered tortures with a corn. Sometimes she was actually lame, her feet hurt so badly."

"Did she say why she persisted in wearing shoes that were too small?"

"Naturally I did not ask her such a question," the nurse said, the charm and gaiety fading from her face. "I knew my—place," she told him, pausing before that last bitter word. "I suppose she kept on wearing the size that used to fit her because she had been so widely publicized as Hollywood's genuine Cinderella, and to have changed to a larger size would have caused a flood of jokes like the ones they make on Garbo for her big feet. You may look in my closet and luggage, if you think I may have taken the missing slippers—*by accident*. Or that I may have accidentally taken other valuables from a dead woman who was my friend. Captain Strawn has already searched everything I own for Miss Conova's checkbook, which I certainly never saw, if she had one."

"I'm sorry," Dundee said gently, but he went through the sick girl's meager possessions—a fruitless search, as he had known it would be.

The doctor followed him from the room, in obedience to a nod from the detective.

"Is she in any danger, doctor?"

"My dear chap, a severe bronchitis is always potentially very dangerous," Dr. Wayne told him. "However, if her mind were at rest, and if she would submit to correct nursing and hospitalization—"

"Why does she refuse to go to a hospital? Money?"

"No. For the same reason she refuses a nurse, although Mr. Max Weinberg has told me to spare no expense. She contends, hysterically, that any member of her own profession would hold her in contempt as being responsible for the death of her patient. If she doesn't quit torturing herself I'll not answer for the consequences."

"I know. Poor girl," Dundee said in a troubled voice.

He was on the point of taking the doctor into his confidence. For he was forced to tell himself: "I could set the poor girl's mind at ease. If she knew that her patient had not committed suicide—" But then he shook himself into realism: "It would certainly be cold comfort to a nurse to know that her failure to guard her patient as she had been hired to do resulted in her being horribly murdered, rather than in death by choice."

Aloud he said to the doctor: "You may tell Miss Patton that Captain Strawn and I attach no blame to her whatsoever, so far as Miss Conova's suicide is concerned." But he was careful to give the word, suicide, no faintest underlining of emphasis.

And, again, he was on his way downstairs, his eager mind abandoning Louise Patton to her physician and to her tortured conscience, to leap ahead with an almost savage joy to the prospect of quizzing Madge Smith's former husband. For one ramification of the amazing truth about the dead girl vitally concerned that extremely unpleasant creature.

XIII

"WHAT AM I CHARGED WITH?" Garnet was shouting hoarsely at Captain Strawn as Dundee entered the parlor of Suite 2-A temporary headquarters for the homicide squad and the special investigator. "That's all I want to know, see? What am I charged with?"

"Good work, Miss Loring," Dundee congratulated the girl, who held an enormous scrapbook across her knees. "May I see?"

"Are you all deef?" the ignored man screamed. "What am I charged with? I got my rights—"

"I don't like your hat," Dundee said softly, and plucked the offending green velours object from its owner's melon-shaped head. "Nor do I like your manners. Will you forgive him, Miss Loring? And I most emphatically do not like your cravat, Mr. Garnet. Orange, believe me, is not your color, Mr. Garnet. *Yellow*, yes, but not orange—"

"Cut it out!" the pool-hall proprietor snarled, his bluish lips curling back from long, stained teeth "I'm asking you for the last time—what am I charged with?"

"Oh, pardon!" Dundee bowed. "I thought I was clear. You are charged with having the most abominable taste in clothes, manners, and personal habits. Or perhaps you're letting your beard grow—"

The man's pale eyes blinked, then shifted. The hand that automatically went up to feel of his chin stubble trembled more than a little.

"You're nuts," he croaked, but his voice was almost feeble. "I didn't come here to be insulted, Mr. Dundee—"

"Come here?" Dundee repeated. "I was under the impression that you were brought here. All right, Garnet! Where were you last night and this morning until you went to keep your ten o'clock appointment at *The Sun*?

Don't bother to lie about being at home and in bed. You haven't had your clothes off all night, or if you have, you put the same shirt and tie back on, and you didn't shave—or bathe, if your face, neck and hands are fair evidence"

"None of your damned business where I was," Garnet blustered, but his thin, unwholesome cheeks had taken on a deeper tinge of gray. "What am I charged with?"

Dundee took from his pocket the warrant with which he had provided himself. "With nothing—so far," he answered curtly. "But if you insist upon being regularly charged, I can arrest you specifically upon this warrant, and book you on a charge of attempted blackmail and of malicious persecution. That is, if you insist. But if you want to answer a few questions without being officially charged—"

"Blackmail!" Dink Garnet exploded, then laughed unpleasantly. "That's rich, that is! That's one for the book, all right! Just wait till I tell *that* to the newspapers! If a man can't try to get an interview with the mother of his own son—"

"Oh!" Kay Loring gasped "Oh, you horrible liar!"

"Hush, Ginger!" Dundee commanded sternly. "Suppose you explain, that statement, Garnet."

"I'll do my talking to the newspapers if they can meet my price for the scoop of the year," Garnet retorted, reaching for his hat with pretended confidence "And I might as well tell you that I've already put the whole matter in the hands of a lawyer. My attorney," he elaborated pompously, "assures me that the law is on my side, and that I can't lose. I'm the boy's father, and I'm his natural guardian, now that his mother is dead. But what's a lot more important—"

"My! How you do run on!" Dundee marveled. "Maybe we'd better give him a sobriety test, Captain Strawn."

The grim old chief of the homicide squad spat out the remains of a toothpick which he had chewed thoroughly, and reached into his breast pocket for another.

"Didn't know you was a proud papa, Dink," he drawled. "Mighty sorry to hear that Bessie has passed away. Kinda sudden, wasn't it? She was looking right pert when I saw her a couple clays ago."

"You know damned well I'm not talking about Bessie!" the badgered man snarled. "I'm referring to my first wife, Yola Conova."

"Well, well! That *is* something for the newspapers!" Captain Strawn agreed admiringly. "Don't blame you for wanting to sell that news to the highest bidder. Colvin," he snapped at a member of his squad. "Fetch Arundel. Geoffrey Arundel," he added, turning back to Garnet. "A poor, misguided actor-feller that's laboring, under the delusion that he's the lawful, wedded widower of Yola Conova"

"Who said he wasn't?" Garnet retorted "I'm married again, too, ain't I? But I got proof that I was legally wedded to to— "

"To Yola Conova?" Dundee prompted softly. "A very pretty name."

"That was only her stage name, and you damn well know it," Garnet protested "When I courted her and married her she was using her own name, Madge Smith."

"Are you sure that *Smith* was the name your bride signed to the application for a marriage license?" Dundee asked, with a quick, warning glance that swung from Captain Strawn to Kay Loring.

To the detective's surprise, Garnet drew a packet of legal-looking papers from an inner breast pocket, separated them nonchalantly, and then proffered a marriage certificate.

"The justice of the peace that married us gave my wife a marriage certificate, as soon as the ceremony was over," Garnet explained, "but later I got a copy for myself, and here it is. You can see for yourself that my wife got married under the name of Madge Smith."

Something sly and guarded, as well as a little anxious, in the man's manner prompted Dundee to remind him sharply: "You evaded my question, Garnet. I asked, you if Smith was the name your bride signed to the application for a license."

Ugly spots of color suddenly appeared in Dink Garnet's cheeks

"She didn't sign the application," he admitted sullenly.

"Oh!" Dundee whistled softly. "You got the license yourself, as a big surprise for Miss Smith, I presume?"

The man swallowed convulsively, then gave a confidential leer. "Well, no, gents," he said. "Tell you the truth, the whole wedding was sort of a jumped-up affair. I got to admit I was kind of a gay dog when I was younger, no better than the next one where a pretty, *willing* girl was concerned—"

In spite of herself, Kay Loring took a step forward, small fists clenched, her brown eyes blazing out of a deathly white face. Garnet grinned. "I told you this girl could vouch for the fact that the dead woman is Madge Smith, and was once my wife."

"You're jumping to a rather absurd conclusion, Garnet," Dundee assured him contemptuously. "Miss Loring realized last night that you thought Yola Conova was Madge Smith, or rather that she had once been known here as Madge Smith. She told me that a number of Hamilton citizens might make the same error. You see, Garnet, I was all for pulling you in last night on a charge of—well, let's say 'mashing,' which happens to be rather a serious offense in Hamilton, but Miss. Loring told me all about Madge Smith, of whom she was extremely fond, by the way, and I concluded that you might be honest in your mistake. Now I wish I had followed my impulse, before you could do any more harm—"

"What harm have I done?" Garnet retorted. Then, craftily: "If you mean to insinuate that Yola Conova committed suicide because of anything I said or did, then you're admitting that Yola Conova and Madge Smith Garnet were one and the same person."

Dundee's young face became suddenly, very hard and as grim as old Strawn's. "That was not what I had in mind, Garnet. Not exactly. But now," he resumed. "Let's get back to your 'jumped-up' wedding. I gather that neither you nor your bride applied in person for a marriage license; that, in fact, both of you were honor guests at a surprise party. Who got that license, Garnet?"

"None of your business!" the badgered man retorted.

"You might check on this by telephone, Captain Strawn," Dundee suggested, "but I feel confident that the name signed to the application was that of J. W. Kenyon."

Garnet's breath left his lungs in a sharp hiss. His lashless eyelids blinked rapidly. A trembling hand scraped the stubble on his chin. "Well, so what?" he blustered. "Old man Kenyon was looking out for the girl's best interests. She was working as a maid in his home, see? When he put her on the carpet and hammered away at her, she up and admitted that she was going to have a kid—my kid, see? So old man Kenyon hotfoots it down to the city hall and takes out a marriage license for us, and I—well, what the hell? I liked the girl well enough, was pretty and a good girl, too. I knew I was the first—"

"Shut up!" Dundee commanded harshly. "Yes? What is it?" he called, as the door opened a crack.

"Mr. Arundel, sir. Are you ready for him?" asked Colvin, without entering.

"Just a minute," Dundee decided. "Step into the bedroom with Mr. Arundel. We'll call you when we want him. Right, chief?"

"O.K.," Strawn agreed. "But get along with this business, boy. I don't know just what you're getting at, but—"

"I think Garnet knows," Dundee assured him, his narrowed blue eyes fixed with cold contempt upon the pool-hall proprietor. "Sir Galahad Garnet. The perfect knight!"

"You ain't got no right to get sarcastic!" Garnet protested. "I don't set myself up to be any better than the common run of men, but you know damned well that not every man will marry a girl after he gets her into trouble—"

"Maybe every man would, if he got paid well enough,' Dundee suggested "But we'll skip that for the moment I'm not interested just now in how much Mr. Kenyon gave you for a wedding present. What I should like to know is whether you have any proof, whatsoever that your one-time wife, Madge Smith Garnet, later gave, birth to a. son. My understanding is that your wife left you—and Hamilton—for parts unknown immediately after the ceremony."

"Not *immediately*." Garnet corrected him, significantly, "We spent our wedding night together in the bridal suite of the Hamilton Hotel—"

Captain Strawn snorted. "Kenyon wasn't taking any chances on the girl getting the marriage annulled, I reckon."

"Answer my question, Garnet," Dundee commanded sharply. "What proof, if any, have you that your wife gave birth to a child that lived?"

"Because I was later served with papers in a divorce suit brought by my wife, and in the papers she asked for custody of the child—*our* son."

Dundee's nostrils flared. "I see! Legally speaking, any child born to Madge Smith after she married you and before her divorce was your child, regardless of actual paternity. I take it for granted that you did not so love this child of your brief 'union' that you contested the divorce and asked for custody yourself?"

Garnet laughed. "Wasn't any need for that!" he crowed, "You see, Dundee, I'd already got a divorce myself, *and*—hold on to your hat, Mister Smart Guy! *I had already been awarded custody of the child myself. Any* child, male or female. Or twins, or triplets. In fact, of any or all offspring or progeny born to the said wife of the said plaintiff, during the existence of the said marriage— or words to that effect. Legal? Why, there wasn't a loophole in them papers big enough for a germ to crawl through!"

"Well, I'll be damned!" ejaculated Captain Strawn, and an unusual surge of emotion made him put a fatherly arm about the shoulders of the listening girl. Or perhaps he realized she needed the support of that arm rather badly.

"Was your wife served with those papers? Did she have a chance to contest?" Dundee demanded.

"Not in person. We couldn't locate her," Garnet admitted. "But she was served legally—through advertising in a dozen big cities, at least. More than the law requires. Don't worry! Them divorce and child-custody papers are all in perfect order. I used the same lawyer as my old friend, Kenyon, always used. A high-priced man, but he knows his business inside out. As full of legal tricks as a dog of fleas. You know him, I guess," he added nonchalantly. "Apperson."

"Henry Bigelow Apperson," Kay Loring breathed, with awe and despair. Even Dundee looked somewhat crushed by the weight of the famous lawyer's reputation.

"Had a long powwow with my attorney this morning," Garnet continued; swaggering to the nearest ashtray to flick the ash from the first cigarette he had dared to light. "We had another laugh over how funny it was for Madge to sue me for divorce and custody of the boy when I already had a divorce and legal custody."

"Very funny," Dundee almost snarled. "Funny as an advanced case of leprosy. By the way, where was Madge living when she sued for divorce?"

"Chicago."

"The name of the child appeared in the papers with which you were served, of course," Dundee said. "What name had she given him?"

He had to ask the question, but he could not look at Kay Loring as he waited for Garnet to answer.

"What if she didn't name him after me?" Garnet blustered. "That don't prove nothing. Nikolai was the

name in the divorce papers. That's Polack or Bohunk for
Nicholas, I guess."

"I suppose you immediately journeyed to Chicago to
find and claim the child whose custody the court had
previously awarded you?"

The man's pale eyes blinked and shifted. "I wasn't in
no shape then to do right by the boy, not being married
again yet. Besides I figgered it wouldn't be right to take a
tiny baby away from its mother's breast."

"What the hell did you want to get the court to award
you custody for, anyway?" Strawn roared.

"That's not hard to guess, Captain." Dundee relieved
the witness of answering mendaciously. "J. W. Kenyon
was bossing the show and was taking no chances on
anyone's blackmailing him or his son Bruce. I imagine
Garnet's publicly avowed paternity—by way of the
divorce and custody suits—was part of the original
bargain."

"I don't know what you're talking about," Garnet
protested sullenly.

"I think you do!" contradicted Strawn.

"Aw, let up on me!" Garnet cried with futile anger. "I
was awarded custody of my son nine years ago, and all
the whys and wherefores don't cut no ice now. Apperson
says there ain't a judge in the world can find a loophole in
my case against the Conova estate."

"'Conova?'" Dundee repeated. "There you go again! I
may be stupid, chief," and he turned to Strawn with a
deprecating shrug, "but I fail utterly to see that this—this
person has established any connection whatsoever—
legally speaking, since he's so fond of the law—between
Yola Conova and his former wife, Madge Smith Garnet."

Strawn took his cue promptly. "Plainly a case of
mistaken identity," he grunted. Then: "By the way, Dink,
if you honestly thought Miss Conova was your former
wife, and the mother of your dear little son, whose
custody you were legally entitled to, did you make any

effort—up until yesterday—to communicate with Miss Conova and to get hold of your son?"

The man's, pale eyes blazed with sudden fury. "You bet your bottom dollar I did I wrote her time and again, when she first started in pictures about eight years ago. She didn't answer, but finally she sicked a lawyer onto me; and like the fool I was, I let him bluff me out of my legal rights. He threatened Federal action, because he said I was using the U.S. mails in an attempt to extort moneys. And of course I wasn't certain in my own mind that Yola was Madge. Nobody else was, either. Bruce Kenyon hooted at the very idea that the screen star was Madge, and so did the old folks—the Kenyons, I mean. The joke on me is that I was all set to go to Hollywood and have a showdown with her in person, when I got interested in Bessie—that's my present wife, and she threw a duck fit when I told her my plans. Jealous. But soon as I laid eyes on Yola Conova yesterday, at the depot, I knew I'd been made a monkey of, and I swore to myself that I'd—I'd—"

"That you'd get even with her for tricking you out of a nice little fortune all these years?" Strawn interrupted with mock softness.

Garnet swallowed twice before answering. "I didn't give a whoop about getting even," he said finally. "All I wanted yesterday and all I want today is my rights. I want that son of mine, and I aim to have him. My lawyer's getting the papers drawn up to serve on Arundel, or whoever's the executor of the estate."

"You haven't wasted any time, have you?" Dundee asked contemptuously. "But let me remind, you again, Garnet, that you have advanced no proof, whatever that your former wife and Yola Conova were one and the same person."

"Proof, hell!" the harassed man exploded "I recognized her, I tell you, and she recognized me. But it wasn't only me that recognized her. Bruce Kenyon and Helen Kenyon knew her the minute they clapped eyes on her, and so did

that pair of old schoolmarm fossils, the Martins. Just ask
'em!"

"*Proof*, Garnet? Legal proof?" Dundee persisted.

"I got you as a witness," the man reminded him
triumphantly. "You and this Loring girl. You both seen us
together last night. At the stage entrance of the theater.
Yola Conova, as she was calling herself, was scared
nearly to death at the sight of me, and you know it. But
did she call the cops to have me pinched for annoying
her? I'll say she didn't!"

"No," Dundee said, very softly. "No, she didn't ask for
help, and—she died a few hours later. No, no! I'm not
accusing you of anything, Garnet. Not yet. But since you
made absolutely sure of recognizing your former wife in
Yola Conova, I think you'd better tell us just how you
convinced yourself. Did you find a telltale scar on her
right arm? Or a strawberry birthmark? Or a beauty spot
mole?"

"She didn't have no scar or birthmarks," Garnet
admitted "But there was a cross mark on the inside of her
right arm, just below the bend of the elbow joint, made by
a couple of prominent blue veins. First time I ever saw
Madge I noticed that funny cross mark, like the letter X—
"

"Where and when did you first meet her?" Strawn
interrupted.

"At a parochial dance," Garnet answered "Me and
Madge belonged to the same church—St. Joseph's. I'm
free to confess I don't make a practice of attending
regular, like I ought. But I go to Mass twice a year at
least, and when I was single I used to go to some of the
block parties and charity bazaars and dances. Father
Sheehan introduced me to Madge, when I asked him to.
We danced together, and I noticed the odd cross mark her
veins made. For a joke, I called her 'Madame X'—"

"When did you meet her?" Strawn repeated
impatiently.

"Lemme see. . . . I don't keep no diary, worse luck. The papers'd eat it up now, wouldn't they?" Garnet bared his yellow, horsy teeth. "But, it was the fall of the year—just about this time ten years ago. Oh, I remember now! It was a masquerade party, for Hallowe'en. Yes, sir! We met in the fall and married in the spring. On May tenth. Not a long courtship, but just a little too long, if you're particular about such things. But better late than never—"

"Have you any other so-called proof?" Dundee interrupted coldly.

"'So-called proof'?" repeated Garnet angrily. "I can produce a dozen witnesses to that blue cross of prominent veins on her right arm—"

"Don't bother," Dundee advised curtly. "I can assure you, Garnet, that the right arm of the woman who lies dead in the Hamilton morgue, the woman who has been identified by Geoffrey Arundel as his wife, Yola Conova, has no such blue cross visible upon it."

Garnet's grin froze against his yellow teeth "You're lying!" He he shouted. "You've been got at! You've been bribed! But you can't trick me! It was there last night. I seen it, I tell you! I seen it with my own two eyes! You was there, and you!" and he whirled upon Kay Loring. "Both of you, seen me push back her fur coat and look for it! And there it was, I tell you! I'll have the law on you, if you've been mutilating a corpse to destroy evidence—"

Dundee remained imperturbable. If he had not loathed the man so thoroughly he would have been enjoying himself. "It is quite possible that Miss Conova had a pair of veins in her forearm that crossed to form an X. It is also equally possible that your former wife, Madge Smith Garnet, had a somewhat similar pattern of veins. All of us have veins that cross to form odd and interesting patterns, quite noticeable when our veins are strutted with blood. But just now, Garnet, let me advise you of a very elementary fact: *there is no blood pressure in the veins of a corpse!* If, as you say, you *saw* a pair of prominent crossed veins on the right arm of Yola Conova last night, no one, I assure you, will ever see them again."

Garnet began to tremble violently. "I'll demand an autopsy!" he cried jerkily. "I won't be tricked again, I tell you! I'll fight—"

"And so, I imagine, will Yola Conova's husband," Dundee cut in. "With possibly more money than you can muster. Not being a cook, Garnet, you've probably never read that ancient recipe for rabbit pie, which begins, sensibly enough, 'First catch your rabbit.' . . . I mean to say, the child you love so deeply that you will fight for him—and his share of the Conova estate—may no longer be alive."

"He's alive, all right!" Garnet answered triumphantly. "She admitted as much last night. Not that she meant to let the cat out of the bag, but I guess I caught her off-guard—"

"Alive!" Kay Loring did not speak or even whisper the word, but Dundee saw her pale lips form it. And in her suddenly wide but unseeing eyes the young detective read a strange conflict—of horror and pity, repulsion and fascination, hatred and love.

He felt sorry for her. And angry with himself. For it was he who, in line of duty, had opened her eyes to the possibility, or rather the extreme probability, that her own father had been desperately in love with the girl who had become known in Hamilton as Madge Smith. Now, in facing the possibility that Madge Smith's child, born in unholy wedlock as the son of this obscene creature before them, was really Christopher Loring's son, and hence her own half brother, Kay Loring was obviously passing through a personal hell. Dundee felt tears of pity for her sting his eyelids. Life had chosen a cruel way to force her to grow up.

Dundee wrenched his eyes away from the girl, who had not been aware of him at all. Strawn had already pounced upon Garnet.

"When and where did you see Miss Conova last night, Dink? We've had enough beating around the bush. Spill it!"

"O.K.," Garnet agreed, almost conciliatingly. "I ain't got nothing to hide nor to be ashamed of. You found me trying to slip the dope to the newspapers, didn't you? It ain't my fault if she got panicky and bumped herself off. I didn't make no threats nor nothing; just demanded my rights—"

"Cut out the embroidery and get down to brass tacks, Garnet," Strawn ordered as ruthlessly as he mixed his metaphors.

"Just a moment, chief," Dundee apologized. "Did you make that demand for your 'rights,' as you put it, through the attorney who had procured custody of the child for you?"

Garnet was nonplussed for a moment, then managed to look virtuously indignant. "You don't think I wanted to make things tough for her, do you? Legal action would've meant a smear of bad publicity, and no matter if she had cheated me out of my boy all these years I didn't want to gum up her career for her—"

"Nor her income," Dundee cut in. "I think we understand quite thoroughly, Garnet, why you didn't go to your lawyer until you knew that the girl was dead, and that legal action was your last hope of cashing in. But I must admit that I'm surprised at Apperson's taking your absurd case against the Conova estate."

Garnet grinned. "He took it, all right! Jumped at it, as a matter of fact. Took it on a contingency basis. I didn't have to put up a red cent of retainer fee. You see, Apperson was at the theater last night, too. Says he recognized Madge the minute she stepped out on the stage 'in person'—"

"Was he acquainted with this Madge Smith you're talking about?" Strawn wanted to know, phrasing his question with elephantine adroitness.

"I'll say he was! Old Kenyon had him at the girl hammer and tongs for a couple of weeks, trying to get her to tell who the daddy of her kid was—"

It was Kay Loring who interrupted then, her voice high and shrill with emotion that threatened to become hysterical.

"But she wouldn't tell, would she? She never told! Never!"

Garnet shot her a look of complete understanding— and hatred. Perhaps, after all, thought Dundee, this foul creature had been infatuated with Madge Smith himself, had wished futilely and jealously for a chance to father a child of hers, had nursed all these years a corroding hatred of that unnamed man.

"No, she never told," he was admitting now. Then, with a quick resumption of his servile nonchalance: "She was a good little kid—a square shooter. She'd stepped out of bounds and she was willing to take the consequences. But when word got around to me that the kid was in bad trouble, and that she wouldn't name the man, and that old Kenyon was scared to death it was his son Bruce, I stepped forward and took the blame like a man—"

"That'll be enough of that tripe, Dink," Strawn said, and spat out the remains of the second toothpick. "Let's get back on the track, if there is one. I take it that you made your demands on Miss Conova in person. When and where did this interview take place?"

"On the telephone," Garnet answered sullenly. "I called from my own private 'phone in my office over the pool hall. I had to call three times before I got Madge herself. First two times some other female answered the 'phone—that blondined broad that was traveling with her, I guess. Upstage as hell, she was. You'd have thought *she* was the movie star, instead of my wife—my *ex-wife*, I mean. Of course I wouldn't give my name or state my business; I figgered if I tried long enough I'd get hold of Madge herself. And sure enough I did. Must've been between half past twelve and a quarter to one. I recognized her voice as soon as she said hello. And I'd swear she knew who I was, soon as I spoke. Got panicky. Tried to pretend she was the other dame. Said, 'I'm sorry, but Miss Conova has retired. This is her secretary speaking. May I take a message?"

"You're giving a very painful performance, Garnet," Dundee commented. "I'm sure we'd all be grateful if you did not try to imitate Miss Conova's voice."

"So you fell for her, too, did you?" Garnet leered, then retreated, with the agility of an alley cat, before the swift menace of the detective's clenched fist. "Keep your shirt on, mister!" he pleaded. "I didn't mean no harm. Well, I was afraid Madge'd hang up on me, so I put the heat on instanter. Without beatin' around the mulberry bush, I says, 'Listen, Madge! Don't pull that line on *me*! I know you—and you know me,' I says. 'But you ain't got no call to be afraid of me, Madge,' I says. 'All I want,' I says, 'is my legal rights. I want my son., The courts awarded me custody of the boy when I divorced you, and now you got to hand the boy over, or I'll take him by law,' I says. Well, she knew there wasn't no use stalling, and she didn't try. She just said—My God, it gives me the cold shivers to repeat it now, after what's happened—"

"What's the pay-off, Garnet?" Strawn cut into the melodramatic recital. "What do you claim Miss Conova said?"

"She said," Garnet began again, and again he hesitated. The silence was absolute after Kay Loring had caught her breath with a quick sharp gasp. "I swear I'm not making this up," the man continued, his stubbled cheeks very pale now. "After I said I'd take the boy by law, if I had to, she said—" and his voice dropped to a whisper that seemed loud in the otherwise silent room,"— '*Over my dead body!*'"

Across the deep hush that followed those horridly prophetic words fell the unmistakable sound of a human body toppling to the floor.

XIV

DUNDEE PLUNGED ACROSS THE PARLOR of the hotel suite which he and Strawn were using as headquarters for their investigation into the death of Yola Conova. As he had suspected, the door into the bedroom was slightly ajar. He thrust it wide and knelt beside the blue-lipped body on the bedroom floor.

"Gosh, Mr. Dundee!" Detective Colvin was terror-stricken. "He ain't dead, is he? We could both hear every word that was said, that door being open a crack, and I didn't see how it was affecting this bird—this gentleman, I mean, until he folded up on me—"

"Who opened this door?" Captain Strawn roared. "By criminy, I'll break the flatfoot that—"

Colvin was getting hold of himself. He dared the wrath of his chief by making an explanation of his apparent crime of eavesdropping. "It was open when I brought Mr. Arundel in here, from the hall, like Mr. Dundee told me. I figgered you and Mr. Dundee opened it a-purpose, so's Mr. Arundel could hear without being seen, or something like that. Is he dead, Mr. Dundee? He sure looks it."

"A bad fainting spell is all, I think," the special investigator answered. "Got your emergency flask with you, Brede?" he called to the stenographic member of the squad. "Fine! Careful! Keep his head down. You're spilling most of that, Brede. Give it to me. There! He's coming 'round already. Don't crowd, fellows. How about a window? You're all right, Arundel. Take it easy. What's that?" and he bent his head close to the bluish lips that were moving slightly. "Strychnine? Oh, I see. In your vest pocket, eh?"

He found the little flat glass phial, with its skull and crossbones label, and rolled one of the tiny pellets into the palm of his hand.

"Water? Thanks, Ginger! One tablet enough, old man?"

"Quite!" Geoffrey Arundel whispered weakly, and over his recumbent body Dundee and Kay Loring exchanged a rather rueful smile. A bit shamefaced, perhaps, on Dundee's part. For no matter how much you dislike a person, if you are playing the Good Samaritan for his benefit when he is helpless, you feel a bit proprietary, even kindly.

"You keep this stuff on hand all the time, do you?" Dundee asked, returning the bottle of strychnine tablets to the actor's vest pocket.

"Right you are," Arundel answered, with feeble jauntiness. "The good old pump has a habit of giving out on me. Nothing organically wrong, the doctors say. Just a bit on the tired side. Strychnine three times a day keeps it chugging away in fair shape, unless an extra burden is put upon it. Sorry to be a blasted nuisance while you're so busy—"

"Don't apologize," Dundee stopped him brusquely. "I'm afraid it's the other way 'round. I mean, I'm afraid we owe you an apology. You were not meant to hear that fellow's charges against Miss Conova—"

"Your arm, please." The reviving man struggled to his feet. "I'm sure I shall find a chair more comfortable than the floor.

"Thank you. I admit that the shock was a severe one, but it was better that I know as soon as you did what that—that unspeakable person had to say."

Now that Arundel was looking almost normal, except for extreme pallor, and now that he was sitting quite at his ease in a very comfortable chair, Dundee was returning to normal too. He did not now feel at all kindly toward the husband of Yola Conova.

There was no time to waste in cursing the bad luck or the carelessness which had resulted in that door's not being quite closed. Dundee had counted enormously on what he might learn from Arundel's face—from minute and uncontrollable facial and blood vessel reactions—as the actor-husband heard Garnet's accusation. He had expected, at the very least, to be able to form a definite opinion, watching Arundel's face intently, as to whether the actor knew the truth—that astounding secret which the dead woman's clothes had told him. If Arundel knew—.

Dundee shook his head slightly, as if to clear it of a thousand swarming possibilities. He went to stand in front of Arundel, looming over the actor, dwarfing him, but he spoke with a soothing, sweet reasonableness.

"You use the word 'shock,' Arundel," he began, very slowly. "You say, in effect, that Dink Garnet's charges, which you overheard, were so 'shocking' to you that your heart couldn't stand the strain. Please! Let me make my point, sir. I assure you there is a point! The point is, Arundel, Garnet's charges that Yola Conova was the erstwhile Madge Smith, and his former wife, as well as the mother of his—son, legally speaking, did *not make you angry*."

A muscle in the actor's cheek had begun to twitch spasmodically, uncontrollably. Now he put trembling hands upon the arms of his chair and attempted feebly to hoist himself to his feet.

"Sit down, Arundel," Dundee commanded curtly. "We don't want you fainting again. I think it is a universally acknowledged fact that anger galvanizes even the weakest, tiredest muscles, Arundel. We speak of getting 'fighting mad' —never, never of being 'faint with anger.' Now, will you tell us why you were not angry at Garnet's charges? Was it perhaps because you knew them to be— true?"

The actor became, suddenly, an excellent proof of the detective's argument. He sprang to his feet, color flooded his pale face, his voice came strong and sharp:

"You fool! Are you blind as a bat? Or do you think I am? I fainted because I could not bear the realization that suddenly forced itself upon me. If you had a wife whom you adored, sir, how would the sudden news of her *murder* affect you?"

Dundee was utterly taken aback. So, obviously, were Captain Strawn and Kay Loring.

Arundel's gray eyes were almost black and very brilliant as he rushed on:

"For it was murder! Oh, I was fooled at first! That fiend was clever enough to take advantage of my poor darling's too well-known suicidal depression. How he must have congratulated himself! Everything played into his vile hands! But not only did he hang *her*! He's hanged himself! You gave him enough rope! Maybe you're not a complete fool, Dundee. Maybe you played the rope into his hands, knowing he would hang himself if you let him talk long enough. Look at him! There's guilt written all over him."

All eyes followed the actor's dramatically pointing forefinger, to focus on a momentarily stunned, open-mouthed Dink Garnet.

"She defied you, didn't she?" Arundel cried, in that curiously strong, vibrating voice. "My darling girl chose death rather than submit to blackmail. My brave girl—"

"Why, you—you—" Garnet was gasping, as he lunged toward the actor across half the length of the big parlor.

Captain Strawn stepped into his path and gripped him by both arms. Garnet struggled for a moment, then relaxed, with a shrug. An ugly smile settled, like a deformity, upon his features. "Pretty good show, eh, Cap? But did you notice he hasn't denied my 'charges,' as Dundee calls 'em? And why not? For a damned good reason! He knows they are true! But listen to me, you Broadway ham!" He turned with sudden snarling venom upon the actor. "You ain't gonna cheat me out of my share of the Conova estate, by pinning *murder* on me! Think you're pretty damned smart, don't you? But it takes more'n *your* say-so to turn suicide into murder. It ain't my fault if she was yellow, if she couldn't face the music, if she'd rather die than fork over—than give me the kid, I mean," he corrected himself.

Dundee was studying Arundel with more interest than he was giving Garnet. A greenish pallor had again spread over the actor's thin face. Again the man seemed about to faint, when normally—Dundee thought—his reaction should have been an upsurge of fighting anger. His gray eyes became bleak and almost colorless. His beautifully manicured right hand pressed hard against his chest, as if to support the tired muscles of his heart.

"The whole thing is quite clear now," he said slowly, in a shallow, tired voice. "I remember about you now. When we were engaged Yola told me that a crook or a nut—she didn't know then which you one were—had made a fantastic effort to blackmail her, on the grounds that she was his former wife and the mother of his son. We laughed at the episode. Every motion picture star has more than one 'double'—"

"Arundel," Dundee cut in, "can you say definitely, from *personal* knowledge, whether or not there is any truth in Garnet's contentions that Yola Conova and Madge Smith, once Madge Smith Garnet, were one and the same person?

As the detective posed his question he watched the actor intently. If Arundel was in on the amazing secret which Yola Conova's clothes had betrayed to Dundee, then he was indeed perched precariously upon the twin horns of dilemma. And the slightest accident might disturb his painful balance. If he was innocent of all knowledge of that secret, but not so innocent of the dead girl's murder—

Arundel's slow, shallow, tired voice interrupted the detective's dizzying whirl of conjecture. "Naturally," he

was saying, "I have no *personal* knowledge of Yola
Conova's life before I met her. But knowing my wife as I
do—or did—and having implicit faith in her, in every
sense of the word, I can only say that this man's charges
are utterly false."

"Yeah?" Garnet snarled. "Well, we'll let the court
decide that. I tell you, Dundee, I can bring a dozen
Hamilton citizens into court to testify that they
recognized Madge Smith in Yola Conova. And *she* knew
it! That's the reason she killed herself."

"You mean," Arundel interrupted bitterly, "that that's
the reason you killed her! Dead, she couldn't take the
stand and prove that all your witnesses were absurdly
mistaken And *you*, you—you—" he choked, "you vile toad,
could count on the love and grief of a bereaved husband to
dictate a settlement of your lying claims out of court."

Captain Strawn decided to take a hand. Out of almost
closed eyes he studied the actor shrewdly as he put his
question:

"What if Garnet's right about the girl, Arundel? What
becomes of your murder theory then?"

Arundel was very pale but his eyes were blazing.
"Very well!" he conceded, his voice again quick and
clipped. "Merely for the sake of argument, let us suppose
that Yola was once this man's wife, that a child was born
to her while they were legally married; that, last night,
when he reached her by telephone, she agreed to meet
him outside and talk the matter over with him.
Something my dear girl might very well have done," he
interrupted himself to interpolate, "if she had never seen
this deluded or criminal blackmailer before in her life. A
screen star cannot survive adverse publicity of the kind
which this creature could have brought upon her. Indeed,
I believe that this is the explanation of Yola's being out of
her room last night. All morning, since the dreadful news
of her suicide was broken to me, I have been horribly
grieved and puzzled by the means she chose. I told myself
that it was not like my wife—not like any screen star, to

choose to die in such a way as to destroy her beauty. Also, I told myself, Yola was a coward about pain. I could not visualize her as having the physical courage to fit a noose about her neck and leap from an icy bridge. She couldn't bear the cold," he added, and his voice broke for the first time. "She was like a—like a lizard," he explained, his eyes suddenly red with tears. "So quick and happy and alive in the sun; so—so—"

It was with considerable difficulty that Dundee kept himself from falling under the spell of that marvelously trained voice. But if it was the actor speaking and not the bereaved husband, how was it that Geoffrey Arundel had not become a sensational success on the stage?

"Baloney!" Garnet ejaculated, with profound disgust. If he was frightened at the turn events had taken, he was a better actor than Arundel, Dundee concluded. "It ain't so easy to commit suicide without mussing yourself up some. Especially when you're in the limelight all the time, and everybody's watching every least little thing you do. Besides, according to the newspapers, she'd tried poison a time or two and it hadn't worked. This time she wasn't taking no chances. You can't change your mind when you're dangling from the loose end of a rope."

Arundel drew himself up very straight, so that he seemed quite tall, and wrapped himself in a magnificent cloak of dignity. "Gentlemen," he began, bowing in the Continental fashion, first to Captain Strawn and then to Dundee, "I think I am well within my rights when I ask you to do your duty—to arrest this man. He is obviously, and by his own confession, vitally concerned in my wife's death. Whether he drove her to suicide with his cowardly blackmail scheme or whether he murdered her when that scheme failed and she promised to be worth more to him dead than alive—"

Captain Strawn raised a silencing hand. "Hold on, Arundel. I'd like to ask you a question. Did Garnet, so far as you know, make any effort to see you this morning after the news of Miss Conova's death was in the papers?"

The actor looked blank. "Why, why—no, not that I know of," he answered.

"On the contrary," Dundee pointed out, after waiting a long, courteous minute for Strawn to continue, "Garnet went to the newspaper office with his story."

Arundel's pale face became greenish white, and he swayed slightly. Obviously his heart was not quite equal to this new shock. Dundee, out of common decency, hastened to reassure him.

"Don't collapse again, Arundel," he said, not unkindly. "We picked Garnet up before he had a chance to spill his story. The point Captain Strawn and I should like to make is that Garnet, whatever his motives in demanding custody of the child who is legally his son, is apparently utterly sincere in his conviction that Yola Conova was once known as Madge Smith, and that as Madge Smith she became his wife—whether wife in name only is quite beside the point now. Garnet, in short, is so sure of his facts that he was willing to let a court pass upon them. Are you just as sure that Garnet is mistaken—that Yola Conova was never known as Madge Smith?"

The actor dropped his eyes to his trembling, moist hands, which were struggling to dry, themselves with a fine linen handkerchief. The muscle in his cheek twitched more violently than before.

After a nerve-racking length of time, during which the only sound was Kay Loring's sharply indrawn breath, Arundel raised his eyes and looked steadily at Dundee, with a sort of quiet despair.

Dundee waited, as breathless as Kay Loring. Was Arundel about to be wrecked forever, on one of the horns of his terrific dilemma—supposing that he was in a dilemma?

"I can't be sure," he said very quietly, with no emphasis upon any single word.

Dundee relaxed. Mentally, he shrugged his shoulders. Arundel, if indeed he had any guilty knowledge of that astounding secret of the dead woman's—a secret which, possibly, no one else in the world knew, except one person, had not impaled himself upon either horn of his dilemma. He was still safe, whatever conclusion Dundee might draw from his admission.

But Garnet was laughing, a brief, sardonic snort of unholy mirth; "Oh, yeah? Then why did you come all the way from New York to Hamilton, of all places? Sure he knew! At least, I'll bet my last dollar he knew that Yola Conova had bucked like a bronco against including Hamilton in her itinerary! I'll give you any odds you want that she tried to back out of the tour when she found she'd have to come to Hamilton. And she won't tell him why! That's it! So out he paddles to get the dope on her past. Everybody knows they was about to split up—"

"That's a damned lie!" Arundel cried hoarsely. "I came because my wife was not well, and I wanted to see personally just how she was standing the strain of the tour. The—nurse I had engaged to look after her had written me of the Tuesday incident—Yola's attempt to commit suicide by leaping from the balcony outside her room in their hotel in Chicago. Naturally I was terribly worried—"

"Scared simply to death that she'd make a go of her next suicide try and leave you a million cold smackers, eh?" Garnet sneered.

"Why, you—" Arundel gasped, and lunged toward the pool-hall proprietor.

"None of that, you two," Strawn ordered, as if he were speaking to a couple of the town's habitual drunk-and-disorderlies. "Now, Arundel, what about it? Did Miss Conova object to coming to Hamilton on the tour?"

The actor was again himself, apparently—coldly, superciliously dignified. "As a matter of fact, she did," he admitted readily enough "On her last day in New York she appealed to the president of World-Wide Pictures, to have Hamilton taken off the list of cities she was to visit. Feldman was not in an obliging mood; in fact, I'm afraid he took no pains to hide his impatience and displeasure with what seemed—to me as well as to him, I confess—to be a foolish caprice. The only reason she would give either Feldman or me was that she had dreamed a horrible dream of a catastrophe which had overtaken her in Hamilton. One can hardly blame Julius—Mr. Feldman, I mean, president of World-Wide Pictures—for not taking the matter seriously or sympathetically. I, however, knowing the condition of the poor child's nerves, and being, I must confess, rather superstitious myself, as most members of my profession are, I believe—Well, I had to come along and stand by, if she needed me—"

"And so here you are," Dundee took up the tale, as the actor's voice faltered and broke. "And superstition stands justified. Or does it? However . . . Arundel! Did your wife make that request of the picture magnate in person, or did you make it for her, as her—well, manager, shall we say?"

The actor's bleak eyes registered mild bewilderment. If he even dimly guessed the reason behind the detective's question he was far too much the master of himself to betray panic.

"I thought," he said icily, "that I made it quite clear that Yola herself made the request of Julius—of Feldman. He and Bertha—Mrs. Feldman—were dining with Yola and me, in our suite at the Savoy-Plaza. Because she was not well, Yola was seeing as few people as possible while in New York. It was a very quiet week—" Again his voice broke, and he closed his eyes for a moment. "I might add," he went on, "that my conviction that my wife needed a nurse—constant, intelligent, trained supervision and care—had come to a head that morning after she had told me of her dream. She was so hysterical, so morbidly sure that her dream would come true that I was frightened, frankly. I advertised, discreetly, for a nurse, and thought myself lucky to secure the services of a person apparently so suitable as the Patton woman," he concluded bitterly.

Dundee chose to ignore the actor's last words. "Did your wife tell you the details of her dream?"

Strawn snorted. "Criminetty, boy!" he expostulated. "What the devil difference does it make what she dreamt?"

"I think I understand the motive behind the question," Arundel took it upon himself to answer. "And I agree with you, Mr. Dundee, that if we knew the details of that most disturbing nightmare of my wife's, and that if we were psychiatrists competent to analyze them, we might arrive at the true reason for her—suicide, if it was suicide. Unfortunately, she did not tell me her dream. Nor did she tell Julius or Bertha Feldman. I remember, distinctly, that they both urged her to do so. Bertha—Mrs. Feldman—reminded her that a dream told *after* breakfast would never come true; that it would 'go by opposites;' that if she had dreamed of a disaster happening to her in Hamilton, she might be very sure that just the opposite would come true—a marvelous triumph, a colossal ovation," the actor concluded. And with only the most delicate suggestion of dialect and with almost imperceptible gestures he had brought into the prosaic room a large, kindly, matronly daughter of Israel.

"Aw, hell!" Garnet exploded. "I, for one, have got my bellyful! All this hooey about a dream! Naw, I won't shut up!" he snarled, as Strawn called his name warningly. "I got a right to speak my piece, same as this Broadway ham. Everything he's told you bears out my story, and you know it! Yola Conova don't dare come to Hamilton, so she makes up this phoney yarn about a nightmare. Arundel here smells a rat. He don't fall for the dream bluff, but he knows his dear little wifie would almost rather die than show up in Hamilton. When he gets here and she won't even let him see her for a minute—yeah, it was all in the papers, Arundel!—he knows damned well there's something rotten in Denmark. And he's had plenty of reasons to have his doubts about her before, more'n likely. You can't hide away a kid and support it without leaving a few traces for a jealous husband to pick up along your trail—"

"Right you are!" Arundel snapped, his words cutting across the angry pool-hall proprietor's tirade like the lash of a rawhide whip. "No wife could hide such a secret completely from a husband, a devoted husband who is with her almost constantly, and who is also her business manager. Since that is true, and since it is equally true that never during my entire life with Yola Conova did I stumble upon the slightest clue to such a secret—"

"Oh, yeah?" Garnet snarled. "You think you can brazen it out, now that she's dead and I can't put *her* on the stand when my custody suit is tried! A good thing my boy has a father left, to look after his interests! But you don't have to take *my* word for it that Yola Conova was Madge Smith Garnet! Why do you think your wife wouldn't see you last night? Because she had other plans, see? Because she had a date with a man she knew long before she ever heard of *you*! And make no mistake about this, Arundel, Dundee, Strawn!" he cried, pointing a shaking forefinger at each man in turn. "In keeping that particular date, Yola Conova might as well have signed a complete confession of her past in Hamilton."

It was Strawn who asked, in a matter-of-fact, impatient voice: "Did anybody witness her meeting with you, Garnet?"

"With *me*? Didn't I tell you she hung up the receiver on me?" Garnet was frankly contemptuous of Strawn. "But I had a damned good idea what she'd do, after she hung up. More'n likely she'd planned all along to see Bruce, but if she hadn't, I'll bet it didn't take her half a minute to decide he was the one man to help her—"

"Why?" Dundee demanded, silencing Arundel's sputtering.

Garnet flushed splotchily, and dropped his eyes. "Because he—well, hell, he's a smart young man, and rich, and knew her when she lived here, and it was his own daddy that helped her when she was in trouble," he floundered. "But regardless of why she wanted to see Bruce Kenyon or regardless of anything, her baby was born after she was legally married to me. The kid's my son legally, and any court will—"

"Yes, yes, Garnet. That point seems to be sufficiently clear. You've made it often enough," Dundee said. "Having been so noble as to take the blame for getting a servant girl into trouble; having been so saintlike as to marry her and give the child a legal name, you now intend to reap any additional financial reward that can possibly come your way. You know, Dink, you must find it heartbreaking—that you can't eat your cake and have it, too, I mean. You can't establish claim to Nikolai Garnet, and, at the same time, levy a tax upon Bruce Kenyon to keep his name out of the old scandal. Too bad! Now, how do you know that Miss Conova kept an appointment with Bruce Kenyon last night?"

"Because I saw 'em together," Garnet answered triumphantly. "Like I said, I figgered what she'd do—run to Bruce for help. And I was dead sure she wouldn't run the risk of having him call on her at the hotel at that time of night. I figgered she'd sneak out and make tracks for a meeting place somewhere, and it seemed to me the only logical place, the only safe place, was Bruce's office, down in the most deserted part of town after nightfall, like it is. But I wanted to get at her first, or join her and make her let me in on the conference with Bruce. I was willing to listen to reason—"

"Meaning you were willing to listen if money did the talking," Strawn cut in, and spat out another chewed toothpick.

"I wanted my rights," Garnet reiterated doggedly. "I— so I got into my car and drove over to the Randolph. I parked and strolled from one entrance to another, looking for her to come out. I figgered she'd bundle up—wear a veil, or try to disguise herself some way, and hop into a taxi she'd phoned to be ready for her. That's what I was prepared for. Somehow I hadn't counted on her taking out the rented car from the Randolph Garage. So I wasn't watching the alley, and she got past me, unless she'd already gone by the time I got there. Anyway—"

"Just a minute, Garnet," Dundee interrupted. "Did you see any member of the Conova party leave the hotel while you were watching for Miss Conova?"

Garnet shook his head. "There was a good deal of coming and going through the main entrance on State Street, but I didn't pay any attention to parties, or even couples, or, men alone, for that matter."

"What time did you arrive for your vigil?" Dundee wanted to know.

"A little before one o'clock," Garnet replied readily. "One reason I hung around as long as I did was that the lights were on in the rooms I knew she was occupying. I'd looked at the hotel register before I went to the theater, and saw that she was in Suite 4-B, along with the Patton woman. Pretending like I was just a movie fan, I went up to the fourth floor and had a look around. My old side-kick, Steve Branagan, was busy shooing the lovesick gals away from that Risher guy's door—down the hall from 4-B. Why, actually one fool girl had tried to bribe a chambermaid to let her hide under his bed—"

"Get along with your own story, Garnet," Strawn commanded sharply.

"O.K., O.K.," the man answered with mocking humility. "So the lights was on, as I could see from the sidewalk. The way I figgered, she was waiting for it to get late enough so's she wouldn't be in much danger of running into folks that might recognize her. Also, there was a chance Bruce had told her he'd have to wait until Helen was sound asleep before he could sneak out to meet his old sweetie. Anyway, it was dose on to a quarter to two when I give it up as a bad job, and started home. But just on an off-chance I decided to drive past the Kenyon produce house. More'n a block this side of it I seen that my luck was with me. There was lights on in the offices on the second floor—Bruce's private office as well as the general offices. Well, I parked my bus a block away and around the corner on a side street—Center Street. I was afraid the sound of a car drawing up to the Kenyon building might put Bruce and Yola on their guard. By this time it was so late that there wasn't a sound down in the wholesale district, except the rustle of papers blown along by the wind. In front of the Kenyon produce house there was a couple of cars parked—"

"A *couple* of cars?" Dundee repeated, with a quick glance toward Strawn, who was grinning in anticipation of saying "I told you so!" Although, as a matter of fact, the old detective had only scoffed mildly at the younger man's elaborate deductions in regard to the *three* cars which must have stood in that particular block after half past twelve when the streets had been washed.

"That's what I said," Garnet assured him, with rather resentful surprise. "Bruce Kenyon's dark-blue Lincoln cabriolet—everybody in town knows that custom-built job of his—and a black Cadillac sedan. I recognized the sedan as the one Yola Conova had left the theater in. At first I was scared to go near; afraid she'd got the chauffeur out of bed to drive her. Then I told myself it wasn't likely she'd do that; she'd not dare. So I walked on up to the building, silent as a cat on my rubber-heeled shoes."

"Just a moment, please, Garnet," Dundee interrupted again. "Was there any other car—across the street, say, or up or down the block a bit?"

"Not that I could see," Garnet told him positively. "And I had my eye peeled, you can bet. Well, I could see at a glance that there wasn't nobody in the sedan, or in Bruce's car, either, for that matter—"

Again Dundee interrupted, trying hard to keep all eagerness, all betraying tenseness out of his voice: "Did you take the trouble to search the cars thoroughly? That is, did you open the doors and look inside them?"

"No. Why should I? I give both the cars the once-over, and that was that. There wasn't nobody in either one of them. So, I was starting for the stairs, see, to go up and join the happy little reunion, when I heard voices and footsteps. Bruce's voice, and Madge's, though I couldn't hear what they were saying. Quick as lightning I ducked behind a big stack of empty crates piled up to the left of the doorway to the stairs. I could see and hear without being seen. And that suited my book for the moment. I figgered the more I got on her before she seen me the better I could play my cards, see?"

"Yes. I think we do," Dundee answered coldly.

Kay Loring was biting her nails in an agony of suspense, and Dundee could guess at the prayers that were whirling out of that red-crowned little head, prayers that her faith in her father might be given back to her.

Geoffrey Arundel had not moved a muscle for a long time, not since Garnet had begun his story of the Kenyon-Conova tryst. If he listened he gave no sign. His head was bowed wearily, to rest against the spread fingers of his right hand. And his face was so bleakly pale, so gray and ill-looking, that Dundee felt a pang of genuine pity for him.

"Well, they come on down the stairs and out onto the sidewalk," Garnet continued. "I could a-reached out and touched her. She was wearing a tweed coat and a kind of a tight red cap on her head. She didn't look a bit like no famous movie star, dressed plain and simple that way. And she didn't look hardly a day older than she did on our wedding day. There was a light at the foot of the stairs. I reckon Bruce had turned it on from upstairs, to light their way down. And when they come out on the sidewalk they didn't close the door behind them, so there they stood in the light, plain as you please. Of course they didn't dream anybody was looking on and listening—"

"Make it snappy, Garnet," Strawn cut in impatiently. "Leave off the trimmings. What did you hear and see?"

"I got a right to tell it my own way, ain't I?" the man protested. "The first words I could make out was Bruce saying, 'But dear girl, you *must* let me see that you get back to the hotel safely.' And she said it was too risky. Somebody might see 'em together. He said he'd just follow in his car, and keep her car in sight until she got back to the hotel. She agreed to that and Bruce helped her into the sedan, and then he stood talking a while, holding the door. I heard him say, 'Whatever you decide to do, Madge, you can count on me. You know that.' Yes, sir, he called her 'Madge' right out plain as day."

"What did she answer?" Dundee prompted impatiently, as Garnet paused for dramatic effect.

"She said, 'I'll never forget that,' and then he said, 'Of course, you'll divorce Arundel just as soon as possible.' And then—"

"Yola, Yola!" Geoffrey Arundel groaned, and hid his face completely behind trembling hands. And so tragic were the deep tones of the actor's voice as he pronounced that name that even Dink Garnet was moved.

"I'm sorry, mister," he apologized surprisingly.

"Get along with your story!" urged Strawn. "What did the lady answer?"

"Well, believe it or not, she laughed—kinda hysterical-like," Garnet obliged. "Then she said, 'That's impossible, Bruce! If you only knew *how* impossible!' Yes, sir, them was her very words! And take it from me, they handed me a jolt, the way she said it and all, after what the papers have been saying about her and Arundel—"

"We can do without your comments, Dink," Dundee interrupted coldly. "I suppose it was at this point that you made your presence known?"

"That was my intention," Garnet answered sulkily. "But just as I was going to step out a telephone started to ring. You could hear it plain, the night was so still. The wind had died down for a minute. Like I said, the door to the stairway was open, which made the sound come so plain, of course. Bruce says to Madge, 'That must be Helen. Wait! I'll be right back,' and then he went racing up the stairs. But before you could say Jack Robinson, Madge had the car moving. She'd started up the engine when she first got into the car, and it was all warmed up, see?

"Well, I was so took by surprise that I didn't know what to do. I figgered I didn't have a chance to catch up with the sedan by running after it, because Madge would speed up when she saw me in her rear vision mirror. Likewise, I didn't dare take a chance on crossing the street and making for my own car until she was far enough away not to notice me. She was heading the way she'd parked when she drove up to Bruce's place. Well, before the sedan had got a block away I heard Bruce throw open an upstairs window. I figgered he'd stepped to the window with the 'phone in his hand, and had seen her drive off. I heard him yell out, 'Hi, there! Wait!' but of course Madge couldn't hear him. I expected him to come tearing down to follow her, but he didn't; not just then. I reckon he thought if she was so all-fired set on him, not seeing her home he'd better let her have her way."

"Stick to the facts, Garnet!" Strawn ordered. "You're trying to say, as I understand it, that you stayed in hiding behind that stack of crates, with your head stuck out to see which way the woman was going. Did you keep your eyes on the car?"

Dundee knew what the old detective was getting at. That bumped tire. . . .

"Sure! Till I made up my mind to make a break for it. Looked like Bruce wasn't aiming to follow her. I figgered she'd turn off at Delaney Street and head toward the Randolph by that route, or that she'd make a U-turn and double on her tracks, and maybe wait for Bruce. But she passed Delaney Street and was still heading away from the Randolph —and toward Old Bridge. Though, of course, I didn't think about Old Bridge until I heard about what happened. I couldn't dope out what the heck she was up to, but it looked like she was going some place besides the Randolph, which was why, she hadn't wanted Bruce tagging her. All this passed like lightning through my mind. I knew if I wanted to talk to her I'd have to take a chance. So I left my hiding place and hugged the wall of the Kenyon building till I was clear to the corner—out of range from Bruce's office windows, if he was still on the lookout. Then I streaked across the street to where I'd parked my bus—"

"How far away from you was Miss Conova's car when you started out?" Dundee asked.

"Nearly three blocks, I guess But my boat's pretty fast and I thought I could swing around to Beacon Street and catch up with her," Garnet answered. "Well, I hopped into my car and stepped on the starter—*and*—" He paused o shrug dramatically. "No, go! No soup! Battery dead!"

Captain Strawn grinned at Dundee, as if to say, "So that's his story! I was wondering what kind of alibi he'd cook up!"

But his words to Garnet were: "Battery dead, eh? Now wasn't that just too bad! Battery dead!"

Garnet was furious, and apparently completely bewildered by the old detective's heavy-footed sarcasm. "What's the big idea?" he snarled. "I said my battery was dead, and it was dead. If you don't believe me, check with the garage—Jimmy Short's, First and Houston. I've got a rented battery in my car this minute—"

"You know how to crank a car, I suppose," Dundee suggested.

"That's what I tried to do," Garnet retorted sullenly. "Damned near broke my arm. Then I tried to roll the car till the motor started, but no go. The way I was parked on Center Street my bus was headed uphill, away from the river, see? Well, while I was trying to crank her up Bruce Kenyon drove off in his car—"

"Did you see him?" Strawn asked. "Or did he see you?"

"No," Garnet answered. "But it was so still I heard him when he started up his engine. I was scared he'd make a U-turn and see me, so I got into my car and laid low. But I guess he went along River Street till he hit Delaney and then turned off—"

"But you don't know which way he went, or even that it was his car that you heard, do you?" Dundee insisted.

"Not to swear to, no," Garnet admitted. "I laid low till I was sure the coast was clear, then I got out and begun to swing on that crank again. When the damned thing finally started I knowed it was too late to try to follow Madge. It must have been a full ten minutes by that time since she'd drove off. So I decided to call the whole thing off—"

"Which way did you go?" Strawn cut in.

"On up Center Street till I hit Maple," Garnet answered readily. "I never passed Old Bridge. If I had, I'd a-seen the sedan there, and I guess there ain't no doubt I'd a-stopped. That's one break I got! It wasn't me that found her! Whew! Course," he admitted, after mopping his forehead with a grimy handkerchief, "I might a-been in time to keep her from doing it—"

"Yeah?" Strawn's eyes were menacing slits. "Lucky's no name for you, Dink. Went right on home to Bessie, didn't you?"

"Sure I did! Sure!"

"Oh, no, you didn't!" Strawn contradicted. "We've checked that angle, Dink. Come clean!"

The man's sallow face reddened. "I spent the rest of the night with a—a friend. And there ain't no use asking me who, because I ain't telling, see? I ain't half as much afraid of a cop as I am of Bessie—and you can laugh all you damned please!"

But neither detective was laughing. It was Dundee who took swift advantage of the opening that Garnet had unwittingly given him. He had to act swiftly, for he could see that, in Strawn's opinion, the case was solved; that nothing remained but to arrest this unpleasant creature for the murder of Yola Conova. And, for many reasons, Dundee had to prevent that denouement—temporarily, at least.

"So you're afraid of Bessie, are you, Dink?" he said, and made a little clucking sound of mock sympathy that brought a ghost of a giggle from Kay Loring. "She isn't jealous, is she, Dink? . . . You know, Dink," he continued chummily, "I've observed that second wives are prone to be unreasonable about their husbands' first wives—and their husbands' children by their first wives. Now, I'm wondering, Dink, if you've thought of that angle."

"What are you getting at?" Garnet snarled, but he looked more disturbed than at any time during the long, inquisition.

"Oh I was just thinking," Dundee said sweetly, "that your Bessie may not be exactly overjoyed If you succeed in locating that *legal* son of yours, and bring him into your home—for her to take care of, and sacrifice for. Growing sons are expensive, I've heard. Hard on shoes; large appetites; schools and college to be paid for—"

"Sure it's expensive to raise a kid," Garnet agreed, but uneasily, for Dundee's tone was not one to inspire confidence. "That's why I'm gonna sue for a big slice of the Conova estate—in the kid's name, as his legal guardian, of course"

"And I don't blame you," Dundee almost purred. "I'm glad to see you have the boy's good at heart. Personally, I'm convinced that there really was a boy born to Madge Smith Garnet, and that you have legal custody—and all the *legal responsibilities* toward that boy, wherever he may be—"

He paused and the intense silence that followed was broken by a smothered cry from Kay Loring. Captain Strawn put an arm about her shoulders and whispered something which made her swallow her sobs and stare at Dundee with tear flooded brown eyes.

"Yes, Dink, I'm personally relieved that you are prepared to take your responsibilities as a father so seriously," Dundee continued. "For, to tell you the truth, I've been worried about that boy ever since you insisted on convincing us of his existence?'

"What do you mean—worried?" Garnet asked

"Why, simply this," Dundee began, raising his eyebrows and shrugging "The boy is going to need your help—your *financial* help, as well as the fatherly love and devotion and wise guidance that you are prepared—I trust—to give him. Of course—"

"*Financial* help? From *me*?" Garnet croaked. "His mother's estate—"

"Do you by any chance mean the estate of Yola Conova?" Dundee asked.

"Aw, what the hell!" Dink Garnet almost sobbed with anger. "You know damned well I mean the Yola Conova estate."

"I thought so," Dundee admitted, commiseratingly. "Mr. Arundel, will you be kind enough to forget, or to put aside for the moment, all your grief and your, very understandable, anger toward this man, and answer a few questions about the Conova estate?"

Geoffrey Arundel's face had again become as pale as tallow, and as expressionless. He bowed slightly.

"Thank you. Now, Mr. Arundel, if you had been asked yesterday or last week, let us say, to draw up an entirely truthful report upon the financial status of Yola Conova, would that report have shown her solvent or insolvent?"

The answering words scarcely stirred the actor's blue-gray lips: "She was insolvent. That is, her liabilities exceeded her actual tangible assets by a good many thousands of dollars."

"Then her *intangible* assets were all that kept her going, I presume," Dundee commented. "I mean, her potential earning capacity as a star—and credit which she had not yet exhausted. Right?"

"That is correct," Arundel told him stiffly. "I may add that many motion picture stars live far beyond their means. Few die leaving great estates—".

"Who gives a damn about what Yola had last week or last year?" Garnet cut in. "Everybody knows she had a million dollar insurance policy—"

"I'm afraid Garnet is in for a rude shock, Arundel," Dundee confided to the actor, almost chummily. "Will you tell him the unfortunate news about that million dollar insurance policy—or shall I?"

"News?" the actor repeated, eyes and face completely blank. "Unfortunate news? I don't understand—"

"Oh, my dear Mr. Arundel!" Dundee seemed to be bowed down with contrition 'I'm so sorry. Naturally I thought you knew. I thought that was the reason—the real reason—why you'd, come to Hamilton posthaste to see your wife. To get her to issue another check on the correct bank to keep the policy from lapsing—"

"Check? Policy—lapsing?" Arundel croaked.

"I'm so sorry," Dundee repeated. "You see, Mr. Arundel, Miss Conova inadvertently issued a check on the wrong bank to cover the premium on her million dollar policy."

The actor was swaying on his feet, when sudden anger—or hope—galvanized him.

"I don't believe you! It's a trick—some absurd police trick—"

Dundee took from the breast pocket of his coat an envelope, and from the envelope the worthless check and the insurance company's letter to which it was pinned.

"This arrived yesterday for Yola Conova," he explained curtly. "Mr. Risher has told us that he saw Miss Conova read this letter; that she put it together with this check—see? Quite a worthless check!—into an envelope addressed to you at the Friars' Club, New York—see? here's the envelope—and that she gave that envelope to him to mail; and that he forgot to mail it. Quite properly, he turned it over to us. No, there's no trick, Arundel. A glass of water for Mr. Arundel, Colvin! No trick at all, Mr. Arundel. But there is something that we don't quite understand. Since Miss Conova wrote her own checks, why did she attempt to pass this particular matter on to you? *Why didn't she herself write a check to cover, to keep that policy from lapsing?"*

The water came just a moment too late. For Geoffrey Arundel had escaped all questions by the simple expedient of fainting. And it took far more than a glass of water to bring him back again.

XV

CAPTAIN JOHN F. STRAWN and Special Investigator James F. Dundee were alone for the moment in the second bedroom of Suite 2-A. Kay Loring had been ordered, against her will, to take time off for lunch, and was, presumably, eating it somewhere as far as possible from the Randolph Hotel and its swarm of reporters.

"Whew!" Dundee whistled, and flopped upon one of the twin beds, from which an anxious hotel housekeeper had had all coverings removed, except a mattress pad. "For a while there I had visions of going to jail myself, on a charge of homicide. No kidding! I really thought Arundel wouldn't survive the shock of the lost million."

Strawn, sprawled in an incongruously dainty "boudoir chair," with a little end table crowded with food close at hand, spoke thickly through one-third of a chicken sandwich:

"I thought he was standing up under it fine—till you sprung that question on him, about why didn't Yola write a new check, instead of passing the buck to him. That's when he keeled over."

Dundee reached for a glass of milk on the night table beside the bed. "It was a very significant question, my dear Strawn," he said lightly, but his eyes were intent upon the older detective.

"I reckon there wasn't nothing so all-fired mysterious about her sending the bum check and the insurance letter on to Arundel," Strawn hazarded. "Simple enough. She didn't have the jack herself. Issued a check on the wrong bank so's to gain a little time. Then when it bounced back, she simply tossed it to him—him being the beneficiary. She musta figgered he'd dig up the cash somewhere before he'd take a chance on losing a million.

Anyway, I'm powerful glad Arundel's not going to die as a result of your ruthless third-degree tactics—as the newspapers would've called 'em. And our case is solved. Sewed up. In the bag. And a very neat job, too. I give you, credit, Bonnie lad."

"Solved?" Dundee repeated, apparently astonished.

"To my entire satisfaction!" Strawn was emphatic. "We'll go ahead and check his story, of course. The Kenyons ought to be along any minute now. I sure hate to have to drag them into this mess, but we gotta have corroboration of Garnet's story. Boy! I don't think anything ever tickled me more than the sight of Dink Garnet's face when you made him realize he was sawin' off the limb he was sittin' on."

"'T'was funny, all right. Talk about a dying man living his whole life over in a flash! Dink saw a motion picture of the next ten or twelve years of his life unwind like lightning—a comic tragedy with him as the sole support of a son he had nothing to do with begetting! For a minute there I thought we were going to have two fainting men for Dr. Wayne to shoot adrenalin into."

"If Dink had had an inkling of the truth about that insurance policy, we'd never have stood a Chinaman's chance of hearing his story, or even of pinning the murder on him—if it turns out that neither Bruce nor nobody else saw him on or near the scene of the crime at the crucial time."

"As it was, Dink could hardly wait to tell his story," Dundee contributed, with a grin. "And a smart move it was, whether he's guilty of murder or not. Dink, yellow toad as he is, is still nobody's fool—though he's feeling like one right now! He realized that the only proof he could offer of Yola Conova's identity with Madge Smith was the fact that she kept a date at an ungodly hour with her former lover Bruce Kenyon. Now he's kicking himself to Timbuctoo for having proved it so thoroughly that he's stuck with a son to support. Personally, I hope the law makes him do his duty by Madge Smith's child—financially, I mean."

Strawn belched loudly, without thought of apology, then settled lower in the silk boudoir chair. "As a matter of fact, Bonnie, the very cornerstone of the plan that Dink Garnet had to think up in such a hurry last night, after he'd killed the girl, was his intention to publish the story of Madge Smith, including his own demands upon her for custody of the child, and including her tryst with Bruce Kenyon. Her murder had to look like suicide, and that story of his was absolutely essential to establish an ironclad motive for suicide!"

"You're endowing Mr. Charles Arthur Garnet with a most fascinating mentality, Captain," said Dundee.

Strawn's thin lips twisted downward. "I think Dink Garnet is a hell of a smart rattlesnake," he retorted. "But we've got him pinned under a forked stick and he can't wriggle out."

Dundee yawned and stretched with luxurious thoroughness before rising from the hotel bed "It does look bad for Dink. The beauty of it is that it nearly all fits in—his whole story as he told it himself, up to the crucial point, of course, and with one slight variation. You believe, of course, that Dink did not hide behind a convenient stack of boxes, but under the laprobe in the Conova sedan. Even the ten minutes he claims to have devoted to an attempt to crank his engine fits in. That was ample time for him to have driven the sedan onto Old Bridge, fitted the tow-rope noose to the poor girl's neck, and yanked her over the railing. And—Dink Garnet being a smallish man has rather a small hand."

"Sure!" Strawn agreed eagerly. "It wouldn't have been no trick at all for him to get her gloves on. I don't mind telling you that I'm tickled pink that you see eye to eye with me, Bonnie lad. We've worked together a long time—"

"But I don't agree with you, Captain, my Captain," Dundee said softly and regretfully. "I only wish I could. In fact, I find the reptilian Mr. Garnet so repulsive that I am afraid I could be tempted to remain silent while you present your case to the grand jury, if it were not for the fact that the real murderer may be quite as unfit to live as Dink Garnet is. Hence, I don't want him to live; therefore we must catch him. Or her."

"I'm satisfied," Strawn repeated angrily, his leathery old cheeks darkly flushed. "Dink Garnet's as good as in the jug now, with two of my best men on his tail. Why don't you agree with me? Just to be contrary?"

Dundee smiled. "For the kind of reasons that always irk you when I have occasion to state them. Psychological reasons. Dink Garnet is psychologically a misfit for the role in which you've cast him. As a blackmailer he's perfect, but even as a blackmailer Dink Garnet would make sure that the law couldn't touch him. By the way, Dink did not write that blackmail letter that Ginger Loring and Conova received. But let's skip that for the moment. Dink's a petty lawbreaker; runs a gambling club in connection with his pool hall, and no doubt keeps a book on the races. But it's significant that he's so cagey and so bush-league in his piddling little operations that he's never been caught red-handed. Right?"

"I'm not on the vice squad," Strawn reminded Dundee sourly.

"In this Conova business, Dink was technically within the law," the younger detective went on, not at all perturbed. "It is noteworthy of his character that when he attempted, by means of correspondence, to shake down Yola Conova a number of years ago, her attorney was able to scare him off without half trying, by merely threatening him with Federal action. No, chief! Dink isn't a courageous soul. And it takes courage of a sort to plan and commit murder—"

"I don't argue that he *planned* to murder her," Strawn protested. "Leastways, not till he was already guilty of kidnapping and liable to swing for it, under the Lindbergh law. As I see it, after he socked her on the back of the head with that auto crank, and took over the car, and drove her in it, while she was unconscious, he suddenly realized what a jam he was in. He figgered you can only hang once, and it had a damned sight better be for murder than for kidnapping—when there was a chance he could make murder look like suicide, and there ain't a thing you can do to make kidnapping look like something it ain't. If you get what I mean—"

"Now we're getting to the crux of my objection to your theory, Captain," Dundee told him. "Why on earth should Dink Garnet, if he really had hidden himself under the lap-robe, do anything so dangerous—dangerous to himself as well as to the girl—as banging her over the head with a heavy crank?"

"To keep her from screaming, of course," Strawn answered promptly.

"Rather a drastic means of silencing her, wasn't it?" Dundee asked "How much simpler it would have been to rise up behind her and clap a hand over her mouth! Or to throw a coat over her head, to muffle her screams. No, chief! Sorry, but I just can't visualize Dink Garnet knocking her unconscious as a prelude to holding a conversation with her in regard to his 'legal rights'. No, Dink would never have clouted her over the head. Not because he is too chivalrous, heaven knows! But because he would have been afraid to."

"When a man's angry, he don't count the consequences," Strawn offered.

"Granted! If he's angry enough, he'll do any fool thing, even commit murder. But surely you don't picture Dink Garnet as seething with rage for nearly two hours, on a cold November night, just because his one-time wife had defied him and hung up the receiver! He had scarcely expected anything more cordial. And most certainly he was not jealous because Madge had gone calling on Bruce Kenyon. There was no love lost between Madge Smith and Dink Garnet. But he'd made money out of her once, by means of marrying her, and all he cared about was another wad of dough. And he thought she was magnificently able to pay.In fact, he thought he'd hit the jackpot of his life. But I'm convinced he did not murder her—either accidentally or with malice aforethought. But, Captain, *someone* did hide under the laprobe— someone who had just as much opportunity to reach her parked sedan unseen as Dink Garnet had—"

"Far as I can see, anybody in Hamilton that wanted to could have done that," Strawn growled.

"Exactly! And that someone did strike Madge Smith senseless with the well-known blunt instrument. Probably that crank. And since perforce that 'someone' was in hiding *before* Dink Garnet arrived, that lurking 'someone' heard the same words that Dink Garnet heard pass between Bruce Kenyon and Madge Smith."

"Why don't you come right out and say you mean Helen Kenyon?" Strawn demanded angrily. "I ain't forgot any more'n you have, that there was a third car, parked across the street from the Kenyon building after the street was washed around twelve-thirty. But I also ain't forgetting that Dink said there was only two cars when he got there."

"The answer to that is very simple," Dundee said. "If the 'someone' came in a car, and then hid himself—or herself—then the car also had to be hidden. Certainly until we know a bit more there's no use in building up a case against Helen Kenyon. But I must tell you now that I checked and found that the tire treads on Helen Kenyon's car correspond with the marks that Shear and I found."

"I had 'em checked, too," Strawn admitted. "But—"

"But you'd much rather arrest Dink Garnet for murder than to jail a charming woman, who also happens to be both a Winter and a Kenyon. And I don't blame you. I much prefer Dink as the goat! But we're not looking for goats, chief. We're looking for the truth, whatever it maybe. And wherever it may lead us. Come in!"

It was Police Detective Cain who entered the hotel bedroom, carefully shutting the door. "About Mr. and Mrs. Kenyon, Captain—"

"You don't mean to say they've given you the slip?" Strawn roared.

"Oh, I brought 'em along all right, chief," Cain assured him soothingly. "But they went on up to old Mrs. Kenyon's apartment on the sixth floor. The old lady's gone to California for the winter, but it seems she keeps the rooms on a yearly lease, and Mr. Kenyon said him and his wife would be much obliged if you and Mr. Dundee would join 'em there, to avoid the reporters, and I—"

"Splendid!" Dundee was enthusiastic. "What was their attitude, Cain? Surprised? Resentful? High-hat?"

Cain scratched his head. "I suppose you'd say they was surprised," he decided. "But they didn't say much. And folks like them—well, they don't wear their minds on their sleeves, no more'n their hearts. I found Mrs. Kenyon at the office with her husband. They'd just had lunch together, Mr. Kenyon said," Cain reported, his voice and manner showing a deep respect, even awe, for the people of whom he was speaking.

"All right, Cain," said Strawn. "Tell Brede to join us up there. And tell him to bring a transcription of all the Dink Garnet stuff. I told him to rush it, and it ought to be ready by now."

The two detectives managed to reach the service elevator without being stopped by reporters. The efficient Mr. Brede, with his stenographic notebook and a briefcase, joined them just as the doors of the lift were opened, to discharge a waiter carrying a tray.

"Are they working you hard, Bartholomew?" Dundee asked casually.

The waiter, who looked very tired, smiled wanly. "Yes, sir. All of the movie gentlemen seem to need quite a lot of coffee. Mr. Risher and Mr. Weinberg have had three pots each. But this tray is for Mr. Arundel. The others haven't cared for any solid food to speak of—"

"I see that Mr. Arundel is now feeling equal to taking a little nourishment," Dundee said softly, eyeing the heavy tray which seemed to tax the strength of the slight young waiter. "Has Miss Patton had any lunch?"

"Some chicken broth and toast Melba, sir. Pierre took her order up half an hour ago," Bartholomew answered. "He said the young lady's breathing seemed to be a little less difficult, sir. After the doctor left this morning Pierre prepared a mustard plaster for her chest and set up a kettle on an electric plate, so that she could take steam inhalations, sir, without getting a nurse."

"Pierre is, I gather, a humanitarian and a gentleman," Dundee commented dryly.

"Oh, no, sir!" Bartholomew was shocked. "Mr. Risher, the handsome young actor, has paid Pierre well to assist the young lady. He has also tipped me generously to lend a hand when she needs one. The chambermaid, likewise, although Hester would gladly do anything to win just one little smile from the glorious young man. Mr. Risher is indeed a prince, sir."

As the elevator ascended Strawn remarked to Dundee, in a voice too low for the operator to hear: "Weinberg and Risher are both behaving like princes. Not a single beef out of 'em for being kept to their quarters. But it won't be long before they begin kicking—and who could blame 'em? Sixth floor out, please! Which is the Kenyon apartment boy?"

The entire sixth floor of the Randolph Hotel was devoted to semi-housekeeping apartments, whose tenants were all more or less permanent. The suite leased by the widowed Mrs. Kenyon was one of the smaller, less pretentious apartments, but the living room into which the detectives were admitted was large and homey, although a bit overcrowded with the personal belongings of the absent woman. It was clearly the abode of an elderly woman who has reluctantly "broken up" housekeeping.

As the opening commonplacenesses were exchanged between the Kenyons and their undoubtedly unwelcome guests, Dundee was reflecting: "Clever of them, if they have anything to hide—this putting of Strawn and me in the position of guests."

And, naturally, he told himself, they both had something to hide. If they were both as innocent as angels of Madge Smith's death, they still must be frantic at the prospect of the ancient scandal becoming public in so spectacular a manner as through police investigation into the suicide of an internationally famous motion-picture star. Yes, literally frantic, and determined to prevent it, no matter what the cost to veracity and justice. Naturally! And who could blame them? Dundee sighed. That was the beastly thing about murder. Murder never stopped at murder—at the simple death of a human being. It always went on and on with its bloody work, killing the happiness of the innocent, destroying the decent privacy of all who had the misfortune to be even remotely involved. And Dundee, whose chief business was murder, grew hot with a terrible anger against murder.

On the surface, Helen Kenyon seemed to be at ease. But that, he was sure, was the result of long and rigid training. Here was a woman who gave unmistakable evidence of having lived for years in a state of extreme nervous tension. Her fair skin, which should have been dewy-fresh and lovely at her age, looked as if it had been parched with a fever. That fever, hotter than any clinical thermometer could have registered, had burned so long in her blue eyes that almost all the color had been consumed, but still it burned. The fever of jealousy, Dundee guessed. He had seen many a woman, in the course of his professional life, who had been scorched in the fires of that dread fever. To some extent, of course, the blaze of the fire in her veins was damped by fear of what this questioning might mean to her—or to her husband. Or to both of them.

Dundee felt suddenly resentful on behalf of this woman. For she must have been a very lovely young girl. She still had beauty of line, of bone formation. And that dread fever had left her wonderful hair undamaged. It was honey-colored hair, as natural in its pale, shining blondeness as Louise Patton's was synthetic; and it was woven into a wide braid that encircled her small, proud head in the coronet fashion of a bygone day. A perfect hairdress for Helen Kenyon.

Bruce Kenyon's handclasp was strong and quick. Dundee liked the feel of the man's lean, warm, steel-strong fingers gripping his. And yet he was sure that Bruce Kenyon was not a congenital handshaker. Tall, dark, almost as thin as his wife, somberly handsome, with a habit of dour reticence, Bruce Kenyon was so unusual a type that Dundee had noticed him particularly whenever he had seen him in public places—at symphony concerts, charity balls, political rallies. As a Republican national committeeman he was prominent in politics, but he was not a politician, in the oridinary sense of the word. Dundee could not imagine him as currying favor.

"Mr. Kenyon," Strawn was beginning with solemn formality, "we are very sorry to trouble you and your good lady, but Mr. Dundee and I are investigating the death of the motion-picture star, known as Yola Conova, and certain facts or alleged facts have come to our attention which indicate that you will be able to help us arrive at the truth of this sad business."

The fair face of the woman and the dark face of the man became as still and expressionless as masks. In the hushed silence of the room there was no noise but the pages of a stenographic notebook in Brede's matter-of-fact hands.

Strawn coughed when it became apparent that the Kenyons were not going to volunteer any information. He shot a glance of almost comical appeal to Dundee, who was glad to oblige. For Dundee had formed a plan of approach, in that minute of deep hush.

"As Captain Strawn has told you, Mr. Kenyon," he began, with brisk courtesy, "I represent the district attorney in this investigation, in which Captain Strawn and I are co-operating with each other. We are investigating the death of a woman who came to Hamilton yesterday under the name of Yola Conova, but who was once known in Hamilton as Madge Smith. It is only fair to tell you that we are already convinced of the dead woman's identity as the former Madge Smith."

After another breathless hush Bruce Kenyon spoke: "In your opinion, sir, is it necessary to bare a woman's past, because she happens to have committed suicide? Is it not possible that the—unfortunate woman chose suicide in preference to exposure of that past? If that is so, I am afraid I shall have to refuse to contribute toward making that desperate choice a futile gesture."

"That," said Dundee, in the same colorless, emotionless manner that Kenyon had adopted, "is a sentiment that does you credit. I suggest, however, that it is not entirely altruistic." His voice suddenly became hard. "Is it not true that you are far more interested in protecting your own good name from scandal than in shielding a dead woman from unsavory publicity?"

"Oh!" The word was a quick gasp from Helen Kenyon's dry lips. "I told you, Bruce, that they'd have heard. Everyone must be talking—"

"Hush, Helen! I'll handle this situation," her husband interrupted sternly. "Gentlemen, you may think what you please, but I have nothing to say. And my wife has nothing to say."

Dundee considered for a moment, then: "Frankly, Mr. Kenyon, I can understand and appreciate your attitude. And I can assure you that Captain Strawn and I have no intention whatever of introducing into the inquest any irrelevant material. Nor do we intend to make a newspaper picnic out of this tragedy. For instance, we have not given the reporters any inkling of the fact that the deceased's name was formerly Madge Smith, that as a very young girl she lived here and worked for several Hamilton families as a servant, that she married a Hamilton man and disappeared immediately after the rather strange wedding. Please!" he begged, as Kenyon was about to speak. "But in view of all the circumstances it is extremely unlikely that the newspapers and the coroner can be kept in entire ignorance of the dead woman's past. If she had died anywhere but in Hamilton it is probable that her past would have remained a secret, guessed only by a few who knew her in Hamilton, but who could never be sure. But Madge Smith, under the name and under the fame of Yola Conova, did dare return to Hamilton. And she—died."

Dundee turned his back upon the Kenyons for a moment, to take a sheaf of manuscript from Brede's briefcase.

"To save time, and to convince you of the absolute folly of keeping silent, Mr. Kenyon," he continued, "I'm going to do something that is a trifle irregular. Here is a transcription of the evidence introduced into this inquiry through the questioning of one Charles Arthur Garnet, better known as Dink Garnet, temporary husband ten years ago of Madge Smith, and, legally speaking, the father of her child. I will also tell you that Captain Strawn and I are in possession of other facts from a number of sources which involve both you and Mrs. Kenyon in this investigation. I believe, after you both have read this transcription, that you will see the wisdom of telling us frankly anything you know."

Since neither the man nor the woman made a move to accept the typed sheets, Captain Strawn spoke up heartily. "Now you two just sit down in that big chair—room enough for both of you, so's Mrs. Kenyon can read right along with you, Kenyon. And, folks, I think it would be fine if you'd both read that stuff straight through without flying off the handle or taking up time to deny little things as you come to them."

It was odd to see those two still-faced people, so tensely on guard, obey the old detective with the docility of the hypnotized. But Dundee was sure that Helen Kenyon was grateful for the chance to sit so close beside her husband, to feel his arm about her thin shoulders as she read.

Captain Strawn possessed, to an immense degree, the virtue of patience—when patience was called for. He could sit now, stolidly waiting, without even twiddling his fingers, his eyes fixed upon the two people in the big armchair. Only his jaws moved as he chewed another toothpick. But Dundee could not sit still. Hands in pockets, he strolled about the big room, studying the pictures—a crowded collection of etchings and fairly good oil paintings, glancing at the titles of books, picking up a magazine now and then, only to drop it restlessly, without reading a line. For the room, he discovered, had something to tell him. And he was listening. Suddenly the message came through.

This room had been used very recently. Someone else within the last few hours had prowled around in it, picking up books and magazines and ashtrays, and setting them down again in slightly different places, leaving faint signs in the film of dust which had collected since the senior Mrs. Kenyon had left for Pasadena.

But it was a discarded newspaper, lying almost concealed where it had been dropped between the end of the big sofa and the wall, that spoke most loudly to the detective. It was a copy of *The Morning Star*—an edition which had come out on the streets the night before, a pre-date, he believed it was called. Since it had been printed several hours before the tragedy there was no word of Yola Conova's "suicide," but there was a large news picture of the two stars—the dark-eyed woman and the golden young man, Clinton Risher—accompanying the front page story of their arrival in Hamilton. Someone

who had been on the streets of Hamilton late the night
before had bought this paper, had brought it to this
apartment whose mistress was far away. And someone
had done a rather curious thing: *the eyes in the large
picture of the movie star had been punched out!* Feeling
oddly moved, Dundee straightened, leaving the telltale
paper where it lay, and he fixed his attention upon the
Kenyons.

They were reading rapidly and, Dundee judged, had
almost finished. From being chalky pale, the thin face of
Helen Kenyon had become suffused with the red tide of
anger. She remained in her seat only because Bruce
Kenyon held her, down with an iron grip on her
shoulders. He, on the other hand, had become so pale that
his dark skin looked like aged ivory.

At last the State's produce king put down the script in
a neat pile on a small table beside the chair, and looked
at his wife steadily, his black eyes holding her blue ones
until she seemed almost calm again. Then he turned
quietly to the two detectives.

"Gentlemen," he began with grave courtesy, "I have
nothing of importance to add to Garnet's story. For a
number of reasons I am glad that Dink Garnet has gone
on record in your investigation as the father of Madge
Smith Garnet's child. I very much doubt that he will push
his custody claim, however, in view of the circumstances
surrounding the lapsed insurance policy. But we are not
concerned with that phase of the matter now.

"The point is, you do have Garnet's statement. After
all—if you do not insist upon airing an ancient scandal—
the worst that need be said of Yola Conova is that when
she was very young and poverty-stricken, she married so
unromantic, so—low-class a person as Charles Arthur
Garnet. The world need not know, as does Hamilton, how
strange a choice she made of a husband, nor the
circumstances of that wedding. It is certainly not unusual
for a picture star to have made an early, unwise

marriage, and to have kept that marriage a secret both from her second husband and from her public."

Dundee and Strawn exchanged a glance which was a mutual confession of admiration and amazement.

"That is quite true," Dundee admitted. "But I am afraid we are concerned with the events leading up to the—tragedy. And those events include the visit she paid to *you*, Mr. Kenyon—in your office in a district that is peculiarly deserted at night. A visit made at the extremely unconventional hour of one A.M. *At your invitation!*"

Again Bruce Kenyon kept his wife from violently entering the conversation, by gently pressing her hand for a moment.

"Shall we say," he began evenly, his agitation betrayed only by the extreme pallor of his lips, "that Miss Conova decided to confer with me, as an old friend—the son of her former employer and benefactor—after she had become alarmed by the demands of her divorced husband? As for the lateness of the hour: the Garnet telephone call itself came very late, and she was so frightened that she acted immediately."

"And the fortuitous circumstance of finding you at your office, alone, at such an hour?" Dundee asked softly.

Kenyon answered so promptly that Dundee wondered if he was not telling the actual truth at last: "Miss Conova set out, in her car, to call upon my wife and myself at our home, but, as she was passing my place of business she saw lights on in the offices and stopped, on the chance that it was I who was working late. And it was. And we had our—conference."

Again Dundee and Strawn exchanged a meaning glance, and again Dundee got the signal to go ahead on his own initiative.

"Then you deny, do you, Kenyon," he asked, without undue weightiness of tone or manner, "that you telephoned to Miss Conova at the Randolph Hotel and insisted that she meet you?"

"It is quite true that I telephoned Miss Conova shortly before midnight last night," Kenyon said, in that even, expressionless voice. "It is not true that I 'insisted' upon a meeting. Shall we say that I paid my respects, extended the appropriate compliments, and expressed the hope that my wife and I could have the pleasure of a visit with her before she left Hamilton?"

"I think we shall not!" Dundee retorted curtly. "I suggest that we say, instead, that *you*—not you and your wife!—wanted an interview with Madge Smith, because you were vitally interested in news of her son, for reasons that seem to be quite well understood in Hamilton. Yes, Mrs. Kenyon?"

"I have something to say! Oh, yes, I have, Bruce! And you can't stop me! And *you* are going to talk, too, at last! Do you hear? *You're going to tell the truth at last!* You've made me suffer the tortures of the damned for ten long years, and now you're going to tell! Oh, yes, you are! It's not just your wife that demands to know now! The law wants to know, Bruce! *And you're going to tell!*"

The hysterical woman, once having slipped the frail leash of her self-control, was fighting off her husband's restraining hands. Dundee, embarrassed, turned his eyes from the pair.

"Very well, Helen," Bruce Kenyon said finally. "I think it will be just as well if I let you say anything you like— now. Of course you have a right to talk if you wish to."

The woman was suddenly almost calm. Her husband's capitulation, made with indescribable gentleness and compassion, had accomplished what restraint had failed to do. But she availed herself of his consent, and began to speak.

XVI

"TEN YEARS AGO," Helen Kenyon began, "a maid in the home of the John W. Kenyons got into the usual sort of trouble. But she seems to have been a most unusual girl, judging by the profound effect she had upon the lives and hearts of a number of Hamilton's citizens, and judging too by her later success as a motion-picture star. A girl who could exchange house dust for star dust is not ordinary, gentlemen!"

"Please, Helen, be brief!"

"Just before Bruce and I were to be married, ten years ago in June," she continued, as if she had not heard her husband, "I received an anonymous letter which told me that my future father-in-law, to avoid a scandal, had bought a husband for the maid, Madge Smith, so that her child would be born in wedlock. The anonymous letter-writer advised me to ask Bruce to tell me all about it. I asked Bruce if it was true that he was the man responsible for the girl's plight. And—"

As her voice broke on a sob, Helen Kenyon paused and groped for a handkerchief, which her husband found and put into her hand.

"He said he was not the man!" she sobbed. "But when I asked him if he knew who the man was, he refused to tell me. He didn't say he didn't know. He just keeps saying—all these years—that he can't tell me. And he said that if I couldn't trust him, there was no foundation for a marriage. He said I should not even have had to ask him if he had—had betrayed our love, by betraying a servant girl. So," she continued, between racking sobs, "we quarreled. Bruce went abroad and we were not married until fall. I asked him to forgive me. I thought he'd tell me the truth after we were married, but he didn't. Madge Smith ruined our happiness! And I'm glad—glad!—that she wasn't happy either!"

"I reckon," Strawn began heavily, with the air of a judge profoundly passing upon a case, "nobody could blame you, under the circumstances, for having your doubts of your husband. His own father thought he was the guilty man, or he wouldn't have paid Dink Garnet to marry the girl. And if the girl let old Mr. Kenyon think it was his—"

That drew fire from Bruce Kenyon. "Madge Smith said nothing whatever when my father and mother questioned her except, 'I won't tell!' And she stuck to it, regardless of whose name was mentioned to her. I explained to Helen at that time, and I've explained since, that a girl who finds herself in such dire trouble as Madge Smith did, will snatch at any straw of help. My father's arrangements, which he made without Madge's consent, by the way, and entirely without my knowledge, must have been a godsend to the girl. She asked for nothing, accused no one, but when help and a name for her child were thrust upon her, I think no one could blame her for snatching at them. My father, by the way, did not question me. I was back in college in the East when it all happened, and the girl was married and gone; and I was thoroughly branded by the gossips as a philanderer saved by his rich father, by the time I returned home in June."

A new thought stirred slowly in the depths of Dundee's unconscious mind and worked its way upward.

"Mr. Kenyon," he said, searching painfully for the right words, "do you know any other reason why Madge Smith permitted this injustice to yourself to be perpetrated by your father? As I understand it, the girl reaped no actual financial benefit from the arrangement your father made for her, without her consent, with Dink Garnet. She seems to have disappeared immediately after the wedding, leaving her husband to enjoy the financial fruits of the arrangement."

Bruce Kenyon looked him steadily in the eye. "I cannot answer that question. I'm very sorry"

"That's what he always says!" Helen Kenyon cried out hysterically. "'I can't answer!' 'I refuse to answer!' For ten years—"

"Mr. Kenyon," Dundee began again, ignoring the sobbing woman, "I've heard a great deal about the character and the beauty of this Madge Smith. It occurs to me that, on the surface, her acceptance of your father's aid, no matter how badly it was needed, was out of character. Not like the girl who seems to have been rather a fine person. So, looking beneath the surface, I believe I see a motive. Is it not true that she did this thing in order to protect the man who was really responsible? I mean," he amended hastily, "that it seems quite possible to me that she hoped, *for certain reasons* which you have probably guessed long ago, that the man who was actually responsible would never know that he was the father of her child; that he would think she had been untrue to him, *so that he would not feel responsible!* Am I right, Mr. Kenyon?"

Bruce Kenyon sighed. "I can see no harm in saying— yes! I did guess the truth ten years ago, and she confirmed my guess last night, of her own accord. Without mentioning the man's name," he added hastily. She truly loved that man better than she loved herself. She chose to destroy his love for her, his faith in her, rather than to—to bring disaster upon him."

"And upon others who had prior claim upon him," Dundee added, but to himself alone, and he wished Ginger Loring could know how much Madge Smith had really loved her.

It was Captain Strawn who spoke, with grim matter-of-factness. "This is all very, fine, folks, but it ain't evidence. It ain't getting us anywhere. I'll have to ask you to tell me who the man was, since you are convinced that you know."

Bruce Kenyon stiffened. A hard light of determination, with which his wife must have been all too familiar, glinted in his dark eyes. "I must refuse to answer that question, whenever and wherever it may be put to me. I have no proof whatsoever that my conviction concerning the man's identity is correct and, if I did have, I should still refuse to answer."

"You've got to tell!" Helen Kenyon screamed, completely beside herself. "For my sake, for your own sake, you've got to tell the truth, Bruce! Publicly! Oh, you don't know how horrible it's been!" she cried, whirling upon Dundee. "Ever since that woman became a picture star, it's been in everyone's mind that Bruce used to love her, that she has a child by *my husband*, and that I have no child! And I'll never have a child as long as all Hamilton believes that Bruce Kenyon is the father of a bastard—"

"Helen!" her husband interrupted sternly. "You're making yourself ill. And—me, too. I can only repeat that I will never name the man. I believe that Madge Smith chose to die rather than to have this whole miserable story become public. For my part, I'll do all I can to see that she did not die in vain. And, gentlemen, if that be melodramatic sentimentality, make the most of it!"

Strawn and Dundee exchanged another glance. Strawn knit his thick white eyebrows, then pounced suddenly upon his unwilling witness:

"Kenyon, don't it strike you as kinda funny that a woman would commit suicide and thus remove the only obstacle in the path of Dink Garnet hell bent on getting custody of her son?"

"On the contrary," Kenyon answered. "Madge took what she believed was the one way to prevent Garnet's ever getting the child or of breaking the story of her life in Hamilton. Consider! Yola Conova, alive, has to admit that she was once known as Madge Smith. Alive, she can be hauled into court to answer Garnet's custody suit. She cannot refuse to tell where the child is. But dead, she does not have to answer anything! Child? What child? Where? For last night she told me that there is absolutely no connection between Yola Conova and Nikolai Garnet!"

"What!" ejaculated both Dundee and Strawn.

"Exactly! She told me nothing of his whereabouts, but she did tell me that he had no faintest idea that Yola Conova was his mother, and that there existed no papers, no checks, no letters—in short, no link whatever between the picture star, Yola Conova, and the boy. Hence, Geoffrey Arundel can say with entire truthfulness that there was never such a child, to his knowledge, and that the only connection between our Madge Smith and Yola Conova was a fairly strong resemblance. That is why, gentlemen," Kenyon continued, "that I urge you to suppress this whole miserable story, if it is at all possible. If not, to put the burden of proof upon Dink Garnet. I think it is quite obvious that he can prove nothing."

Before answering, Dundee took a turn or two up and down the room, hands thrust deep into his pockets, his head whirling with a thousand conjectures and possibilities. Most insistent was the query: Did Bruce Kenyon suspect the whole truth? Or had Madge Smith taken him into her confidence, in that last desperate hour before she went out to meet the "blunt instrument" in the hands of her murderer?

When he did speak it was not to answer Bruce Kenyon's deeply sincere and quite reasonable appeal. He asked:

"Will you tell us now, Mr. Kenyon, what you really said to Miss—Conova when you telephoned her last night? It is obvious that you did not do so to extend a social invitation, on behalf of yourself and wife."

The man considered for a moment, gnawing at his lower lip with the first signs of indecision which he had betrayed.

"Very well," Kenyon agreed abruptly. "I said, 'This is Bruce Kenyon speaking, Miss Conova. It has been ten years since we met, but I hope you remember me.' Or

words to that effect. When I pronounced my name I heard
her gasp, but she did not interrupt. In fact, I was able to
conclude a rather long sentence, before she said, 'I'm
sorry. I didn't get the name.' I repeated it, and she said,
'I'm sorry, but you are mistaken. I have never known
anyone of that name.' But her voice was entirely
unconvincing. Also I got the definite impression that she
could not speak freely because there was someone with
her. In fact, I asked her if that was the case, and she said,
quite eagerly, 'Yes. Thank you so much!' as if I had paid
her a compliment. I understood that she really wanted
me to continue talking, regardless of what she said in
answer, so—I forget the exact words I used—I told her
that it was vitally important for me to see her as soon as
possible. She listened, without answering, and I
continued. I told her that there were certain conditions in
Hamilton of which I must warn her immediately—
conditions dangerous for her. I emphasized the fact that I
was speaking as a friend, but that it was to our mutual
advantage that she see me."

"Just a moment, please," Dundee interrupted. "Have
you any idea whether anyone was listening in—either on
an extension telephone or from the hotel switchboard?"

Kenyon knit his brows. "I really can't say definitely.
Since I knew I was running the risk of being overheard in
some such manner, I believe I should have been aware of
the fact if a receiver of an extension telephone had been
picked up. But I should not like to go on record one way
or the other."

Dundee looked at the man with increasing
admiration. "Thank you, Mr. Kenyon. It is true, is it not,
that you telephoned to Miss Conova about midnight?"

"A few minutes before midnight," Kenyon answered
positively.

"And that you telephoned from this suite—your
mother's hotel home, to which you have a key?"

"That is correct," the man answered promptly. "I
thought it would be much safer for Miss Conova to come

to this apartment, only a couple of flights of stairs from her own suite, than for me to go to her rooms, which I understood she shared with her companion."

"Mrs. Kenyon, I take it, was not with you?"

"No. I drove her home from the theater, to which we had gone upon her insistence," Kenyon told him, with reluctance. "For the last few years I have had to refuse to go with my wife to see any motion picture starring Miss Conova. Of course she went anyway—alone or with my mother, who, I am afraid, hates—or rather, *did* hate— Yola Conova as violently as does my wife. One reason I consented to go last night was that I was very much afraid something unpleasant might happen if I was not there. My presence, I hoped, would act as a brake upon— runaway emotions."

Captain Strawn snorted. "Mean to say you was afraid your wife'd rise up in the audience and interrupt the show to ask Yola Conova who the father of her baby was?"

A dark flush, whether of anger or of embarrassment, spread over the lean face of Bruce Kenyon. "There were a number of extremely unpleasant possibilities," he answered steadily. "If you really have delved into the past as much as you seem to have done, you know that a number of people besides my wife believed they had cause to hate Yola Conova. It may seem strange to you that a ten-year-old scandal can still be so alive in a city the size of Hamilton. Ordinarily, the misfortunes of a maid-servant, no matter how prominent the families she worked for, are soon forgotten, except, possibly, by the person responsible for her trouble. But in this case, just as the scandal was about to be forgotten, even by my wife, whose happiness had been so tragically affected—"

"All you ever had to do was to tell me the truth!" Helen Kenyon cried, bitterly. "If you hadn't thought more of *her* than you did of *me*, you wouldn't have shielded her at my, expense—"

"Hush, Helen! Hush, dear!" Bruce Kenyon pleaded, but there was no love in his voice; there was only pity. And his wife knew it, and sobbed the more desolately.

"As I was saying," Kenyon continued resolutely but wearily, "just as the scandal was being forgotten a new star appeared in the motion-picture sky—as the publicity writers phrase it. That star was Yola Conova to all the rest of the world so far as I know: to Hamilton, she was Madge Smith. Actually, many people spoke—especially to *me*, and to Helen—of going to see the latest Madge Smith picture. The Madge Smith legend grew and spread. My wife and I had to bear the brunt of the gossip, and it was Helen who suffered the more, naturally. But there were other women who thought they had good cause to hate Yola Conova, and they proved themselves good haters and tireless gossips. You see, gentlemen, they could have forgiven a luckless servant girl her sin, but they could not forgive her her fame and success."

"Certainly not!" Dundee agreed. "By the way, were the people concerned absolutely convinced of Yola Conova's identity with Madge Smith?"

"No," Kenyon said. "They pretended to themselves and to others that they were. You see, it made their nasty little scandal so very big and important. And they were not going to endanger their obscene fun by putting their conviction to too severe a test. I mean, no one, so far as I know, ever went to Hollywood to see Yola Conova in person, and make sure. Yesterday was their first opportunity. And mine, I should add."

"You recognized Madge Smith at the station yesterday?" Strawn asked.

"I did. And she betrayed the fact that she recognized both me and Dink Garnet," Kenyon answered. "There were others at the station for the same purpose as I was. And I saw that they, too, had their eight-year-old suspicions confirmed."

"I will ask you to name those persons," Strawn said, with grim formality.

"And I must decline to do so," Kenyon retorted firmly. "I have never stooped to gossip in my life, and I do not intend to begin now."

"And yet, Mr. Kenyon," Dundee began slowly, "you were willing to 'gossip,' in a certain sense of the word, with Yola Conova last night. That, as I understand it, was the object of your telephone call."

Anger flashed in the man's black eyes. "I did not gossip! I told her, when I talked with her at my office, that there were certain forces at work in Hamilton against her, which would result in a calamitous barrage of publicity, if in nothing more serious."

"'If nothing more *serious*,'" Dundee repeated significantly. "You were afraid, were you not, that Miss Conova's life was in danger?"

Kenyon was not startled or surprised. "I don't think I actually feared for her life," he said slowly. "But, frankly, I did have a rather fantastic fear that some woman who— hated her —and I most emphatically state that I do not mean my wife!—might make an opportunity to create an extremely unpleasant scene, or even throw vitriol in her face, to destroy her beauty. Please do not ask me to name any woman or women in this connection. I should have to refuse. After all, gentlemen," he urged anew, "the case, on the surface, is very simple. Yola Conova, who has made previous attempts upon her own life, has succeeded in committing suicide in Hamilton. It is within your power to keep practically all other facts out of the coroner's inquest proceedings—if you wish."

"Unfortunately, Mr. Kenyon, it is not quite so simple as that," Dundee retorted. "Newspapers have a genius for digging far below the surface. And I must remind you that Captain Strawn and I are only doing our official duty—by the living as well as by the dead. Now, please go on. You were saying that you had driven your wife home from the theater."

Kenyon sighed. "Very well. When we got home I suggested to my wife that she take a sedative. She was—

quite upset. But she agreed, and we went to our separate rooms. When I thought it likely that my wife was asleep I left the house in my car, coming here to the Randolph and to this apartment. I telephoned Miss Conova, and she herself answered."

"Immediately?" Dundee asked, having Risher's testimony in mind.

"No," Kenyon answered promptly. "I thought they must be out and was about to hang up when Madge herself said hello. When I had explained that I was calling as a friend, and that it was vitally important to her that I see her, I asked her to join me here in this suite. I gave her the apartment number—6-D, and told her I would wait for her here. She laughed and said, in a falsely gay voice intended to deceive the person who was with her, 'Awfully sweet of you! Maybe I will—just to prove that you are wrong.' Or words to that effect."

"I'm sure you have a very good memory, Mr. Kenyon."

"I have. I waited until around twelve-forty-five, and then I tried to call her again. The operator told me Miss Conova had retired and was not to be disturbed. I thought, of course, that she had left that order with the desk as a blind, and was on her way to meet me. But after waiting for about ten minutes more I gave it up and started to leave. But I found a note pushed under the door to the living room."

"A note—from her?" Dundee was oddly incredulous.

"Why, yes," Kenyon said. "Just a scribbled line or two, saying, I believe, 'On my way to your office. Please meet me there.' It was not signed. Naturally I complied immediately."

"Oh, *naturally!*" Helen Kenyon echoed, with heartbroken bitterness.

"May I see that note?" Dundee asked, holding out his hand.

"I'm sorry," Kenyon answered, with apparent sincerity. "Madge asked me for it and of course I gave it to her. She asked me for a match and burned it. I arrived at my office first, and left the stairway door unlocked, so that she could come up without delay. She arrived within two minutes after I did."

"Was she very much agitated?" Dundee wanted to know.

"She was!" Kenyon answered curtly. "She was afraid she might have been followed, and immediately ran to the window to look out. But there was no car and no pedestrian in sight. She said she had been suspicious that not only one car, but two, had been following her as she drove here. But apparently she had been mistaken."

"Apparently," Dundee repeated dryly, with a glance at Strawn. "Did she describe the cars? Or say who she thought might have followed her?"

"No—to both questions," Kenyon answered "She began to tell me immediately about Dink Garnet's call and his demand for custody of her son."

Dundee was only half listening to Bruce Kenyon. The rest of his mind was absorbed with a vitally important question, to which he could as yet see no answer. That was: Why had Madge Smith chosen the greater risk of leaving the hotel and driving alone to a lonely rendezvous, to which she could so easily be followed, in preference to snatching a chance of slipping unseen into an apartment in her own hotel. It did not make sense, apparently. But there must be a reason—an excellent reason.

"Did she say she had had any difficulty in getting away?" he asked. "It happens that her companion, Louise Patton, is a nurse, and that she was hired by Conova's husband to protect Yola Conova from a suicidal mania."

Kenyon smiled slightly. "She seemed to be amused at something she had said to Miss Patton—something designed to make sure her too-zealous companion would not follow her. But she did not say what it was."

Why did she go to Bruce Kenyon's office? Why? Why?

Afraid, possibly, that Helen Kenyon might suspect the rendezvous and surprise the conspirators? No, that wouldn't wash. Helen Kenyon would be even more likely to seek for her husband in his peculiarly isolated place of business than in a hotel apartment.

Whatever it was that Bruce Kenyon was saying was interrupted then by James F. Dundee, whose precocious inner-signal apparatus was at work. He knew that feeling well, and he respected it.

"Mrs. Kenyon, what time was it when you came to this apartment last night?" he asked with startling abruptness, but his voice was matter-of-fact.

"About one o'clock—a little later, maybe," she answered, then looked so frightened that Dundee felt a qualm over having trapped her with the suddenness of his attack. "I—I—suppose the elevator operator or someone told you I was here. But why shouldn't I be? I have a key. My mother-in-law likes me to keep an eye on things while she's away—"

Dundee betrayed no elation over the accuracy of his guess "You came here in the expectation of finding your husband with Yola Conova, didn't you?"

"I was terribly worried," she evaded. "We had quarreled and I couldn't go to sleep. I didn't take the sedative, as I'd promised Bruce. I thought he wanted me to take it just to make sure I wouldn't follow him. He saw me take it—but it wasn't a sedative tablet; it was an aspirin."

"Poor Helen!" Bruce Kenyon groaned under his breath.

"You didn't find him or Miss Conova here," Dundee went on quietly, watching her intently. "You knocked at Miss Conova's rooms, too, didn't you?"

"I—Yes, I did," she whispered, her lips bluish gray under a trace of rouge. "There wasn't any answer. I was afraid I'd wake up everybody in that wing of the fourth floor, I knocked and called so loudly. But I didn't much care if I did."

"Did anyone come out of any of the other rooms?" Dundee asked quickly.

"I heard a door open somewhere as I was leaving, but I couldn't tell which one it was. It was behind me, and I didn't turn 'round."

"So then you went to your husband's place of business?"

"I did not!" she denied. "I'd already been there, before I came here. The place was dark. I haven't a key to the building, so I didn't go up. I waited in the car for about ten minutes, thinking he might come. You see, I reasoned that if Bruce was not trying to see Yola Conova he was taking a long drive at high speed, to calm his nerves after our quarrel, and would wind up by doing some work at the office before coming home. He's done just that so many, many times. So I waited and I prayed that that was what was happening, but it was so—so eerie there on the waterfront, with the wind shrieking. And it was cold. And I—Well, I drove on to the Randolph. I couldn't make myself believe that all my fears and suspicions were unfounded."

Dundee and Captain Strawn exchanged a long look, and the former shrugged slightly. It was the old man who put the next question.

"What did you do, Mrs. Kenyon, when you couldn't find your husband or Miss Conova at the Randolph? Did you make any inquiries about either of them at the desk, or of the elevator operator?"

"No, of course not. I—there was nothing to do but to go on home. So I did."

Dundee saw Captain Strawn gravely make a note on the pad of paper he held on his knee. "El Op," the captain wrote, then he asked: "What time did you get home, Mrs. Kenyon?"

"I don't know exactly," she answered. "Not later than a quarter to two, possibly several minutes earlier. I—I didn't look at a clock."

"Now, Mrs. Kenyon, on your way home, you again went past your husband's office, to see if he was there,"

Strawn stated flatly, as if he had an eye witness to the fact.

"I did not!" she cried, her eyes flashing. "If I had done so, I would have seen their two cars there. And I'd have gone straight upstairs and had it out with them both! I only wish I had! Maybe *she* would have told me the truth! I'd have made her name the man—if she could! Maybe she didn't know herself—for sure!"

"Helen!" Bruce Kenyon said sharply. Then, with helplessness and despair he turned to the detectives: "Gentlemen, I beg you to forget some of the things my wife has said. She is not herself. She's under a great strain—"

"So we see," Strawn agreed dryly, but a hand was in his pocket and Dundee felt sure that it had closed, metaphorically at least, upon a pair of steel bracelets. For it was obvious now that the old detective was just as convinced that Helen Kenyon was guilty as he had been sure that Dink Garnet had murdered Yola Conova.

Certainly the motive in the case against Helen Kenyon was glaringly apparent, Dundee told himself. And almost forgivable.

"Did anybody see you arrive home?" Strawn was asking

"Why, no, I suppose not. The grounds are quite extensive so there are no close neighbors," Mrs. Kenyon told him. "I parked in the driveway near the front of the house, so as not to awaken the servants who sleep in a third-floor wing at the back of the house."

"Now, Mrs. Kenyon," Strawn went on, his mouth grimmer than ever, "if you didn't pass by the Kenyon building on your way home, what route did you take?"

Her blue eyes blazed. "I fail to understand the necessity for all these questions! Very Well! I drove home by way of Riverside Park. That's the shorter route, as you should know."

"Riverside Park!" Dundee repeated softly. "That would have been between half past one and a quarter to two, wouldn't it?"

"I think so," she answered, running the tip, of her tongue over her dry lips. "I've told you I don't know just what time I got home, but that's approximately correct."

"Did you see anyone—*anyone at all*—in Riverside Park as you drove through?"

"No. I—oh, I don't remember!" she cried desperately. "I was not on a sightseeing drive! There could have been a dozen people crossing my path and I wouldn't have known it. I'd just have avoided hitting them, as automatically as I shift gears. What difference does all this make? *I* didn't see that woman last night after the theater! *I* didn't have anything to do with her committing suicide! And I refuse to answer any more questions! I'm going home! Hand me my bag, Bruce! And my coat!"

"Just a minute, Mrs. Kenyon!" Strawn commanded sternly. "How many times did you telephone Yola Conova last night —or try to speak to her on the telephone?"

"I've said I'll answer no more questions," she retorted. "If you won't show me the courtesy to hand me my things, Bruce, I'll get them myself." And she strode, with curious, quick jerkiness across the room to where her things had been left—her mink coat across the back of an occasional chair, her large handbag on the seat of the chair.

"I'm afraid, Mrs. Kenyon—" Strawn began again, when the raucous yells of newsboys screaming an extra in the street six floors below came through the partly opened window.

In a moment the four men—for Brede abandoned his notebook for once—were crowding each other at the window, which Strawn flung wide.

"Yola Conova Murdered!" screamed a newsboy. "Read all about it! Extry! Extry! Police investigating murder, not suicide! *Movie star murdered!* Read all about it! Extry!"

Strawn and Dundee glared at each other in mutual suspicion. "That Ginger-girl's double-crossed you!" Strawn snarled, and Dundee snapped back at his old colleague with "The hell you say! One of your boys has tipped off the papers. It's not the first time it's happened, and—"

"I'm going to have one of those extras sent up," Bruce Kenyon said, and went to the telephone which stood on the desk near the occasional chair.

"Tell 'em to send up a flock of 'em," Strawn ordered. "Damn the luck! I wonder if they've got the whole mess in. Listen!" and he leaned out of the window to harken to the jumbled squawks of the competing newsboys.

Dundee leaned out to listen too, but with only half an ear. For he was trying to hear what Helen Kenyon was saying to her husband. And he wondered if the telephone call had been a ruse on Kenyon's part, to give him an opportunity to speak to his wife, across the large room from the group at the window.

But if so, he must be whispering to her beneath her monotonous reiteration of "Murder. . . Murder. . . . Bruce, did you hear? . . . Murder. . . . Murder. . . . Bruce!"

The telephone call to the desk downstairs, for copies of the extra, was never made by Bruce Kenyon.

Afterwards, Dundee blamed himself bitterly for having divided his attention. If he had not been looking out the window, straining his eyes toward the enormous headlines, he might have been able to reach the insane woman before she could fire those two shots.

One bullet from her little .25 caliber automatic went straight into the heart of Bruce Kenyon. The second bullet—fired before the stunned men at the window could make a move toward stopping her—drilled a neat little round hole in her blue-veined temple, and severed a curling tendril of honey-colored hair.

"Horrible! Horrible!" Captain Strawn kept muttering, after the bodies had been removed on sheeted stretchers. He looked very old—nearer seventy-five than sixty-five. "I guess it's about time for me to retire, Bonnie." He sighed heavily. "Getting too old for my job."

"No more your fault than mine," answered Dundee. "Not so much, in fact. I had reason to know her state of mind better than you did." But he did not tell Strawn of that discarded newspaper, with the pictured eyes of a woman punched put. Frankly, he was sparing himself until he felt less sick.

"You know, Bonnie, I can't blame her a hell of a lot. Can you?"

"No."

"Looks like she never intended to face the music—not after she realized what she'd done But she wasn't gonna leave Bruce behind! No, sir! He'd be with her in death, even if she had lost him in life. Funny thing is, I don't believe Bruce tried to stop her—or wanted to."

"I don't think he did," Dundee agreed. "I think it's even possible that he told her to do what she did. That he remembered there was an automatic in the drawer of that telephone table; that he pretended to want to telephone for the extras, just to be near her—and that gun. That he showed her the gun by opening the drawer. That he whispered to her, 'If you want to go, I'll go with you!'"

"Good Lord! Have you gone nuts?" Strawn snorted.

"Maybe. At least, I'm crazy-tired and sick at my stomach," Dundee admitted. "If a man believes his wife has committed murder, and if he knows that even though she may escape conviction her life is ruined—" He groaned. "Oh, hell! I'd like to strangle with my bare hands the reporter that tricked Doc Price into spilling the beans."

"So would I," Strawn said. "But after all, boy, it wasn't *news* to her that Yola Conova had been murdered. She must have known we suspected her, by the questions we asked—"

"Speak for yourself, Captain!" Dundee said harshly. "I didn't suspect her! I tell you, that word 'murder' shouted down there on those streets crashed through her poor brain like a bolt of lightning. I heard her saying it over and over—'murder. . . murder . . . murder.' She was dazed. She couldn't take it in at first. Then—the gun. And realization. And an obedient finger, on a trigger—"

"What in God's name do you mean?" Strawn pleaded. He was trembling.

"I mean," Dundee said slowly, "that I firmly believe they both died innocent, and that each thought the other was guilty."

Captain Strawn ripped out a mighty oath. Then, somewhat relieved, he reasoned: "Look, boy! One or the other of the Kenyons murdered Yola Conova. Maybe they was both in on it. I mean to say, maybe Bruce come upon the sedan after Helen had cracked Yola, or Madge, or whatever, you want to call her, over the head with the crank—or with the butt of that gun of hers, if she was carrying it then. A gun butt makes a swell 'blunt instrument'! Bruce comes up on the sedan, where it's rammed the curb, and got a flat. He finds his wife there, scared stiff at what she's done. So he pitches in and helps her by framing that fake suicide with the tow rope. Anyway, I'm satisfied that the case is solved. Now it's up to the coroner's jury. I hope they'll hold an inquest on all three of the bodies tomorrow, and get the whole mess over with. What's that you're muttering?"

Dundee looked up with a placating grin. "Sorry to be getting on your nerves like this, chief. The fact is, I was muttering to myself that I wished I could have asked Bruce Kenyon one more question."

"All right, all right! What question?" Strawn asked glumly.

"He probably would have refused to answer, but I wanted to ask him this: Why did Madge Smith choose to meet him in his office, rather than in this apartment? You see, chief, there was some good reason for that apparently insane choice of hers. Why on earth did she choose to make a trip outside the hotel, risking the danger of being followed, or at least of being seen and recognized, when he was waiting for her here? You can't say it was because she was afraid of Helen Kenyon. I'll bet a month's pay that Madge Smith didn't know, until after she talked with Kenyon at his office, that she had been the cause of a ruined marriage. I doubt if Kenyon told her even then."

"Oh, why worry about a little thing like that?" Strawn growled. "Maybe she wanted a little fresh air," he suggested with elephantine sarcasm.

Dundee shook his head as if to brush away a buzzing mosquito. "What conceivable advantage did his office have over this apartment?" he worried.

His eyes wandered around the spacious, comfortable living room of old Mrs. Kenyon's apartment, where her only son and her daughter-in-law had just died. *What did it lack that the office afforded?*

And suddenly he was on his feet, exultation routing fatigue.

"I've got it! What a sap I am! See you later, Captain! I've got work to do! And no time to talk about it! There's not going to be another death in this case if I can help it! If I haven't monkeyed around until it's already too late!"

XVII

"NO SIR. Dr. Bowen is not at home," an elderly parlor maid told James F. Dundee. "He's over at the hospital. Go one block east and then turn to your right. The big gates—"

"Let me show him, Minna! I'm all through with my supper. Honest. Come along, sir."

"No tricks now, mind you, young man!" the parlor maid called after them sternly, but the admonition was obviously for the small boy who was dragging Dundee along the path at a great rate. "If you try any more shenanigans, the doctor won't let you step foot on the hospital grounds—"

But she closed the front door of the doctor's cottage upon her own words, for the twilight was bitter cold. The child slackened his pace and looked up at Dundee with a wide, triumphant grin.

"Ginger!" the detective exclaimed involuntarily. But that was absurd, of course, for this bit of a boy had curls that were many shades darker than Kay Loring's ginger-colored mop. The kind of red hair that, for want of more accurate synonyms, is labeled burnished copper. His freckles, too, were fewer but darker than hers, and his eyes were a much deeper, more purple black than Ginger's brown-velvet eyes.

"The kids call me 'Red,' not 'Ginger'," the boy corrected him, beaming. "I like nicknames, don't you?"

"You're Nikolai," Dundee stated. "I never expected to find you here. What a stroke of luck! What's your last name, Nikolai?"

The boy had withdrawn his hand. He was not beaming now. "I don't like to be called Nikolai. All the kids at school laugh and poke fun at me for being named Nikolai Rodovsky. Some of 'em call me Sheeny, and some call me a Polecat, 'cause I told 'em my mother says it's a Polish name."

"Rodovsky," Dundee murmured. "Is your mother's first name Polish, too?"

"Yeah," the red-headed youngster admitted. "But it's the beautifullest name in the world, and my mother's the beautifullest lady. Her name is Modjeska. You spell it M-o-d-j-e-s-k-a, but like Mother always 'splains, the *d* is silent. My mother was named after a great Polish actress, she was! And she'd be a great actress, too, if it hadn't been for—Fate! What is Fate, mister?" But the boy did not wait for an answer. "How did you know my name, mister?"

"Because your hair is so red and your eyes so black," Dundee answered enigmatically. "Are you living at Dr. Bowen's, Red?"

The child beamed again. "Sure! It's swell there! I have been living at Dr. Bowen's nearly two weeks. Dr. Bowen's my guardian now. A judge said he could be my guardian till my mother, gets all well and able to take care of me again."

The detective was careful to keep any trace of startled surprise or excitement out of his voice. "I'm sorry your mother's sick. Where is she?"

The boy looked at him out of rounded, breath-taking black eyes. "Gee! You *are* dumb!" he marveled. "Where else would she be but in Doctor Daddy's hospital? And soon's she's feeling good again, I'm gonna pay her a long visit every day, and play Chinese checkers with her, and read out loud to her, and—"

"How long since you've seen your mother, Red?"

"Oh, I don't know," the boy answered. "More'n a year, I guess. She didn't get to come home last Christmas, but I betcha she'll be well by this Christmas, I betcha my bottom dollar! My mother works in New York. Did you ever hear of a lady miner, mister?"

"A—*lady* miner?"

"Minna says my mother must've turned into a digger for gold, and anybody that digs for gold and silver and coal and all like that is a miner. I betcha the work was too hard for her, and that's why she got so sick. There's the hospital, mister. It's awful funny you didn't know where it was. I betcha everybody else in Cardinal City knows where Dr. Bowen's Hospital and Sanitarium is."

"I've never been in Cardinal City before," Dundee told him. "I live nearly three hundred miles from here, in a city called Hamilton. I flew here in a plane owned by a friend of mine."

"What kind of time did you make?" Nikolai asked nonchalantly.

"Pretty fair. We took off from a Hamilton field at half past three and planed into Cardinal City at ten minutes past five. Then I took a taxi from the airport to Dr. Bowen's house, and—here I am!"

"Gee!" the boy breathed, those round black eyes glowing with admiration. "I'm gonna be an airplane pilot when I'm big. Mother wants me to be the greatest violinist in the whole world, but I'd rather be a test pilot, like Clark Gable. Did you fly here with some serum for one of Dr. Bowen's patients, that's lying at the point of death?"

"No," Dundee answered gravely. "I'm working in another scenario this time." He stooped and spoke from behind a cupped palm: "Don't give me away, Red, but—'*I Am the Law*'!"

"Gee! Gosh! Are you a racket-buster or a G-man?"

"A racket-buster—I hope. Now, Red, you cut along home and I'll tackle Dr. Bowen—"

The child's freckled face looked paper-white in the gathering dusk. "You ain't come to pinch Doctor Daddy, have you, mister?" he quavered. "He's a swell guy. Honest he is! He's awful good to me, and so is Mama Bowen. My mother is crazy about Doctor Daddy, too. He's a straight guy—"

"Don't worry, Red," Dundee said reassuringly. "And mum's the word! Don't let on to anybody—not even to Dr. Bowen—that there's a racket-buster in town. Promise? Word of honor?"

Those great eyes, like purple pansies, gazed into Dundee's blue eyes with deep solemnity. "I promise! Cross my heart, hope to die!"

"That's the stuff!" Dundee applauded, his hand on the boy's slim shoulder. "What did Minna mean—about tricks and shenanigans?"

"Aw, she don't need to worry!" Nikolai said, flushing. "I promised Doctor Daddy today I'd not try to sneak into Mother's room again. She's kinda out of her head, she's so sick. I want to see her so bad I can't hardly stand it, but my mother says you'd better die than break a promise you make on your honor, cross your heart, and hope to die. There's Dr. Bowen now, pulling the curtains across the windows in his office. So long, Mr. Racket-Buster! Be seeing you!"

"Yes, I'll be seeing you, Red," Dundee answered gravely, and watched the small figure until it blended with the shadows of shrubbery near the big gates.

There was no formality or delay. Inside the big, warm, cheerful hall a passing nurse waved toward a closed door, saying, "Dr. Bowen's in his office. Just go right in!"

If ever a man looked kindly and guileless and trustworthy, that man was Dr. Howard Bowen. With his curling fringe of white hair, his smiling, bespectacled eyes, his rosy cheeks, his rolypoly, pot-bellied little body, he was so perfect a Mr. Pickwick that it was with difficulty that Dundee remembered his real name.

"Dr. Bowen? My name is Dundee. I've just flown here from Hamilton to see a patient of yours."

Dundee was watching closely, and he could have sworn that there was no change in the beaming friendliness with which the doctor was regarding him. Apparently the name Dundee, and the city of Hamilton, meant nothing to this Pickwickian little medical man.

Perhaps he did not listen to the radio news broadcasts or read crime news in the papers.

"Have a seat, Mr. Dundee. So you flew, eh? Ideal weather for flying, after last night's terrific storm. A gale like we had last night is always dreaded by those in charge of the sick. We lost a couple of fine old trees on the sanitarium grounds, and the roof of a hen house. Was there a bad blow where you come from, sir?"

"A bit of wind, but we missed the storm," Dundee told him. "I knew, before I left Hamilton this afternoon, that Cardinal City had been quite hard hit. The telephone and telegraph service was interrupted for about three hours after midnight."

"You don't say!" the little doctor ejaculated politely. "I hadn't realized it was so bad. But it was fortunate—for business—that the wires were down at night, rather than during the day."

"Dr. Bowen, a woman tried desperately last night to reach you by long distance," Dundee said. "She put in a call for you at your home at fifteen minutes after one o'clock, and not until two o'clock did she give up hope of reaching you. She had taken a tremendous risk to get to a telephone over which she could not be overheard, for her message was for your ears alone—not for the curious ears of a hotel switchboard operator. So she went out into the night, alone, to a business office, where she was permitted to use a telephone in the utmost privacy. But the risk she took was worse than wasted. She was not able to reach you, and so—"

"My dear sir," the rotund little doctor interrupted, "I should much appreciate it if you would be brief and to the point. I am due now to begin my rounds of the sanitarium patients. I might explain that we have both a hospital and a sanitarium here, housed in different buildings and with different staffs. My chief interest is the sanitarium. The patients there are very restive if I am late—"

"I am sure I am in as great a hurry as you, doctor," Dundee said. "You have a sanitarium patient registered as Modjeska Rodovsky—"

The rosy old face became grave, even a little sad. "Yes, Modjeska's here. But her condition is such that she is not permitted any visitors. Frankly, I am puzzled at your knowing that she is here. She told me that absolutely no one who had ever known her was in her confidence and we pledged ourselves to protect her secret. Not one of her Cardinal City friends has attempted to see her—"

Dundee smiled slightly. He was remembering the links in the chain of strange clues and incredible deductions that had brought him out of the Kenyon apartment in the Randolph Hotel into this doctor's office three hundred miles from tragedy-stricken Hamilton. And he relaxed a bit. Apparently he was not too late.

"I have known for only a few minutes that your patient is using the name of Modjeska Rodovsky," he said. "I had no idea under what name I would find her, yet I came as fast as a chartered plane could bring me. By the way, doctor, do you know why your patient is calling herself Modjeska Rodovsky?"

The little doctor's eyes snapped fire behind their thick lenses. "For the usual reason, sir! Because it happens to be her name! Many patients, under similar circumstances, use an assumed name, but Modjeska did not resort to that subterfuge. But, really, sir, I must ask why—"

"A moment, please, doctor!" Dundee begged. "Would you be prepared to swear, in a court of law, for instance, that your patient is Modjeska Rodovsky?"

"Certainly, sir! I've known Modjeska Rodovsky seven or eight years. That is why she came to me in her present misfortune. But I must insist, sir—"

"Dr. Bowen," Dundee said gravely, as he presented his card, "I am here in an official capacity. And I have a warrant for the arrest of your patient, known here as Modjeska Rodovsky."

The doctor's pudgy little hands shook as he held the card close to the thick lenses of his spectacles.

"What are the charges against Modjeska, Mr. Dundee?" he asked quietly, but his Pickwickian cheeks were less rosy.

"You don't seem particularly surprised, sir."

"A doctor, Mr. Dundee, is seldom surprised at anything a confirmed alcoholic may do." He sighed deeply. "I suppose the poor girl is charged with grand larceny?"

"Grand larceny?" Dundee echoed.

"Perhaps I'm wrong, but I've been puzzling over the source of the poor girl's rather large supply of cash. She arrived absolutely penniless. I had to pay the taxi driver who brought her out. But she assured me that a package would arrive for me in the next mail, containing cash. It did, and I was dumbfounded to find that the ordinary parcel post package contained two thousand dollars in greenbacks. Her explanation was that she had sent the cash on to me so that, if she did not come here for treatment, the money would be lost to her. She did not trust herself with the money, for fear she would change her mind and use it up in drink. Frankly, sir, I had a notion, when you arrived, that you were the man in the case—a rich young man who had fallen in love with Modjeska and had financed her treatment for alcoholism. She is a widow, you know, with a nine-year-old son. But you haven't told me the charges, sir."

"There are several," Dundee answered, "including impersonation with criminal intent, obtaining money under false pretenses, and criminal conspiracy. Dr. Bowen, how well did you know the woman who is your patient, before she entered your establishment this time?"

The little medical man was quite pale now, but his voice and his near-sighted eyes were steady. "When I was in private practice I was the family physician of the Rodovskys—Modjeska and the boy, Nikolai. I believe I was first called in when the baby was about a year and a half old. The mother was conducting a little day school and day nursery then, in the basement of the First Methodist church. She also had a few older pupils for French and piano. Her fees were small and I understood that she barely made a living for herself and the boy, who was always rather delicate, without being exactly sick."

"Was Modjeska Rodovsky a healthy young woman herself?"

"Oh, yes. Extraordinarily so," the doctor replied promptly. "But I sometimes feared she was not getting enough to eat. A school like hers really had no chance during the depression, but she hung on as long as she could, largely because she was determined to earn her living in such a way as to be with the boy constantly. Their devotion has always been a beautiful and touching thing."

"Yet the boy is not permitted to see her now," Dundee said.

"Naturally not!" the doctor said sharply. "No mother who adores her boy and who wants him to respect her would permit him to see her in the condition into which Modjeska Rodovsky has got herself. Frankly, I am at a total loss to understand how so fine a girl became so quick and so complete a prey to the disease of alcoholism. An inherited predisposition, I suppose. You understand, sir, that I am violating professional ethics to talk in this way, but under the circumstances . . . I want you, sir, to realize that Modjeska Rodovsky is not exactly responsible, and that she is far too ill to stand trial now for any offense that she may have committed, since she has been a victim of the demoralizing disease of alcoholism."

"You are willing then to tell me to what extent the disease has progressed?" Dundee asked.

"'Extensive tests have been made during the seven or eight days that Modjeska has been with us," the doctor answered, "including a spinal puncture. Without going into technical explanations, I can say that there is definite mental deterioration or degeneration, and marked physical degeneration. Stomach, heart, kidneys and liver all show morbid changes, and in some instances alarming impairment."

"What are the mental symptoms?"

"In addition to the normally expected impairment of mental faculties," the doctor explained, 'the patient shows a definite psychopathic condition, making her almost unrecognizable—"

"Ah!" Dundee breathed. "Go on, doctor, please."

"If this were not clearly a case of alcoholism in advanced stages, I should suspect schizophrenia. Dementia praecox rarely manifests itself for the first time at Modjeska's age—she is twenty-eight, but of course there can be no hard and fast rule. And it is certainly not impossible for an alcoholic to be a D.P. as well. There are, however, certain tests to which she does not respond positively—"

"Is she a victim of manic-depressive insanity, by any chance?"

"I am sure she has a tendency to the particular type of mental and nervous and emotional imbalance which, at its worst, is called manic-depressive insanity," the doctor answered carefully. "But the symptoms so frequently associated with dementia praecox are much more prominent in her case. For instance, she has marked delusions of grandeur—"

"Ah!" Dundee said again. "For instance—?"

"She seems to think she's a queen—not literally, of course, but to behave as if all ordinary mortals should bow down and worship her," the doctor told him sadly. "Her nurses—she insisted, with a grand gesture, upon a day and a night special, which I confess have been needed—find her intensely trying most of the time, and occasionally very charming and ingratiating. In her efforts to get a drink of whiskey or gin she tries to bribe nurses, attendants, maids or tray boys—anyone she can manage to speak to—with promises to get them into the movies, as soon as she is out of here."

And again Dundee said, "Ah!"

"Quite typical, but distressing," the little doctor lamented. "And, like most confirmed alcoholics, she finds it almost impossible to differentiate between truth and fantasy. In fact, she seems to prefer a lie to the truth."

"Any hallucinations?"

"Definitely! She goes completely berserk at frequent intervals, laboring under the delusion that she is trapped, that she is 'buried alive,' that she will be 'railroaded' to an insane asylum, and that some man—whom she refers to only as 'he,' never using his name—has plotted to get rid of her. At other times—"

"Good Lord!" Dundee breathed, not at all blasphemously.

"Yes, it is a pitiful case," Dr. Bowen agreed "At times, as I was about to say, she seems entirely lucid, and very sensible. For instance, I was afraid she would be terribly difficult about the child, Nikolai, but not even in delirium—she suffered a rather acute attack early in the week—has she called for the boy. The core of her fineness seems to be unimpaired. The real Modjeska Rodovsky would never harm a hair of that boy's red head."

A lump pressed hurtingly against Dundee's tonsils. "I'm sure of that," he said, in a low voice. "The boy is with you. I had a talk with him. He says you are his guardian now. How did that happen, doctor?"

The little doctor flushed to the rims of his spectacles, which he now took off to wipe thoroughly. "I've always had a soft spot in my heart for Nicky," he admitted. "Modjeska —she would never let anyone shorten that mouthful or give her a nickname—Modjeska has been away from Cardinal City for most of the time these last two years. In fact, it happens that I hadn't seen her for more than two and a half years when she wired me from New York that she was coming here for treatment in my sanitarium. Naturally it never occurred to me that the poor girl was in trouble, except physically. And, while a hospital is a good hiding place, a fugitive might be expected to use an assumed name."

"In this case, your patient *had* to be known as Modjeska Rodovsky," Dundee said cryptically. "Anything else would have defeated the whole scheme."

The doctor restored his spectacles to his nose. "I take it, sir," he said, with the first touch of real belligerence, "you mean that my diagnosis of mental incompetence was essential to her defense, if she was arrested upon some of the charges you have hinted at?"

"Exactly." Dundee nodded emphatically.

"If you are implying, sir, that my diagnosis could under any circumstances be arranged for; that I could be bribed in any manner whatsoever to conspire to defeat justice—"

"Please, doctor!" Dundee interrupted the little man's almost apoplectic outburst. "Since I have been in this room I have become convinced that you are an innocent accomplice of the woman who is here under the name of Modjeska Rodovsky! I do not question your diagnosis, doctor! On the contrary, I was sure of the diagnosis of your patient before I came here today. On no other basis, as a matter of fact, could I have made the deductions which led me straight here, once I had the essential clue."

"Thank you," Dr. Bowen said stiffly, but his ruffled feathers were beginning to lie smooth again. "You were asking, sir, how I came to be in temporary charge of the child, Nikolai Rodovsky. As I told you, Modjeska found it almost impossible to make enough money here in Cardinal City to support herself and the boy, especially after she determined upon a musical career for him. He is a violinist."

"Has he talent?" Dundee interrupted, strangely hoping for a negative answer.

"He's our local child prodigy, our own Infant Heifetz," the doctor told him. "But whether the lad has genius or mere childish precocity, it is hard to say. About four years ago, after she had become convinced that Nikolai was a genius, Modjeska began to spend nearly all of her time in Chicago and New York, trying to earn enough money to give the boy the best musical education. The boy boarded with his teacher, Signor Safarini, once a famous concert violinist, I, believe, but reduced to extreme poverty in his old age. His granddaughter kept house for him and Nicky. The old man adored the boy, but the cold truth was, as I learned when Maestro Safarini died about two weeks ago, that poor Modjeska had been supporting all three of them. God knows how!"

"But you don't?" Dundee asked quickly.

"No. That's one subject she stubbornly refuses to discuss. But let me continue about the boy. I was sent for when Safarini died. His granddaughter was going to California, to try her luck in the movies, and she couldn't be bothered with the care of a child, even if he should turn out to be a genius, and hence a gold mine for her."

"Pardon me, doctor," Dundee interrupted. "But I have a rather strange request to make of you. There will be a most distressing amount of publicity connected with— Modjeska Rodovsky, I am afraid, and hence Nikolai will become involved. Personally, I think it is of paramount importance that the boy continue to develop normally and—well, sweetly and privately, unhampered by newspaper exaggerations regarding his 'genius.' Will you agree now to refrain from all mention of his musical ability to reporters?"

The little doctor had become quite pale. "Publicity! Reporters! I confess I'm dismayed. Mr. Dundee. Nothing is more harmful to a doctor and his legitimate career than newspaper headlines—regardless of how he happens to get into them. Certainly I agree with you that Nicky must be protected. Since I am legally his guardian for the present I shall be more than glad to comply with your request."

"That's fine!" Dundee breathed with deep gratitude, for he was sure that if Dink Garnet smelled the sweet odor of fame and fortune for the boy who was legally his son, he would battle for him through every court in the land. But if the red headed youngster looked like nothing more than a ten or twelve year drain upon his purse. . . . "Did Modjeska suggest your temporary guardianship of the boy?"

"Ultimately, yes. Nina Safarini, in her hurry to make a clean sweep of everything after her grandfather's death, had burned all his papers, including Modjeska's letters. And she didn't remember the poor girl's address. She knew I was particularly fond of the youngster, so she sent for me and I promptly brought him home—tickled to death at the chance to have him with me. Before a week had passed Modjeska wired me that she was coming here for treatment—"

"May I see that telegram, doctor? Please!"

The doctor started to protest, then shrugged his plump shoulders and went to a large steel filing cabinet, which he unlocked.

"I keep my case histories here," he explained. "The telegram is attached to Modjeska's history. Here it is, sir."

It was a day letter, from New York, dated November 9, a Tuesday. Dundee read:

ARRIVING WEDNESDAY ELEVEN P.M. TO UNDERGO FULL COURSE OF TREATMENT YOUR SPECIALTY DETERMINED ON LASTING CURE STOP HAVE CHANGED TERRIBLY AFRAID YOU WILL BE SHOCKED BUT KNOW YOU WILL HELP FOR NICKYS SAKE DONT LET HIM SEE ME TILL I AM WELL HAVE PLENTY MONEY BEST REGARDS

MODJESKA RODOVSKY

Without a word he handed the yellow sheet back, but under his breath he muttered, "Clever! Oh, clever, clever!"

"I understood what was wrong," Dr. Bowen explained, glancing at the message as if to refresh his mind. "My specialty in the sanitarium is the treatment of alcoholism, by a method of my own, which has been rather unusually successful, I believe. I was actually stunned by the message, Mr. Dundee, for while I had not known Modjeska Rodovsky very well, I had formed a very high opinion of her. But I attributed her downfall to psychological causes, and when she came I was determined to get at the psychic cause of the poor girl's terrible misfortune. I found, however, that she had offered herself for treatment too late."

"Too late?" Dundee echoed. "You mean she can't be cured?"

"Oh, she can be cured of addiction to alcohol, I think," Dr. Bowen answered, "but the physical and mental ravages of the disease are so great that she can never be a healthy woman again. It was partly because I was convinced of this that I had myself appointed Nikolai's guardian. Modjeska signed the necessary paper—quite willingly and gratefully."

Dundee made an inarticulate ejaculation which Dr. Bowen mistook for an expression of pity.

"Yes, I am afraid Modjeska Rodovsky will never be fit in any sense of the word—to take personal charge of her son again," Dr. Bowen said, sighing. "Of course, since you are here with a warrant for her arrest on grave charges, I am the more glad that the boy is protected—"

"Tell me, doctor! Would you have recognized your patient as Modjeska Rodovsky if she had not apprised you of her coming by wire?"

The little doctor considered. "Why, yes," he said, after marked hesitation. "Her features, her general physical characteristics, are not radically changed. I should say that the most decisive change is in personality. And in— spirit, if I may be pardoned the use of the word. Of course, since she is mentally ill, her soul is in hiding behind the intruding personality—if you get what I mean."

"I think I understand perfectly," Dundee said, quite truthfully. "Do you find her memory seriously impaired?"

"Definitely. That is, of course, one of the unfailing symptoms of alcoholic insanity. Also her inability to concentrate. She cannot read for more than a minute at a time, or listen to what anyone says—"

"Pardon me, doctor!" Dundee cut in eagerly. "But has she taken an interest in the newspapers since she arrived? Or in radio news broadcasts?"

"Ah! You think she may have been expecting your arrival—or someone's coming to arrest her?" the doctor deduced. "Quite likely, Mr. Dundee. As a matter of fact, her nurses have reported that she can hardly wait for her copy of the morning and evening papers to which she subscribes, but that she hardly does more than glance at the pages before she flings them away. She has no radio in her room. Patients furnish their own, and Modjeska of course did not bring one from New York and has not been well enough to initiate the renting of one. She is really a desperately sick woman, Mr. Dundee."

"I'm sure she is," Dundee said grimly. "Have you seen her today?"

"Certainly! I see all my patients twice a day. She was having a very bad time of it—had spent a sleepless night, according to her chart, walking for hours in a state of extreme apprehension. Typical of an alcoholic denied the accustomed stimulant. By my method the patient is taken completely off all intoxicants. I do not subscribe to the graduated-dose type of therapy. Her condition of exhaustion, coupled with extreme depression, was so great that I prescribed a narcotic hypodermically. You see, her obsession that she is 'trapped,' 'plotted against' and 'buried alive' had reached the point of acute mania."

"I see," Dundee said. "I see—a great deal. Have you a copy of your morning paper, doctor?"

Dr. Bowen shifted a mass of papers and books on his desk, peeped into his overflowing waste-baskets, stuffed mainly, it appeared, with pharmaceutical house advertising, then rose and trotted briskly to a glass-doored bookcase, on whose top lay the folded paper.

"I confess," he said, rather ruefully, "that I haven't looked at the paper today. I seldom have time before I go to bed at night, and usually I'm too tired to do more than glance at the foreign news and Washington datelines and the editorials. My medical journals—But I beg your pardon! Here is the paper."

Before accepting it Dundee knew that, since it was a regular edition of the Cardinal City morning paper, "put to bed" at least a couple of hours before the news of Yola Conova's "suicide" had been out on the leased wires, it would of course contain no reference to that tragedy. Nor was it likely that Cardinal City newspapers would have issued extras on the suicide of a motion-picture star who was no longer of top rank, even though the tragedy had occurred within the state.

He was right. The front page contained no mention of the name of Yola Conova, but as he turned the pages of *The Cardinal City Press* he came suddenly upon a large close-up of the star, dominating the page devoted to motion-picture reviews and gossip, as retailed by a syndicated Hollywood columnist, the famous and feared Lucretia Patrick. The caption beneath the picture was, "Yola Conova, shown above as she appears in *Magnificent Sin*, gives Cardinal City the go-by on her personal appearance tour. Her latest sex 'opera' is *not* packing them in at the Grand Theater."

The viciousness of the feeling against the star was apparently strictly local—a case of sour grapes, possibly—for Lucretia Patrick was rather astonishingly fulsome in her praise. Dundee's eyes leaped down the paragraph printed entirely in italics, which appeared under the syndicated heading, HOLLYWOOD HIGHLIGHTS, by Lucretia Patrick, Motion Picture Editor, International Feature Service:

"All of Yola Conova's old friends in Hollywood—and this writer has been one of Yola's most intimate friends for years and years—are delighted that she and that amazing youngster, Clinton Risher, are standing them in the aisles

on their personal appearance tour. As was predicted in this column about a month ago when Yola was rather discouraged, her greatest success lies ahead of her, not behind her. Hollywood producers, please take notice! As for Clinton, that boy certainly has what it takes, and if those two manage to get back to Hollywood without having come to an understanding which will involve a divorce for Yola, then the little birds we have working for us in New York, Chicago and Hamilton, where the couple are this minute, are all wrong. But when it happens, remember you read it here first! Good luck, Yola and Clint! . . ."

As Dundee read he was conscious that the little doctor was peering over his shoulder.

"Tchk, tchk!" clucked the doctor. "I wonder . . . Mr. Dundee, I've been very frank with you. Now will you please answer a question for me? You said that one of the charges against Modjeska Rodovsky was impersonation, I believe."

"Impersonation with intent to defraud," Dundee answered, "is one of the charges against the woman who is now your patient."

"It occurs to me, Mr. Dundee, that a certain queer trick that Fate played on Modjeska Rodovsky became the basis of an obsession that took hold of the poor girl quite a long time ago, and which has now become a definitely psychotic delusion. Am I right in my guess that Modjeska Rodovsky has been guilty of impersonating this motion-picture actress? This"—he looked again to confirm the name—"this Yola Conova?"

Dundee chose his words carefully. "I think there is no doubt that Modjeska Rodovsky assumed the name of Yola Conova."

The Pickwickian little physician sighed and shook his head. "And now you're thinking of her as a criminal, and I'm thinking of her as a psychiatric case. And when we meet in court the poor girl will be as resentful of and bewildered by my analysis of her as by your charges.

Modjeska's is rather a strange story, Mr. Dundee. Some of it I heard from the girl herself years ago, some I've learned this last week through her nurses, who've picked up a bit of local gossip somehow. Modjeska came here from California between seven and eight years ago, as near as I can remember without consulting my files. She had just been through an odd experience, which had quite naturally embittered her. It seems that she had worked very hard to get into motion pictures, and had actually been signed by one of the less important studios on a short-term contract, when suddenly this star"—he pointed to the picture of Yola Conova in the paper— "made her appearance in a startlingly successful picture produced by one of the major studios. Poor Modjeska's modest little career died a-borning. Her studio—one of the 'independents,' I believe they're called —had to stop production on the picture which was half finished, until a new and entirely different girl could be found for Modjeska's role, and when her short-term contract was finished she was out of pictures—forever. She never appeared on the screen. There was of course no room in the industry for two Yola Conovas, and since the major studio had brought out the first of the two who looked so much alike as to be able to double for each other, it was their star who rose to fame and fortune. As I understand it from movie fans, there can be no greater handicap than to resemble a star—if you want to get into pictures. Modjeska found that to be true. Merely by existing, Yola Conova kept Modjeska Rodovsky from making a living in the fields where her assets normally would have been marketable at a good figure."

Dundee nodded. "I see. She was cut off from the legitimate stage and musical comedy, as well as from pictures. For the same reason she could not get a job as a commercial photographer's model nor as a clothes model. Tough luck! And she took it hard, I suppose?"

"Much harder, it seems now, than anyone, suspected," Dr. Bowen answered. "Her resentment against the accident of fate which had elevated Yola Conova and condemned her to obscurity, in which she could live in no peace because of everyone's saying, 'Why, you look just like Yola Conova! You're the image of her!,' must have gone very deep, until it warped her mind. After she became an alcoholic, as a means of escape, *she definitely 'escaped' from her true self into the personality of the woman who had wronged her merely by looking like her.* I believe that at last Modjeska Rodovsky came to believe that she was Yola Conova, and that she is guiltless of criminal intent if she has publicly impersonated the real star."

"I take it, then, doctor, that *if your patient here had ever openly contended that she was Yola Conova,* you would not have been surprised?"

"Certainly I should not have been surprised!" the doctor retorted. "I should have considered it an entirely normal manifestation of her *abnormal* mental condition."

"Then tell me, doctor, what would have happened to your patient if she had still been here when all of that two thousand dollars was gone—paid out for treatment, hospitalization and special nurses? Would you have certified her as a lunatic and asked for her admission to the state asylum for the insane?"

The little man's rosy cheeks were scarlet now, but not with shame. His voice was strong with righteous anger. "I fail utterly to understand the drift of your remarks, sir, but if Modjeska had failed to respond to treatment, if she had persisted in her delusion of being another person—this Yola Conova—then continued hospitalization would of course have been essential. Our state institution for the care of the mentally ill is efficient and humanitarian to the highest possible degree. However, your question seems to be hypothetical. If you are right, and Modjeska Rodovsky has committed a serious crime, or crimes, her future home will probably be our state institution for the *criminally* insane. That prospect, I am frank to say, grieves me deeply."

There was a knock at the door, but without waiting for an answer a pimply adolescent panting with excitement loped into the doctor's office, an evening newspaper in his hand.

"Gee, Dr. Bowen!" the boy gasped. "Did you hear what happened to me? Gosh! I'm still shaking! That Polack must be nuttier'n a chocolate bar! I betcha it'll be the locked ward for *her* tonight!"

"What are you talking about, Benjy?" the little doctor demanded, reaching for the newspaper.

"I'm taking papers to the patients in the sanitarium, see?" the boy began. "Nearly everybody's waiting at their doors to take the papers away from me, patients and nurses both, all steamed up over this pitcher star murder in Hamilton, see? Well, I—"

Dr. Bowen was staring at the front page. His hands were shaking. "Yola Conova—murdered!" he read aloud. "I've got to get to Modjeska, Mr. Dundee. She'll need me—"

"I'll say she does!" Benjy panted. "She was waiting for me, too, like she always does. But she didn't know nothing about the murder, because soon as she read the headlines that says this here pitcher star didn't commit suicide, but was murdered in cold blood—"

"Make it snappy, Son!" Dundee ordered sharply.

"I am, ain't I? This Polack that everybody's knows is a dead ringer for that Conova dame takes one look at them headlines and then she goes cuckoo! Screaming and everything. Miss Pruitt, the general, come running. Seems like the patient's special was down to supper . . . Well, the Polack grabbed Miss Pruitt and shook her and then begun to pound her with her fists. And all the time she was gabbling a lot of silly stuff—"

"What did she say?" Dundee demanded tensely. "Try to repeat her very words!"

"Well, she kept yelling at Pruitt, 'Look! Murdered, it says, nurse! Murdered! But I'm not dead!' she screams, over and over. You see, mister, looks like she thought she was this here Conova dame! Gosh!" he breathed, his eyes and mouth wide with juvenile relish of horror. "It must be somepn fierce to be off your base and think you're *murdered but not dead!*"

XVIII

A FEW MINUTES LATER, after Dundee had told Dr Bowen all that it was necessary for him to know, the special investigator waited outside the slightly open door of Room 327, listening.

"Doctor, please, please!" a husky voice was pleading. "If I tell you something very strange and—and incredible, but true, doctor, true as life and death are true!—will you at least listen to me as if I were not a patient, as if you had not made up your mind that I'm crazy?"

"Later, my dear," Dr. Bowen's voice answered. "But now—"

"Oh, I know!" Her, cry was so tragic, so hopeless that Dundee's eyes stung with sudden tears. "Your mind's made up! And who could blame you? I *am* an alcoholic! *I'm* to blame for this trap I'm in, not you! But I only wanted to be cured of—of my habit, like my husband was! But I'm *not* insane! I haven't delusions or hallucinations or—Listen, doctor! I've simply, got to put in a long distance call! Immediately! You can listen in, if you like! Then you'll know that what I tell you is true, that I'm— Oh! What if Geoff says I'm crazy, too? What if he's expecting me to call, and refuses to talk to me? Oh, oh, my *God!*"

"Listen, child," Dr. Bowen interrupted, pityingly. "Prove to me that you're mistress of yourself, else I can't let you see your visitor."

"Visitor?" that husky voice repeated. "A visitor! Is it—?"

"A visitor from Hamilton. He flew here to see you," the doctor said, obediently following Dundee's instructions.

"From—*Hamilton*? Oh! Oh, Geoff! Geoff! Oh, my darling! Where are you, Geoffrey?" she cried with hysterical rapture.

And before Dundee could realize what was happening a sobbing, laughing woman was hurling herself against his breast, her small hands clutching at his coat lapels as if they were life lines thrown to her in a shipwreck. Her face was pressed so hard against his vest buttons that minutes later their imprint still lingered on her unhealthily puffed cheek "I didn't mean what I was saying, Geoff!" she sobbed and laughed "But I've been so frightened. Even before that terrible girl got herself murdered? I should have known you wouldn't leave me to rot here, locked up like a crazy person!

"Darling Geoff!" her words rushed on, in a torrent that Dundee had no wish to dam. "It must have been horrible for you today, but why didn't you tell them right off that it wasn't me? Imagine, Geoff, reading about your own murder. And such a horrible murder, Geoff?" She shivered violently, and clung to Dundee more tightly. "But it's all right now, isn't it, darling Geoff! Why don't you say something? Why don't you kiss me, darling?"

"I'm sorry, Miss Conova," Dundee said gently. "Shall we go into your room?"

The little doctor and the special nurse had slipped away. Without waiting for an answer Dundee put his arm about Yola Conova's waist—oddly thick it was, in comparison with the dead girl's—and half carried her to a chair, kicking the door shut behind them. She was limp and unresisting as he settled her in the big chair, making rather a fuss about it, so that she could gain a measure of composure without his eyes upon hers. The ridiculously tiny feet—disfigured now with the puffy ankles that indicate kidney trouble—he lifted and set upon a footstool.

"What—did you—call me?" she whispered at last.

"'Miss Conova.'   But perhaps you prefer to be known as Mrs. Arundel in private life," Dundee told her matter-of-factly.

In the second before realization dawned on her Dundee had a chance to study her, to compare her face, her body, and her personality—insofar as it could be read under the circumstances—with that of the girl who had come to Hamilton falsely as Yola Conova, a girl whose real name was Modjeska Rodovsky, but whom Pauline Loring had rechristened nearly twelve years before, giving her the humble name of Madge Smith.

There was, of course, a strong resemblance, a likeness which must have been far more striking before this woman's beauty had been impaired with disease and alcoholism. But they had never been, he was sure, "as like as two peas in a pod." No wonder there had been so much doubt in Hamilton that the lowly and erring "Madge Smith" had become the glamorous star! Dundee had seen that other woman only once, off stage, when she was being taunted and threatened by Dink Garnet at the stage door, but his heart had gone out to her. She had seemed—well, *good.*

Not that this woman—this real Yola Conova—looked evil. But she did look disillusioned, selfish, imperious, spoiled, bitter. And not so beautiful, really, as Modjeska Rodovsky. There were puffs under her famous eyes— dark, stormy eyes on the screen, but dulled now, and slightly bloodshot. A roll of soft fat around her waist that his supporting hand had felt and flinched from. Puffy ankles. Betraying tremors in her small, gaudily manicured hands.

Suddenly hot anger surged in his blood. That this one should be the real Conova, the star who had had the equivalent of a lifetime of success, fame and adoration, while that other girl had known only disgrace, frustration, and death at the hands of a murderer!

But now Yola Conova was fully alive again, her marred face glowing, her dulled eyes glittering with tears of joy.

"Geoffrey sent you!" she cried. "He couldn't get away from that miserable little hick town, I suppose. But why on earth, I ask you, did Geoffrey do such an insane thing as to go to Hamilton? Never mind! You won't tell him I

was so—frightened, so suspicious of him, will you? Sick
people are likely to have sick fancies—"

Dundee looked at her searchingly, trying to make sure
that she was not acting. "Were you really terrified to the
point of insanity by the suspicion that Geoffrey Arundel
meant to abandon you to a living death—committed to a
madhouse?"

She nodded, biting her lips that had acquired the
habit of trembling like an old, old woman's. "Wasn't I
foolish?" she quavered. "The only thing was, he was so
terribly enthusiastic about our plan—his plan, it was
really!—to send a double to take my place on the tour
while I took *her* place and put myself in the hands of *her*
own doctor to take a cure for—for a nervous breakdown. .
. . Of course, it seemed to me the only thing to do, too,
until after I was here, and the—the cure began, and was
so horrible, and I couldn't sleep—" And she began to
shiver again, hugging herself pitifully with her crossed
arms, as if she were cold with a fatal chill.

"It must have been bad," Dundee said, almost dumb
before her complete absorption in herself, her lack of
realization.

"Thank you, darling," and she smiled—a flash of the
Conova he had admired on the screen: a smile that was a
glimmer of glory. It was, to Dundee, like seeing a lovely
child peering from behind a dark curtain for one dazzling
moment.

"But everything's all right now," she went on, and the
lovely child was gone. "Don't look so sad, darling. The
report of my death has been grossly exaggerated, as Mark
Twain said. Now I can stay here a bit longer, as my true
self. It'll be fun to see my nurses and doctors change their
tune! I can really give myself up to getting well now. But
be sure not to tell Geoff I doubted him—"

Dundee's blood ran cold. "I can understand your
relief," he said. "But there are other aspects—rather
serious ones—"

"Old sobersides, you!" she chided, with a sudden gamin grin that was painful to see. "Of course I know all this publicity is terrible, but it may not be so bad, really! One never knows how the public will react, but I wager they'll fight to see my next picture. After all, it's not my fault if that wretched girl was murdered—"

Dundee could stand no more. "But she *has* been murdered! While hired by you to take *your* place!"

She suddenly became very much the offended queen. "*I* did not hire her. My husband did. With my consent, but the plan was his. And he certainly did not hire her to get herself into such a mess, and ruin my career!"

Dundee's lips felt stiff and strange against his teeth. "Had it occurred to you, Miss Conova, that the police will believe *that Modjeska Rodovsy doubled in death for you— as well as in life? That she was hired for that purpose?*"

"What do you mean? It sounds like a riddle. . . . Who are you? You don't sound like a friend of Geoffrey's—"

"I'm afraid, Miss Conova, that I deliberately took advantage of a very natural mistake on your part and permitted you to talk freely—"

"A reporter!" she cried, torn between dismay and gratification. Swiftly she surveyed herself and apparently was satisfied with what she saw—magnificent lounging pajamas of scarlet-and-black satin, pointed scarlet fingernails, tiny black satin slippers—slippers that did not quite match, since one was trimmed with, gold kid, and the other with silver. Slippers whose mates had led Dundee straight to this room. From the pocket of her pajama coat she whipped out a vanity case and tiny, comb.

"Thank heaven you didn't bring a photographer," she said, as she pulled the comb through the sleek blackness of her hair that was coiled in a great, shining loop on her neck. Her hair, at least, seemed to have suffered no loss of beauty through her illness. It was, he noted, with surprising resentment, more beautiful than poor Madge Smith's.

"Please don't bother, Miss Conova," he said coldly. "I'm not a reporter. I'm a special investigator from the office of the district attorney of Hamilton County. In other words, Miss Conova, I'm a detective!" he added, with intentional brutality "My name is Dundee."

"A—*detective*?" She looked almost idiotically puzzled, but not at all frightened. "I'm afraid I don't see why you've come to see me—"

"I've been trying to make you realize why I'm here. A murder has been committed, Miss Conova. So far, everyone who reads newspapers and listens to radio news broadcasts thinks you have been murdered—"

She shivered and again hugged herself with her crossed arms "I know! Isn't it *ghastly*? But now that you've seen that I'm really alive you'll tell the press, and—Oh, yes! Please tell them, if you see the reporters before I do, that I shall of course arrange it so that Modjeska Rodovsky's little boy—she has a son, you know—never wants for anything. That's not a bad idea, really! It will simply, save the day for me, wipe out all the bad effects of the wrong kind of publicity. Listen!" and she actually seemed about to clap her hands. "'Star will double as mother for dead double's son!'" she improvised "Really, I'll be awfully glad to do it. I understand he's a wonderfully clever little boy. Sings like an angel, they say! I'll devote myself to his career—make another Bobby Breen out of him!"

"Miss Conova, please give me your attention!" Dundee commanded harshly. "When you thought I was your husband you said, 'Why didn't you tell them right off that it wasn't me?' I think you know the answer to that question!" and his blue eyes held her dark ones relentlessly, until comprehension dawned in them, widening the pupils alarmingly.

"Oh!" she whispered, and one hand went slowly to her throat. "You—mean—? But—but Geoffrey *told* you where to find me, or you wouldn't have known! If he—he'd meant to—to—"

"Geoffrey Arundel did not tell me or anyone else that Yola Conova is alive," Dundee answered her, his eyes refusing to let hers waver. *"He identified the body as yours!* He meant never to tell the world that you are alive!"

"I—I—" she gasped, but her throat was locked in a spasm of terror.

"You asked me why Arundel went to Hamilton. I suggest that he went to Hamilton in order to be on the ground so that he could make a false identification—an identification that none could question! That he arrived in Hamilton and waited quite confidently for that corpse to be brought into our morgue, and to be called upon, by the police to view that cold, stiff body, to identify it as yours!"

"No; no!" she whispered.

"You asked me why I came here to see you," Dundee went on. "I am sure you can guess now the answer to that question, too. Miss Conova, you can refuse to answer my questions if you wish. It is my duty to point out your rights and privileges under the criminal code—"

"But—" she gasped, her scarlet fingernails cutting into the flesh of her throat. "*I* haven't committed any crime! I haven't anything to hide! Oh, I don't know what to say! I'm frightened again! I'm terribly frightened!" she whispered hoarsely, and this time it was a desolate child that peered from behind the dark curtain, to plead with her accuser for reassurance and comfort.

"You have committed not one crime but several, Miss Conova," Dundee told her gravely. "One of the crimes with which I stand ready to charge you is impersonation with intent to defraud—"

"Impersonation?" she repeated. "Oh, hiring a double, you mean! But out in Hollywood everybody uses stand-ins and doubles. Maybe not for personal appearance tours, darling, but—"

"My name is Dundee," he reminded her grimly. "The major crime with which I am ready to charge you, Miss

Conova, is conspiracy to commit murder in order to defraud the Reliance Life insurance Company of one million dollars. Again it is my duty to warn you that anything you say be used against you."

To his intense amazement she laughed suddenly. "It sounds just like a movie! But you're being awfully silly, you know! Why on earth should I conspire to murder *myself*? I'd have to keep permanently out of the way, wouldn't I? Be *'murdered but not dead'*. Talk sense!"

"A million dollars affords remarkable scope for traveling in very distant lands," Dundee reminded her "What more natural than that the bereaved husband of poor Yola Conova, who had succeeded at last in committing suicide, should travel in foreign countries? And what more natural than that, after a decent interval, he should marry again—a woman, oddly, enough, who happened to look a lot like his dear, dear screen-star wife. I suggest, Miss Conova, that you saw no reason to doubt that you could get away with it—*provided your husband did not cash in and keep the whole million, leaving you to rot in a madhouse!* It was a desperate scheme, Miss Conova! So well-plotted that you thought you were forever caught in a trap of your own making! *Because you did not trust your accomplice!"*

She held out her hand. "Please!" she said, like a well-mannered little girl. "I want a cigarette. I've smoked all my own."

Dundee took a pack from his pocket, held a match for her while she got her cigarette going, then lit one for himself. A small, rather shy smile rewarded him. He tried to shake off the spell which her vanishing charms still had power to cast. He must not forget that she was an actress of long experience.

"You *are* being silly, you know, darling," she said with more confidence. And the spell was broken for Dundee. "Why on earth should Geoffrey go to such trouble and risk to murder my double, when it would have been so simple to murder me without ever being suspected?"

"The answer to that is that Arundel did not want to murder you, because he loves you, but he wanted to enjoy all the advantages of your death without your being actually dead."

"If you think Geoffrey actually did murder Modjeska Rodovsky, and planned to let the world believe forever that it was me, then you have a strange idea of love," she told him scornfully. "And if Geoffrey was too impatient to wait for me to drink myself to death, he could have slipped a high-powered poison into one of my sleeping powders, and no one would have questioned the verdict of suicide. I tried more than once to commit suicide—*half* tried, anyway. I left suicide notes that weren't dated, and Geoff could have kept one of them instead of destroying them each time he found me still alive in the morning. He could have kept one and used it—easy! So why on earth, I repeat, should my husband have gone this roundabout way to murder—not me, but my double! Taking a *double* risk of detection, by the way, if you'll pardon the pun."

Dundee felt limp and helpless. And not a little foolish. For this small creature, sick though she was, her mentality impaired by chronic alcoholism, had put her scarlet-nailed finger right on the weak spot of his whole theory, which was really concerned with Arundel, not with her, as the murderer. He would have to be more on his guard with her, he decided. She was far cleverer than he had given her credit for being. A complex and dangerous person, this Yola Conova!

And then suddenly he had the answer to her question. By betraying to him the fact that she was actually enjoying herself in this new role—probably the most dramatic of her long career—she had given him the essential clue. For she was typical, he was sure, of that strange, unreal land known as Hollywood. And Geoffrey Arundel was no less an actor. He too had the psychology of Hollywood!

"Geoffrey Arundel," he began, "is an actor. Nothing is very real to him except himself—and you, because you

are a part of himself. You've been his wife for a good
many years—six, isn't it? A lifetime in Hollywood! You're
part of his only reality—himself. To kill you would be
murder. It would be real to him. Real murder. He couldn't
pretend it was anything else. And very probably he is still
rather fond of you. No, let me go on! But cry if you like.
And I'm sure Geoffrey Arundel wouldn't want to feel
guilty of murder. I don't think he could stand the reality
of knowing himself a murderer. But a stand-in—a double!
That was a different matter! Modjeska Rodovsky was
never *real* to Geoffrey Arundel—nor to you! You've
betrayed that essential fact a dozen times since I came
into this room. She wasn't *real* to you, *and it isn't real to
you yet that she is dead!* To you, to Geoffrey Arundel, she
existed only to 'double' for you in a sequence that was too
dangerous for you to risk your precious skin by acting in
it personally. When she had served her purpose it was as
if she had never been. That's the truth, isn't it, Yola
Conova? All of it?"

She nodded obediently, even admiringly. "I'd never
thought of it that way, but it is true. Doubles aren't
people. You don't know them, really. They're just—sort of
like props, for us to use as we need them, and then to
discard and forget. Somehow," she confessed, wrinkling
her white forehead with its fascinating widow's peak. "I
still can't make Modjeska Rodovsky seem real. Just
think, darling, she was a living human being—not just a
shadow of *me*! And yet she isn't real to anyone except—
you! All the world think she's me! She doesn't exist—even
as a corpse, *until I give the word to make her real!* Then
everyone will try to pronounce her name and wonder a bit
about her and forget her name, and—*remember me!*"

"You're not only the 'Incomparable Conova'; you're the
'Incredible Conova,'" Dundee said, his blue eyes icy. "If
you wish you may make a statement, which will be taken
down in shorthand for you to sign—a statement which
may be used against you—"

"Oh!" she gasped 'Oh, *darling*' Don't frighten me to death. What did you say your name is?" She put a pitiful hand to her forehead 'I can't remember. I'm—a little forgetful—sometimes—"

"Dundee is the name," he reminded her "It is not darling.'"

"I beg your pardon," she said with surprising humility. "I don't mean any harm. It's just a—a Hollywood habit. I shan't mind signing a statement later, but, please, won't you just let me tell you things first, without worrying about how they'll sound when they're written out? Couldn't we sort of make a—a synopsis of my story later and let me sign that?"

"Of course," Dundee said stiffly, but his heart was melting toward her in spite of himself.

"Then, listen!" she begged, still with childlike humility and sweetness, "if I can *prove* to you that when Modjeska Rodovsky died I had absolutely no motive for conspiring to murder her, but every reason in the world to want her to live, you'll have to believe I am innocent of any conspiracy to—to murder her, won't you?"

"I shall be glad to listen."

She had kept Dundee's pack of cigarettes. Now she took the third and lit it, as if the action were purely automatic. "I once had a little dog that had to go into a hospital for an operation," she began slowly. "He was absolutely terrified that I meant to leave him there, so the vet told me my poor dog would rest easy, that he wouldn't be frightened, if I left something of my own in his cage that he knew I valued. I left my gloves. You see, dar—I mean, Mr. Dundee—my little dog thought that even if I didn't want him again, I'd come back for my gloves." Heavy tears brimmed in her eyes and dropped upon the hand that was clenched in her lap.

"I see," Dundee said, and cleated his throat. "What measures did you take to make sure that your husband would not leave you here?"

"I wrote a check for the quarterly premium on my insurance on Wednesday morning before I left New York. The last day of grace would be Friday. Geoffrey kept reminding me to write it, so that he could mail it himself, before I left to come here. No one can sign checks on my bank account but me. So I wrote the check. But Mr. Dundee, *I deliberately wrote that check on the wrong bank!"*

Dundee's heart felt suddenly light, for the first time in many hours. He did not know why he was so glad, that this strange, selfish, tormented little creature had cleared herself, in his eyes, of the charge of conspiracy to commit murder. There was no question that she was speaking the truth. She had had no opportunity to learn the facts of the returned check, marked "Account Closed." And she had cleared up a mystery that had puzzled him sorely— how such a mistake could have been made, when so much depended on the insurance policy.

But he said, coldly enough, "Were you not afraid the policy would lapse, because of the check's being on the wrong bank?"

"Once before I made the same mistake, but not intentionally, and they simply sent the check back and let me draw one on the correct bank, although the last day of grace had passed. I knew Geoff would receive notice from the Reliance company, because it was arranged that Modjeska was to send all my mail on to him. And I knew Geoff wouldn't permit that policy to lapse. So, since he was making so damned sure I'd come here and take the cure, *I* made damned sure *he* would have to come to me— to get me to sign a new check on the right bank."

"Didn't you realize he could have written you?"

"Of course! And a letter would have been evidence that I was really Yola Conova! He'd have had to send me the returned check and the notice from the insurance company, and a request that I make it good. You see, Geoff had made me agree that it wouldn't be safe for him to write me—and that was one thing that frightened me so, when I woke up cold sober that Wednesday morning and knew that soon I'd be Modjeska Rodovsky and Modjeska Rodovsky would be Yola Conova, and I'd be shut up, and—"

"Yes, I see," Dundee cut in hastily, for she was verging on hysterics. "You were afraid that your husband not only meant to leave you here, but to murder your double and profit by your 'death'?"

"Of course I didn't think he meant to do any such thing!" she cried. "I thought he meant to substitute Modjeska Rodovsky for me *permanently*, because— because I wasn't able to go on any longer."

"Did you seriously suspect that Modjeska Rodovsky would be party to such a fraud?" Dundee asked. "Did she seem like that sort of person to you?"

Those great, tormented black eyes stared at him. "So you fell for her, too," she said wonderingly. "I liked her myself. I realize that now. She was awfully good to me. She treated me as if I were a sick child, not as if I—But I've got so I don't trust anybody!"

"Was it Modjeska Rodovsky who asked for the job of double, or you who asked her to take it?"

"What? . . . Didn't I tell you about that?" She was looking extremely tired. Dundee was afraid she might collapse any minute. "Geoffrey happened to run into her outside the theater where I was appearing in New York. Some fans had mistaken her for me and were begging her for my autograph."

"So it was your husband who made her a business offer to double for you?"

"I don't remember much about it all. I was—well, I was drunk, you know. That's why Geoff thought he simply had to do something. I think he had her wait in a taxi until he came up to my room in the hotel and got some of my clothes —street clothes, for her to wear. But the first I knew there she was in my room, in my,clothes, taking care of me, and Geoff was urging her to double for me on the tour, while I took treatment. That was four or five days before I was to leave for Chicago. She was with me constantly until she left for Chicago, as *me*, and I left for Cardinal City as *her*. Oh, I'm so tired, so tired!"

"I know," Dundee admitted contritely. "And you're being splendid. I appreciate your cooperation more than I can tell you."

"And *you're* sweet," she told him, reviving. "Not at all like detectives in movies, except Bill Powell, of course. Well, Geoff taught Modjeska the lines of the one-act play and coached her on being *me*. I gave her nearly all my clothes, that I wouldn't need here, and a diet my doctor had given me two or three years ago, when I first began to put on a pound or two. Geoff thought she ought to have some documentary evidence that she was me. And he made me address a bunch of envelopes in my own handwriting, so that she could forward my mail to *him*—"

"Geoffrey Arundel seems to have thought of everything," Dundee said grimly. "Your handwriting on those envelopes would be a very handy bit of legal proof that you had been in Hamilton, that you were the dead woman—if a question arose as to her identity!"

"Oh! I see!" she gasped, her lips going white around their rouged edges. "He thought of something else, too. He had Modjeska give me *her* birth certificate and her little boy's birth certificate. He told her they would be safe with me, and that she simply must not risk having them found in her possession while she was *me*. I gave them to Dr. Bowen when I checked in here. I'd never in the world have convinced him that I wasn't Modjeska Rodovsky, if you hadn't come, would I?"

Dundee ignored that question. It was too poignant.

"How did the two of you—two Yola Conovas—manage to get out of the hotel without exciting comment?"

She smiled with pride of profession. "I'm an actress, remember. And Geoff is amazingly good at make-up. He made Modjeska look like me to the dot, and he fixed me up to look like no one in particular. Modjeska gave me a marcel wave—she used to be a beauty operator in New

York, I think—and Geoff put a lot of flashy looking rouge on my cheeks. I never wear my hair curled and I never wear cheek rouge, so that I looked entirely different, and nothing else was necessary except my glasses, which I always wear for reading. Modjeska and I left my suite together and walked right out through the lobby together. If anyone gave me a second glance they took it for granted that I was some friend of Yola Conova's, or a woman reporter, come to see her off. In fact, I kissed her good-by!"

"Superb!" Dundee commented sincerely.

"Oh, it was Geoff's idea, but I admit I did a good job," she told him, so pleased with herself that life was coming back to her lips and she was no longer trembling. "We took separate taxis, and we both went to Grand Central station. Geoff had bought our tickets and had checked both sets of luggage for us that morning. I had my ticket and my baggage checks, but otherwise I had nothing— absolutely no money at all, not even for a tip for the red cap or Pullman porter. Modjeska paid my taxi fare in advance, just before we left Geoff made her do it. He wanted to make absolutely certain I'd go through with it, and not have money to get drunk on before I got here."

Dundee whistled. "He *is* a thorough chap. How did you manage about money for this place?" he asked, as if Dr. Bowen had not already told him.

"I checked out nearly all the money I had in the bank, except enough to cover the insurance check," she told him. "Geoff cashed the check for me. After I'd paid all my bills, I gave Modjeska five hundred dollars, Geoff five hundred, and kept two thousand for myself. Geoff made me make a package of it and address it to Dr. Bowen here, and then he let me watch him, from the door of our suite, while he dropped it down the mail chute in the hall. Modjeska was to get another five hundred at the end of the month. You see, Geoff had promised me—Oh, I forget! . . . My head hurts! I can't think! . . . Listen, darling! Be a good sport and toddle out to get poor Yola a drink. Ni-i-ce boy! That pompous little idiot of a doctor wouldn't suspect you—"

"No drink!" he told her firmly but not unkindly. "Dr. Bowen warned me that you'd try to coax a drink out of me, and I gave him my promise. You see, Miss Conova, he's not kidding you when he tells you that if you take a drink now the consequences might be—well, very serious indeed. Possibly fatal. Whiskey and the drug he's administering to you to cure you of the habit simply don't mix. They make a violent poison."

"Like whiskey and strychnine?" she surprised him by asking. "Somebody sent me a clipping out of a medical journal about that. I guess it was somebody who didn't want me to run any risk. Or maybe it was somebody who thought, if I wanted to kill myself, I'd better know how to do a good job of it!" she added bitterly.

Dundee was startled. He remembered something vividly. "I suppose, then, it made you afraid to take strychnine, if you'd been using it as a tonic?"

"I never took a dose of strychnine in my life!" she protested. "I always thought it was dangerous for Geoff to take so much of it, but his heart's tricky, and mine's not," she added, with sublime ignorance of the true state of her health. "I once saw a dog die of strychnine poisoning. It was horrible!"

"There was a little glass phial of strychnine tablets in your suitcase, which Modjeska Rodovsky was using, and she found it, and was frightened and puzzled," Dundee told her, his eyes, and mouth very grim. "Did you put those tablets in your suitcase?"

"Of course I didn't! Don't be absurd!"

"Did you keep the envelope in which your anonymous 'friend' sent you that clipping about the lethal effects of strychnine and whiskey?" he asked tensely. "Or, the clipping itself?"

"No," she whispered, and she began to shiver so violently that Dundee was frightened. "I remember the envelope was addressed on the typewriter and it was sent to my home address, which isn't known to the general public. There wasn't any writing—just the clipping—"

"What magazine was it clipped from?"

"I don't remem— Oh, yes, I do!" she discovered with pleased surprise. "It was *The Journal of Clinical Pathology*. The clipping was all about the discoveries of some doctor who had made a report to some medical convention. I remember it told about how a man had been murdered with a combination of strychnine and corn whiskey, and about how another man, who was an habitual strychnine user, had died after drinking only half a pint of whiskey."

"Cheerful reading," Dundee commented. But to himself he remarked, "Clever! Clever! Fiendishly clever!" Aloud:

"Where was the envelope mailed?"

"I noticed that, too. New York. I asked Geoffrey if he could imagine who would send me such a thing, and he said it was probably meant for him, instead of for me, because he takes strychnine, you know, and used to drink."

"Then Mr. Arundel saw the clipping!" Dundee said, trying not to sound too triumphant. "You were in New York yourself at the time, I suppose?"

"Why, no! I was in California. So was Geoff, of course, so you see it couldn't have been he who sent the clipping! It came, I remember, just a few days after I'd got into the papers for having tried to commit suicide, though the reporters just hinted that that was what I'd done, saying it was 'the well-known overdose of sleeping medicine,' and things like that."

Dundee was silent so long, so engrossed in a new train of thought and theory that she sprang to her feet and began to pace the floor with quick, jerky steps, her shoulders slightly hunched as if she were bitter cold. She was smoking furiously, her lip curling as if she hated the taste of the tobacco.

"Miss Conova," the detective said suddenly, "you said your husband was once an alcoholic and had been cured. When and where did he take treatment?"

"Let me think. . . . Don't let Geoff know I told you, for God's sake! It was a deep secret. . . . Three years ago, I think—. Yes, three years. He was in a play, *Lord Algy*, a comedy, that was an awful flop, and I was in Hollywood in the middle of a picture. He was so depressed that he went on an awful bat that landed him in the psychopathic ward at Bellevue. Later he was transferred to a private sanitarium up in Westchester—the Good Samaritan."

"Was he there a long time?"

"Yes, he was pretty well shot, and somehow he managed to get hold of liquor during the course of the treatment. Some employee of the hospital was suspected, and discharged, I believe. Geoff nearly died, after one relapse, and it frightened him so badly that he has never taken another drink. He was in the hospital about eight months."

"Do you know Max Weinberg?" Dundee asked abruptly.

"Weinberg? . . . *Weinberg?* . . . Never heard of him! Oh, yes, the manager of the tour! No, I never saw him. Geoff says he's a pleasant, harmless little fool. Geoff registered a kick about the chap World-Wide first had lined up to send out with me, and made them change, just so that it would be some man who didn't know me personally."

"A very thorough man—Arundel," Dundee commented again, with genuine respect. "Was it your husband's idea, by the way, that a registered nurse go along with Modjeska, pretending to be a lady's maid?"

She paused in her quick pacing. "Nurse?" she repeated vaguely. "Oh, yes. I'd forgotten. She was a nurse, wasn't she? Geoff had some awfully good reason— Oh, I remember now! If Modjeska pulled an awful boner, Geoff was to wire the nurse to grant an interview to the reporters, saying that I—or rather, Modjeska doubling for me—was not exactly herself—I mean, *myself*. Oh, it sounds mixed up, but you see what I mean. If a registered nurse told the newspapers that Yola Conova was not— well, not exactly responsible because she was so ill that it was necessary for her to have a nurse in Constant attendance, well *anything* could be forgiven!"

"Then Modjeska knew that her companion was in reality a nurse who would help her over the rough spots, if necessary?"

"No, stupid!" Yola Conova cried impatiently. "The psychological effect on Modjeska would have been terrible. I expressly cautioned Geoff not to tell her. You see, he was preaching to her—and so was I—that she simply *couldn't* fail!"

"Then the nurse, Louise Patton, was in on the conspiracy?"

"What do you mean? Geoff told her I was a 'mild mental case,' so that she was prepared to expect any sort of crazy mistake that Modjeska might make. Really, we did have to take ordinary precautions, to keep from having a scandal over my using a double on the personal appearance tour. Geoff suggested these things, but I freely admit I agreed to them."

"I meant—did the nurse know that Modjeska was a double, not the real Yola Conova?" Dundee asked.

"Of course not, idiot!" She was emphatically contemptuous "Do you think Geoff would have taken a chance on having me blackmailed for the rest of my life? Or on having *himself* blackmailed?"

"I suppose not," Dundee admitted. "Did you know Miss Patton yourself?"

"Of course not! It was absolutely necessary to get someone who had never seen *me*. Geoff found— what's-her-name, through a classified ad and arranged to have her meet me at the train—Modjeska, rather, not me I never saw her at all. But it seems to me that if she'd been on the job, as she was paid to be, Modjeska wouldn't have been killed. It's all her fault."

"Exactly what Miss Patton herself says," Dundee assured her, without smiling "But if you are going to consider all the 'ifs' in this case, you must remember that if you had not hired a double to take your place, that double—Modjeska Rodovsky—would not have been murdered. So—shall we then say it's all your fault?"

"But I've told you and *told* you I didn't mean to do any harm!" she protested, with sudden childish petulance.

"Miss Conova, why did you want to commit suicide? What did you want to escape—through alcohol or through death?" Dundee asked suddenly.

She stopped and stared at him, her eyes pitifully defenseless. 'I didn't want to die, really," she said slowly. "But—*Geoff wanted me to.* I didn't realize for a long time what he was doing to me, but he was—he was constantly putting the thought of suicide into my mind. He'd do a thousand little things to hurt me and humiliate me and break my nerve and rob me of all pride, all self-confidence. Then always there would be something to make me think of suicide. I can't explain, but—listen! Just for instance: one night, when I couldn't sleep, because the reviews had been so terrible on a picture I'd counted on to save my career, Geoff sat beside my bed *all night* reading poetry to me!"

"Poetry?"

"You think I'm crazy, don't you?" she flung at him passionately. "Well, I am nearly crazy. I've had enough to drive me mad! The poems Geoff read to me, to soothe me, to comfort me—his beloved wife, who was worth a million dollars dead!—were all about death! And most of them about death by suicide. Oh, they were lovely poems! Geoff is a marvelous reader! And, quite obediently, I tried to end it all after he'd gone to his room. But I took either too much or too little veronal and—well, here I am, telling you a wild tale that you don't believe, but—*it's true,* I tell you! Geoffrey Arundel is a fiend of subtle cruelty—and I—God help me!—I'll love him more than I hate him—till I die!"

He let her weep until the fury of the storm had abated. In fact, he was only half conscious of the fact that she was flushing the poison from her mind and nerves in a torrential flood of good salt tears, for he was reconsidering his whole case in the light of this last revelation.

"You've already arrested Geoff, haven't you?" she asked at last, startling him out of his profound reverie.

"Your husband is—detained by the police," Dundee answered, with literal truthfulness, since Arundel had had orders to remain in his hotel rooms, and since a plain-clothes member of Captain Strawn's Homicide Squad was on duty to see that he obeyed those orders. "Why do you ask, Miss Conova?"

"Because I'm glad he's safe," she said, incredibly.

"Safe?"

"Of course! You're being stupid again!" she scolded. "Geoff didn't kill anybody himself! I know Geoff too well! He wouldn't run such a risk and he—he wouldn't like doing anything so obvious and—and messy as murder— not even if she was just a stand-in! So of course he managed it so that somebody did the—the job for him. I'll bet anything he has an ironclad alibi!"

"For the actual deed—yes! He was playing bridge with three other men for hours before and hours after the murder was committed. But one who *conspired* to commit murder is just as guilty as the member of the conspiracy who actually deals out death to the victim. If you cannot prove to the satisfaction of a jury that you were not a party to this conspiracy to murder Modjeska Rodovsky and to collect on that million dollar insurance policy, you will be held as guilty as Arundel and his fellow conspirator or conspirators—"

To his amazement she smiled. "I've convinced you!" she reminded him. "And I'll make another bet with you. I'll give you any odds you like that Geoff won't be convicted. Because I still love him, like the fool I am, I'm glad he's safely locked up, where he'll have a chance to stand trial and make monkeys out of you all—and especially a monkey out of the poor fool that actually did the job for him!"

Dundee got to his feet, which he had to restrain with extreme effort of will from running toward the nearest telephone.

"And—if he were not safely locked up?" he asked, trying to appear casual and matter-of-fact.

"You really can't be as stupid as you're trying to pretend!" she replied. "If Geoff weren't safely locked up, his life wouldn't be worth a nickel—when his accomplice, his tool finds out that Yola Conova is *not* murdered, *not dead!* That there won't be any million dollars to split up! *That Geoff can't pay for services rendered!"*

Dundee's scalp tingled, but he forced himself to say cheerfully, "You have a vivid imagination, Miss Conova, but—well, you're *not* crazy! If you ever need an insanity defense I'm afraid you'll be out of luck!"

She brushed that aside. "Do you know who did the actual killing, Mr. Dundee? Have you got him under arrest, too?"

"I know now. *You* have told me!"

XIX

"SEEMS TO ME like you took a chance—leaving her in the sanitarium, instead of clapping her into the jail hospital," District Attorney Sanderson grumbled. "I told you, Bonnie, when you talked to me long distance—"

"I know," Dundee said. "I had to use my own judgment, Sandy. I couldn't tell you everything on the telephone. I couldn't make you realize how dangerous it would have been to remove that girl to jail—no matter how efficient the jail doctor might be. Not only would it have endangered the actual life of Yola Conova; it also would have made it practically impossible for us to keep reporters from getting hold of the truth before we are ready for it to break. I should have had to book her under her real name—either as Yola Conova or as Mrs. Geoffrey Arundel, and police reporters would have spotted her almost instantly. Not only that! She might have been recognized by the desk sergeant and by any other member of the police force she came in contact with—including, of course, the matron. I wouldn't trust one of 'em to keep a secret like that, even for a couple of hours. Look how the news got out here that it was murder, not suicide—resulting in the Kenyon tragedy."

"All right, all right!" Sanderson agreed wearily. "But how did you make sure she wouldn't have a chance to commit suicide, or to telephone Arundel and tip him off, or escape?"

"Easily enough! I gave her her choice of jail or the locked ward at Dr. Bowen's sanitarium. It's harder to get out of that than out of a city jail—believe me! I had a good look at it. Her night nurse was told that Modjeska Rodovsky was under arrest for having impersonated Yola Conova—suffering from the delusion that she was Yola

Conova. Also the nurse was warned by. Dr. Bowen that she would never get another case in his outfit—which is tops in Cardinal County —if she talked, even among the nurses. . . . But Sandy, that girl is amazing! Conova, I mean. I think she's going to snap out of it now, regardless of what hell she has to go through. Arundel has been a sort of Svengali, and she has broken his spell over her by confessing that there was a spell. God knows whether her career as an actress is over forever! I don't! And nobody can tell which way the wind will blow in Hollywood—"

"You're looking pretty far ahead," Sanderson reminded him. "Personally, I'm interested right now in booking Arundel and whoever it was he hired to commit the actual murder. And if you have any real proof against Arundel, or, know who his accomplice is, you haven't honored me with your confidence. Of course, I'm *only* your, boss, and *only* the district, attorney—"

"I didn't tell you over the telephone who his hired hand is, because I'm determined not to say the name out loud, for fear I'm a human radio broadcasting station that the murderer can tune in on. But before I left Cardinal City I took time to put in a long distance call for Bob Pendergast, in New York, and I expect to hear from him any minute. I told him I'd fly back here and to call me with some sort of report by half past ten tonight, our time—an hour earlier than Eastern Standard, of course. It's five minutes to the half hour now—"

"Who the devil is Pendergast?"

"You remember, Sandy. Dewey sent him to Hamilton on one of his racket-busting jamborees—the 'Spider' Spinelli case. We did him a good turn or two, and I asked him to reciprocate. He's one of Dewey's best special investigators. I gave him three chores to do for me, but of course I didn't tip him off as to what I expect to prove. He's as tight-mouthed as an old con man, so there's nothing to fear from that quarter. You got in touch with Strawn, of course?"

"Yes," Sanderson said. "And the old boy is huffy at you. He wouldn't believe me when I said you'd lammed out of here right after the Kenyon shooting without saying 'May I please?' or 'Go to hell!' to me."

Dundee grinned. "I didn't want to take time off to listen to you and Strawn. I was in a desperate hurry, both to prove that my deductions were right, and that Yola Conova was hiding in the only place that she could be safe—"

"In Madge Smith's shoes?"

"Literally speaking, Madge's or Modjeska's shoes were a whole size too big for Yola, which was my main clue as to the swapped identities of the two girls. But I reasoned that a famous screen star can't just disappear. She's too damned conspicuous. So she had to be hiding where she wouldn't be conspicuous—where people were accustomed to the fact that they had a fellow citizen who looked amazingly like Yola Conova. Elementary, my dear Sandy. If the murder had occurred anywhere else but in Hamilton, or in Cardinal City, Arundel had a fair chance to succeed with his quite simple plan. Remind me to tell you all about the ins and outs of it sometime. But now, tell me, what does Strawn know? Did you tell him that it was a double who was murdered?"

"I had my orders from you," Sanderson said, without any real resentment. "So of course I did not tell him. Or anybody else. He's satisfied with the obvious solution— that Helen Kenyon killed the girl in a fit of jealous rage. But when I told him you said you had a 'pot on to boil,' and that you expected it to boil over tonight, he agreed to stand by. He's superstitious about your hunches, and, I confess—blast your conceited grin!—that I am, too."

"This is more than a hunch, Sandy," Dundee told him, the grin fading and his blue eyes taking on that icy hardness that always startled those who thought him a peculiarly mild and sweet-tempered manhunter. "All I need to go ahead is—Ah! Hand me the 'phone, Sandy.

That ought to be Pendergast. And make sure nobody cuts in on the switchboard, won't you, please?"

The district attorney left his private office to obey his subordinate, and returned after Dundee was deep in conversation with his long distance caller.

"Yes, Bob, I got that," the young detective was saying, as he made shorthand notes on a pad of scratch paper. "No, not quite so fast. My shorthand's not what it used to be.

"Yes. Go ahead. What? Oh, swell! Talked your arm off, did she? Remind me to buy you a new one, old son. Sure I'm tickled! In a state of exaltation, if you must know. And so are you. Why? The county's paying the bills, and cheap at the price. Well, what about the doctor? Find him in? Yeah. Yeah. Boy, is this our lucky day! You rate a double hot fudge sundae for this. What's that? Repeat that, Bob. Good boy! I'm getting more kick out of that than anything else you've told me. They all make mistakes, don't they? Oh, before midnight, I think. In time to make your Saturday morning newspaper fairly interesting reading. Oh, sure! We squash reporters and sob sisters and cameramen with every step we take. They make greasy green spots on the pavements of Hamilton. That's why I'm in a hurry to close up this case. Thanks a million, Bob. I'll be sure they spell your name right. Hell, why should Dewey get all the publicity? O.K. Hope we can return the favor soon. Good-by."

"Well?" Sanderson prompted. "Got what you wanted, I suppose?"

"You know, Sandy, speaking of reporters reminded me that I haven't seen Ginger Loring for—good Lord, it must be ten hours!"

"Practically a lifetime! Considering the fact that you only met her—let's see—yeah, twenty-six hours ago!" Sanderson gibed. "As a matter of fact, she's waiting in the outer office for you now. Grayson wouldn't announce her, told her she'd have to wait till you and I were through with our conference. She's been trying to get you since four o'clock."

"Why didn't you tell me?" Dundee was on his feet and making for the door. "Ginger! Hey! Grayson! Show Miss Loring in, you fathead!"

"Can't she wait until you tell me—? Oh, come in, Miss Loring."

She slipped into the room, shutting the door behind her, and then leaned against it. In her shabby little old muskrat coat and a cheap but cocky brown suede hat with a speckled quill she was certainly neither beautiful, nor smart, but something about her made Dundee's heart melt with an almost unbearable tenderness. Her rust red curls, her freckles, her smallness, her little-girl quality, and, perhaps more than anything else, her very lack of beauty, were so dear, so lovable, that he wanted nothing quite so much as time off, just to look at her and realize her. After Yola Conova—and yes, after the trouble making beauty of Modjeska Rodovsky—she was as delicious and satisfying as good, crusty, yeasty homemade bread.

"Jimmy," she was saying, "I've got something to tell you. Something awfully important. Please listen and, keep an open mind till I've finished."

"You're trying to tell me that it was your stepmother who wrote that letter to Yola Conova, aren't you. I was sure of that hours ago, child. Somehow you made the discovery last night when you were about to turn the letter over to me."

"Oh, yes. *That!*" she astonished him by saying, as if she had almost forgotten the whole incident. "I saw that someone else besides me had been using my desk, and that a new sheet of carbon paper, lying there business-side up, had nothing but that letter, cut into it. So of course I thought Pauline had written the letter, and I had to have time to think. I knew if she had written the letter she wouldn't do anything more serious. Then came the murder, and—well, I was afraid you or Captain Strawn would arrest Pauline. But it wasn't Pauline that, wrote the letter, Jimmy. It was Mrs. Martin."

"Mrs. Martin! On *your* typewriter?"

"Yes. She got into conversation with Pauline at the station and then went to our apartment. It seems that she doesn't have any classes on Thursday afternoons, except to supervise typewriter practice, so she left a student assistant in charge and went to see 'Yola Conova' arrive, and then insisted on following Pauline home. They talked about her—about Madge, I mean, and it was Mrs. Martin's idea to write the letter, just to frighten Madge. Pauline told me about it when I went home for dinner tonight. She's terribly upset, Jimmy. She firmly believes Madge committed suicide and that she and Mrs. Martin drove her to it. But that isn't what I—"

"Just a moment, Ginger, please. Was it your stepmother who made those weird calls to the Conova suite—the ones that Louise Patton answered?"

"No. It was Mrs. Martin. I made Pauline go with me and face her in the whole bad business," Ginger told him "But Mrs. Martin didn't kill Madge, Jimmy. And it wasn't that beastly little old masher of a husband of hers. Captain Strawn had already been at them both, giving them the good, old-fashioned third degree without rubber-hose trimmings, and he'd found that they could furnish a watertight 'alibi.'"

"An alibi for each other doesn't mean much," Dundee pointed out.

"It happens that the Martins have neighbors on one side that live embarrassingly close, so that they can hear each other's bedroom secrets, if voices are raised above a whisper. And it seems that the Martins did not whisper last night—or rather, this morning. Professor Martin got home about twelve-thirty; the neighbors will swear to hearing Big Bertha's stormy reception of him, and their subsequent quarrel which lasted until the milkman came. I also understand that the neighbors—thoroughly charming people, if you like toads—didn't try to stop the row, by calling out that they were being kept awake. They were afraid they'd miss something. As it was, they had a wonderful time. But the Martins didn't kill Madge, Jimmy, and neither did Pauline. My stepmother, in permitting Mrs. Martin to frame that horrible letter to poor Madge, did something I'll never forgive, but I honestly believe it was the first petty, underhand thing she ever did. She's so ashamed she can hardly bear it, and she's sincerely grieved that Madge is dead."

"I don't think there'll be any need for this angle of the business to get into the papers or into the case, when it goes to trial," Dundee said, taking her small, icy hands between his. "Do you, Sandy?"

"Heck, no!" Sanderson said explosively. "No use stirring the mud any deeper. But I intend to see that that Martin dame is kicked out of her school job, right out onto her fat hoot-nanny."

Ginger giggled shakily and withdrew her hands. "Thank you both. But there's something I'm trying to tell you, Jimmy, and you, too, of course, Mr. Sanderson. Something vitally important! And I've got my scrapbook to prove it. Jimmy! Mr. Sanderson! Madge Smith was not Yola Conova!"

Dundee shot a quick glance at Sanderson, who raised his pale eyebrows until they almost met his sandy hair.

"I thought," Dundee said, choosing his words very carefully, "that you were 'surer than sure,' as you put it last night, that our visiting star was your own Madge Smith."

"I was! I still am! It was Madge Smith who came here as Yola Conova, but she was not Yola Conova! And I can prove it!" she protested passionately, as the two men remained silent, eyeing each other. "You remember, Jimmy Dundee, you sent me over to my office to get my scrapbook on Yola Conova?"

"Yes," Dundee said guardedly, with a vivid picture of Ginger as she had sat with the big book on her lap, patiently waiting, while Dink Garnet and Arundel had been under fire.

"Well, I took my scrapbook with me when I went to lunch. You were so busy you'd forgotten that you wanted it, and those news pictures taken in Chicago and here in Hamilton. I thought I might be able to help somehow, so I studied them, and I guess I must have known all the time, subconsciously, that Madge wasn't Yola, because I began to compare the close-ups of Yola with some of the candid camera pictures of Madge that she hadn't been able to escape having taken, though she tried to avoid the cameramen, and so—"

"So what?" Dundee prompted, as she paused uncertainly.

"You're not angry with me for finding out something you missed, are you?" she pleaded. "You see, I knew Madge, and you didn't, and all these years I've never more than half believed that Yola was Madge, because of the great difference in personality, so of course I had something to go on—"

Dundee laughed, a wholehearted laugh that was as kind as his eyes. "Idiot! I'm just worried for fear you've spilled the beans to someone else, or that, if you've found out the truth, someone else will, too—before we're ready."

"You know—already? Oh, that's where you disappeared to! You went to see the real Conova, didn't you?"

"Yes. But tell me how you proved your hunch."

"The hairline was different," she said simply. "I remembered what a hairdresser said to me once, when I was talking about twins that you couldn't tell apart, and she said no two hairlines were ever exactly the same. And she laughed about a story she had been reading in which a man masqueraded as another, so convincingly that he fooled the man's wife. She said he wouldn't have fooled her for a minute, because she's hair conscious—"

"Just as our friend Shear, of the Randolph garage, is 'car conscious,' as he puts it," Dundee cut in. "Which reminds me!" and he took up the telephone. When the connection was completed he said, "Shear? . . . Dundee speaking. Yes, very terrible. But, Shear, there's something I'm not quite clear about. As we were driving to Old Bridge this morning you told me that Miss Conova turned back and asked for some maps. Yes, that's right. Now I want to know, Shear, if she had already got into the car and was ready to drive away, then got out and came back into the garage? She did? Then listen, Shear! Did you follow her back in without keeping the car in sight? You did? You mean anyone who had followed her— or anyone who happened to be passing, for that matter— might have hidden in the back of the car, under the rug, let's say, while she was inside the garage getting the maps? Fine! Fine! And, Shear, don't talk! Not a word to anyone, even to your buddy working there with you, you understand? Gosh, no, man! Nobody could blame you if that's what happened! Don't be foolish! And thanks, Shear!"

He hung up the receiver and looked at Sanderson, forgetting Ginger Loring for the moment. "Well, Sandy! Our case is complete, except—"

Sanderson looked completely mystified. "*Our* case? It's darned decent of you to include me, but—"

"Except," Dundee went on, "that I don't know how the devil I'm going to get the rope around Arundel's neck! Yola Conova is right, I'll bet you a month's pay. Unless we can get a confession of conspiracy and complicity out of Arundel, he'll wiggle clean out of this and get a medal as America's most devoted husband."

"Do you mean to say Yola Conova would stand by him?" Ginger asked, utterly incredulous. "When he let the world think she was dead?"

Dundee grinned. "She is annoyed, but—laugh, if you like —she loves him. No, she warned me that she'd not help, even if the law permitted, to convict him of anything. The only thing we have on him now is conspiracy to defraud, and we'll have to prove even that.

If he's got nerve enough—and I think he has—he'll brazen it out, saying that Conova herself arranged the whole business without his knowledge. As a matter of fact, according to Conova's own story, the actual switch was made just before train time and so carefully was the thing planned that I doubt that we can get any actual corroboration of Conova's charge that Arundel managed the whole business of the impersonation. Madge was the only other person in on it—and Madge is dead. If Conova changes her story, and takes full blame for the employment of a double, which she might do, since she would have every chance of getting off with a suspended sentence, and she could not be punished any harder for having done it alone—"

"Why the devil didn't you get her statement in writing before you left?" Sanderson demanded with sudden fury.

"Because I was frightened stiff that Arundel's hired hand would get wind of the fact that it wasn't Yola Conova who was murdered, but her double, and of the additional and vitally important fact that there'll be no million dollars to split up between the plotters. I didn't relish the thought of Arundel's being murdered in, revenge and anger, and believe me, he'll be killed as soon as his accomplice knows the truth—if we're not on our toes to save him—for the hangman's rope, I trust!"

Ginger shivered. "Maybe it would be better—and neater, for him to be murdered. And his murder would be the final proof of the guilt of the—accomplice."

"True, my sweet! But the state frowns on such informal justice. I'm afraid we can't let Geoffrey get bumped off tonight. But we've got to act quickly—"

"But Jimmy," Ginger interrupted, color coming back into her milk-white, freckled cheeks. "Can't we let him get almost killed? We'd know as much if an attempt was made to murder him as if it were successful. You haven't said who the 'hired hand' is, but suppose you arranged to have the news broken to—to him, as if you didn't suspect him—Arundel's hired assassin, I mean, of any complicity, and then—well, let nature take its course, up to but not including the point of Arundel's actual murder."

District Attorney Sanderson beamed upon her. "Isn't she cute, Bonnie?" he asked "And smart! It's nice working with you, Dundee You involve such nice girls in your cases. I married one of 'em, Ginger."

"And I'll tell Penny on you if you don't behave, you reprobate. Remember I've got 'dibs' on Ginger. You took one of my girls, as you openly admit. You know, sweet child, you've got an idea there, but for certain reasons I'm afraid it won't work. You see, if Arundel is attacked by the person I have in mind—attacked in a sudden gust of fury, I mean—and we gallop up to his rescue, we still haven't got anything on Arundel himself. It won't do us any good for the hired hand to accuse Geoffrey of having instigated the whole thing. Under the circumstances, providing always my theory is correct, Arundel could simply deny everything the accomplice—the actual assassin—said, and we'd have the devil of a time proving anything at all against him. You see, we again come back to Yola Conova's warning, Sandy, that Arundel played so safe—"

"Listen!" Ginger Loring cried. "I've got it! Let's work it the other way 'round! *No, wait!* Let me tell you my plan! I'm a reporter. Arundel knows that. He also knows that his life will be in danger, if the news gets out that Yola Conova is still alive. That's why he fainted today. He thought you were going to reveal the fact that Madge Smith was Yola Conova's double!"

"Yes. I knew the truth then, and he sensed that I did. Also the story Garnet was telling was dynamite under Arundel's careful scheme."

"He was scared almost to death—literally speaking," Ginger rushed on. "And he was even more terrified when he found out that the million dollar insurance policy had lapsed. Even if it was never discovered that a double had been murdered, Arundel knew he could not pay the assassin he had hired. Now, I think we're agreed that

Arundel would not run the risk of hiring an underworld gunman, aren't we? The risk of being blackmailed for the rest of his life was far too great. He had to hire someone whom he could pay off permanently; someone he need never fear—if he paid as agreed, for services rendered!"

Dundee's blue eyes blazed with sudden sheer joy in the excited girl who had come so close to him that he could measure her height by his own vest buttons.

"I believe you're reading my mind again, you brat!" he scolded.

"No, thanks!" she retorted, her impish face tilted upward, so that her chin rubbed against the gay Scotch plaid of his tie. "I've one of my own to read! And interesting reading it is, too."

"No one ever tells me anything," Sanderson mourned.

"As I was saying," Ginger continued breathlessly, "Arundel knows I'm a reporter. I'll go to him now, and ask for an 'exclusive' interview. Then I'll tell him that I've discovered something that nobody else knows but me, and then—"

"No! It's too dangerous!" Dundee protested, cupping that eager, upturned little face in his hands. "God knows to what lengths he'd go, to shut you up—"

"Don't argue! Just listen!" she commanded. "And then make all the arrangements with Captain Strawn you like, so that everything will go off all right. I'll get him, Bonnie Dundee! If it's the last thing I ever do!" Then she laughed shakily. "See? The acting bug has bit me, too! Slap me down next time I spout off, like that, Bonnie Dundee! Now, listen! And don't look at me like a dying calf. I'll be all right. You're going to take care of that, you old super-sleuth!"

XX

IN THE CLOSET of the bedroom of the suite which Geoffrey Arundel had deemed necessary to sustain his dignity as the bereaved husband of a famous star, Investigator Dundee waited tensely, his right hand warming the steel of a snub-nosed automatic.

Beside him, invisible in the darkness of the closet, was Detective Sergeant Holloway of the Homicide Squad, as much in the dark as to what Dundee expected to happen, but ready for anything. Arundel should be returning any second now, for Captain Strawn, down in his temporary headquarters in Suite 2-A, had agreed to detain the actor only long enough to allow Dundee and Holloway time to enter and secrete themselves.

It gave Dundee a grim sort of pleasure to imagine the relief, the sense of security, which Arundel was now enjoying, for the greater that relief the more unprepared the actor would be for the shock which was soon to overtake him, and, consequently, the more revealing would be his reaction,

For it had been planned that Captain Strawn should clearly intimate to Arundel that the police were ready to go before a coroner's jury with the tragic story of Helen Kenyon's final moments, as adequate solution of the slaying of, Yola Conova. Indeed, it was ostensibly to confer with Arundel on just how much of the dead woman's past need be revealed and how much could safely be consigned to the three graves of the tragically dead, that Strawn had summoned the supposedly bereaved husband.

"There he is!" Holloway whispered, as a muffled sound told of a door's being opened in the parlor of the suite. "If he decides to go to bed immediately and comes to this closet to hang up his clothes—"

"Not likely," Dundee whispered. "Midnight's only the shank of the evening for an actor. Listen! He's turned on the radio! Damn! If he keeps that dance music blaring we won't be able to hear anything."

But the hot swing band broadcasting from the ballroom of a New York hotel was suddenly snapped off.

"He's remembered that he's supposed to be in mourning," Dundee muttered. "Or—yes, she's here! Hope he doesn't notice that the door is ajar, and close it—"

He was not referring to the closet door, which was also slightly ajar, but to the door between the parlor and the bedroom. They were in luck, as the closet was not more than three feet away from that open door.

"Come in!" they heard Arundel call. Apparently he had forgotten for the moment that there was no longer a detective on guard outside his door to protect him from the invasion of the curious or of reporters, as well as to watch his movements. Strawn was to have made it quite clear to Arundel that all supervision of the members of the Conova party by the police was at an end; that they could come and go at will.

"Hello, Mr. Arundel!" they heard an excited voice greeting the actor. "I'm Kay Loring. Remember me? I was present when you were being questioned by the police today. But I'm not a policeman, or that is, a policewoman, or anything like that. I'm a reporter, you know. On *The Sun*, and I—"

Arundel's clipped English voice cut across her flood of words. "I have refused all day to see reporters, Miss—er— Loring, and I must insist upon your respecting my privacy, my grief."

Dundee gritted his teeth and listened

"Of course I understand how you feel," Ginger was rushing on, pretending to be absolutely breathless with joyous excitement. "And I'm not really here just as a reporter, but, oh, Mr. Arundel! I have the most wonderful news for you! Honestly, I can hardly talk, I'm so excited, and so happy for all those who love Yola Conova, and are grieving for her death, just as you are, only of course not quite so much—"

"What are you talking about, young woman?"

"Oh, Mr. Arundel! Prepare yourself for a shock—a wonderful piece of news! Mr. Arundel, our darling Yola Conova is not dead!"

Dundee and Holloway could hear Arundel gasping like a fish out of water; could imagine a hand going to his heart. Then his voice, curiously thin and piping: "Not— dead? Do you mean she has—has been revived after so long a time, with a pulmotor, for instance?"

Dundee's heart ached for Ginger as he heard her say with apparent nonchalance: "Oh, you mean Madge Smith, or whatever her real name is! She's dead, of course! Why, they even performed an autopsy. Remember? But Mr. Arundel, Madge Smith was not your wife! She was not Yola Conova! Madge Smith was Yola's double! Isn't it marvelous!—Please don't faint, Mr. Arundel! I'm not a nurse. I don't know how to take care of people with queer hearts–"

"Be quiet!" Arundel croaked. Then, "Where did you get such a fantastic idea? Who told you any such rot?"

Ginger's' voice sounded aggrieved. "Nobody told me, Mr. Arundel! I discovered it all for myself! I came to you first, just as soon as I knew the truth beyond the shadow of a doubt—"

"You mean to say nobody else knows your idiotic— notion?"

"It isn't a notion," said Ginger stoutly. "It's just a plain statement of fact, and I can prove it to the police in two minutes. But I thought you'd be so happy, and I felt so awfully sorry for you, because you were so terribly shocked by all the things that Dink Garnet said about Madge, thinking she was your wife and had been his wife—"

"For God's sake, stop talking for a minute!" Arundel commanded. "That is, don't keep running on like a—a babbling brook. Just answer my questions."

"Yes, sir, but—" came Ginger's meek voice, and Dundee knew just how she must look to Arundel—very tiny, very childish, very easy to silence.

"You're absurdly mistaken, child," the actor said, with something remotely like kindliness. "Pitifully mistaken, I mean. Cruelly mistaken. Now tell me without fuss and all this hysterical excitement what makes you think the— the dead woman is not Yola Conova?"

"I don't think you're going to be glad," Ginger said sadly. "I don't know what to think of you, Mr. Arundel—"

"I'm not interested in what you think of me, young woman!" the actor said harshly. "I asked you a plain question. You've come to me with a cock-and-bull story, and I'm asking you for proof. Either give me some proof or I'll—

"Here are two photographs, Mr. Arundel," Ginger said with sudden brisk firmness. "You see, they are both quite large. One is an autographed portrait study of Yola Conova. It happens to be mine. And it happens to compare in all essential details with all other photographs of Yola Conova that I have in my scrapbook. Now, here is an enlarged photograph of the face of the dead girl—of Madge Smith. A close-up taken by the police today. It's not pretty, but—"

Dundee wondered how Arundel was taking it. Recklessly he thrust his head beyond the door of the closet; then, daringly, he tiptoed to that other door which was also ajar. As he had suspected, Arundel was too frightened, too absorbed in terrific speculation, to sense the nearness of a hidden and uninvited guest.

"You see this hairline, Mr. Arundel?" Ginger was proceeding inexorably. "Both Yola and Madge wore their hair brushed straight back from their foreheads and off the ears. Therefore the entire hairline as it can be seen from full-face is exposed on both photographs. The eyebrows also are clearly photographed, but of course on a retouched photograph such as Yola's they could not be considered as decisive evidence. But I want you to consider these points. See here? . . . And here? . . . And look at the widow's peak. Madge's is the deeper peak. If Yola's were the deeper, the more pronounced, I mean, I might think it was due to make-up or retouching. But it's Madge's widow's peak that comes lower down the middle of the forehead, see? And look at the shape of the ears, Mr. Arundel! The lobes could be hidden with large earrings, but the tops of the ear, and the shape of the shell itself—"

"Miss Loring, do you want to get into pictures?"

"What?" Dundee heard Ginger gasp, as if she were totally unprepared for the one denouement they had confidently counted upon.

"Miss Loring, I see that it is folly for me to try to deceive you further," the actor said, his voice clipped and icy. "You have stumbled upon a secret that I would have given my life to protect. Yola Conova's sad secret!"

"I don't understand, Mr. Arundel."

"My dear child," Arundel began suddenly on a new tack, and Dundee had difficulty in restraining himself as he saw the actor lay a kindly hand upon her shoulder. "My wife is alive. True! But hers is a living death, a fate far worse than the one which overtook the poor girl who begged for the chance to act as stand-in for my dear wife in the forlorn hope that somehow, sometime, a scientific miracle could bring her out of the hell of madness, and let her resume the career that the public need never know was interrupted. It has been hard for me today, bitterly hard, Miss Loring—"

Dundee, from behind the door, saw Ginger take one backward step, so that Arundel's hand dropped from her shoulder. He saw how white she was, but how valiant she looked her in scorn.

"You mean, Mr. Arundel, that you intended to let everyone go on believing that Yola Conova was dead?"

Arundel bowed his head in histrionic sadness. "Yes. Yola is incurable. I could not bear the disgrace for her of the public's knowing that the 'Incomparable Conova' has

joined the other great artist, Nijinsky, in the land of the
living dead. As for the other girl, she is dead. Nothing can
bring her back to life. She will be buried with honors she
never hoped for in her humble life. Her child will be
taken care of as she never dreamed he would be. I shall
see to that, of course, I give you my word—"

"Then you know where the boy is?" Ginger pounced.
Dundee saw the actor go mushroom white again. "No, no!
Certainly not! But I shall have private detectives seek
until he can be found, and I shall adopt him legally—"

"Where is Yola Conova, Mr. Arundel?"

Dundee saw that Arundel was so relieved by the
question that he wanted to shout aloud in his exultation.
But he controlled himself almost instantly. "I'm afraid I
shall have to refuse to answer that question, my dear. My
poor wife is being cared for by the best of doctors, who, of
course do not know her identity, but who are well paid to
give her every protection against her suicidal mania and
to—"

"You mean, Mr. Arundel, that you still don't intend to
a admit publicly that Yola Conova is not dead?"

Arundel shrugged and spread his hands in a theatric
gesture of appeal. "What earthly good would result, my
dear? Away from reporters, from the pitiless glare of
publicity, she will be far happier, will have that millionth
chance to recover from madness. I am sure you agree
with me, Miss Loring. You love her. You want the best for
her. And you are a clever writer, I'm told. A very superior
type of motion-picture critic and an outstanding feature
reporter. Hollywood, Miss Loring, needs women of your,
type, to bring new blood into the writing of original
stories for the screen. I can guarantee you a contract as a
writer for a major studio at a starting salary of three
hundred a week, and—"

"In exchange for my silence, of course," Ginger said
matter-of-factly. "It's a wonderful offer, Mr. Arundel, and
I appreciate it, but Mr. Clinton Risher has already given
me a job as his personal press agent and sort of press

bodyguard, and Mr. Weinberg has wired the coast about a job for me out there with World-Wide. So you see your bribe doesn't interest me. May I use the telephone, please?"

"No!" Arundel said curtly, and seized the thin little wrist that went out to lift the telephone from the desk near which they stood. "You're lying about Risher and Weinberg. You're just trying to raise the ante. All right! I'll see that you get five hundred a week, if you keep your mouth shut."

"You know, Mr. Arundel," she said sweetly, but she was rubbing her wrist. "I simply can't understand why you are so afraid of the story's getting out. Of course I know you can be prosecuted for conspiracy to defraud, but even if you bribe me successfully, how can you be sure nobody else will get wise? Of course, I admit I'm awfully clever, but you know, Mr. Arundel, I believe you are afraid of something else! Or—shall we say of—somebody else? Afraid of the murderer of Madge Smith? The murderer who still believes that the dead woman is Yola Conova? The murderer who must not know that Yola Conova is still alive, that you can't pay? In other words, the murderer who will get you if you don't watch out!"

Dundee's blood turned to ice water. The little fool! She had promised to be careful, not to taunt him into—

"Ginger!" Dundee shouted, his voice hoarse with terror, as he flung wide the door between parlor and bedroom and raced after Arundel. Detective Sergeant Holloway's heavier feet pounded after him.

"Drop that girl, Arundel!" Dundee commanded. "But not out of that window, as you planned! Now, hands up! Bracelets, Holloway! And very becoming they are, Mr. Geoffrey Arundel! You realize, of course, that you are under arrest, charged with a number of crimes, including—*murder!*"

Ginger, who had fallen to her knees just below the open third-story window from which Arundel would have tossed her to certain death if Dundee had not risked being against that door, got to her feet and crept to Dundee's side, leaning against his bigness for comfort

"You were grand, my sweet," he told her, rumpling the rust-red curls from which that cocky little felt hat of hers had fallen. "But a fool, too, for disobeying orders. What's that, Arundel?"

"I said," came a thread of voice from bluish lips, "that I think you had better give me a strychnine tablet."

"And I think we'd better not," Dundee said brusquely. "Got a fake pill there—sure death of some kind? You've been reading too many detective stories, Geoff darling. Your wife, by the way, sends you her love. She was tremendously relieved to see me. Had been quite upset over the idea of spending the rest of her life in a madhouse. Incidentally, she told me how very clever you had been in arranging for Madge Smith—or Modjeska Rodovsky, to give her her real name—to double for her."

Arundel's pale, icy eyes met the detective's steadily. Dundee was forced to admire his nerve. "You were eavesdropping, apparently. Therefore you heard me admit that I knew of the impersonation, knew that my wife was alive when I identified the dead body as hers. And you heard my reasons for aiding and abetting the impersonation. Legally, I suppose, I am guilty of conspiracy to defraud the public and World-Wide Pictures Corporation But I am absolutely innocent of any other crime—"

"Did I remind you that anything you say may be used against you?" Dundee asked cheerfully "By the way, Ginger, you were wanting to telephone, weren't you? 1 seem to remember that this ham actor objected. There's the telephone. Hop to it, honey!"

"Oh, yes!" Ginger said brightly, but she was still far too pale. "Room 316, please. Hello, Miss Patton? How are you feeling now? Oh, I'm so glad! This is Kay Loring. Yes, that's right Remember? Well, I just couldn't wait a minute longer to tell you the wonderful news! Oh, I'm at the newspaper office!" she lied, her voice blithely sincere

"What do you think? I know you'll be so awfully glad! Oh! Well, we're getting an extra ready right now, so of course you'd have had the news soon anyway, but I wanted to get your reaction for a feature story. I've just talked with Mr. Arundel, and he admitted—just a minute, please. Hold the line—"

And she stood there, one hand covering the mouthpiece of the telephone, until Dundee and Holloway between them had subdued Arundel, who was struggling like a maniac.

"Hello, Miss Patton. Sorry. My boss wants me to hurry up and write the story. Listen! Yola Conova is *alive*! Did you say something, Miss Patton? Oh, I know how you must feel! How glad you are that it wasn't the famous star that was murdered while she was under your protection, but just a stand in, a double. Are you listening, Miss Patton? You sound awfully queer. I'm afraid the good news is too much for you. Yes, that's what I said. It was a double who was murdered. Not Geoffrey Arundel's wife at all! Not Yola Conova! Yes, he knew all about it all the time! I've just been talking with him, and he admits it was a trick—Miss Patton. Miss Patton— She's hung up on me!" Ginger told them, her eyes wide with surprise, which only Dundee knew was entirely assumed.

"Take me on to jail!" Arundel screamed in a sudden frenzy of terror. "What are we waiting for? I demand my rights—"

"The right of jail protection?" Dundee asked softly. "Afraid of someone, Arundel?"

"Take me out the bedroom door! I won't stay here and be—"

"Murdered? No, no! We won't let her hurt you, Geoff darling! Ah! I think we have a visitor! Imagine anyone's dropping in at this hour!"

Before Dundee could reach the door the knocking had become a frantic pounding, which he was afraid would attract unwelcome attention from the hotel's other third-floor guests.

"Come right in, Miss Patton!" he invited. "We're having a little party. Nice of you to drop in—"

The nurse had taken time to don a dark-blue satin housecoat, which fastened with a zipper from hem to throat. Her blonde hair was arranged in pinned curls beneath a permanent wave cap, worn at night to protect the "set." Cold cream glistened on her cheeks, innocent now of rouge, powder, and the becoming flush of fever.

"Geoff! Is it true? Did you trick me? If you did, I swear to God, I'll—"

"Shut up, you fool!" Arundel tried to seize her hands with his own, but the manacles defeated him.

The woman seemed to see nothing, not even those chained steel bracelets on the man she was now shaking with the violence of acute hysteria.

"Is that woman alive, Geoff? Tell me the truth, I say! The truth! If you've tricked me, I'll—"

"Miss Patton!" Arundel interrupted her, his voice suddenly low and sharp as an icicle. She stopped as if that icicle had penetrated her heart. "It is quite true that my wife is alive. I fail to see why I am accountable to you for that fact! Simply because the woman I hired you to guard and to assist in every way possible happened not to be the real Yola Conova, but a double! Why you should be so upset over this deception on my part is utterly beyond me, Miss Patton. I freely absolve you of all complicity in the conspiracy to defraud the public and the motion picture company. I have not tricked you into breaking any laws, Miss Patton! Do you understand?" he insisted tensely, his pale eyes holding hers. "You are guiltless in this matter. I take all the blame! I think these gentlemen have been convinced by your manner—more than by anything I could say—that you did not conspire in the deception! Now, get a hold on yourself, Miss Patton!"

Dundee had listened with unadulterated admiration. Yola Conova was right! This man was surely a genius in his own way!

"Bravo, Arundel!" he applauded. "Holloway, ask Captain Strawn to come in now. I'd like him to hear the last act of our little drama. He ought to be just outside the door. Oh, hello, Captain! All's well so far. Thanks for your expert timing. Is Brede coming, too? Fine! Then we're all set."

"Good evening, Miss Patton," Captain Strawn said, awkwardly. "Feeling a lot better, I see. Able to be up and about again, eh?"

The nurse had had time to get a measure of control— too much control, Dundee was afraid. A confession made things so much simpler!

"Good evening," she answered, her voice oddly monotonous. "Yes, I'm better, thank you."

"Then I hope the change won't cause a relapse," Dundee said, not unkindly, though his heart was hardened against her. "We're going to have to take you to jail, Miss Patton—"

"Jail?" she echoed. "But Geoff—Mr. Arundel said—".

"Unfortunately for you, Miss Patton, Mr. Arundel is not the law of Hamilton County, nor the district attorney, nor the police force," Dundee told her. "Louise Patton, I arrest you for the murder of Modjeska Rodovsky, known also as Madge Smith, and it is my duty to warn you that anything you say may be used against you."

She stood stone still, her hands at her sides, against the dark blue satin of her housecoat.

"Was that her name?" she said strangely, and then turned as slowly as if she were a mannequin, her eyes resting deliberately, searchingly on Detective Sergeant Holloway, on granite-faced old Captain Strawn, on young Dundee, and, finally, upon small Kay Loring, huddling against a table.

"That child ought to be at home and in bed," she said, amazingly, then those searching, inexorable blue eyes traveled on, to rest upon Geoffrey Arundel, and to realize that his hands were manacled.

"Have they arrested you for murder, too, Geoff?" she asked.

"I want to get out of here!" Arundel shrilled. "This woman's dangerous. If she killed my—if she killed that poor girl, there's no saying to what lengths she may go—"

"Is he under arrest for murder?" Louise Patton asked.

"Yes. Arundel will be charged with conspiracy to commit murder," Dundee told her, light breaking upon him. He knew now what Louise Patton wanted, and he would give it to her! "I can assure you that we have enough evidence against him to indict him, and that, if a jury finds him guilty, he will be held as guilty as you— that is to say, as guilty as the person who actually killed Modjeska Rodovsky, believing her to be Yola Conova."

"I see. Well, Geoff, it looks as if we are going to have a nice long time to at last—. You see, Mr. Dundee, Geoff has promised me so many things and has disappointed me so frequently, that I shall be grateful for the long 'date' together that the trial will give us. Of course it will be too bad that we can't get married—as we'd planned—"

"Shut up, you fool! You'll talk yourself onto the gallows!" Arundel cried, and Dundee wondered if the man really cared for this woman at all.

"Oh, but you'll be there with me, too! Up there, Geoff, we'll be together at last!" and she laughed. "Mr. Arundel suffers from a hangover from silent pictures, when they used subtitles," she explained. "He talks like the actor he is! A bad actor, if you'll pardon the pun! You are a bad actor, Geoff! A damned, double-crossing, black hearted, egg sucking—"

"She's mad!" Arundel screamed "Get me out of here!"

"You've fallen into a habit of calling sane women mad, Geoff," Louise Patton said, in a sudden, deceptive calm. "Remember how you kept telling me that Yola was insane, until I believed you? You couldn't divorce a mad woman, you said. Otherwise, you would divorce her, and marry me. But—if Yola should die, poor Yola, poor, mad Yola, then there wouldn't be anything at all to prevent our getting married, you said! Geoff talks well," she explained pleasantly to Dundee and to Strawn. "He could always get me to do anything he wanted. Couldn't you, Geoff, my darling"

"It's not true, not true!" Geoffrey Arundel moaned "I tell you, she's determined to involve me with her when I have done nothing—"

"From the time I met him," the nurse went on, almost dreamily, not addressing her partner in crime, "he could twist me around his long nailed little finger. He lost me my job in the sanitarium where I was happy and well thought of—in line for post of head nurse. He was an alcoholic. Did you know that? Maybe *he's* the mad one! Probably you won't believe me, but it's true that I never meant to kill Yola Conova. I didn't think I'd have to. And Geoff made me think it was only a question of waiting, waiting, giving her opportunities to commit suicide when she was *apparently* well guarded—"

"I hired you to guard her, not to kill her!" Arundel broke in.

"Isn't he funny?" she inquired, still with that eerie air of pleasantness. "Won't it go over big with a jury when he explains how he hired his mistress—the woman he had been promising to marry for three years!—to watch over the wife whose very name she loathed?"

"Do you want to tell us all about it, Miss Patton?" Dundee asked, almost gently. "I have already warned you that anything you say may be used against you. But if you wish to confess—"

"What do you think I've been doing? Of course I'm going to tell you all about it!" she answered with sudden blazing fierceness. "You kept me from killing him when I found out that he'd tricked me into doing murder for him. The only way I can get even with him now is to make sure he swings with me—if I've got to swing. What constitutes premeditation, Mr. Dundee?"

"Good Lord!" Dundee breathed. "Premeditation, Miss Patton? I'm not a lawyer, but I believe that if five minutes elapse between the impulse to kill and the performance of the deed, it is premeditated murder. I think I know what you're referring to. When you struck Miss Conova—I mean, Miss Rodovsky—on the head with that automobile crank you thought you had killed her, didn't you?"

"Yes," she answered readily. "But I did it in a sudden storm of anger and disappointment. It wasn't— premeditated. But I did deliberately plan how to make it look like suicide. I couldn't think of any way on the spur of the moment but to hang her. I hated doing it. I—I— turned on Geoff as soon as I'd done it. My infatuation for him died when she died. Even if he hadn't tricked me, I honestly don't believe I'd ever have married him or touched a penny of her money. But the very thought that he'd made a murderess out of me by lying and trickery drove me wild when Miss Loring told me the truth tonight, so—"

"I understand," Dundee said. "You followed the woman you thought was Conova when she left the hotel, didn't you? Instead of going just before she did, I mean. You had listened to her on the telephone, and had heard her make a tentative appointment with Bruce Kenyon. Also you had taken some very strange telephone calls for her, which gave you the idea for that absurd story of yours about Yola Conova's sending you out on an errand with money to appease a blackmailer."

She looked, surprised. "I didn't think it was an absurd story, under the circumstances. That Garnet fellow *was* trying to blackmail, her, and she had received some sort of threatening letter—"

"You eavesdropped when she was burning the letter?"

She did not resent that. "Of course! I had to know everything she said and did—and thought, if I could read her mind. You see, Geoff had made me believe she actually did have suicidal tendencies, and it was my job to *encourage* her to suicide, to do what Geoff had done—to keep the thought of suicide fresh in her mind always. It was sort of hard to do. I wondered why it was so hard. Now of course I understand. Since she wasn't Yola Conova, she didn't have any suicidal tendencies, and Geoff knew she wouldn't have them; knew that it would take murder to get rid of her—"

"Did Geoffrey Arundel ever *suggest* to you that you murder Yola Conova, if she did not oblige, you both by committing suicide?" Captain Strawn asked

"Of course I didn't!" Arundel said.

"I shall say that you did," Louise Patton told him calmly. "I shall cite times and places when we said what we should do when you were free. I shall tell the jury how you had me steal poisons from Dr. Alexander's medicine chest and send them to you for months—months and months, I say!—before you succeeded in getting her into a suicidal frame of mind."

"And I shall deny everything you say, because there's not a word of truth in it!" Arundel was gray with rage and fear.

"There's one little detail that can be corroborated," Dundee interrupted. "You remember, Miss Patton, how you clipped an article from a medical magazine—"

"Oh, yes!" she agreed eagerly, so avid to put the noose around Arundel's neck that her own did not feel the tug of it. "From *The Journal of Clinical Pathology.* Geoff asked me to send Yola, anonymously, any medical articles I ran across showing easy ways to commit suicide. He said if she was determined to end her life she would be better off dead, but that she actually didn't seem to know how to make a go of it; that the only things she would try to kill herself with—overdoses of morphine, atropin, and veronal—failed for some reason or other."

"Miss Conova says she did not try very seriously," Dundee told her. "She did not quite agree with Mr. Arundel that death is a sweet lover, whose embrace she must hasten to enjoy."

"How did you know about the clipping? From—her?"

"Yes. Then from Dr. Alexander. He checked and found that the article in question—concerning the lethal properties of whiskey and strychnine in combination—had been clipped from the medical journal on file in his office. He remembers having called your attention to the article, Miss Patton."

A shadow passed over her cold-creamed face, which suddenly looked haggard. "I'm sorry Dr. Alexander has to know about—me. He was splendid to me. Geoff told me how Yola acted when she got that clipping. He said she kept reading it over and over; as if it fascinated her. She didn't know whether it was a warning from a friend, or a—a suggestion from an enemy, he said."

"It's a lie. I said nothing of the sort," Arundel protested.

"It happens that you did," Dundee told him curtly. "Go on, Miss Patton, if you wish. You were saying that when you followed your patient you had no intention of killing her. Why, then, did you follow her?"

"I had to keep her in sight I was curious. But I was also determined to get everything on her that I could," Louise Patton told them "I would have blackmailed her cheerfully enough into giving Geoff a divorce. But I had been so happy for days I thought everything was going to settle itself without—without any trouble for anybody."

"Meaning that you didn't want to murder her unless you had to?" Strawn pressed "In other words, you admit your intentions were to kill her and to make it look like suicide, if she didn't do sit herself?"

She flung up her head. "Yes I might as well admit that, too. I started out with that intention. From New York, I mean. Not when I followed her out of this hotel twenty-four hours ago. I was happy for days, as I said, because I was sure she was going to divorce Geoff and marry Clinton Risher. I did everything I could to encourage the match. I wrote Geoff that Yola was in love with Risher, and, while anyone could have read the letter, because I pretended it was just a nurse's report on a patient, I knew he understood That's why he came out here? I know now but I didn't understand last night, when he whispered to me at her dressing-room door not to be a fool. He said Yola was just playing with Risher, that she would never divorce him. I thought he was just conceited, too sure of his hold on Yola. I heard her promise Clinton Risher last night to marry him a month after the tour was over, and, God! I was so happy I could have died. And I wish I *had*."

"You mean, Miss Patton, that you were glad to forego the million dollars insurance money?" Strawn demanded skeptically.

"I'd never thought of the money!" she cried "I swear I hadn't! Geoff didn't talk about it either—much, because he knew it wasn't her money I wanted. I never wanted anything but to be Geoff's wife publicly, as I had been in secret for three years, whenever he could get away from her and come to New York. But I know now that all Geoff thought of was the million dollars! That he wanted her to live, for some reason I can't understand—unless he's been lying to me all these years, and he still loves her."

Dundee did not bother now to propound his theory of why Arundel chose to incarcerate his wife in a madhouse, rather than to slay her.

But a sudden thought had struck Louise Patton—the inevitable conclusion. "She was in on it! She tricked me, too! All of it, all—*all of it*—was just a trick, a long-planned scheme, to get me to do murder for them!"

"Please, Miss Patton," Dundee pleaded. "I give you my word that Miss Conova was an innocent victim of Geoffrey Arundel's foolish and wicked plotting—as innocent as Modjeska Rodovsky was. She did nothing worse than lend herself to fraud, because this man had made her too ill to go on, had literally driven her to drink and to attempted suicide."

"Rot!" Arundel exploded, striking his manacled hands against his knees. "I've had enough of this—"

"Oh, but we haven't!" Dundee assured him. "We find it enormously interesting, Mr. Arundel. By the way, Arundel, you know that it was Modjeska Rodovsky herself who unconsciously sealed her own death warrant last night, don't you? Oh, yes, you do! You heard Garnet when he told us her last words. Will you remind him, Miss Patton?"

The nurse was staring at Dundee, her jaw dropped. "You do know everything about it, don't you? I was hidden under the fur-lined laprobe in the tonneau of the sedan. I got in when Yola—I mean, Miss Rodovsky—left the car after she'd started to drive away from the garage and went back to get something. I was only a few steps behind her all the way. Twice I thought she heard me, or sensed my nearness, on the long flights of stairs. But a nurse learns to walk softly, and I always wear rubber heels. I stayed under the laprobe for a long, long time, more than an hour, while she was up in Kenyon 's office"

"Pardon me, Miss Patton. Did you hear Garnet when he arrived?"

"No. I read in the paper this afternoon what he said he did, but sounds were muffled by the rug," she told them. "But I did hear the door open and I heard the conversation between Miss Conova—I mean, Miss Rodovsky—and Mr. Kenyon. Of course I know now why she said what she did, but then—"

"Repeat the words that were used, if you remember them, please," Strawn directed.

Arundel made an ugly sound "What a fool you are, Louise!"

"Yes, you made an awful fool of me," she said, with her new calmness. "Mr. Kenyon said to her, 'Of course you'll get a divorce from Arundel now, as soon as possible, and Yola—or whatever her name was— said, 'That's out of the question, Bruce! It's simply impossible!'--or words to that effect. I can't remember exactly, because I was suddenly so sick with anger that I felt as if I were drowning in the blood that had rushed to my head. I remembered nothing except what Geoff had said, that Yola was just playing with Clinton Risher, and I was so angry with her for having led me on into a fool's paradise of hope that I could hardly wait until she drove off to hit her over the head with the crank. I didn't think whether I was killing her or not. I just wanted to hit and hit hard. I wanted to hurt her as badly as she had hurt me by being Geoff's wife and refusing to divorce him—"

"Did you speak to her first?" Dundee asked, to divert the threatened return of hysteria.

"Speak to her?" she echoed. "I was too angry, too drowned in that rush of blood to my head to speak. Now, I'm glad she didn't know. Oh, my God, how glad I am she didn't know it was me! Poor thing, *poor thing!* Why, why, why, I killed a girl who had never done me a wrong in her life! She liked me! She trusted me! Oh, Geoff! How could you do this to me? I hope to God they hang me quickly! I'm not fit to live! I don't want to live!"

But as Dundee said, later, to Sanderson and to Ginger Loring, who stubbornly refused to go home until Dundee himself would take her: "She doesn't want to live now, but she'll fight the gallows fast enough when she comes to trial. It's one of nature's little tricks on us that we can quickly get used to anything—even to the astounding and atrocious fact that we have committed murder. Before she gets in the witness box she will have talked herself into believing that she was justified."

"Oh, Jimmy, no!" Ginger protested "She's genuinely sorry—"

"*Sorry?* Sure! But we can't live with sorrow. We have to live with ourselves. And nobody could live with himself as a *murderer*—if he were not abnormal. And Louise Patton is not abnormal."

Ginger shivered. "I know what you mean. She was already returning to normal, before you tricked her into another homicidal rage. No, don't remind me that I tricked her! I'm trying to forget it. I don't like being a manhunter. Did you notice, Jimmy? She'd cold-creamed her face and had 'set' her hair under a permanent wave cap, just as if she had done nothing awful! She was already getting used to it. That's what you mean. Oh, Jimmy! I think that's horrible! To know that human beings can be so vile—"

"If you'd seen as many 'human beings' fight for their lives, when their lives are too vile for saving, as I have seen, you would not wonder at anything," District Attorney Sanderson told her "Dat ole debbil self-preservation bats a thousand per cent in all of us, sweet thing!"

"When did you first suspect Louise Patton, Bonnie Dundee?"

He grinned at her. "To be true to my profession as represented in fiction, I should say that I suspected her from the first. And I'd be lying in my teeth. One doesn't, somehow, expect a nurse to kill her patient. Which is of course why Arundel chose a nurse for the job."

"Do you think he intended to marry her when he got her into it?" Ginger asked. "If all had gone well, from their standpoint. If the verdict had been suicide, and the million dollars insurance money had been paid over—"

"The Lord only knows! But if I am any judge of Mr. Arundel's character, I should say no. He would have stalled Louise Patton along for the required year of mourning, and by that time would have been very far away indeed—possibly with Yola Conova herself! Who can say what fantastic scheme Arundel had hatched under that smooth hair of his—which, by the way, I suspect of being a toupee."

"You know, Jimmy, it might so easily have been the perfect crime," Ginger said "If Louise Patton had struck her on the *side* of the head, instead of on top, so that the concussion would have seemed to be the result of the banging of the swinging body against the concrete supports of the bridge—"

"Perfect crime—in a pig's eye!" Sanderson snorted "It was doomed to failure from any one of a dozen angles.

But get out of here, both of you! I've got to get some sleep if I'm going to have strength enough to work up a case against those two which will rate an indictment, to say nothing of a conviction. So scram!"

Outside it was cold and clear. Last night's wind storm was nothing but a memory. The stars twinkled at them. Before getting into Dundee's car they stood close beside each other for a minute, drawing in great lungfuls of the crisp, clean air.

"Gosh, I'm sleepy!" Ginger discovered, and yawned widely as Dundee helped her into the car. "An hour ago I thought I could never sleep again, that my eyelids would be wide with horror of all I've seen in the last twenty-four hours, and now I can hardly hold them open."

"Me, too," Dundee admitted, his jaws cracking in a yawn that put hers to shame.

"And I can't help thinking what a bang-up story I'm going to write tomorrow, after I get my job back," she confessed. "I'm not forgetting Madge, Jimmy, but—"

"I know." He let the car out a bit in the quiet, deserted street. "Old Dame Nature is a hell of a wench, isn't she? God bless her! Then you didn't mean what you said to Arundel when he tried to bribe you? About going to Hollywood, I mean."

"I meant it then," she said. "I wanted to escape. But now I want to get back to work. My kind of work. I guess I'll always be a newspaperman, Bonnie Dundee. Just as you'll always be a—a manhunter."

He wondered just what she meant, but he was careful to keep his voice casual and cheerful as he answered: "Well, you can't say that never the twain shall meet.' Because this particular twain has done a fair job of meeting in the last twenty-four hours. Life isn't dull for our kind of people, is it, my sweet?"

She did not answer, for she was asleep, her rust-red curls tangling with the nubbly wool of his topcoat, her little freckled nose snubbed flat against his elbow.

Other Resurrected Press Books in *The Chief Inspector Pointer Mystery* Series

Death of John Tait
Murder at the Nook
Mystery at the Rectory
Scarecrow
The Case of the Two Pearl Necklaces
The Charteris Mystery
The Eames-Erskine Case
The Footsteps that Stopped
The Clifford Affair
The Cluny Problem
The Craig Poisoning Mystery
The Net Around Joan Ingilby
The Tall House Mystery
The Wedding-Chest Mystery
The Westwood Mystery
Tragedy at Beechcroft

MORE MYSTERIES BY ANNE AUSTIN

Murder at Bridge

When an afternoon bridge party attended by some of Hamilton's leading citizens ends with the hostess being murdered in her boudoir, Special Investigator Dundee of the District Attorney's office is called in. But one of the attendees is guilty? There are plenty of suspects: the victim's former lover, her current suitor, the retired judge who is being blackmailed, the victim's maid who had been horribly disfigured accidentally by the murdered woman, or any of the women who's husbands had flirted with the victim. Or was she murdered by an outsider whose motive had nothing to do with the town of Hamilton. Find the answer in . . . Murder at Bridge

One Drop of Blood

When Dr. Koenig, head of Mayfield Sanitarium is murdered, the District Attorney's Special Investigator, "Bonnie" Dundee must go undercover to find the killer. Were any of the inmates of the asylum insane enough to have committed the crime? Or, was it one of the staff, motivated by jealousy? And what was is the secret in the murdered man's past. Find the answer in . . . One Drop of Blood

The Black Pigeon

There were plenty of reasons for "Handsome Harry" Borden to be murdered. After all, he had cost numerous investors their life savings with questionable securities.

And he had left his wife for a string of actresses and dancers, only to shed each in turn for a new flame. And the office boy that he had bullied. Not to mention the jealous boyfriend of his secretary to whom he had made unwanted advances. So there were plenty of suspects when was found dead of a gunshot wound in his office. The question is, which of them actually committed the crime?

- The Problem of Cell 13 by Jacques Futrelle
- The Conundrum of the Golf Links by Percy James Brebner
- The Silkworms of Florence by Clifford Ashdown
- The Gateway of the Monster by William Hope Hodgson
- The Affair at the Semiramis Hotel by A. E. W. Mason
- The Affair of the Avalanche Bicycle & Tyre Co., LTD by Arthur Morrison

RESURRECTED PRESS CLASSIC MYSTERY CATALOGUE

Journeys into Mystery
Travel and Mystery in a More Elegant Time

The Edwardian Detectives
Literary Sleuths of the Edwardian Era

Gems of Mystery
Lost Jewels from a More Elegant Age

E. C. Bentley
Trent's Last Case: The Woman in Black

Ernest Bramah
Max Carrados Resurrected:
The Detective Stories of Max Carrados

Agatha Christie
The Secret Adversary
The Mysterious Affair at Styles

Octavus Roy Cohen
Midnight

Freeman Wills Croft
The Ponson Case
The Pit Prop Syndicate

J. S. Fletcher
The Herapath Property
The Rayner-Slade Amalgamation
The Chestermarke Instinct
The Paradise Mystery
Dead Men's Money

The Middle of Things
Ravensdene Court
Scarhaven Keep
The Orange-Yellow Diamond
The Middle Temple Murder
The Tallyrand Maxim
The Borough Treasurer
In the Mayor's Parlour
The Saftey Pin

R. Austin Freeman
The Mystery of 31 New Inn from the Dr. Thorndyke
Series
John Thorndyke's Cases from the Dr. Thorndyke
Series
The Red Thumb Mark from The Dr. Thorndyke Series
The Eye of Osiris from The Dr. Thorndyke Series
A Silent Witness from the Dr. John Thorndyke Series
The Cat's Eye from the Dr. John Thorndyke Series
Helen Vardon's Confession: A Dr. John Thorndyke
Story
As a Thief in the Night: A Dr. John Thorndyke Story
Mr. Pottermack's Oversight: A Dr. John Thorndyke
Story
Dr. Thorndyke Intervenes: A Dr. John Thorndyke
Story
The Singing Bone: The Adventures of Dr. Thorndyke
The Stoneware Monkey: A Dr. John Thorndyke Story
The Great Portrait Mystery, and Other Stories: A
Collection of Dr. John Thorndyke and Other Stories
The Penrose Mystery: A Dr. John Thorndyke Story
The Uttermost Farthing: A Savant's Vendetta

Arthur Griffiths
The Passenger From Calais
The Rome Express

Fergus Hume
The Mystery of a Hansom Cab
The Green Mummy
The Silent House
The Secret Passage

Edgar Jepson
The Loudwater Mystery

A. E. W. Mason
At the Villa Rose

A. A. Milne
The Red House Mystery
Baroness Emma Orczy
The Old Man in the Corner

Edgar Allan Poe
The Detective Stories of Edgar Allan Poe

Arthur J. Rees
The Hampstead Mystery
The Shrieking Pit
The Hand In The Dark
The Moon Rock
The Mystery of the Downs

Mary Roberts Rinehart
Sight Unseen and The Confession

Dorothy L. Sayers
Whose Body?

Sir William Magnay
The Hunt Ball Mystery

Mabel and Paul Thorne
The Sheridan Road Mystery

Louis Tracy
The Strange Case of Mortimer Fenley
The Albert Gate Mystery
The Bartlett Mystery
The Postmaster's Daughter
The House of Peril
The Sandling Case: What Would You Have Done?
Charles Edmonds Walk
The Paternoster Ruby

John R. Watson
The Mystery of the Downs
The Hampstead Mystery

Edgar Wallace
The Daffodil Mystery
The Crimson Circle

Carolyn Wells
Vicky Van
The Man Who Fell Through the Earth
In the Onyx Lobby
Raspberry Jam
The Clue
The Room with the Tassels
The Vanishing of Betty Varian
The Mystery Girl
The White Alley
The Curved Blades
Anybody but Anne
The Bride of a Moment
Faulkner's Folly
The Diamond Pin
The Gold Bag
The Mystery of the Sycamore
The Come Backy

Raoul Whitfield
Death in a Bowl

And much more!
Visit ResurrectedPress.com
for our complete catalogue

About Resurrected Press

A division of Intrepid Ink, LLC, Resurrected Press is dedicated to bringing high quality, vintage books back into publication. See our entire catalogue and find out more at www.ResurrectedPress.com.

About Intrepid Ink, LLC

Intrepid Ink, LLC provides full publishing services to authors of fiction and non-fiction books, eBooks and websites. From editing to formatting, from publishing to marketing, Intrepid Ink gets your creative works into the hands of the people who want to read them. Find out more at www.IntrepidInk.com.